"A charmer."

"Prepare to laugh out loud while reading *The Singles Table*."

—PopSugar

"Hot, bantery, quirky as hell, and so sweetly romantic! I *loved* this book."

—Sonali Dev, *USA Today* bestselling author of *Incense and Sensibility*

"Utterly hilarious and so, so swoony! *The Singles Table* is a fantastic enemies-to-lovers, grumpy/sunshine rom-com. I adored Zara and her slightly chaotic energy, and the Indian wedding setting is perfect escapist fun. A delightful read!"

—Farah Heron, author of *Accidentally Engaged* and *Tahira in Bloom*

"You won't feel lonely at the singles table with this book to keep you company. A charming and hilarious rom-com filled with wonderful characters. One of my favorite books of the year."

—Jackie Lau, author of *Donut Fall in Love*

"Desai does it again. . . . Zara and Jay are a refreshingly self-aware pair, and it's eminently satisfying to see them not just address their business conflicts but seek professional psychological help. . . . Desai's fans will be delighted." —*Publishers Weekly* (starred review)

"Hilarious . . . delicious . . . steamy . . . [a] memorable romance."

—*Booklist* (starred review)

"A beautifully told rom-com that's full of laughs, heart, and scorching sexual tension." —*Kirkus Reviews* (starred review)

"Desai's latest is the best way to dive into a rom-com if you have yet to make it back into theaters. In fact, it's even better."

—SheKnows

"A sexy and fun romance."

—The Nerd Daily

"Outrageously funny, meltingly hot and tender, and wrapped up in heartwarming community, this book will warm you in the best ways. Daisy and Liam are just the kind of sexy joyful magic we need in the world right now."

—Sonali Dev, author of *Recipe for Persuasion*

"A smart, sexy read. If you haven't done so already, prepare to mark Sara Desai as your new fave author!"

—Sajni Patel, author of *The Trouble with Hating You*

"A writer to watch."

—Bustle

"Geek-chic Daisy makes an endearing heroine, and the dysfunctional Murphy family provides believable tension. Desai's fans will be thrilled to reconnect with the eccentric Patels, and new readers will be hooked. This is a gem."

—*Publishers Weekly* (starred review)

"This novel has all the funny banter and sexy feels you could want in a romantic comedy—and, of course, a terrific grand gesture before the happy ending." —NPR.org

TO HAVE
AND
TO HEIST

SARA DESAI

BERKLEY ROMANCE
NEW YORK

BERKLEY ROMANCE
Published by Berkley
An imprint of Penguin Random House LLC
penguinrandomhouse.com

Library of Congress Cataloging-in-Publication Data

Names: Desai, Sara, author.
Title: To have and to heist / Sara Desai.
Description: First Edition. | New York: Berkley Romance, 2023.
Identifiers: LCCN 2022043742 (print) | LCCN 2022043743 (ebook) |
ISBN 9780593548509 (trade paperback) | ISBN 9780593548516 (ebook)
Subjects: LCGFT: Novels.
Classification: LCC PR9199.4.D486 T6 2023 (print) |
LCC PR9199.4.D486 (ebook) | DDC 813/.6—dc23/eng/20220928
LC record available at https://lccn.loc.gov/2022043742
LC ebook record available at https://lccn.loc.gov/2022043743

First Edition: July 2023

Printed in the United States of America
1st Printing

Book design by Daniel Brount

To Sharon, Rana, Adele, and Tarick:
we were our very own heist crew.

TO HAVE

·· AND ··

TO HEIST

PROLOGUE

◇ ◇ ◇

JACK

Imagine you are just an ordinary guy. You have a good job. Your financing is almost paid off on your Ford F150 truck. You have a contact list of women around the globe who delight in your company. Your *Acanthocereus tetragonus* cactus is thriving. And you have your health.

On a cool summer evening in Berlin, you repossess a $10 million Caravaggio painting from a private collector. Don't worry. The collector is a bad guy. On your way to the airport, you are run off the road by four goons in a Saab. They blow up your rental car, beat you, shoot you, and take the painting. With your dying breath, you ask who sent them. Since you are almost dead, they tell you. It was Mr. X. You are not surprised.

One year later you are not dead, but you wish you were. Your new girlfriend wants a commitment. The Ford dealer has repossessed your truck. Your boss has put you on probation even though it wasn't your fault he didn't get insurance for the rental car. And to top it all off, Mr. X is always one step ahead of the game.

You get a lead on a job in a small, obscure European country. You dump the girlfriend and retrieve an ancient artifact from a royal residence. Easy peasy. You make it across Europe to London. While you are waiting for your flight to Mexico, Mr. X's goons find you in the restroom at Heathrow Airport. You know things are going to be bad when they don't even wait for you to wash your hands. You are still in therapy from the last beating/shooting, so you just hand over the artifact. They shoot you anyway. Just for fun.

This time it takes you six months to recover. No work means no pay and no pay means no truck. You finally return to work and get a lead on the perfect score—the Wild Heart, a magnificent necklace containing twenty-six oval-shaped pink diamonds surrounded by diamonds and emeralds with a forty-carat heart-shaped pink diamond pendant center. The necklace was one of thousands of priceless items stolen by the British from India during the colonial period and is now on display in a boutique museum on the Near North Side of Chicago, Illinois.

You haven't been back to your hometown in over fifteen years, although you still call your cousin Lou on his birthday every year. He thinks you work as a conman in New York. Your real job would disappoint him.

This time you play it smart. You travel with a fake passport under an assumed name. You book a room in a fancy hotel and forgo loyalty points at your usual budget hotel chain. Lou hooks you up with a Sig Sauer 45 and two small Beretta M9-22s. He has just been released from prison and now sells black market weapons from behind the peonies in his wife's greenhouse. He's 16 percent certain arms dealing isn't a violation of his parole.

You have a good feeling about this job. When you get back to your hotel, you make two calls. First, you call the Ford dealer and tell him to get your truck ready. Then you call Lou's wife. Her peonies are suffering from botrytis blight. You tell her treatment begins with good sanitation and she needs to prune off and destroy the infected parts of the plants. You doubt she'll follow your instructions, and you make a mental note to buy your peonies elsewhere.

After three days of recon inside the museum, you pay a midnight visit to check out the building and grounds. The garden is thick with unpruned vegetation and smells like piss. Whatever. You aren't there to help with the gardening. You are there to retrieve the necklace, and the thick foliage is a perfect place to hide. You take a few pictures and hide your supplies in the hellebore under a magnificent oak suffering from bacterial leaf scorch. Now you just have to wait for the perfect night.

ONE

◇ ◇ ◇

There are people who need people, and then there are introverts. You don't get to choose that particular personality trait when you're born. You're either the kid who spends recess running around the playground looking for friends, or you're the little angel who sits quietly in the reading corner with a book, lost in another world.

I'm definitely one of the people who need people. Leave me alone for more than a few hours and I'll be speed-dialing my way through my contact list or skulking around the local coffee shop looking for familiar faces. I'm the person who will ask if the chair is free at your table if you look like you need a friend, or chat with you in the grocery line and tell you that you're lucky you've picked this till because Charlotte scans things so fast, a few items always get missed and you might go home with a free can of beans.

I've always admired people who are content with their own company. My bestie Chloe can go an entire weekend without talking to another human being if her daughter is away at a sports game or sleeping over with friends. Actually, that's not entirely true. I don't think we've gone more than a few hours without communicating in some form ever since we met on the school playground in fourth grade. Even in the blackest moments of her favorite romance books, when all is lost and it seems like the couple will never find their happily-ever-after, Chloe will always be there for me.

I don't know what I would have done if she hadn't answered my call the day I, Simi Chopra, almost killed a man.

"Oh my God! Chloe!" I held a mirror over the mouth of the naked octogenarian on the floor to see if he was breathing. People who need people are adept at multitasking, even if it involves getting emotional support from your bestie while trying to revive one of your landlady's many "gentleman callers." Not that I begrudged eighty-year-old Rose her extracurricular activities. She'd kindly rented me her basement suite at a reduced rent in exchange for helping with chores and keeping her company on her rare evenings in. Someone in the house had to be getting some good stuff, and it wasn't me.

"What's wrong?" Chloe's soothing voice crackled over my phone speaker. I was due for a phone upgrade, but between rent, loan payments, therapy, and living expenses, even my entry-level office salary plus a side gig in a candy store didn't pay enough to indulge.

"I think I killed someone."

Chloe didn't miss a beat. "I'll grab some bleach and be right over."

"You'll be late for work."

"It's an IT help desk, babe. We spend most of the day telling people to turn the computer off and on again. I can easily get someone to cover for me."

Chloe is my ride-or-die. No questions. No judgment. Everyone should have a friend whose first thought is to run for the bleach when you call to tell her you might have killed someone.

"Hurry. He's barely breathing." I cleaned the mirror and held it over his mouth again, making a mental note to thank my parents for sending me to a first aid course in twelfth grade. They thought they were paving my way to med school. Instead, the course just confirmed that no one should put their life in my hands.

"I'd better bring a tarp, too," Chloe said.

"There's no blood."

"You might still need the tarp in case he loses control of his bowels."

"Crap."

"Exactly. I've been reading a lot of romantic suspense books," she said. "I know everything about dead bodies."

"I don't think he's that dead." I held the dude's wrist in my hand. "I feel a pulse. I'm not sure if it's his or mine. My heart is pounding so hard, I can't tell."

"Is he only mostly dead? Like in *The Princess Bride*?"

Chloe loves romance. We watch *The Princess Bride* every year on her birthday and rom-coms when it's her turn to choose on movie nights. Honestly, all that mushy stuff is like nails on a chalkboard to me, but this is Chloe. In seventh grade, she took the fall when I brought a set of steak knives to school for my Edward Scissorhands Halloween costume, and in eleventh grade she sneaked me in the classroom window when I overslept and almost missed our final calculus exam. There isn't anything I wouldn't do for her.

"Is there a degree of deadness that involves breathing?" I asked.

"You were the one who was supposed to become a doctor."

I heard cupboards slam, keys rattle on the counter, the click of a lock. Chloe was on her way. She was nothing if not efficient.

"If I'd become a doctor, I wouldn't be living in a low-rent basement suite and drowning in debt." I pressed an ear to the dude's chest, listening for a heartbeat.

"You would have had even more debt," she said over the rapid thud of footsteps and the hum of traffic. A single mom working three jobs to make ends meet, Chloe couldn't afford a car, so she took public transport to get around.

"Yes, but I would also have had the kind of job that would enable me to pay it off before I hit middle age."

"Almost at the bus stop." Chloe huffed into the phone.

I gave myself a mental pat on the back for choosing to stay in our hometown of Evanston, Illinois, when I finally moved out of my parents' house. I had briefly considered finding a place in Downtown Chicago, but rents were high, and I spent most of my free time with Chloe and her daughter, Olivia, so putting almost fourteen miles between us didn't make sense.

"The paramedics are here," Rose called out from the hallway. She'd put on a robe after I called the ambulance, a small mercy for which I was undyingly grateful. I wasn't judging her. I just didn't need a visual of what the future held in store for me fifty years from now.

"Gotta go, babe," I said to Chloe. "Rose needs me. I'll see you soon."

A gorgeous blond paramedic with green eyes and a face so chiseled it could cut glass gestured me to the side while his two equally hot companions crouched down to check out the almost naked dude on the floor—I'd thrown a tea towel over his hips for the sake of modesty.

"What happened?" he asked.

"My basement suite flooded this morning." I smoothed down my hair, acutely conscious that I'd come upstairs with a bad case of bedhead and wearing only PJ shorts and a ratty Chicago Bears sweatshirt. "I woke up with my stuff floating past my bed, so I came upstairs to tell Rose. She gave me keys to her place when I moved in so I could check in on her from time to time."

He smiled, which I took as a good sign. Maybe he liked curvy South Asian girls with long, matted dark brown hair and a little extra lip fuzz because they hadn't had time for the morning groom. Or maybe he was just a Bears fan.

"Unfortunately, I walked in on her and her boyfriend doing it on the couch." The visual had been bad enough, but the cost of the extra therapy I'd need to undo the trauma of what I'd seen was beyond imagining.

"Doing what?" he asked.

"You know . . ."

Respect was the guiding principle of my family. Respect for parents. Respect for aunties. Respect for elders. With respect drilled into me from birth, I couldn't bring myself to use the *S* word when it came to describing the intimate relations of two seniors. But what word could I use? Why did the paramedic have to be so sexy? Did he wear contacts or were his eyes really that vivid green? Was that a medical device in his pocket? I quickly shut down the runaway train of random thought process that was the bane of my existence.

"Boning." The word dropped from my lips before I could catch it.

His finger froze on the tablet he was using to record my information. "Boning?"

"Okay. Fine. Sex," I said quickly. "They were having sex. On the couch. Naked. Curtain ties were involved. And a curtain rod. I also saw a can of whipped cream, which I should really put back in the fridge so it doesn't spoil." I leaned in close, lowered my voice to a conspiratorial whisper. "I didn't know that position was possible after the age of forty. The dude really knew his stuff. I guess that makes sense if you've been doing it for eighty-plus years minus maybe fifteen or so. Of course, I can only guess when he lost his virginity. I didn't have sex for the first time until I was twenty."

His eyes glazed over, a telltale sign that I'd overshared.

"Name?" he asked.

"Simi Chopra. Currently single."

"I meant *his* name."

I bit back a grimace. Why couldn't he have been plain or even average? I could never speak in coherent sentences when a dude was too good-looking. "To be honest, she has so many boyfriends, I can't keep track of their names. She usually goes for younger men—fifties to seventies and occasionally forties if they're having an early midlife crisis. She said the octo—and nonagenarians usually have performance issues—although from what I saw, this dude is an exception. I kinda liked the last guy she was seeing. He runs the Lincoln Park 10K Run for the Zoo every year. He's super fit and has a six-pack, although I did wonder if it might just be his ribs poking out because he only eats raw, especially grass. She liked his stamina, but she got annoyed at meal times because he kept running out to the backyard to graze."

"Would anyone like tea?" Rose had gone to change when the paramedics arrived and was now wearing a tropical print dress with a giant pink belt cinched around her waist and a pair of matching heels. Rose was in theater and still performed onstage. She loved loud colors and bold prints because they matched her personality.

"Maybe not the best time," I called out. "What's this one's name?"

"Stan," she said. "I don't know that much about him. I met him in a bar last week after a show and we've been hitting the mattress hard ever since. He's eighty-eight with the stamina of a man in his fifties. It was nice being with someone mature for a change."

The paramedic coughed, choked before asking, "How did he wind up on the floor?"

"I walked in and scared him," I said. "Rose was on the couch.

Sort of. She saw me and screamed. Stan jumped off her. Well, it was sort of a slow push away followed by a concomitant drop elsewhere. Not that I was looking, but your eyes have to go somewhere, and mine went there, and then I immediately wished they could be somewhere else."

"I'm not here to judge," he said, shaking his head in a way that belied his words.

I could see my chances of getting laid in the back of his ambulance were quickly disappearing. "He lost his balance trying to get up," I continued. "Then he fell and hit his head on the coffee table. I called 911 and checked to make sure he was breathing with a makeup mirror." I hesitated, waiting for an acknowledgment of my skill. None was forthcoming.

A rush of air cooled my heated cheeks before I heard the back door slam.

"I'm here," Chloe called out. "I've got bleach and rubber gloves. The tarp's in the car. Where's the body? We could probably dump him in the river." She froze behind the island counter that separated the kitchen from the living room. "You're not alone."

"Hello, darling." Rose gave her a little wave. "I'm afraid I can't offer you any tea. We're on our way to the hospital."

"That's Chloe," I told the paramedic. "She came to help."

"Good thing we got here in time." He jotted something down on his tablet.

Alarmed, I tried to read his screen upside down. "What are you writing?"

"A note to myself never to be alone in a house with you and your friend." He tucked the tablet away, then held the door while the other paramedics carried Stan out on a gurney. Rose walked beside them, holding Stan's hand.

"Is that a joke?" I called out. "I hope it's a joke. Don't forget I saved him by making sure he was breathing. If it wasn't for me, he'd be mostly dead."

Chloe hefted her bag and a Costco-sized container of bleach onto the counter, then ran over to wrap me in her arms. "Are you okay? Should I call your therapist?"

"No." I shuddered against her. "If you just pour some of that bleach into my eyes, I'll be fine. The things I had to see . . ."

Everything about Chloe is soft and warm, from her organic cotton sweaters to her fuzzy UGG boots. Her bright blue eyes, rosy cheeks, and long, bouncy blond curls are straight out of the Hallmark Christmas movie universe. I could totally see her moving to a small town to run a bakery and falling for the grumpy firefighter / police officer / sheriff who plans to spend Christmas alone until they get trapped together in a cabin during a snowstorm.

Instead, despite having a software engineering degree, she was working days on an IT help desk with a side hustle as a community college teacher and an evening side gig / passion project as a white hat hacker. Even then, between rent, bills, and student loan payments, she struggled to make ends meet every month.

"I'd better call the insurance company for Rose," I said, pulling away. "And then I need to start cleaning."

"Don't you have to be at work?"

"Work" for me was a mid-level position as a pricing analyst for a food distribution company. My job involved sitting in a tiny cubicle inputting data into a computer forty hours a week. Mind-numbing boredom, constant distractions, and a lack of social interaction meant I had to drag myself to the office every morning. I was overqualified, underpaid, and the job had nothing to do with the degree I'd spent four years at college to acquire. I'd had to take on a side gig at a candy store to help cover my bills, student loan payments, and the occasional evening out, which happened only if there was more than one hundred dollars in my checking account after paying back my friends for the Uber ride home I owed them from last week.

"I can't leave," I said. "I need to bail out the water, wait for the emergency plumber, call the insurers, and then I should really go to the hospital to make sure Rose is okay. I also need to salvage my stuff and let my parents know I'm moving back home until everything is sorted." My brain was already in hyperdrive, setting off a rush of endorphins. There was nothing I liked better than having too much to do.

"You'll get fired," Chloe said. "They've already given you two warnings."

"It was going to happen anyway." I'd changed jobs frequently since graduation, struggling to find something that inspired my passion and utilized the skills I'd acquired for my business degree. I had too much energy, a short attention span, and a low boredom threshold. I needed to be moving. I needed constant activity and fast deadlines. If I had fifteen things to focus on at once, I was golden. If I had to sit in a cubicle doing repetitive tasks while faced with constant distractions, I had to work twice as hard as my colleagues just to keep up. Chloe said I was like a duck, appearing to swim effortlessly, but paddling furiously under the surface.

"You could ask for more hours at the candy store," Chloe suggested.

"I've already gained five pounds. If I worked more hours, I'd need a whole new wardrobe." I loved selling candy at Westfield Shopping Mall. I loved the chaos and the crowds. I loved that the owner had seen right away that I could manage the store alone—cash, stock, window displays, shoplifters, suppliers, kids, and tourists. It was a high I never got with my office jobs. Or maybe it was the sugar rush . . .

"I'd better get to work if I'm not needed for body cleanup," Chloe said. "We can chat tonight."

"I'll definitely need some cheering up after I tell my parents all my bad news: I almost killed Rose's boyfriend, I lost my apartment and my job, I might have to declare bankruptcy, and I'm moving back home."

"Just don't tell them you're still single," she warned.

"Of course not. They'd disown me."

TWO

◇ ◇ ◇

What do you mean you need to move back home?" My mother's voice reverberated around the family kitchen, making my sugar hangover one thousand times worse. I'd tried to sneak in the back door after spending the evening helping Rose with her insurance paperwork over a bucket of fried chicken, three bags of candy, and *Murder, She Wrote*. But, of course, they'd caught me.

"It's just until my apartment dries out," I said. "I promise you'll not even know I'm around."

My parents live in a modest raised four-bedroom ranch house on a quiet cul-de-sac in Evanston, or "little Chicago" as no one in Evanston calls our leafy urban suburb. Mom is an English professor at Northwestern University, which is only a few blocks away from our house. Dad has an easy commute on the Metra to his custom tailor shop in the Loop. After my three brothers and I moved out, Dad turned the twins' bedroom into a yoga studio and kept mine as it was for guests and/or my inevitable return.

"We'll have to make a shower schedule if we all have to be at work by nine A.M." My dad looked up from his glossy men's fashion magazine. He was a master tailor and owner of Chopra

Custom Clothiers, so he had to stay on top of all the trends. He'd learned his skills from his father and together they'd built the business into one of the top custom tailors in Chicago, dressing everyone from celebrity chefs to movie stars and even a few Chicago Bears.

"Why do people have to start work at nine A.M.?" I wondered out loud. "Who decided on a nine-to-five workday? Don't people realize that workers are much more productive if they get enough sleep? We're not machines. Everyone has a different biorhythm. I could have been twice as efficient if my boss had let me start at eleven A.M. and work until seven P.M."

I knew I'd given myself away when my father raised an eyebrow. "Could have been?"

"I'm not working there anymore," I admitted. "I didn't vibe with the idea of increasing the efficiency of moving unhealthy food products through the supply chain. There's an obesity epidemic in children."

"What about the candy store?" My mother frowned. "How does that 'vibe' . . . " She said the word with an extra dose of sarcasm. In her line of work, words mattered. ". . . with your beliefs?"

"We're not offering it as real food," I said. "Everyone knows it's just sugar."

"Juice is pure sugar," my father said. "Twenty-five spoons in one glass of orange juice. Imagine that." My father was a health nut. He got up at five A.M. every morning to run, followed by a half hour of yoga and twenty minutes of meditation. For breakfast he had a wheatgrass protein shake and an egg white omelet and then it was a protein bowl for lunch, if he had time to eat at all.

"Who cares about juice, Rohan? She lost another job. We'll never get her married now." My mother turned to me, huffing her displeasure. "What did you do this time?"

"Nothing. The office was a soul-sucking wasteland of despair.

I was overqualified. The work was mind-numbing, and the open plan office meant there were too many distractions. I couldn't have picked a worse possible job."

"How are you going to earn a living?" she demanded. "How will you find a husband?"

Some people had a great relationship with their parents. I did everything I could to avoid spending too much time with mine. Not because they were bad people—they were kind, charitable, generous, and well liked in the community—but because they couldn't help judging me and meddling in my life. Before college, there was the pressure to become a doctor, lawyer, or engineer. Then the resigned sighs when I decided to get a business degree, and the seeming despair after graduation when I couldn't land anything other than entry-level office jobs. Even worse was my marital status. Twenty-nine years old and unmarried. I couldn't have been more of a disappointment.

"I'll take extra hours at the candy store, and I'll look for another job, but it will take time." I grabbed a fluffy pav from the dish on the table. My mom was an amazing cook—an irony since my dad was not a big eater. Luckily my brothers had no food issues and could empty the pantry when they came home to visit.

"How much time?" Dad wanted to know.

"I don't know. I applied for over ninety jobs last time, and the supply chain company was my only option. I really don't want another entry-level position. I want to be able to use my degree, but I need money. I might just take another retail job while I'm looking."

"Don't dismiss entry-level positions so quickly," Dad said. "Do you know how many CEOs started at entry-level positions? Doug McMillon loaded trucks at Walmart and worked his way to the top."

"So now she's going to load trucks at Walmart?" Mom was

already up and tidying the kitchen. She was a woman who got things done, rushing through the house like a hurricane, vacuum in one hand, laundry in the other. Dad liked to linger over his food. Mom ate on the go—a necessity with four kids and a full-time job. I'd never seen her sit down for dinner. Usually, by the time Dad had finished eating, the kitchen was clean, the laundry was done, the floors were mopped, sports uniforms were washed and ready for the next day, lunches were made, and she was getting ready for bed so she could get up and start all over again.

"If you want retail, you can work with me," my father said. "I need help selling to the younger crowd, but people your age don't want to work in a tailor shop. They tell me they want to feel passionate about what they do, and they don't have a passion for suits."

"What about Cristian?" Half Portuguese and half Brazilian, Cristian Da Silva had been working at the store for the last year. When he wasn't selling suits and flirting with the female customers, he worked as a life coach / male escort. For a dude whose entire goal in life was getting laid, I never understood why he worked in a men's tailor shop until he told me about his crippling credit card debt, which came from living a lifestyle he couldn't afford.

Dad waved a dismissive hand. "Cristian isn't interested in a career as a tailor. If he wasn't so good with the customers, I'd let him go. In my day, you were grateful to have a job. Excitement and passion were for hobbies."

"We don't live in the Middle Ages anymore, Dad. People want balance in their lives." My dad's life was consumed by work. If he wasn't on the floor in the showroom, he was supervising the tailors, meeting with buyers, selecting fabrics, and traveling around the world attending fashion shows and visiting designers.

"This unbalanced life bought our house."

"Well, I'm never going to be able to afford a house, so why kill myself trying?"

"She appreciates the offer." Mom shot me a warning look, as if she knew I was thinking of turning Dad down because of the parade of suitors she'd soon be sending through his door. "She can start on Monday morning."

"I need her tomorrow night," Dad said as if the deal was done. "I have to attend a fashion show, and a late shipment of fabric is coming in. I don't trust Cristian to handle it alone. Simi knows the business."

We all knew the business. My brothers and I had to work at the store every Saturday during high school. My dad had hoped one of us would be interested in taking over, but my older brother, Nikhil, had become a doctor and the twins were studying engineering at MIT.

"I've got plans tomorrow night," I said. "Chloe got a gig doing some freelance security hacking work for the Victoria Museum and they invited her to preview a new jewelry exhibition. She asked me to go with her in case the executive director asks her any art-related questions. I took an art history elective my first year of college."

"You would choose Chloe over your own father?" My father slapped his hand over his heart. "Homelessness and unemployment instead of a job?"

"Rohan." My mother looked up from wiping the table. "You can't throw our only daughter out on the street."

"I'll pay time and a half," my dad said. "You won't get a better offer."

My lips quivered with a smile. If there was one thing my family loved, it was the art of negotiation. "I can't believe you think I'd blow Chloe off for money," I said with feigned indignation. "What kind of friend would I be?"

"What kind of daughter would leave her father shorthanded at a critical time?" he retorted.

"A daughter who needs money."

Dad made a show of shaking his head. "Double time."

"Done," I said. "But you'll have to make it up to Chloe. She likes your dal tadka, paneer masala, methi saag, lamb biryani, and chicken coconut curry."

My dad's face softened. He had a sweet spot for Chloe and her daughter, Olivia. "I'll cook on Saturday, and they can have it for Sunday dinner."

"Then we have a deal. Chloe will have to go without me."

◇ ◇ ◇

"Polka dots or flowers?" Chloe held two dresses in front of her phone camera. She'd been cool with me backing out of the museum tour to help Dad at the shop, especially because the consultant who'd hired her online had gone from friendly to flirty in the last few days, even hinting that he hoped their evening would continue beyond the museum.

"It depends on who you're trying to impress." I twirled around on one of the stools in Dad's shop beneath a rainbow wall of thread. "Polka dots are artsy but sophisticated and would appeal to the executive director of a museum, especially one based in a historic building. The flowers are more you, but if you want to hook up with your hacking buddy—"

"He's not my buddy. He's a security consultant who was hired by the executive director of the museum to find ethical hackers to do penetration testing of their new security system to identify and patch up weaknesses. His name is Michael P."

I'd suggested several times that Chloe turn her ethical hacking side hustle into full-time work, but with Olivia to care for, and a deep-seated lack of confidence, she preferred the stability and benefits of her help desk job.

"What about the rest of his last name?"

"We've only corresponded online," she said. "His e-mail address and his handle were all Michael P."

"If you plan to hook up with Michael P, you should wear something that screams, 'Take me now.'"

"Who wants to be taken now?" Cristian looked up from his phone. He was wearing his favorite cargo pants and a skin-tight black shirt with *Social Justice Warrior* written in cursive across his chest. He played competitive soccer in his spare time and claimed to volunteer at an animal shelter, although I didn't know if the latter was true. I preferred to admire his sexy smile, lean toned body, chiseled jaw, and run-your-hands-through-it-while-he's-ravishing-you hair from a healthy distance in case he caught me looking and tried to get into my pants. In the short time we'd been waiting for the delivery truck, he'd called three different women and told each of them that she was his "special baby girl" and that he was coming to see her tonight.

"Go back to your womanizing," I said. "I'm sure you've got a few more 'special baby girls' waiting to hear from you."

"You're jealous." His soft tawny bedroom eyes smoldered. "But don't worry. I can schedule you in next week for a little Cristian love." He checked out his reflection in the window and smiled. He knew he was drop-dead gorgeous. If I hadn't done some social media stalking and seen the visual evidence of his inflated ego and his fixation with sex, even I wouldn't have been immune to his charms.

"Uh-uh no way nope." I checked the street again for the truck, still clinging to the faint hope that it would arrive early so I could catch Chloe at the museum before she left. Traffic usually slows in the Loop after seven P.M. when everyone has left the city for their cozy homes in the suburbs but picks up again at nine P.M. because of airport traffic. Dad often schedules his deliveries for that low traffic window.

"Is that Cristian talking?" Chloe asked.

"Yes. He thinks I'm desperate to get him into bed."

"I'm not going to get anyone into bed tonight," she said. "My wardrobe screams 'struggling single mom.'"

"That's why I left my black dress in your hall closet. It's the one with the lace overlay and plunging neckline. You can put a cute sweater over it to meet the executive director, but when you go for drinks with Michael P—"

"Have I mentioned recently how much I love you?"

"You brought bleach to a possible murder scene. I think that says it all."

"Say what?" Cristian looked up again. "Did you murder someone? I've never slept with a murderer before. I'll give you whatever you need, baby. Cold bath. Knife play. Coffin. I'll even let you put a bag over my head if it gets you off."

"Don't tempt me."

I heard the rustling of hangers, a gasp. "It's perfect," Chloe said. "He won't stand a chance."

"Don't get too excited." I moved out of Cristian's hearing range. Even the slightest sexual innuendo could set him off. "You don't even know what he looks like. He could be a forty-year-old geek who lives in his mother's basement."

"He's a single parent of a teenage girl, just like me," she said. "We have a lot in common—same taste in music, same love of rom-coms, same interest in modern contemporary design, same passion for hacking. I feel like I know him better than I ever knew Kyle."

A shiver ran down my spine when Chloe mentioned her abusive ex. She'd met him when she was sixteen and working as a waitress for the summer at his parents' country club. Kyle was a college sophomore majoring in computer engineering and showed up every day to golf with his dad. He was charming and handsome and swept Chloe off her feet and into a storage shed, where he became her first. Two months later she found out she was pregnant and decided to have the baby. Kyle had initially walked away, but when his parents threatened to disinherit him, he changed his mind and asked Chloe to marry him. Only sixteen and living with her alcoholic mother, Chloe took the lifeline he offered. She would have been better off alone.

"You never really knew Kyle," I said. "He wasn't interested in sharing his life with you. He only married you to get his parents' money. I think that was pretty clear after you left him and he refused to pay child support and then had the audacity to try to reconcile when his parents finally cut him off."

Chloe had spent six horrendous years with an angry and resentful Kyle, caught in a cycle of physical and emotional abuse. When she finally broke free, she worked two jobs and went to college at night to give Olivia the best possible life she could.

"Can you meet us for drinks afterward?" she asked. "I need you to check him out. I don't trust my own judgment. What if he's another Kyle and I just don't see it?"

"Of course I'll be there. Just text me the address." I popped a few Fuzzy Peaches in my mouth. The problem with working in a candy store when you have a sugar addiction is the limitless supply. I was amazed I still had all my teeth.

I tried to stay upbeat, but I was worried about Chloe. Despite everything she'd been through, Chloe was still sweet, gentle, kind, and trusting. She thought the best of people. She believed in romance, love, and happily-ever-afters.

"Maybe he has a friend and they each turn out to be 'the one' and we can have the double wedding we dreamed about when we were kids," she said.

I would have laughed out loud, but my mouth was full of candy. There was no "one." Men thought of me as a pal, or worse, a sister. My dates usually devolved into ad hoc counseling sessions where I gave the dude tips on how to ask out the woman he really wanted to be with. Relationships ended when I beat the men at pickup or humiliated them at pool. With three brothers, I'd learned how to hold my own in the activities they enjoyed.

The delivery truck pulled up in the loading zone outside the store and I motioned to Cristian to open the door. "The truck is here. Gotta go inspect bolts of cloth as my penance for losing my job. If he's hot, send me a picture. If he's under sixteen, send me a pimple count."

"I can't even . . ."

"You forgive me."

"I do."

"Have fun, babe."

"Right back at you."

I tucked my phone away, pushed up my sleeves, and went to have "fun" with Cristian.

THREE

◇ ◇ ◇

Cristian and I had just stacked the last bolt of cloth in the storage room when Chloe called. My pulse went immediately into overdrive.

Chloe never *called*.

We messaged, chatted on apps, commented on social media posts, video-called, or communicated on servers. Voice calls were for the rare occasions our hands were occupied with mostly dead octogenarians, baking disasters, or true emergencies.

"Babe, what's wrong?" Chloe didn't live near any seniors, and she wasn't baking tonight.

"Help! I'm trapped."

My body went from chill to panicked in a heartbeat. "Where are you? I'll be right there."

"What's up?" Cristian had removed his shirt to stack the bolts of cloth, not because the work was particularly taxing, but because he liked to show off the results of his gym obsession.

"I have to go." I tossed the keys to him. "Lock up for me. I'll owe you."

"Does that mean we get to play Murder in the Dark?" he called out.

"You wish." I pushed open the door to the shop and put Chloe on speaker so I could figure out the fastest way to get to her.

"The door's locked." Chloe's voice rose in pitch. "I can't open it."

"Do you know where you are? Did you see the van? Was it white? Were you blindfolded? Did you count turns like we learned in self-defense class? How about sounds? Smells? Did you call the police?"

"I can't call the police," she sobbed. "They'll think I did it."

"Did what? You're losing me, babe. Take a breath and calm down. Where are you?"

"I'm at the museum," she said. "The door was open, and the lights were on when I arrived, but no one was here. I figured they'd started the tour without me because I was late. I was looking for them when I heard breaking glass upstairs. I went up to see what was going on, and as soon as I walked into the upper gallery, the door slammed shut behind me. It can't be opened from the inside. I called the museum phone number, and I sent an e-mail to the museum address, but no one responded. I never communicated with the executive director directly, so I don't have his details. I don't know who else to call."

"What about Michael P?"

"He isn't here . . ." Chloe's voice wavered. "He isn't anywhere. I tried to message him, but I can't find the server he set up for the project. I can't find any of our messages, the digital contract, the work order, or my report. His profile on the freelancing platform is gone, too. It's all gone. It's like he never existed."

My skin prickled in warning. "What about his company?"

"It doesn't exist. There's no record of it online, and I had no direct communication with them. Michael approached me directly through the freelancing platform. He said he'd been hired by the museum to do a red-blue penetration test and I was on the red team, which attacks the system and breaks into defenses. It all seemed aboveboard."

I looked up the address of the Victoria Museum. I usually took the L train to get around, but depending on the location, it was sometimes faster to take an Uber.

"Just hang on. I'm figuring out the fastest way to get there."

"There's something else . . ." Chloe hesitated. "One of the glass display cases in the jewelry exhibit has been smashed—that must have been the sound I heard—and a necklace is missing. There's a trail of glass leading to the window."

"Do you think someone stole it while you were there?"

"I don't know what I think," she said. "Michael told me the museum had just combined their access and security systems into one integrated security management system and they needed to test it for vulnerabilities before the museum opened their new vintage and ancient jewelry exhibition. I hacked into the system, identified the weaknesses, and sent him my report. I recommended they separate physical and cybersecurity because, in an integrated system, a hacker can shut down the security of the entire museum. With the information in the report, it would have been easy for him to turn everything off and walk right in."

"But why lock you in?" I asked. "If the police show up, they'll search you and see you don't have the necklace. You can't be accused of the theft."

"What if they accuse me of being an accomplice?" Her voice rose in pitch. "I didn't make any effort to hide my digital trail because I thought the job was legit. The police will see I hacked the system. And now here I am locked in the museum at night with a smashed display case. They won't look for the real thief because they've got *me*."

No. No. No. Chloe could not go to jail. She was everything that was good and kind in the world. She had a thirteen-year-old daughter who needed her mom and a bestie who needed her strength. After enduring six years with Kyle, she'd suffered enough.

"We need to get you out of there before the police show up so they can concentrate on finding the real thief," I said. "I'm on my way."

"There's nothing you can do." Her voice hitched, and I heard the soft thud of a fist on metal. "It's a security door. It won't open unless the system is turned on, and if you turn on the system, the alarm will go off because the sensors on the glass case will have been triggered." Her words came faster, running into one another in a way I'd never heard before. Chloe was the calm one, the steady one. Just the idea that she was so frightened she could barely put a sentence together made my stomach churn.

"What about the window? If the thief got out, you can, too."

"It's two stories up a sheer brick wall at the back of the museum. You know how I am about heights." She gave a hollow laugh. "I always knew it would be my downfall."

"Babe . . ." I swallowed past the lump in my throat. "We're talking prison if they find you in there. We'll work through the height thing together. I'll see what I can grab from the shop. Definitely some rope . . ." My mind circled back to all the murder mysteries and thrillers I'd watched with Rose over the last year. I was tempted to give her a call. She was a crime show addict. If anyone knew how to get out of a locked museum, it was her.

"I don't know what to do." Chloe choked back a sob. "Olivia . . . she'll be alone."

"I got you," I told her. "Sit tight. I'll be right there."

◇ ◇ ◇

I had too much gear and not enough time, so I called an Uber. "Emma" arrived two minutes later in her black "I'm a single independent woman who needs no man" Ford Flex.

Half Jeep, half SUV, and all muscle, Emma's vehicle was a fitting ride for someone who was the epitome of Elle King's "Chain Smokin, Hard Drinkin, Woman." I guessed her to be in her late thirties, maybe a few years younger. Her short dark hair was cut ragged and dyed with bright pink streaks. She was all curves beneath a black tank cut low to show off her ample cleavage and two full sleeves of ink.

"I'm on a rescue mission," I said after I'd climbed into her vehicle with a doubled-over suit bag filled with ropes, hangers, a blanket, and random things I'd grabbed that might help get the rope up and Chloe down.

"If it's a lost pet, you should know I don't allow animals in my vehicle."

"It's a person, not a—"

"Except my ex, Zack." Her eyes narrowed in the rearview mirror. "He was an animal—in bed, in the car, restrooms, alleyways, boats, forests, beaches . . ."

"Lucky you," I said, more out of jealousy than prudishness. My fingers flew over the screen texting Chloe words of assurance and a status update of where we were.

". . . fields, department stores, concert halls, classrooms, bars . . . and once we went into this confessional at a church and—"

"My friend is locked in a museum in the Gold Coast," I blurted out. "Someone tried to set her up to take the fall for a theft. I need to get there as fast as possible."

Emma turned on the engine and floored the accelerator, sending me thudding back in my seat.

"I need to be alive when we get there." I clung to the door handle when Emma made a sharp left onto East Jackson Drive.

"Chill." She looked over her shoulder instead of keeping her eyes on the road. "I've never been in an accident, and I've driven boats, planes, tractors, combines, transport trucks, RVs, and motorcycles.

I've also got a friend with a limo service, and I help him out when he's overbooked. I've got all the licenses. There isn't a vehicle I can't drive." She sped down the road, weaving back and forth between the two lanes until we hit Lake Shore Drive. I thought the busy eight-lane multilevel expressway that runs alongside the shoreline of Lake Michigan would slow her down, but the challenge of navigating all that traffic just made her drive faster.

"So your ex . . ." I was desperate to get to Chloe but not at the cost of my life. Talking seemed to be a good distraction. "What went wrong?"

"He changed after he got famous and insured his hands," Emma said. "He was afraid to do anything in case he injured them—and I mean anything. What's the point of being a virtuoso violinist if you can't put those strumming techniques to good use? 'Redefining what it is to be a classical musician in the twenty-first century,' my ass. I'll tell you what he needed to redefine—his relationship expectations if he thought I was going to put out for a man who has sex with his hands in the air like he's getting robbed. I had to do all the work. He used to be a Dvořák's Violin Concerto in A Minor—playful and commanding—but then he turned into a boring Bach's Sonata for Violin Solo No. 3 in C Major. Talk about a snoozefest."

"I get it," I said, even though I didn't. Classical music wasn't my thing. I'd made it to level four in piano, and after three months of violin, my father had taken it away to save his sanity. "I'm sorry it didn't work out."

"What's the rope for?" Emma asked, checking out the back seat through the rearview mirror as if she hadn't just shared her heartbreak along with the most intimate details of her life.

"My friend is trapped on the second floor of a building, and I need to help her escape. She's not much of a climber and she's afraid of heights."

"You gotta get the rope up there before she can climb down," Emma pointed out.

"I was going to try and throw it."

"You don't look like you've got much of an arm."

"I have three sports-mad brothers. I know how to throw."

"I like the sporty types," Emma said. "My dad was a professional race car driver so he was always training. He used to take me along to the gym so we could spend time together before he went on tour. I took out a ton of student loans to get a degree in exercise training so I could be part of that world, but it's hard to break in as a woman. The only jobs I could get were holding the coach's clipboard or running out for protein shakes. I didn't spend $90,000 for a stupid degree to run around ordering kale acai green tea chia almond milk smoothies with a triple protein boost hold the shredded coconut. Like strawberry and banana is going to kill you? I had to take this gig just to pay the bills."

It was Chloe's story and my story. It was Cristian's story and the story of countless other millennials we knew. We were living a life where our dreams and passions were always out of reach.

We raced past the Chicago Children's Museum—a primary school field trip favorite—and then past Ohio Street Beach. "Do *you* get the ticket if the police stop us?" I asked. "Or is it my fault because I told you I was in a hurry?"

"Never had a speeding ticket," Emma said. "I go too fast for the police to catch me. Also, I know this city so well, I can easily give them the slip."

We made it to the museum in a fraction of the time it would have taken on the bus or L train, but instead of letting her pull up in front, I asked her to keep going. "Park on the next block. I don't want anyone to identify your car or see me without my disguise."

I threw on a suit jacket I'd taken from the shop and topped it off with a black fedora. Dad said they were coming back in style.

"That's not much of a disguise." Emma snorted a laugh. "You look like you should be tap dancing in the rain."

"It's not a fashion show," I said. "I'm potentially doing something illegal, and I don't want to be caught."

"I'm all over that illegal shit," Emma said. "You need some help? Or do you want me to wait and drive the getaway car?"

"I don't want you to get involved."

Emma handed me her card. "That's my personal cell phone number. I'll stick around the area just in case. And if you ever need an exercise trainer, just give me a call."

"Thanks again." I grabbed the bag from the back of her car and hoisted it over my shoulder.

"This area is mostly one-way streets," Emma called out. "If the police are on your tail and you need me for a getaway, make sure you're running in the right direction."

◇ ◇ ◇

Anyone who has gone to school in Chicago is familiar with its numerous yellow bus destinations—everything from ice cream shops to aquariums and from jousting matches to skydiving in a giant wind tunnel. Our teachers were spoiled for choice when it came to field trip venues, especially museums. After fourteen years of school with multiple field trips every year, it was a shock to discover there was actually a museum I hadn't seen.

Tucked away on a quiet tree-lined street in the Gold Coast neighborhood, the Victoria Museum is three stories high with an elegant but restrained Italian-style limestone exterior. Although I was tempted to just push open the ornate inlaid front door, I pulled my fedora low and snuck around to the side gate leading to the back garden.

It didn't occur to me at the time to wonder why the gate was unlocked or who had left the fresh footprints in the mud. Nor did I bother searching the dense foliage at the back of the yard. I was focused on rescuing my bestie, and there she was, leaning out the second-story window, her face a blur in the drizzle of rain.

"Simi?" Her thin voice carried over the loud crunch of my footsteps on the gravel path below the window.

"I'm here." I held up my bag. "I brought rope and other stuff to help get you down."

"I can't believe you came."

"Of course I came. I'll have you out of there in no time." I forced a smile, but Chloe knew me too well. Even in the semidarkness, she could tell I was worried.

"It's too high to throw the rope, isn't it?"

"Maybe for an amateur." My joke fell flat as did the rope after a few failed attempts. Like I'd told Emma, I knew how to throw, but if I couldn't do it, there weren't many who could.

"I'll tie it to a stick or branch and lift it up," I said. "Or you could climb out the window, and I can talk you down."

"It's too high," she said. "I can't do it."

I heard a crack in the bushes: the rustle of leaves. I looked behind me, but there was nothing but trees and darkness.

"What is it?" she called out, her voice low. "What's the matter?"

"I heard something. It must just be a cat." I walked over to the bushes and picked up the nearest fallen branch. Thick and sturdy, it was almost six feet long.

"I've got the perfect branch," I shouted, tying the rope to the top. Chloe leaned out over the window, and I held it in the air just under her outstretched hands.

"Got it!" She untied the rope and pulled it inside.

"Tie it to something sturdy."

Chloe moved away from the window. Moments later, the shriek of an alarm pierced the silence.

"Chloe?" My heart pounded in my chest. "What happened? You need to get out of there."

"It's too late." She leaned out the window and dropped the rope, her face pale in the semidarkness. "Someone turned on the system or I've triggered one the alarms. The police will be on their way. You need to leave before they get here."

"No." I grabbed the rope and threw it up toward her, over and over and over again. "I'm not leaving you."

"Don't be an idiot." Her face was pale in the moonlight, resigned. "This has nothing to do with you. I was stupid. I didn't do my due diligence and now I have to pay the price. I won't drag you into it."

Sirens wailed in the distance, growing louder by the second.

"The mostly dead man in Rose's living room had nothing to do with you and yet you showed up with bleach." I picked up the branch but my hands were shaking too much to tie the rope. Panic fuzzed my brain. I ran for the wall, clawing at the wet, slippery bricks, desperately trying to find a handhold. If she wasn't coming down, I was going up.

Red and blue lights lit up the trees. Tires screeched. Doors slammed.

"Jump!" Unable to find purchase, I grabbed the bulging suit bag, holding it out as if it would somehow break her fall. My breath burst in and out of my lungs, my face wet with a mix of rain and tears. "I'll catch you. Fall on me. Please. Please. Just jum—"

A hand clamped over my mouth, cutting off my words. Big. Warm. Slightly sweaty and smelling of pine and earth.

Maybe if my brain hadn't already tipped into sensory overload, I might have reacted differently. I'd taken self-defense training. I'd lasted through six judo classes with my brothers until someone had thrown one of the twins on top of me, and I'd suffered a minor concussion and a fractured arm. I knew what to do when someone grabbed me from behind, but instead of slamming my heel into his instep, twisting, and running away, I froze.

Lights swept over the window above and then Chloe disappeared.

FOUR

◇ ◇ ◇

Shhh. I'm not going to hurt you." My assailant wrapped a strong arm around my middle, pulling me tight against his hard body. Step by careful step, he pulled us back into the thick bushes until I could barely see the window where Chloe had been only seconds from escape. Protected by a canopy of trees, the mini forest was dry despite the rain and fragrant with the sweet scent of the flowers.

"Are you okay?" he asked.

My heart pounded a frantic beat. Seriously? Was I okay?

"Mmmph," I mumbled with all the sarcasm and indignation I could muster and then I licked his hand, anticipating a reactive jerk of disgust that would free my mouth long enough to scream. Instead, I got a low chuckle that vibrated deep in his chest.

"If I take my hand away, do you promise to be quiet? You can't help your friend if you get arrested, too."

I nodded. He moved his hand. I drew in a breath of cool air and let out the energy of my panic-infused brain. "Am I okay? No, I am definitely not okay. My best friend is being arrested for something she didn't do. I tried to rescue her and failed. My cheap rental apartment flooded, a naked man was mostly dead, I got fired, and now I have to live at home and work with Cristian, whose only goal in life is to get every woman he meets into bed. My parents are desperate to marry me off, and now I'll be a sitting duck for a parade of losers who can't find a woman on their own. I eat too much candy and I need to exercise more. I'm wet and cold and on the verge of bankruptcy and a stranger just dragged me into the bushes to do God knows what with me."

"Anything else I should know?" His voice, calm and quiet, brought my racing pulse down a notch. What the hell was wrong with me? What had happened to my instinctive fight-or-flight response?

"No. That just about sums up the dumpster fire that is my life."

"Take a breath," he said.

"A breath?"

"Deep breathing helps reduce anxiety. It's been proven in medical studies."

"Do you know what else reduces anxiety?" I struggled against his firm hold—not just because I was desperate to get away from him but because I didn't understand why he didn't scare me. "Not being held captive in the bushes. Why don't you let me go and see how chill I become?"

"I'm saving you from your misguided sense of loyalty and total disregard for your own well-being. The police will be coming back here any moment now, looking for an accomplice." He tightened his hold, and my stupid brain interpreted his warmth and firm grip as "safety and security" instead of "you're going to die."

"Misguided?" I glared over my shoulder, but I couldn't make out his face in the darkness. "That's my best friend in there. She's already gone through more pain than most people experience in a lifetime. Now she's scared and alone and going to jail, and I'm trapped in the bushes with you."

"They aren't bushes," he said. "The shrub to your left is nine-bark. It has a beautiful leaf color, a cinnamon inner bark, and blooms pink in June. It's best kept trimmed to about five feet, but no one has looked after this garden, which is why this one is over eight feet tall. On your right, you've got arrowwood. You might know it as fragrant viburnum. It adds structure to a garden and a wonderful spicy fragrance to your space. Again, lack of pruning is why it has overgrown."

"Are you a gardener? Is that why you were hiding back here?"

"Gardening is just a hobby," he said.

"What's your real job? Kidnapping innocent women? Skulking behind museums?" Something niggled at the back of my brain, and I sucked in a sharp breath. "Or are you the thief?"

"I'll admit I was attempting to acquire a certain item from the museum, but someone got there before me." He stepped back, deeper into the bushes, pulling me with him. I felt him moving, adjusting my position, his hips pressed firmly against my ass.

My muscles tightened, ready to run if it turned out I'd made a serious error in judgment. "What's going on? I watch a lot of crime and mystery shows, so I know that the deeper people are dragged into a forest by a stranger, the lower the chance that they'll make it out alive."

"You were standing on the hellebore," he said. "It's a work-horse in a small garden, but the stems break easily. My favorite pairing is hellebore planted near brunnera and fern for a trifecta of shady textural goodness."

Not what I expected to hear from a stranger in the dark.

"Are you for real? This place is about to be crawling with police. You're a kidnapper and self-professed would-be thief, and you're worried about the plants?"

"You don't like plants?" The disappointment in his voice was unmistakable.

"Sure I like plants. I'd take a house with a garden over an apartment in a high-rise any day, but that's not the point. You need to get your priorities straight."

"What's more important than plants? They give us food, fiber, shelter, medicine, and fuel. The basic food for all organisms is produced by green plants. In the process of food production, oxygen is released into the air we breathe, and as I'm sure you know oxygen is essential to life."

Oxygen was also essential for lowering anxiety, or so my therapist said. Since I didn't seem to be in any imminent danger, I tried my 5-5-5 breathing technique, then 4-7-8, and then I chose a calming focus and tried mindful breathing.

"Are you hyperventilating?" he asked. "Or trying to fall asleep?"

"I'm trying to use the plant oxygen to calm down so I can think. And by the way, people are more important than plants. Specifically, the people you love."

"Is that why you showed up here with a bag full of—what do you have in there anyway?"

I felt his hand move down my arm, fingertips brushing my fist clenched tight around the top of the suit bag.

"Things to help Chloe escape—rope, hangers, a blanket, a roll of duct tape—"

"Tape?"

"I was in a panic, okay? Tape is useful in many situations. It can repair things, close things, seal things . . ."

"I'm aware of the wonders of tape," he said. "I've just never thought about it in the context of escaping from a second-story window in the rain."

"Obviously, you lack imagination."

"I'm imagining it now," he said, "and I'm laughing inside so you don't feel embarrassed."

"I appreciate your restraint."

He shifted behind me, adjusted his hold. "Why a suit bag when there are many more functional bags out there? Gym bags, shopping bags, tote bags, suitcases, travel bags, even backpacks. I've always found handles to be particularly useful."

"My dad owns a high-end suit store. The only other bag options were luxury leather satchels and briefcases, and they hadn't been rain-proofed. I can't afford the thousand-dollar hit."

"Is that why your friend was trying to steal the necklace? You're both desperate for cash?"

I looked back over my shoulder, gave him the side-eye. "How do you know a necklace was stolen?"

"It's the only thing of real value in that museum. There was supposed to be a private security team watching it in anticipation of every low-life amateur trying to steal it when the exhibit is announced tomorrow."

"Like you," I said.

He bristled, his body tensing behind me. "I'm a professional."

"If you're a professional, then how did someone else get to it first?"

"If I could answer that question, we wouldn't be here," he said. "Very few people knew it was going to be part of the exhibit. The thief also had help from someone with extensive knowledge of the security system."

Chloe. But I wasn't going to share that information with him.

"So what happens now?" I asked. "Do you wait until the police are gone and steal something else?"

He gave a snort of derision. "I don't steal; I retrieve and return to the rightful owner."

"Semantics," I said. "If it's not yours and you take it, then it's theft."

"We will have to agree to disagree." He ran his hand up the

sleeve of the suit jacket to tug gently on my fedora. "What's with the hat?"

"It's a disguise in case there were cameras on the street."

"I dealt with the cameras," he said. "No one will know you were here with your suit bag full of tape."

"Tape is underrated."

"So are plants."

I would have laughed except that we were hiding from the police, and I didn't want to draw any attention by raising my voice above our hushed tones. I was also enjoying our conversation despite the curious circumstances. If he wanted to hurt me, he would have done so by now and I'd slowly let down my guard. Passing the time chatting in the arms of a thief in the bushes behind a museum wasn't how I'd imagined I'd be spending my evening.

"How did you get into the retrieval business?" I leaned against him because he was warm and solid, and nothing about him screamed threat.

"Did you ever read *Oliver Twist?*" His free hand dropped to rest easily on my hip, sending a rush of warmth through my body.

"My mother is an English professor. Other kids got picture books at bedtime. We got the classics. I'll give you *Oliver Twist* in a few short words. Orphan. Workhouse. Apprentice thief. Bad things. Worse things. Happy ending."

He paused and said, "That's pretty much my story but without the happy ending."

"Then it's a sad story."

"Depends how you look at it. If you'd met me in a bar and I was wearing a fancy suit and paying for everyone's drinks, you'd think it was a happy story because I'd overcome a difficult childhood and made something of myself. You're making a situational judgment."

"Are you wearing a suit?" I felt behind me, stroked my hand over his thigh. "Feels like jeans."

"You're making it very difficult to be a gentleman," he said. "I think we should keep the below-the-belt stroking for later."

"You're assuming there's going to be a 'later.'" I moved my hand as far away as I could, given my limited range of motion. "How do you know I won't scream and run away as soon as you let me go?"

"Because I intrigue you," he said. "If you weren't intrigued, you could have screamed as soon as I removed my hand and disabled me with a well-placed heel. Of course, I would have released you the instant you indicated you wanted to go, secure in the knowledge that I had done my moral duty to stop you from running headlong into danger."

"Maybe I'm not as intrigued as I am astonished at the size of your ego." There was definitely more to him than he let on—the way he talked, his interest in literature, his knowledge of plants, and his decision to save me from myself when he could just as easily have stayed hidden in the bushes all suggested he wasn't an ordinary thief.

Far from being insulted, he just laughed. "As for me, I'm still here despite the risk to my personal safety because you have me totally enthralled."

"Enthralled?"

"You are an enthralling woman," he said. "You show up in the rain dressed in a fedora and oversize blazer and carrying a suit bag full of rope and tape on a hopeless quest to rescue a friend trapped on the second floor of a museum. Even when the police arrive, you refuse to give up or show any sense of self-preservation until you are manhandled into the bushes by a stranger and still you show no fear."

"That doesn't mean I'm not scared," I pointed out.

"I said I wouldn't hurt you."

"They're just words. You're still holding me prisoner."

"I think we both know it's more for show," he said. "If you wanted to get away, you could."

He was right. Now that my head was clear, I remembered all my self-defense lessons, as well as a couple of judo throws. It wouldn't be difficult to break his hold. I just didn't want to.

"You're forgetting the police outside," I said. "Your screams of pain might attract their attention."

"I have never once screamed in pain." He stiffened behind me. "I've been shot, beaten, tortured, and stabbed and the most they ever got from me was a groan."

I bit back a grimace even though he couldn't see my face. "It sounds like you're in a dangerous line of work. Or are you just that bad at making friends?"

His body shook with laughter. I felt the gentle press of his forehead against the back of my head. "Why did I have to meet you now? Why couldn't we have met on a plane? Or in a bar? Or across a crowded room?"

"It would have been cliché," I said. "You're an interesting man in an interesting profession. You have to meet someone in an interesting way."

He gave a contented grunt. "You think I'm interesting."

"You're a thief who doesn't act like a thief. I'm curious to know more about you. Do you like movies?"

"I'm more of an action person," he said. "I don't like sitting still for very long."

"Me neither." I tipped my head to the side, looked back at him again. "But if you were forced to watch something? If you were tied to a chair and couldn't get up, what would you choose?"

"Hmmm." He twisted his lips to the side, considering. "Not horror, thriller, or mystery. Too much like work. Same with action movies. Every job I do now seems to involve some kind of chase. Not romance—I don't believe in happily-ever-afters—and drama usually puts me to sleep. What's left?"

"Westerns, comedy, science fiction, and fantasy."

"I like a good Western," he said. "And a good laugh. I'm not really into fantasy worlds but superheroes . . . space . . . *Star Wars* was good. I liked Han Solo."

"That makes sense. He's the nexus of true cowboy grit and a cocky, irreverent action hero—flawed, ambitious, egotistical, daring, handsome, and charismatic. I always liked his swagger."

"What's swagger?" he asked.

"The combination of confidence and charm."

"Does he remind you of anyone?" He leaned back against a tree, pulling me with him. I could feel his tension ease, so I relaxed, sinking against his broad chest. "No," I said, my lips quivering with a smile. "No one at all."

"Hummph." He gave a snort of derision. "Are you sure? Maybe you should rethink your answer."

"If you're looking for a boost to your massive ego, I think you're more of a Star-Lord type. He's the inverse of Han Solo. Cocky yet oblivious, womanizing, facetious, conceited, charming but arrogant."

He bristled behind me, his voice thick with indignation. "Conceited? Facetious? You obviously know nothing about me."

"That's true. I haven't even had a good look at your face."

"You'd change your mind if you knew me," he said. "You'd instantly think Han Solo and not Star-Lord."

"I look forward to being proven wrong."

His arm relaxed around me. I could have just pushed it away, but I wasn't inclined to move, especially since the lights were still flashing on the street, and the police had yet to search the garden.

"Do you have an interesting profession?" he asked.

"I have a business degree and a bunch of soul-sucking, mind-numbing entry-level office jobs under my belt as well as a few retail side gigs. I have too much debt to pursue anything interesting, much less find my passion."

"Now, that's a sad story."

"I shouldn't have gone into business." I shrugged my shoulders and sighed. "I'm just not a desk person. I can't deal with all the distractions in an office. My brain bounces around too much. My parents said I was squirrely when I was a kid—always going off on tangents, never in a straight line."

"I like squirrels," he said. "They're sociable, loyal, athletic, adaptable, and intelligent."

His words hit me deep inside. Chloe was the only other person I knew who liked squirrels for their squirreliness.

"Check the back," a man shouted. "She must have had an accomplice."

"You were right," I whispered.

"Professional, like I said." He tensed again, holding me so tight, I could barely breathe. I felt curiously safe with him. If he'd let me go in that moment, I wouldn't have moved.

Two police officers walked into the garden, sweeping their flashlights back and forth in a cursory search. They spent a few minutes studying the gravel path beneath the window and the grassy lawn beside it. One of them squatted to inspect my branch while the other shone his light on the wall. After a little arguing about whether it was worth searching the bushes in the rain, they turned and walked away.

I heard doors slam. Engines purr. Red and blue lights faded away. When the night was still and silent save for the patter of rain on the leaves above, my captor released me, and we walked carefully through the bushes into the dimly lit garden.

"Do I get to look at you properly now?" I asked, turning. "Or is this going to be a case of 'If you see my face, I'll have to kill you'?"

"I promised I wouldn't hurt you," he said. "I don't break my promises."

"I'm glad to hear—" Words failed me when I turned around. He wasn't traditionally handsome but ruggedly so, with a strong jaw, a straight nose, and a wide, stubborn mouth. His eyes were dark and velvety, sprinkled with gold. Gorgeous. Just like the rest of him. Even partially hidden in the shadows, he was simply the most breathtaking man I'd ever seen.

My knees weakened and I struggled to regain my composure.

I was already dead when he smiled. I died a little more when he brushed back the longish dark hair that was a damp tangle around his chiseled face. He wore a leather jacket over broad shoulders and a gray T-shirt stretched tight across the hard, muscled chest I'd had the pleasure of leaning against for the last twenty minutes. I guessed him to be an inch or two over six feet, maybe slightly less if his battered leather boots had heels.

"Hello, beautiful."

My mouth opened and closed, but nothing came out. He looked like trouble. But it was the kind of trouble that sent a delicious thrill down my spine.

He held up a twenty-dollar bill. "Thanks for this. I needed cab fare."

I stared at him aghast. "That's mine?"

"It was in your back pocket. You should really keep your cash in a zippered purse. It's more of a challenge."

"You stole it?" I searched my now empty pocket. How had I not felt his hand? Granted, his hips had been on my ass the entire time, but fingers were different.

"Borrowed."

"Are you seriously playing the semantics game again?" I forced myself to give him a harder look. Were those gold flecks in his warm brown eyes or was it just the glitter of ill intent? Was that a smile or a smirk on his handsome face? Was the devil-may-care attitude masking something more sinister? And were those jeans molded to his narrow hips for ease of running away? Or to entice a sex-starved candy store employee who couldn't remember the last time she'd had a hookup?

"I'd play any game with you, but this isn't the time." He walked back into the bushes, and a few moments later, he was up on the retaining wall.

"Wait," I said. "If you're going to steal my money, at least give me your name."

"Oliver."

"Oliver what?"

"Twist."

FIVE

◆ ◆ ◆

Someone had forgotten to tell Detective Garcia that he was supposed to be middle-aged and balding with a face worn by trauma and heavy drinking. Wasn't mid-thirties—I had to guess when he wasn't forthcoming about any personal details—too young to become a detective? With all the crime in the city, how did he have time to build biceps as big as beer kegs? And why would someone who looked like he should be on a runway in Milan become a detective? What a waste of deep, rich, chocolate brown eyes and a strong square jaw. Millions of women could be fantasizing about him, but instead he was sitting in a windowless interrogation room at Chicago's 18th Precinct questioning a woman who was so clearly not guilty of any crime, it was almost laughable.

"Can we take off the handcuffs now?" I rattled the chain that attached the cuffs to the metal table in the interrogation room. "Look at me. Do I look like a threat?"

He lifted a nicely groomed eyebrow. "It's standard procedure when we catch someone in the back garden of a museum during a theft."

"The theft had already occurred by the time I got there," I

said. "And you didn't catch me. I volunteered to come to the station to corroborate my friend's story. I wasn't expecting to be cuffed, tossed in an unmarked car, and frog-marched through the police station like a criminal. Where is Chloe? She's going to be very distressed. I should be with her."

"She said the same thing about you when I mentioned you were here," he said. "Why don't you tell me the facts, and then I'll see what I can do."

He leaned back in his chair, blue shirt unbuttoned at the collar to show off the corded muscles of his tanned throat, manspreading just enough to make me wish the metal table between us wasn't quite so wide. The dude was solid muscle. He had to spend hours at the gym to get shoulders that huge. And that chest. *Phwoar.* I'd never hooked up with a police officer before, but I liked the idea of being with a man who could protect me with his body alone.

I gave Garcia a brief outline of the facts, since he loved facts so much. Chloe's excitement when she'd been approached about the freelance museum job. Her growing online attraction to the consultant who hired her. The invitation from the executive director to the private viewing and her decision to go with the black dress instead of polka dots or flowers. Her frantic call. My cab ride—I didn't mention the part about speeding. And finally, my failed attempt to rescue her.

"It must be hard for Chloe as a single mom," Garcia said. "Lots of bills to pay and no one to help. Sometimes people get desperate."

My spider senses tingled. This was not where I had expected the conversation to go.

"Olivia is safe, healthy, and happy," I said. "Chloe works three jobs to support her. They're renting the first floor of a nice house that has three other lovely tenants, and although money is tight, the only real issue she has is an ex who has consistently refused to pay child support or alimony. He's someone you should investigate, not Chloe. He's a nasty piece of work. His parents disinherited him after they found out he'd abused her. He barely scraped through college, and now he's involved with a bad crowd."

"No one is trying to take Olivia away," he said, understanding.

"Then I don't appreciate your attempt to insinuate that my friend would resort to theft to make ends meet. It's beneath you and the dignity of your profession."

He bristled, like I'd hit a nerve. Maybe he was one of those TV detectives who'd lost a partner or came home one night after solving a murder to find his best friend sleeping with his wife, and now he spent his days working and his nights drinking whiskey out of a bottle until he fell down drunk on his unmade bed in the dingy apartment he felt he had to live in because it was a reflection of how wrecked he felt inside.

"My apologies." He held up a hand in a gesture of capitulation. Detective Garcia had nice hands. Strong. Tanned. A light dusting of tawny hair on his forearm. I'd never thought about a man's forearm as being sexy before, but something about the way he moved . . .

While Detective Garcia flipped through his black notebook, I silently indulged in a few fantasies. Detective Garcia and I on a tropical island where nudity was encouraged. Detective Garcia and I dancing with our bodies plastered together in my favorite nightclub. Detective Garcia crying with happiness as I walked down the aisle in a red-and-gold lehenga and a pair of gold stilettos with a relieved parent on each arm.

"I have to consider all scenarios," he continued. "We're not talking about the theft of a candy bar. The necklace that was stolen is an antiquity called the Wild Heart. It was loaned to the museum by a private collector for a special exhibit. It's made entirely of diamonds and emeralds and is valued at $25 million."

$25 million. I couldn't even conceive of that amount of money.

How many bags of candy would I be able to buy with $25 million? Or candy stores? I could pay off my loans and Chloe's loans, my brothers' loans, and my parents' mortgage. I could buy a house with a yard and a gate to keep aunties and suitors out. I could hire Garcia to protect me 24-7. I would never have to worry about money again.

Garcia opened his file and slid a picture of the necklace across the table. I'd never seen such a beautiful piece of jewelry. A huge heart-shaped pink diamond surrounded by tiny diamonds rested at the center of a chain of pink diamonds surrounded by diamond and emerald leaves in a floral arrangement.

"Wow. Just wow," I said. "I didn't know diamonds came in pink."

"It wouldn't be worth $25 million if the diamonds were clear, or so I've been told," he said. "Not really a jewelry man. No time for that kind of thing. Crime doesn't sleep."

"Neither do I when my friend is wrongfully accused of a crime and there is no evidence to implicate her." I settled back in my chair, confident in my TV show legal analysis. Detective Garcia wasn't so bad. Gorgeous. Fit. Dry sense of humor. Not particularly threatening. Employed. *Not a professional thief.*

"It could be that she had an accomplice," Garcia said. "Someone who was part of the heist from the beginning. Someone who was there to catch the necklace when it was thrown out the window . . ."

Maybe Garcia wasn't that handsome after all. He had a cleft in his chin and his cheekbones were almost too defined. He'd probably insist on wearing a tuxedo to our wedding instead of a sherwani and there would be no lazy Sunday afternoons eating chocolate croissants in bed because he'd be a sugar hater and health nut like my dad.

"I think this is the part where I ask for my lawyer."

"You have that right," Garcia said. "But I only have a few more questions and then you're free to go. It might take hours for your lawyer to get here."

"That might work for someone who didn't have to binge crime shows with her eighty-year-old landlady to get a reduced rent," I said. "But I know all the tricks. I'll make that call."

◇ ◇ ◇

There were times I hated having a huge family. First, I never had a summer weekend to myself. Why couldn't the Chopras and the Devs (my mom's side of the family) just stop getting married? Why couldn't people just live together and save all the poor single people from having to repurpose old outfits, buy expensive gifts, learn new dances, and eat too much food when they'd rather be lounging on the couch eating handfuls of expired candy, drinking fancy cocktails, and watching romantic comedies with their bestie?

Second, I couldn't go anywhere in Chicago or the burbs without a relative spotting me and reporting back to my grandmother or my mom.

"Simi ate three pieces of pie at the Big Papa Pie Company on West Chicago Avenue last night at seven twenty-eight P.M. and that was right after she had pizza across the street—an entire medium vegetarian special. She won't find a husband if she eats like that."

"Does Simi have the flu? I saw her throwing up in an alley outside Bruno's Pub on North Clark Street last night. She only had one shoe and she couldn't walk straight. I can send over some chicken soup."

On the other hand, a big family meant that no matter the problem, someone had the expertise to help you—especially if it involved law, medicine, engineering, or IT.

A criminal lawyer with a prestigious boutique firm, Riswan Dev was one of the family success stories—tall, handsome, professional, employed, and now looking for a wife. For bonus points, he'd bought a four-bedroom house down the street from his parents and then moved them into the suite downstairs so they would be near their future grandchildren. He was also damn good at his job, and he owed me a favor.

"I'm still waiting to hear why you think my client is involved in the alleged theft," Riswan said. Slim and lanky, with a pair of wire-framed glasses perched on a prominent nose, he'd made it down to the station a mere half hour after I called, along with another attorney from his office to represent Chloe in case there was a conflict of interest.

Garcia had kindly given us a chance to talk in private and had removed the handcuffs at Riswan's request. I liked Riswan's tough, snarky attitude. This was why people paid him the big bucks. It occurred to me that I had no big bucks to pay him, and we hadn't had a chance to talk about his fees—for Chloe or me.

"She was in the garden behind the museum when the alarm went off." Garcia shot me a pointed stare. I mentally crossed the nightclub fantasy off my list. It would clearly take a small fortune in drinks to loosen Garcia up enough to get him onto a dance floor.

"The theft could have occurred anytime after the museum closed," Riswan said. "My client could have been there enjoying the plants, for all you know."

"In fact, I was admiring the ninebark," I said, sending a silent thanks to Oliver for the botany lesson. "They have a beautiful leaf color, a cinnamon inner bark, and bloom pink in June. They are best kept trimmed to about five feet, but clearly no one looked after the museum garden, which is why the one at the back was eight feet tall. Similarly, the arrowwood—you might know it as fragrant viburnum—wasn't pruned, which is why it was over-grown."

"I see." Garcia wrote something in his notebook. His biceps

weren't as big as I'd initially thought, and upon reflection, his forearms were a bit too hairy.

"We didn't take the necklace," I blurted out. "Why don't you write that down?" I didn't like Garcia anymore. It was, in fact, possible to be too handsome.

"I'm not the thieving type," I continued. "When I was a kid, I would break out in hives when my brothers stole laddu from the pantry. I couldn't even eat them. My therapist thinks it comes from deep-seated anxiety issues. I've spent most of life trying not to make waves."

"Then who took the necklace?" Garcia fixed me with a stare.

"Maybe it was the man who was hiding in the bushes at the back of the garden."

Garcia stopped writing. "What man?"

"When the police showed up, he grabbed me from behind and dragged me between the ninebark and the arrowwood. He had his hand over my mouth so I couldn't scream, and he pinned my arms to my sides. I accused him of being the thief, but he said it wasn't him."

"I thought his hand was over your mouth. How did you have a conversation?" Garcia tipped his head to the side and gave me a quizzical look. Damn he looked fine.

"He took his hand away after he said he wouldn't hurt me. His name is Oliver. He said he was there to retrieve the necklace and return it to its rightful owner but someone else beat him to it. He convinced me to stay in the bushes with him because he said I couldn't help Chloe if I was arrested, too. I believed him until he stole my money and ran away. That's when I came to my senses and surrendered myself. Why would I abandon my friend and listen to a thief?"

Garcia did a lot of writing in his notepad. Kicking it old-school. I wasn't a big fan of the old pen and paper, but it fit his personality—the real straitlaced no-nonsense one, and not the sex god fantasy.

"At any point did he let you go? Did you see his face?"

"Near the end, after he'd taken my money, he released me, and I got a chance to look at him. He was gorgeous but in a devilish way."

"Gorgeous but devilish?" He heaved a sigh. "Can you be more descriptive? Hair and eye color. Weight. Height. Clothes."

"Leather jacket. Very worn. Boots. Also worn. His hair was tousled like he'd just got out of bed. It looked good on him. Sexy." I licked my lips, imagining Oliver in place of Garcia in my tropical island fantasy. "He was about the same height and build as you, but leaner. I don't think he spends as much time in the gym as you probably do . . ." I trailed off when Riswan shook his head. "Or not. It's nothing to do with me how much time you spend in the gym. Or don't. Or whether you even like gyms. Maybe you were born with biceps the size of watermelons—"

Riswan cut me off with a shake of his head. "That's enough."

"Did he give you a last name?" Garcia asked.

"Twist." I shrugged. "I think he was lying because he said his name was Oliver, so Oliver Twist? I don't think so. We were just talking about Oliver Twist so I'm pretty sure he made it up. Or maybe it's just his modus operandi for when he holds someone hostage in the bushes behind a museum. He reveals his sad back story. And boom. Punch line at the end. 'My name is Oliver. Last name is Twist.'"

"I think we're done here," Riswan said.

But I couldn't stop. I'd come here thinking I just had to corroborate Chloe's story and then all this would go away. I'd thought Garcia was a nice guy—a worthy subject of a naked fantasy—and he'd been playing me all along. I hadn't done anything wrong and now I was being accused of a crime. My anxiety level had hit "high intensity" and thoughts were bouncing around my head like pin-balls before pouring out of my mouth unfiltered.

"He's the criminal," I said. "He's the droid you're looking for. Ha-ha. *Star Wars* reference. Three brothers and two parents who are all *Star Wars* stans. What can I say?"

"Simi . . ." Riswan put a firm hand on my arm, but it was too late. He should have dragged me out of there as soon as I started talking about the laddu.

"He said he was there for the necklace and then he stole twenty dollars from me," I said, my words tumbling over one another in a desperate attempt to get free. "I don't know why you're still here wasting time with me when you should really be at the museum looking for footprints or checking the surrounding area for sur-veillance footage that will lead you to the real criminal, and not a woman whose own mother laughed when she said she wanted to murder her brother."

Riswan stood so quickly, his chair almost fell over. "I need a few moments to confer with my client."

Garcia snapped his book closed. "I'll bet you do."

"I thought you were nice," I said to Garcia. "I thought you were decent and honest and an upstanding member of the police community. I even thought you should be a model but now I un-think it. I also unthink—"

"Simi." Riswan shook his head. "Stop. Talking."

"Why? I don't have anything to hide. I'm an open book. Ask me anything."

Riswan drew in a long breath and cleared his throat. "I believe what my client is trying to say is that she is a brutally honest person who has told you the truth about what happened that night. She did not steal the necklace and was not part of any plot or plan to remove it from the museum. If you have any evidence that sug-gests otherwise, I look forward to seeing it."

Garcia have a curt nod. "I'll be in touch."

After Garcia left, Riswan gave my hand a squeeze. "Don't worry. We'll figure this out."

"I am worried," I said. "I thought it couldn't get worse and then it did."

◆ ◆ ◆

Chloe didn't speak for the entire train ride back to her place after our respective lawyers had arranged for our release from the police station. I'd never seen her so shaken. She was my rock, my touchstone. Nothing rattled her. She'd had a baby at sixteen and still finished high school and got a college degree. She'd lost jobs, run low on cash, and sat with Olivia in emergency rooms countless times without ever losing her cool. But this time was different. This time I was the one being calm, even though I was an anxious mess inside.

"Riswan is the best at what he does," I said after pouring two glasses of white wine in her kitchen. "He was the gold medalist in his class. His parents wanted him to be a corporate lawyer or a big-time litigator so he could make a lot of money, but he chose criminal law because he wanted to do legal aid and help people who couldn't help themselves."

Chloe lit a calming scented candle and sat on a stool at the small counter separating the kitchen from the living area. She'd lived in the ground floor suite of the cheerful character home with Olivia for the last five years and had decorated it in a nautical theme to match the white-and-blue kitchen. Her rent took up over half her income every month, but she was determined to stay to give Chloe stability and the benefit of the shared backyard.

"My lawyer said Detective Garcia called the executive director of the museum." Chloe took a big gulp of her wine. "The director said they didn't hire a security consultant. They've used the same security firm to handle cyber and access security for years. He didn't know anyone called Michael P. He didn't know me. And he didn't arrange a tour of the museum. In fact, private viewings were expressly forbidden in the contract the museum signed with the owner of the necklace and his insurance company." Chloe dropped her head to her hands. "I was set up. Why would someone do this to me?"

"I don't think it was personal," I said. "Michael P could have chosen any of the ethical hackers advertising on the freelancing platform. It was just bad luck he picked you." I breathed in the soothing scent of lavender, doing my best to keep my impulse to scream under control.

"He picked me because he must have known I'd be so excited to get a big job like this that I wouldn't bother to do my due diligence, and then he made me think we had a connection. I was stupid and trusting just like I was with Kyle and so many of the other guys I've dated." She banged her forehead with the heel of her hand. "Why does this keep happening to me? Why can't I find a nice guy? Someone protective and caring. Someone who makes me feel safe and loved. Someone who isn't trying to hurt me or rip me off."

"He's out there." I drained my glass. It could have been gasoline, or it could have been a $5,000 bottle of Screaming Eagle Cabernet. Already in sensory overload, my taste buds didn't care. "But maybe you should focus on—"

"I won't find him in prison." Chloe moaned. "And you can't come with me because you have to look out for Olivia. Kyle's parents are her godparents, and I know they'll take good care of her, but they don't know me like you do. I'm worried Kyle might try to worm his way back into the family if she winds up with them."

"Why would he care? He's never wanted anything to do with

her." I hated talking about Kyle. I hated his name. I hated the man. If I ever did murder someone, it would be him. Even his parents didn't like him. After the divorce, when the truth came out and Chloe was awarded sole custody of Olivia, they'd disinherited him and kicked him out of their house.

"Kyle's grandparents set up a very generous trust fund for Olivia's education before they passed away," Chloe said. "If something happens to me, he could petition for custody so he can get his hands on that money. I don't want him anywhere near her. I think he'd hurt her. I feel it in my bones."

"If he ever touched her, my criminal career would get off to a flying start." My hands closed into fists. I'd known Olivia since the day she was born. She was like my own daughter. There was nothing I wouldn't do to protect her.

"That's the only thing that makes this bearable," she said. "She would always have you."

A sliver of guilt slid through my heart. If I'd gone to the museum with Chloe, she wouldn't be sitting here worrying about Olivia. I would have known something was wrong when no one showed up. I would have dragged her out of there, and the only problem we'd be trying to solve tonight would be whether to tell Cristian's girlfriend about his three "special baby girls."

"I have to think it through." Chloe twisted a thick strand of hair around her finger, her classic stress move. "The police might show up any minute to throw me in jail."

"I'm going to stop you right there," I said. "No one is going to prison. The lawyers will clear all this up and then we can get back to living our lives. And even if they can't, there is no way I would let you go to prison alone. You need someone to have your back in the joint or you might get shanked in the shower. It has to be someone hard, tough, and street-smart. Someone forged in the hell of being the only girl in a family with three boys."

As I'd hoped, Chloe finally smiled. "You've been watching too many shows with Rose."

"We'll have to beat a few people up when we get there," I continued. "We have to show our dominance; otherwise we'll appear weak, and that's when they take your stuff and turn you into somebody's bitch."

"I'm nobody's bitch." Chloe finished her glass and slammed it on the counter.

"Now we're talking." We were a little bit tipsy. Good thing Olivia was sleeping over at a friend's house. She didn't like to see her mother acting anything other than parental.

"I would look terrible in an orange jumpsuit." Chloe grabbed the bottle and drank straight from the top. "It's not my color."

"That's because you were never meant to wear it." I didn't mention that I looked great in orange. It made my skin glow and set off my dark hair.

"I've never shanked anyone before." She pushed herself up, her forehead creased in a frown. "I don't think I could do it."

"I got you, babe," I said with the confidence of someone who'd spent their childhood playing cops and robbers with her brothers and having pretend sword fights with sticks.

"It's going to be okay," she said, half to herself.

"Of course it's going to be okay."

I said the words, but I didn't believe them.

SIX

◇ ◇ ◇

Chloe and I walked into my parents' house the next morning just as Nani was rolling roti, smoothing a small ball of dough over a marble base. My grandmother spent every Saturday preparing a big meal for the weekly family lunch on Sunday and every Sunday complaining about how tired she was after doing all that cooking.

"Howdy, ladies!" Nani said. "Pull up a chair. Get 'em while they're hot."

"You're not a Texas cowboy," Dad said from behind his newspaper. He liked actual paper when it came to the news. He didn't like my slightly abrasive grandmother. Dad usually made himself scarce when Nani was around. He must have been taken by surprise. To say they didn't get along was an understatement. Nani was not the kind of person to keep her views to herself and she hadn't liked my dad from the day they met. My mom was supposed to marry a doctor or an engineer. She'd married a suit salesman instead.

"I've been watching Westerns at the gym," Nani said. "It must have rubbed off."

Nani was my mother's mom, but she shared my dad's obsession

with fitness. Lean and slim, she worked out twice a day and had the biceps to show for it. Her jet-black hair—a result of cheap boxed hair dye—was a contrast to her softly lined face, but there was no hint of senility in her dark brown eyes.

"I love warm roti." Chloe reached for the freshly fried flatbread, and I slapped her hand away. Although she'd spent as much time at my house as she had at home when we were kids, she still didn't recognize a trap when she saw one.

"We can't stay." I sensed an impending storm and even one roti would lead to an invitation to sit down for a meal. "I'm just here to change because I spent the night at Chloe's, then we're heading out for coffee."

"Don't forget we're having a special dinner tomorrow night," Mom said, tucking loose strands from her graying hair behind her ear. "Be home by six P.M." She gave me the smile she used on her students when she was giving them a pop quiz. She had her usual English professor look going, with thick purple glasses, a beige sweater pulled over a white shirt, a colorful scarf, and an artsy necklace. Work. Casual. Party. Business. My mother dressed the same for every occasion.

"Oh, and by the way . . ."

The hair on the back of my neck prickled. My muscles tensed, ready to run.

"Nani got a call from Annika Auntie." Mom and Nani shared a look that screamed trouble. "Annika said she heard from Meera Auntie who heard from Satya Auntie who heard from a friend of a friend of a friend that you were at the police station last night." Mom raised an eyebrow. Nani looked over her shoulder. Dad lowered his newspaper. Chloe shoved a warm piece of roti into her mouth.

"That's very interesting." But not surprising. Nani was the center of gossip in our local South Asian community. Chicago.

Naperville. Burr Ridge. Lombard. Downers Grove. Evanston. Oak Park. She knew someone who knew someone who knew someone who would tell her what was going on no matter the time of day or night.

"They said you were talking to Riswan Dev," Mom continued when my immediate response was not forthcoming.

Chloe handed me a piece of roti. I stuffed my mouth so conversation would be impossible. Anything to avoid having to answer the question I knew was coming.

"Do I hear wedding bells?"

Gah!

"He's my cousin," I said between chews. "Did you forget that part?"

"He's a distant cousin." Nani threw a roti into the pan, and it sizzled in the oil, sending up a scent so delicious, it made my stomach rumble. "At your age, you can't be picky."

Dad lowered his newspaper and peered over the top. "Is he the lawyer?"

"Yes," I said.

"Lawyer is okay. I approve. Just let me know the date. Don't get married during Fashion Week."

"Most parents would be concerned if their daughter had been spotted outside Chicago's 18th District police station in the middle of the night," I said, bristling. "They'd wonder if I'd been hurt, attacked, held up, even assaulted. Maybe I committed a crime. Did you think about that? I could be a criminal."

Mom and Dad shared a laugh. Even Nani joined in.

"Not you," Mom said. "You're not the type."

"What type is that?"

"You've always been a good girl, Simi. Yes, you're impulsive, easily distracted, and overanxious, but you're a team player—a follower, not a leader. You encourage others, but you never reach for the stars. It's not a bad thing. Lots of people walk that middle road, but you won't find any criminals on it. That kind of person is willing to take risks and cross lines you would never cross."

"I could be a criminal," I muttered. "I could do bad things. I've watched so many crime shows with Rose, I could commit the perfect murder."

"You'd be a great criminal," Chloe whispered. "You almost committed a crime last night. You definitely have it in you."

"Thanks, babe. I can always count on you."

"If she committed a murder, we could hire Riswan to defend her," Nani mused. "Then they'd get to spend some time together."

My parents nodded as if they were seriously considering asking me to kill someone to find a husband.

"But if he loses the case, then all that time is wasted," Dad said. "They can't give us grandchildren if she's in prison."

"They can have conjugal visits." Nani flipped her roti again. "After my husband died, I started seeing an ex-con, and when he was sent back to the joint—"

"I can't believe we are seriously having this conversation," I said. "What if I was arrested last night for stealing a $25 million necklace from a museum? What if the police handcuffed me and dragged me downtown? What if I had to call Riswan to get me out, and that's why we were outside the police station?"

"If you're not interested in the boy, just say so," my mother huffed. "You don't need to make things up."

"I'm not interested." I reached for a roti, heedless of Nani's frown. I'd show them bad. I'd take a roti meant for tomorrow's dinner and eat it today. "Riswan is a great guy and good at what he does but he's a bit too nice for me."

"She likes her men with a bit of rough," Nani said, pulling the plate out of reach. "Add that to her online marriage résumé and we'll have her married in no time."

"We're leaving." I grabbed Chloe and dragged her down the hall.

"Don't forget about dinner tomorrow," my mother called out. "We're having a special guest."

◆ ◆ ◆

At first, I wasn't alarmed when I saw the cars parked outside the house on Sunday night. My parents are very social and love hosting family dinners. It was only when I walked into a house filled with silence that the warning bells began to ring. We Chopras are a loud bunch. Even two of us make a lot of noise.

My dad joined me in the hallway, where I was adding my shoes to the pile by the door.

"What's going on?" I knew exactly what was going on but I wanted him to say it.

"You mother has invited a few people over for dinner."

"Do they happen to have an unmarried son who can't find his own wife?"

"Your mother loves you," he said. "She just wants you to be happy."

"She wants grandchildren, and she thinks of me as a brood-mare." I couldn't hide my bitter tone. "The other day she whipped out the tape measure and wrapped it around my hips."

"Beta!" Annika Auntie waved from the door to the living room. "It's so nice to see you."

"She invited the aunties, too?" I groaned. "Can I pretend I have a work emergency at the candy store and have to run to refill the Swedish Fish bin?"

"Too late," he said. "Here she comes."

Annika Auntie was short and round, her smiling face surrounded in a mass of black curls. "The Kapoor family is already here." She lowered her voice to a conspiratorial whisper. "Their son Anil is such a nice boy. He likes fried food, model planes, video games, and he makes jewelry. Good teeth. Nice smile. And he has all his hair."

"That's a low bar, Auntie. But it reminds me that I need to wash my hair. Please give them my apologies for missing what I'm sure will be a scintillating evening."

No chance. Annika Auntie grabbed my arm and dragged me to the living room.

"Here she is." Satya Auntie clapped her hands. She was a tall, thin version of her sister Annika but with the same determination to see every last single relative wed. "All ready for tomorrow when she'll be working with her dad in the family business like the dutiful daughter she is."

I should have known they wouldn't let me escape. Annika and Satya were worse than a WWE tag team. They dominated every family get-together, bouncing off one another to herd young singles into the center of the room. Many of Chicago's therapists had this Legion of Doom to thank for their busy client lists.

My dad introduced me first to Anil's parents, then two of his aunts, three of his uncles, his sister, and his cousins who were visiting from Delhi. Finally, I got to meet my mother's latest find.

Anil was twenty-five but looked nineteen, this being a result of the twice-daily moisturizer he applied to his skin, according to his mother. I briefly considered making a *Silence of the Lambs* joke but decided against it when she gifted me a jar of his miracle cream. He was taller than me by a few inches and lean, but with a long face and narrow chin. His thick black hair stood straight up like he'd recently been electrocuted, and his bushy eyebrows were raised in a permanent state of surprise. No one seemed concerned about our four-year age difference, but I felt like I'd be robbing the cradle if I married a man who wore Mickey Mouse shoes.

I sat across from him while his family extolled his virtues. Not only was he a mechanical engineer, he also worked for a 3D print-ing company, played the French horn, and was a mathematical ge-nius with a photographic memory. He was very close to his family—so close, he still lived at home to save money to pay off his student loans. There was more than enough room in his base-ment suite for two—or three, or even four if they were baby-size. Nudge. Nudge. Wink. Wink.

"Simi is a business graduate," my mom said with none of the despair and disappointment she'd shown when I first told her about my decision to study commerce. "She is getting real-life ex-perience in retail to understand the business world from the ground up while she is saving to do her MBA."

I wasn't sure where all this MBA nonsense had come from. My school days were over. I was all about earning money to get out of debt so I could move on with my life and find my passion.

"Is that a long program?" Anil's mother asked. "Anil is want-ing to have a family right away."

Before I could answer, I heard a buzz overhead. A small white drone circled the room before hovering in front of me.

"Anil builds drones and model planes in his spare time," his mother said. "He's good with his hands."

I put a mental tick in the "redeeming features" box, although I was pretty sure we weren't thinking the same thing.

The drone descended and dropped a diamond bracelet in my lap.

"Uh . . ." I didn't know much about jewelry, but Dad did sell one-carat diamond cufflinks for $4,000 a set. Using that as a guide, I figured I'd just been given at least $1 million worth of diamonds. I didn't know what to say to someone who had randomly drone-dropped an insanely expensive bracelet in my lap. Was he trying to buy my love? More importantly, was I for sale? $1 million would solve all my problems and Chloe's, too. And all I'd have to do is marry Anil, move into his parents' basement suite, and have a couple of kids.

He is good with his hands.

Was that enough to give up my independence and my dream of finding my one true love? Would Anil be able to make me laugh while holding me hostage in the bushes? Or engage in the fast-paced banter that made my brain dance in delight?

"Thank you, but I can't accept—"

"It's fake," Anil said. "I made it at work. Our 3D printer technology is so sophisticated, you can't tell our imitation jewelry from the real thing. That bracelet is made from a pre-ceramic polymer with a nanoparticle filler."

"How fun." I put the fake diamond bracelet on my wrist and an even more fake smile on my face. The toy drone beeped and flashed its lights before flying back to Anil's lap. It returned a few moments later with a paper note attached to an apple.

"Anil loves apples," his mother said as I unrolled the note. "He never leaves home without one. Very healthy. Good for the teeth."

Help. Marry me. I want to be free.

"Anil asked if I liked the bracelet and I do," I said, balling the cry for help in my fist. "But I'm afraid—"

"Wait!" Dad jumped up. "I heard the doorbell."

He returned a few moments later, his forehead wrinkled in a frown. "Simi, a police officer is here to talk to you."

Curious, I went to the front door. The police officer turned out to be Detective Garcia, and he wanted to ask me a few questions.

"You've come a long way," I said.

"You mean from low-income housing in Pilsen to being a detective for the CPD?"

I wasn't sure if Garcia was joking or if I'd insulted him and he was trying to be polite.

"I didn't mean—"

"Just messing with you." A slow smile spread across his face. "Driving out to talk to potential suspects is part of the job."

He leaned against one of the pillars by the front door, arms crossed over his chest. He was wearing a long-sleeved gray Henley with the top two buttons undone, and a pair of jeans that were snug in all the right places. Casual looked good on Garcia. Too good.

"Do I need my lawyer?" I clutched the railing on the front porch, trying to appear cool and calm while screaming inside.

"I only have a few questions, but it's up to you. If you want him to be present, we'll have to meet at the station."

My pulse was already hammering. I didn't want to drag this out for the hours it would take to travel into Chicago and wait for Riswan to show.

"Okay, shoot." My brain pinged a warning. "I mean, don't shoot. I assume you've got a weapon under that shirt, although it's tight enough to see every ripple of your abs and I don't see a holster, but maybe you've got a low-profile holster, or maybe the gun is in your pocket, or under your jeans . . ." *Stop. Stop.* But I was in the spiral and the only way out was down. "I meant on your ankle under your jeans and not under your zipper part of your jeans because I wasn't looking there. At all."

"Simi." He placed a hand over my hand, the warmth of his skin and the firm steady touch instantly calming me down. "I just wanted to ask you about the man in the bushes."

"Oh." I took a deep breath. "What do you need to know?"

"We found a print in the garden. It was a boot, just as you said. Do you know where we can find him?"

"No."

"See here's the thing," he said. "If you cooperate and tell us where he is, then we'll be able to retrieve the necklace and I can convince the DA to give you a reduced sentence."

"Reduced?"

"That's right."

"What about no sentence because I'm not guilty of anything?"

His hand dropped away, and he studied me with such intensity, I was sure he knew part of my brain was still thinking about his zipper. "My theory is that Chloe used her hacking skills to take down the security system. She went inside, took the necklace, threw it down to you, and you gave it to your accomplice—"

"He's not an accomplice. He's a stranger named Oliver Twist. I never met him until that night." I pulled out my phone. "I'm calling Riswan."

"I'd be happy to give you a ride into the city," Garcia said in a tone that suggested it wasn't a request.

"Are you going to put handcuffs on me again?"

"No."

"Could you?" I looked back over my shoulder. "My parents are trying to set me up, but I'm not interested in getting married. My life is a mess. If I were a criminal, then I'd be off the hook, not just for tonight but maybe forever. There aren't many families that want a criminal for a daughter-in-law." I heaved a sigh. "Unfortunately, I'm not a criminal, and I'm running out of excuses why I can't get married."

Garcia's mouth dropped open. I got the feeling from the shock on his face that women didn't often beg him to be cuffed. Or maybe they did . . .

Don't go there.

"What if I run into the living room?" I said before he could refuse. "Could you tackle me and throw me to the ground then snap the cuffs around my wrists and read me my rights like you did at the museum?"

His brow creased in a frown. "No one has ever asked me to do anything like this."

"Then you mustn't know many single almost-thirty-year-old South Asian women with marriage-obsessed parents." I grabbed his hand. "Please, Detective Garcia. I'll owe you one."

"Is that a bribe?" His voice rose from deep and low to just low. "Are you trying to bribe me to handcuff you in front of your family?"

"Is it illegal? If so, then yes. I can't take it anymore. Everywhere I go, there's an auntie dragging along some hapless suitor. They show up at my work, my gym, even the dentist's office. Once they caught me getting onto a ride at Six Flags and I had to talk and scream at the same time."

Garcia shook his head. "I don't—"

"You can't take me, cop!" I raced for the living room, but not too fast because I needed Garcia to keep up.

"Jesus Christ," Garcia muttered, following behind me.

"What's going on here?" Dad shot to his feet. "Simi?"

With the slightest shake of his head, Garcia pulled his cuffs off his belt. "Simi Chopra, I need you to come to the station. You're under suspicion as an accessory to a burglary."

"You can rough me up," I whispered when he came near. "It's okay."

Garcia spun me around and snapped the cuffs around my wrists. My heartbeat quickened at the way he held me, confident and commanding.

"Oh no." I put as much fear into my voice as I could. "What's happening? How could you do this to me? I'm innocent, I tell you, *innocent*."

Garcia yanked me back, his lips warm on my ear. "You're overdoing it."

"You'll never make this stick," I shouted as he marched me out the door. "You've got nothing on me."

"You're a terrible actor," he said quietly. "I hope never to see you onstage."

"Have you ever seen a Bollywood film?" I retorted. "This is positively repressed."

Dad rushed out to the porch, waving his phone in the air. "Don't worry, beta. I'll call Riswan."

"We'll never get her married now," my mother wailed.

Garcia opened the door to the police cruiser and put a gentle hand on my head. "In you go."

Just before the door slammed, I heard Annika Auntie say, "It's okay. Nothing to worry about. She was an *accessory* to the burglary, not the actual burglar. Everyone knows accessories don't count."

SEVEN

◇ ◇ ◇

Where have you been all my life, sunshine?" Cristian blew me a kiss from the other side of the tie display when I walked into Dad's store Monday morning. I'd only spent an hour at the police station the night before. Riswan got me out of there after Garcia admitted he still had no evidence to tie me to the crime. After a sleepless night, turning over all the possibilities of my worsening situation and fantasizing about being cuffed by Garcia but this time in bed, Cristian was the last person I wanted to see.

"Hiding." I made my way to the workroom, keeping my distance from his octopus hands.

I love my dad's store. It's everything you could imagine a traditional tailor shop would be, with its dark wood paneling, gold accents, and deep red upholstery. He expanded a few years ago when the sandwich shop beside us went out of business, increasing the size of his workshop out back and adding a spacious and discreet fitting area behind a wall of frosted glass. Suits of all types are displayed on racks in the center of the bright and airy space, with shirts and accessories neatly folded on warm wooden shelves lining the walls. The scents of fresh linen, wool, and leather are so much a part of my childhood, the store feels like a second home.

"Don't be like that, Sim." He followed behind me, his Sperry boat shoes thudding softly on the plush carpet. He was wearing a pink and white striped shirt with a blue polka-dot tie and a pair of slim navy dress pants that broke perfectly at the tops of his shoes. On anyone else, it would have been too much. On Cristian, it was style perfection, and he knew it.

"I'm not like other guys," he continued. "You're special to me."

"Like your three special baby girls from the other night?"

"Five," he said, totally unashamed. "I broke up with my girlfriend and I needed some love."

"And now you're trying for six?" I pushed aside the curtain separating the workroom from the sales floor. "I'm not in the mood."

"Want to play the question game?" He leaned against the sewing table while I took off my coat.

"No."

"Handcuffs or roses?" He followed me back into the shop and across the floor to the tie table.

"Cristian . . ."

"I want to be ready when you realize you're desperately in love with me. Should I show up at your place with a bouquet of roses or a shiny pair of handcuffs?" He studied me, considering. "I think it'll have to be roses. I can't imagine you'd let anyone put you in cuffs."

I was tempted to tell him about me and Detective Garcia last night but then he'd never leave me alone.

"Save your money. It's never going to happen."

"I can't say I've ever heard those words from a woman." He held up a tie and tilted his head to the side. "What do you think about me in yellow?"

"Not your best color," a deep voice said, as smooth and deep as the top-shelf whiskey my brother Nikhil had bought to celebrate my college graduation. I've never been a whiskey drinker, but I did appreciate how good it made me feel.

It took me a few long moments to process the fact that Oliver Twist was standing in front of me. If I'd thought he was gorgeous in the dark and rain, he was breathtaking in the light of day, taller, broader, his jaw more defined. He'd even had a shave. His eyes, now that I could see them clearly, were a kaleidoscope of buttered chocolate and golden caramel, the color shifting to green when he smiled.

"What are you doing here?" I drew him away from Cristian and over to the cashmere socks.

"I came to return the money I borrowed." He held out a twenty-dollar bill. "As promised."

I tucked the money in my blazer pocket, still struggling to process the fact that he was in my dad's store. "How did you find me?"

"The name of the shop was on the suit bag you were using to carry the tools of your trade." His lips curved in a smile. "I'm very observant."

"You really shouldn't be here." I kept my voice low. "I told the police you were there. They're looking for you."

Far from being angry, he just shrugged. "I wouldn't be good at my job if I was so easily identified. They won't be able to link me to the scene of the crime."

"Unless I called them . . ."

"But you won't," he said. "Because that's not who you are."

"You don't know anything about me," I snapped. "Maybe I'm not the good girl everyone thinks I am. Maybe I like cuffs and not roses. Maybe I'm a criminal mastermind disguised as a suit salesperson. Or I could be a terrible person who is self-centered, entitled, and rude, and everywhere I go, I ask to speak to the manager."

"We both know that's not true," he said. "Not after what you did for your friend. And if your idea of a bad person is someone who's rude, you'll have a long way to go to change my opinion of you."

"Did you just come here to return my money or is there something else you want?" Why did he have to be so irritating? I had a bad side. I'd turned down at least six arranged marriage proposals in the last year alone.

"A suit." He shrugged off his worn leather jacket to reveal arms so perfectly muscled, they would have put Nani to shame. "Where do we start? I've never had a custom suit before."

Cristian had disappeared. My dad was on the phone in his office. Except for a man trying on hats, we weren't busy, so I showed Oliver to the fitting area behind the glass.

"I'll take your details and measurements, then you'll need to sit down with one of the tailors to discuss fabric, style, and cut."

"I am delighted to be in your very capable hands."

I grabbed a tablet and joined him in front of a three-way mirror. "I'll need your details for the form. Name." I raised my eyebrows. "And don't tell me Oliver Twist because I don't believe you."

"Jack."

"Last name?"

"Let's just leave it at Jack," he said.

"Unfortunately, the online form insists on a last name before it will allow me to move to the next page." I held up the tablet to show him the screen. "How about Jack Spratt? Jack Frost? Jack Sparrow? Jack Horner? Do you have a beanstalk? Do you kill giants? Have you built a house? Are you nimble?"

"How about something not fantasy-based?" With a soft chuckle, he moved closer to study the screen.

"Jack Dawson? Jack Skellington?" I tried to ignore the heat of his body, the warm breath across my cheek. "Jack-Jack Parr? Jack Torrance? Jack Pearson? Jack Reacher? Jack Ryan?"

His laughter, deep and rich, filled the room. "You know your Jacks."

"I like movies. I'll watch anything so long as I'm not watching it alone. Sharing snarky comments is all part of the fun."

"I think doing anything with you would be fun." His smile made me smile. I couldn't stop it. Were we flirting? Was that a flirting smile? Was I flirting with a thief?

"How about Danger?" he said. "It's got a good ring to it. Strong, brave, but also daring."

"Jack Danger." I put the name into the form, my lips quivering with amusement. "How about an address?"

"I'm staying at the Pendry in the Carbide & Carbon Building."

My finger froze over the keyboard. "You don't live in Chicago?"

"Not for a long time. I'm just here on business."

I felt a curious little stab of disappointment. It wasn't that I was in any way attracted to the kind of man who would hide in the bushes outside a museum to steal a $25 million necklace. He was simply different from anyone I'd ever met. "The suit will take a few weeks," I said quickly to hide my lapse. "If you have to leave, we can send it after you by courier."

"Let's assume I'll be here to pick it up. If not, I'll call with a forwarding address."

He gave me his cell number and paid the deposit in cash. After I'd filled in the rest of his details, I pulled out the measuring tape.

"We take a lot of measurements to ensure the suit is a perfect fit." I wrapped the tape around his broad chest. He was all rock-hard rippling muscle, so unlike the soft pasty bankers and potbellied lawyers who made up most of my dad's clientele.

"Do what you need to do." His voice dropped, low and rough. "I look forward to the experience."

Electricity pulsed in the air between us. My breath hitched and heat pooled low in my belly. I took a deep breath and thought about orange jumpsuits.

"Is there a special occasion coming up or is the suit for work?" I measured his shoulder, neck, arm width and length with only the barest tremble from my rattled nerves. I'd never enjoyed touching a client more.

"I may have to pay a visit to a country estate in Lake Bluff," he said. "I don't think my usual clothes are appropriate."

"Not unless you're trying to make the Kessel Run in less than twelve parsecs." I didn't expect him to get the *Star Wars* reference, but he laughed.

"Funny. You're very funny, Simi."

I froze with the tape around his waist. "How do you know my name? I never introduced myself."

"It's on your name tag." He tapped the gold tag on my chest. "Simi Chopra."

"Jack Danger." I repeated his name for no reason other than the press of his finger on my chest had sent a zing of electricity straight to my core. Hands shaking, I tightened the tape measure. He was built like a Greek statue—all smooth, hard perfection. "What kind of suit are you looking for?"

"I want to blend in."

"You're not really a blend-in kind of guy." He wore a tarnished pendant on a black leather string around his neck over a vintage Led Zeppelin shirt from the band's 1979 concert at Knebworth House. His biker-style boots were black, polished, and shiny, and very unlike the mud-covered boots he'd been wearing the other night.

"You didn't see me until I grabbed you the other night," he pointed out.

"That was, perhaps, the most terrifying moment of my life." I tapped the last set of measurements into my tablet.

His face softened. "I was trying to help."

"I know. Sometimes when I'm highly stressed, my brain loses the ability to executive function, and I run purely on impulse. If you hadn't grabbed me when you did, I probably would have done something crazy."

"You tried to scale a wall with your bare hands in the pouring rain," he said. "I was silently cheering you on."

No laughter. No mocking. No frustrated sigh or head shaking with disappointment. I'd always been a source of exasperation for my family, but not for him.

I moved behind him, as much to hide my surprise as to take measurements from the back.

"Are you going to frisk me?" he asked when I stepped in close to measure the width of his shoulders. He smelled of pine and leather and the fresh ocean breeze—wild and free.

"This is a custom tailor shop, not a police station."

"I might have a dangerous weapon in my pocket," he teased.

I pulled the measuring tape tight under his arms, reminding myself that I was a professional. I was totally unaffected by the rock-hard pecs that flexed under my hands or the fact that I was now so close, I could feel the heat of his body. It was disconcertingly intimate. I'd measured many clients over the years for my dad and not once had I ever felt like I needed an immediate date with my vibrator.

"I felt your dangerous weapon when you were holding me hostage in the bushes," I said. "I wasn't impressed."

Laughter rumbled in his chest. "I have a feeling it would take a lot to impress you."

I squatted behind him to get the waist-to-floor measurement.

He looked over his shoulder. "While you're down there . . ."

"Behave." I glared up at him. "Or I'll ask Cristian to take over."

"Cristian's more interested in *your* measurements," he said. "I'm going to have a word with him on the way out."

"A word?"

"Very civil. Very polite. I'll let him know you're out of his league and he should stop wasting his time."

"Now who's the funny one." If there were leagues, Cristian and I were miles apart. He may have been a womanizer, but he was as comfortable at a gala as he was at a pub crawl. He knew how to dress, what to say, and how to navigate every echelon of society. I was lucky if I made it out of a social event with my dignity intact.

"Simi?" His deep voice pulled me out of my downward spiral of self-loathing.

"Yes?"

"Are you planning to take any more measurements? Usually when a woman spends that much time staring at my ass, I buy her a few drinks and invite her to my hotel room to get naked."

Mortified, I stood and entered his measurements into the online form. "It would take more than a few drinks to get me naked in your hotel room."

His smile broadened. Seriously, nothing seemed to faze this guy. He could take whatever I threw at him and gave it right back. "How many?"

"You wouldn't be able to keep up." I'd been blessed with a fast metabolism and a high alcohol tolerance. Not one of my brothers could outlast me when it came to drinking games.

"You complicate my life when you say things like that," he said. "I'd appreciate it if you could be less interesting."

I didn't know if he was flirting or joking or just trying to pass the time, but I was as far from interesting as a person could get. My job didn't involve danger or excitement. Paparazzi weren't hiding in the bushes every time I stepped outside. I wasn't jetting off on foreign vacations or hitting a home run at Wrigley Field.

"Which side do you dress?" In tailor speak, it was a delicate way of asking which way his private parts hung—to the left or right of his zipper. Some men thought we asked the question to put a little extra room on that side of their pants. In fact, we asked it before taking the inseam measurement because we didn't want to get too personal when working in that region. The few times I'd forgotten to ask, I'd had an unexpected surprise.

Something wicked flickered in his eyes. "I thought you'd know since we've already been intimately acquainted, or were you wiggling your ass against me in the bushes for another reason?"

"I wasn't thinking about pants at the time."

"Neither was I." He licked his lips, his devilish grin drawing laughter up my throat.

"Behave," I said, although I knew I'd be disappointed if he did. "Right or left?"

"I don't give out that kind of information until we've had at least one kiss."

I called his bluff with one of my own. "I'll get Cristian to finish up."

"Left."

Without glancing up at him, I ran the tape up the inside of his right leg, and then low over his hips. There was a bulge that I hadn't noticed before. Not that I'd been looking.

After I'd inputted all the data, I checked with the tailors. Only Cristian had time to help Jack after we were done.

"Cristian must be on a break," I said. "He should just be a few minutes. Feel free to browse."

"Maybe you could help me narrow things down while I'm waiting. What would you recommend?"

"It depends on the event. Cocktail party? Charity fundraiser? Bar mitzvah? Is it indoor or outdoor? Formal or casual? Is there a theme? A celebration of any particular culture? My summers are taken up with weddings, so there's very little I don't know on that front. I haven't seen an original wedding idea since my cousin smuggled an elephant into Huntington Beach so he could ride it for his baraat. It's a procession for the groom."

Jack shrugged on his jacket. "Were you there?"

"It was an elephant. Of course I was there. After the baraat, I went to see him up close and the trainer let me ride him back to the truck."

"Interesting." He stroked his chin, considering.

"Why?"

"I wondered if you were the kind of woman who would run toward an elephant or run away from it. Now that I know you're up for a little adventure, we may be able to help each other."

After spending half an hour with my hands on his magnificent body, I was up for help of any kind. "Will we be naked?"

"Much as I would like to say yes, I was thinking about your other problem." He leaned down and whispered in my ear. "I know who took the necklace."

A wave of relief washed over me. Chloe was safe. The horrible ordeal was finally over. "Oh, thank God. I can call Detective Garcia and—"

"You can't call the police," he said quickly. "The thief no longer has the necklace. He gave it to a fence—that's a middleman between a thief and the consumer of stolen goods."

"I know what a fence is." Rose was going to be so jealous when I told her I'd met a thief who knew a real-life fence. "Do you know who he is?"

"Yes, but he's very well connected at all levels of government—mayor's office, governor, a senator or two, maybe even the White

House. If we gave his name to the police, the necklace would disappear before they could get to it, and we'd never see it again."

"I don't understand . . ." Hope disappeared under a tidal wave of disappointment.

"I know where he's keeping the necklace," he said. "But I can't get to it on my own. I need help."

My hand flew to my mouth. "You want me to help you steal the necklace from someone else?"

"I like to think of it as a retrieval, or better yet, a repossession," Jack said. "It doesn't belong to him. It needs to go back to the rightful owner."

"Beta," Dad called out. "I need you in the back. Cristian can take over if you're done with the measurements."

"I'm not a thief," I said, turning back to Jack. "I don't know the first thing about pulling off a—"

"Heist." Jack smiled. "That's what we call it in the business."

"I'm not in the business."

"Not even to save your friend?" He trailed an idle finger along my jaw, warming my skin. "Or yourself? If the necklace is found, say, in a corner of the museum where it might have been overlooked, there would have been no theft. I doubt the gallery director would want to press charges for the trespass if nothing was taken."

I turned over the possibilities, the risks, and the rewards. "Altruism doesn't suit you. Why wouldn't you keep it for yourself?"

"I'd be willing to ensure it was returned to the museum so you and your friend would be cleared of all charges," he said. "What happens to it after that would not be your concern."

So he was going to steal it again. Not that it mattered. Chloe and I would be free. But the risk of going to jail was very real. This time we would be committing an actual crime.

"I don't know you," I said. "We met under suspicious circumstances and now you show up with a proposal that could get me into real trouble. My cousin is one of the best criminal lawyers in the city. I'm going to take my chances with him."

"Think about it," Jack said. "I'll be at the Black Dog in the West Loop on Wednesday at eight P.M. if you change your mind. Bring your friend. If we go ahead with this, we'll need her help. In fact, we'll need a crew."

Cristian still hadn't returned, so I brought Jack to the waiting area. "Good luck with the suit. I hate to say it, but you're in good hands. Cristian knows his stuff when it comes to tailoring."

"There's a reward," Jack blurted out after I turned away.

"I don't think even a few thousand dollars will change my mind."

"What about five million?"

EIGHT

◆ ◆ ◆

The Black Dog is a dimly lit, seriously sexy bar located in a basement beneath the Hobie Hotel. The bar's interior is decidedly British, with red velvet banquettes, tufted couches, prints of London, and bookshelves filled with leather-bound books. But what makes the Black Dog unique is the seating configuration that gives every party a sense of privacy. It's a great bet for a secret rendezvous, or when you're meeting a thief to discuss a heist.

"This is just a fact-finding mission," Chloe said for the third time. "We're not agreeing to anything. We're just assessing the risks." She sipped her Negroni, one of sixty cocktails on the beautiful hand-drawn menu. We'd already worked our way through the daiquiris and margaritas. I was taking the sugar down a notch with a gin-based, floral-scented concoction that tasted like cherry liqueur, but Chloe was full steam ahead with her cocktail extravaganza.

Chloe rarely went out, so she took advantage of every opportunity. She'd blown out her hair into soft waves and dressed up in a gorgeous flowy mauve slip dress that had a boho crochet lace bralette top and a light and airy skirt with a tiered hem. I felt almost underdressed in my favorite shimmery silver camisole, big hoop earrings, and a pair of black jeans.

"We've talked through the risks for two days," I said. "We could go to jail. Our lives could be destroyed. Olivia would be on her own. Fences are not nice guys. We might get hurt if we're caught. Maybe even killed."

"On the other hand," she said. "If Jack knows what he's doing—and it sounds like he does—we could walk away with our freedom and a share of $5 million. My attorney said it was a bad sign when you got called back to the police station. She thought we should start thinking about a plea deal. And you said Riswan was concerned."

To say Riswan was concerned was an understatement. He'd told me in no uncertain terms that if I hadn't mentioned the man in the bushes, the police wouldn't have been able to make a case for anything other than trespassing. But throw a third person into the mix, and suddenly there was a plausible explanation why neither Chloe nor I had the necklace in our possession.

"It's a life-changing amount of money," Chloe said. "It would mean no more loans and no more debt. I could buy the house I always dreamed about. I could set up a trust fund for Olivia where there would be no risk of Kyle waiting in the wings to steal her money. I could travel, buy nice clothes, get another degree. I could get a pet. Olivia's always wanted a dog . . ."

I finished the rest of my drink. Why hadn't I ordered something with more alcohol, like a Long Island Iced Tea? My nerves were still jangling, and Chloe wasn't helping by sharing her plans to spend money we didn't even have. "Or we rely on our lawyers to get us out of this mess and move on with our regular lives," I countered.

"Is that what you want?" She put down her drink. "A regular life? Debt? A basement apartment that floods every few months?

Bouncing from one job you hate to another? Humoring your family's attempts to find you a husband when it's the last thing you want? You had dreams about how your life would be when you didn't have to play second fiddle to your brothers. You don't have to be the 'good girl' anymore. Live life on your own terms. Be bold. Be brave. Find your passion. Where's your sense of adventure?"

Chloe clearly hadn't come for facts. She'd made her decision. I wasn't surprised. She'd been through so much in her life, she wasn't afraid to take risks. I was the one who'd been suffocated by familial expectations. My small attempts to break those chains—business instead of law or medicine, a rental suite instead of living at home, refusals of proposals from decent men—had come at the high cost of family disappointment.

"We're not going to a lost city to find a hidden treasure," I said. "This is real. The risks are real. If it all goes wrong, a wise-cracking, irreverent-but-devilishly handsome archaeologist with a wry, witty, and sarcastic sense of humor and a fear of snakes won't be swooping in to save us."

"Ladies." As if on cue, Jack joined us at the table. He was wearing a perfectly fitted gray button-down shirt beneath his leather jacket, a pair of vintage jeans that hugged his hips, and brown Blundstones that had seen better days. On another man, the look might have been too casual. On him, it was thirst trap sexy.

"He's just missing the hat and the whip," Chloe whispered under her breath after I'd introduced them.

Jack had also brought along a friend he introduced as "Gage."

There were only two words to describe Gage: deadly and dangerous. He had military-short dark hair above a wide forehead, glacial blue eyes, and a chin so square, he could have been a model in geometry class. The dude was all lean hard muscle poured into black jeans, black boots, and a Hellraiser graphic T-shirt. He was raw and rugged, and he drew attention through the force of his presence alone.

"Does this mean you're in?" Jack asked after we'd ordered a fresh round of drinks.

"We're collecting facts." I looked over at Chloe. Her gaze was fixed on Gage and his gaze was fixed on her. There was too much gazing and not enough talking so I gave her a nudge.

"Chloe? Facts. Remember?"

She shook herself and took a big gulp of her Tequila Sunrise. "Facts. Yes. Risk assessment. Where is the necklace?"

"At the home of Joseph Angelini, a real estate and casino mogul who has sold and developed some of the largest undeveloped tracts of land within the city limits." Jack steepled his fingers. He had nice hands—strong and tanned with just enough hair to give them a decidedly masculine finish.

"I read about him," Chloe said. "He was indicted on charges alleging bribery and corruption in the rezoning of an industrial site last year."

"The DA dropped the case when the key witnesses all died in unfortunate accidents." Jack shrugged off his jacket and rolled up his sleeves. I stirred my drink, ogling his exposed forearms in a circumspect way. He wasn't trying to be sexy, but I suddenly understood why the Victorians got excited at a forbidden glimpse of an exposed ankle.

"Why would someone like that take the risk of acting as a fence?" I asked. "It's not like he needs the money."

"He trades in favors. This is one of them."

"So he's an amateur fence, not a professional." I didn't want Jack and Gage to think we were totally naive about underworld crime.

"Does it make a difference?" Jack's lips quivered at the corners, like he could see right through me. Given we seemed to have some kind of rapport, I had suspected he would.

"Less risk if he's an amateur." I leaned against the banquette and examined my fingernails, all chill and relaxed like I had experience meeting shady characters in poorly lit bars to discuss heists and different kinds of fences.

"Why haven't we heard about the reward?" Chloe frowned. "Or the theft, for that matter? It hasn't been in the news."

"The museum director pulled a few favors to keep it out of the papers because he was concerned that the other donors would pull their pieces before the exhibit opened," Jack said. "The provenance of the necklace is also in question and the owner didn't want to draw any unwanted attention. He arranged with the insurance company to offer a reward to people who are in a position to locate and retrieve the necklace and discreetly arrange for its safe return."

"You?" I asked.

"Among others."

"If you could retrieve the necklace, why would you return it for a reward? Why not just sell it?" Chloe proved once again her super smartness and I was proud to be her friend.

"It's not easy to sell jewelry on the black market," Jack said. "You have to know people. You also have to be able to keep it secure. There are people who would kill to acquire something of that value."

He spoke with the confidence of a man who dealt in stolen jewels and murderers every day. I couldn't believe I was having this conversation. Me. The "good girl." Talking about heists, fences, dirty real estate moguls, the criminal underground, and secret rewards. That's when it really hit me. Jack was from another world. A forbidden, exciting, dangerous world. A world I'd only ever watched on TV. A world where people died for real.

"I'm not signing up to get murdered," I said.

"That's why Gage is here." Jack tipped his head in Gage's direction. "He keeps people safe."

I could imagine. Intense masculinity seeped from Gage's pores. His arms were like twin pythons, intricate tattoos covering his smooth, tanned skin.

"How do we know the reward is real?" Chloe asked. "You could just be using it to lure us into helping you, and the minute you get your hands on the necklace, you'll disappear into the ether."

"Fair point." Jack glanced over at Gage. "You want to show her?"

Gage's voice was a rough rumble that emanated from deep in his chest. "You got a Dark Web ID?"

Chloe snorted a laugh. "What hacker doesn't?"

They exchanged the kind of information non-computer-literate people like me don't understand. Moments later, Chloe was scouring the dark side of the Internet on her phone. "He's not lying. The reward has been posted on several Dark Web forums. But this just means we won't be the only people after it."

"They don't know what I know," Jack said.

"What's that?" I sucked the lime from my gin and tonic and immediately wished I hadn't.

"The location."

"What's in it for you?" I asked him, drawing on my vast knowledge of crime shows and murder mysteries featuring middle-aged women who lived in crime-ridden towns. "Why would you help us?"

"That's my business."

That right there was the crux of the problem. We would be throwing in our lot with a man we didn't know—a self-professed thief with underworld connections. I could have shut it down right then, but a spark of giddy anticipation rushed through me—the same rush I'd felt when I'd gone to help Chloe. I felt alive in a way I hadn't for years.

I looked up and caught Jack's gaze. Whether it was altruism or self-interest, he'd tried to save me at the museum. I could still remember the warmth of his body against mine, his solid strength. Against all odds, I'd felt safe with him. I'd trusted him when a childhood of being mercilessly teased by my brothers and overlooked by my busy parents had left me unable to trust at all.

"If you're so experienced, why don't you do it yourself and hire your own crew?" Chloe asked. "Why do you need us?"

"I can't take the risk that someone will tip off Angelini. Like I said, he's well connected."

"And you trust us?" Chloe asked.

"The kind of people who would have an interest in the necklace don't know who you are, so if you go nosing around, they won't be suspicious. And I'm not worried you'll tip anyone off because you wouldn't know who to tell."

He had an answer for everything, and his explanations made sense. My mind raced. Maybe I could do this. Save Chloe and get out of debt. Live life and find my passion instead of struggling every day just to keep my head above water. For once, instead of being the "good girl," I could take a walk on the wild side.

I looked at Chloe and she grinned. That's the thing about having a best friend. You can communicate without using words. We were doing this. Together.

"Okay," I said. "We're in."

Jack held out his hand and we shook, heat sizzling through my veins at his brief touch. "Now, about your crew . . ."

◇　◇　◇

It was surprisingly easy to find information about assembling the perfect heist crew. All it took was dinner with Rose after work on

Friday night. I had no hesitation telling her what was going on. Rose and I had shared many secrets, although hers were the kind I didn't really want to know.

"The most important thing is trust," Rose said over smoked salmon timbales, confit duck with redcurrant sauce, and fondant potatoes. With Stan in the hospital, she'd wasted no time finding a replacement and had hooked up with a French chef who had offered to prepare dinner so we could chat.

Always a fashion icon, Rose had dressed in her favorite Leopard Jeanne dress with a plunging neckline and multiple strands of white pearls. Her hair was cut into a neat shoulder-length bob and dyed silvery blond. It was hard to believe she was eighty years old. I felt positively unkempt in my T-shirt and jeans.

"In almost every heist, there is a twist, a betrayal, or some unexpected surprise," Rose said. "As a result, you don't want strangers in your crew."

"Should we be having this conversation in front of Chef Pierre?" Chloe dropped her voice, her gaze cutting to the short, balding, round-faced gentleman in the kitchen. "If he tells anyone . . ."

Rose waved a dismissive hand. "He's an exchange student from a seniors' culinary school in France. He's here to learn how to cook American food. He doesn't speak much English."

"How do you communicate?" Chloe asked.

"At my age, dear, you don't waste time talking." She blew a kiss to Chef Pierre. He caught it and pretended to eat it. Then he licked his hand. Suddenly the confit duck didn't look so good.

"I can't think of anyone I know who would be willing to commit a crime," Chloe said.

"People will surprise you when money is involved." Rose sucked on a chicken bone, her gaze on Chef Pierre. He murmured something that ended in a groan. I have never been so glad to have failed French.

"The most important role is the driver," Rose said. "There's no point putting in all the work to steal the necklace if you can't get away. You need someone who can think fast, drive faster, and evade the police or whoever will be chasing you from the scene of the crime."

My fork froze in my salmon timbale. "What do you mean, 'whoever will be chasing you'?"

"You won't be the only people after something that valuable," she said. "If one person knows where it is, others will know."

"Jack says no one knows."

"The thief from the museum knows," she said. "He's probably at a bar right now bragging to his friends. Someone overhears. The message gets passed along. Suddenly, everyone is planning a heist. The key is to get there first."

"How many heist movies have you watched?" Chloe nibbled her duck. She was such a dainty eater. I just opened my mouth and shoveled the food in.

"All of them. I did a little murder mystery dinner theater between Broadway shows, and the movies helped me get into character. I also played a cat burglar in a fringe production a few years ago. I was nude except for a tail and a pair of ears. They dropped me from the ceiling to steal a diamond with my teeth." She mimicked the motion with her hand, fingers splayed.

Chloe choked on her duck. I handed her a glass of water and thumped her on the back. Out of the corner of my eye, I saw Chef Pierre stagger back against the stove. Either his language skills were better than he let on, or the concept of naked cat women falling from the ceiling was universally translatable.

"If you need a 'grease man' or in this case 'grease woman' on your crew to hide in small spaces, contort around laser beams, and drop down from the ceiling to avoid pressure plates on the floor, I'll be happy to help out," Rose offered. "As Chef Pierre can attest, I'm very flexible, and I still have all my old theatrical rigging. I bought it when the playhouse shut down. I was thinking of setting it up in the garage when Stan gets out of hospital as a 'welcome home' surprise."

"And would you look at the time." Chloe pushed her chair back. "Olivia will be getting home from visiting with her grandparents soon. I should really be there to meet her."

"Stay." I grabbed her arm. "Please."

"You definitely don't want to waste any time," Rose said. "Assembling your crew is only the first step in a successful heist."

"I know someone who might be interested in driving." I pulled up Emma's contact details on my phone. "She drove her Uber to the museum like we were in the Formula 500, and she's struggling with money, too. I'll text her."

"No texts!" Rose held out a warning hand. "You can be traced through electronic records. All communication must be done in person, or you can leave handwritten messages under stones."

"Handwriting?" Chloe chuckled. "They don't teach cursive in schools anymore. This is going to be a modern-day heist. I can set up a secure server, and we can use burner phones to communicate. Leave the tech stuff to me."

"Perfect," Rose said. "Another crew box ticked."

Chef Pierre refilled our wineglasses. I didn't know much about wine, but I did know that only alcohol would burn from my brain the disturbing images of a naked Rose dropping from the ceiling with a diamond in her teeth.

"You'll also need someone to handle gadgety things," Rose continued. "An engineer or a mechanic who is good with their hands and can handle drills, wiring, and power tools. It helps if he's inventive and can come up with ideas to solve mechanical problems."

"Like James Bond's Q?" I asked.

"Exactly." She held up her wineglass and gave Chef Pierre a dramatic wave. "*Magnifique.*"

He put his hand to his heart and gave a mock bow. I closed my eyes in case he decided to lick his palm.

"You have lots of engineers in your family," Chloe said to me. "Do you think any of them would be interested?"

"We can't involve my family unless you want every South Asian person in Illinois to know what we're doing. They can't keep secrets. Gossiping is as natural to them as breathing. My entire family knew I'd met with Riswan less than fifteen minutes after it happened. I can't even imagine how fast the gossip spread when I asked Garcia to arrest me."

"We've all been the subject of criminal charges," Rose assured me. "I have quite the rap sheet. Mostly for mischief and public indecency. I was a little bit wild in my teens and twenties. I had a kink for exhibitionism in my thirties, and in my forties, I just couldn't keep my clothes on because the perimenopausal heat flashes were driving me crazy. In my fifties, it was drugs— menopause will do that to you. You're too young to hear about my swinging sixties. And last year I was picked up for solicitation— but that one wasn't my fault."

Something niggled at the back of my mind. It hummed and buzzed. Like a little toy drone.

"I do know someone." I swallowed back a grimace. "He's a mechanical engineer, and good with his hands according to his mom. He builds toy planes and drones and he works at a 3D printing company that makes fake jewelry."

"Oh, that's good." Rose leaned up to kiss Chef Pierre, who had joined us at the table to serve the strawberry galette. "Did you see *Ocean's 8*? You might want to consider asking him to make a replica of the necklace you plan to steal."

"Jack called it a retrieval," I said. "The necklace will be returned to its rightful owner."

"Of course it will, dear." She gave me a warm smile. "Now how about muscle?"

A blush crept up Chloe's face and she stabbed at her galette. "We have that covered."

"Jack has a friend," I explained. "He looks like he was in the military, probably some kind of black ops. Jack said he keeps people safe."

"That reminds me." She tapped her lip with a manicured nail. "You'll need a key master. Someone who can pick locks, crack safes, open doors . . . that kind of thing."

"Jack said he can do that. He also suggested we find a meeting place. I was wondering if we could use your garage. I'd be happy to give you a share of the reward."

Rose had lost her driver's license five years ago after driving the wrong way down a one-way street and knocking over a fire hydrant. She'd sold her old Volvo and now her garage was empty save for a mini kitchen, a few lawn chairs, odds and ends, and rack after rack of clothes.

"You're welcome to the garage." Rose waved a dismissive hand. "I don't need the money. I have more than enough to get by. At my age it's all about experiences."

We finished our dessert and helped Chef Pierre tidy the kitchen. Rose kissed my cheek at the door.

"I'm looking forward to meeting your man," she whispered in my ear. "I was beginning to worry about you. Use it or lose it. You know what I'm saying?"

"I don't have a man."

"What about your gentleman thief?"

"He's a thief. I can't trust him."

"The bad boys are always the best in bed." Rose sighed. "Stan used to be an enforcer for the mob. He tells me about his hits when we're together. It really gets me going, especially when he's describing arterial spray. If you hadn't walked in the other morning—"

"See you on Sunday." I pushed Chloe out the door. "Hopefully, by then we'll have a crew."

NINE

◇ ◇ ◇

I guess I was expecting something out of a movie the first time I got everyone together: a serious heist crew gathered around a table, sharing their skills and considering the merits of various plans in a thoughtful and professional way.

What I got was chaos.

Chef Pierre had set up a buffet of French pastries on a rough-hewn table between the lawn mower and the tool bench in Rose's garage. He and Rose were engaged in some kind of cream puff foreplay that involved Rose licking cream off his finger and Chef Pierre retrieving the cream with his tongue. My Uber driver, Emma, had jumped at the chance to join the heist and was now throwing balls of yarn at Anil's drone and shouting something about a childhood trauma that involved bees while Anil munched his way through a bag of apples. Chloe was trying to set up a whiteboard that only had one leg and Gage looked like he wanted to be anywhere else.

"So this is your crew." Jack folded his arms across his chest, one eyebrow lifted in what could have been either censure or dismay.

I folded my arms, too. "You say that like you could do better."

"I couldn't do worse."

Emma spotted us at the door, stuck two fingers in her mouth, and whistled so loudly, my eardrums vibrated. I made quick work of the introductions. First names only and a brief description of each person's role in the crew: driver, hacker, key master, muscle, gadget guy, grease woman, and me.

"Simi's our leader," Jack said when I hesitated over my role. "She's in charge of this operation."

"I'm not a leading type," I murmured, keeping my voice low. "I'm a following type. I go with the flow. I'm the fly girl, wise-cracking sidekick, or backup singer in a band. You said you needed a crew; I got a crew. But this has to be your show."

Jack's gaze swept the room. "There're not *my* friends."

"Except for Chloe, they're not my friends, either," I retorted. "They're just people I know."

Emma jumped on a chair, trying to catch the drone. Chloe had found Rose's costume rack and was trying on an enormous feather hat. I couldn't see Chef Pierre and Rose, but there were strange noises coming from the wardrobe at the back of the garage.

"Do you know anyone else?" he asked.

I didn't understand why he was putting it all on me when he was the one with experience. "How can I be in charge if this is my first heist?"

"First heist?" Emma gave a fruitless swat at the buzzing drone. "What about the museum? Are you saying you're a novice?" She trailed off when the door opened. I didn't know who I was expecting, but it certainly wasn't my dad's junior tailor Cristian.

He was wearing cargo pants and Nike slides, a green *Save the Trees* T-shirt, and a Bears cap turned backward. He caught my gaze and shot me a flash of whitened teeth. "Looks like I got here just in time."

◇ ◇ ◇

"This is your fault," I pushed Jack up against the fence in Rose's backyard, where Chloe, Gage, Jack, and I had convened to discuss Cristian's attempt to blackmail us into letting him join the heist.

"My fault?" He gave an indignant sniff. "He's *your* dad's employee."

"If you hadn't come to the store in the first place looking how you look and acting how you act, Cristian wouldn't have felt compelled to hide in the fitting room and listen to our conversation," I retorted. "He's insecure and he's been trying to sleep with me since he started working at the store. You showing up looking all gorgeous and being flirty made you into a threat."

"I get the impression Cristian spends a lot of time hiding in fitting rooms listening to conversations." Jack's lips pressed tightly together. "More concerning is the fact you didn't notice he was sitting in the banquette behind you at the Black Dog."

"It was dark, and he was behind me. You should have seen him."

"I was looking at you."

We stared at each other, chests heaving, tension shimmering in the air between us.

"It doesn't matter how he got here," Chloe said. "He knows about the heist, and he's threatened to tell Simi's family about it. We're going to have to include him."

"I refuse to be blackmailed." My hands found my hips. "Let him tell my family. They saw me dragged out of the house in handcuffs and they still think they can find me a husband."

"He won't stop at your family," Gage said. "I know his type. He's a wild card. Better to have him here, where we can keep an eye on him, than out there making trouble. Does he have any useful skills?"

"Other than preening in front of mirrors and seducing women?" I was positively seething. "Clearly, he's good at spying, hiding, and blackmail. He's also not burdened by scruples, morals, laws, or common decency, so anything goes. I can't imagine what he could contribute."

Jack shared a look with Gage. "I can."

◆ ◆ ◆

"Cristian will be our inside man," I told the crew as I fought back an overwhelming desire to punch Cristian in his beautiful face. "He's resourceful and very good with people. His job will be to form a connection with someone in the mansion so he can get inside and feed us information."

"I'll *bet* he's good with people," Emma muttered. "So long as the people have boobs, money, and utterly no taste."

"You remind me of someone I really cared about." Cristian gave her a smooth, guileless smile that made the hair on the back of my neck stand on end. "We should hang out. I've always enjoyed spending time with older women. You could teach me how to knit."

Emma's face turned three shades of fury. "Give me a pair of knitting needles and I'll shove them up your—"

"We're all here to help Chloe get out of a terrible jam and collect the reward." I positioned myself between them, cutting off Emma's line of sight. "It's best if we try to get along."

Anil raised his hand.

"Yes, Anil?"

"No offense to Chloe but I'm just here for the money and I want to know how many people will be sharing the reward."

"Rose is taking a nonmonetary supporting role for now," I said. "She'll only become part of the heist if we need her services as a grease woman. So that leaves seven of us."

"Six," Jack said. "I'm on salary."

"So that would be $833,333.33 each." Anil's face lit up. "That's enough to get a place of my own far, far away from my parents and start training to be an MMA star."

"You?" Emma snorted a laugh. "In an MMA ring? You'll be creamed more than those puffs on the table."

"Don't be unkind," Chloe said. "I'm sure everyone in this room has a dream about what they'll do with the money."

I sensed the room descending into chaos again, so I turned the floor over to Jack.

"The necklace we are after is called the Wild Heart," Jack said. "It last sold at auction in November 2015 for $25 million. It features twenty-six oval-shaped flawless pink diamonds and a forty-carat heart-shaped pink diamond. Each diamond is enhanced by a cluster of oval-shaped green marquise emeralds supposedly crafted to resemble the leaves of the phalaenopsis orchid, but which in fact are more like dendrobiums that produce leaves that are opposite one another. The diamonds and emeralds are strategically placed to create a floral effect that makes the necklace resemble a lei of Orchidaceae. The gems are set in eighteen-carat white gold and precious platinum."

"He likes plants," I explained when I saw a few blank stares. "We met in the hellebore."

"It wasn't as romantic as it sounds," Jack said. "She trampled it underfoot like a herd of elephants. I had to go back the next night to repair the damage."

"I wasn't trying to make it sound romantic." I heaved a sigh. "I was explaining how I knew that you liked plants."

"They probably understood when you said, 'He likes plants.'" Jack's gaze drifted to Cristian. "At least some of them."

"Can we have nicknames?" Anil asked. "We would call Jack 'Plant Man' and I'll be 'The Butcher.'"

"The Butcher?" Chloe asked me, keeping her voice low. "I thought he was an engineer."

"It's his dream MMA ring name. Self-styled. He said it was ironic."

"What butchering are you going to do wiggling your plastic joy sticks and flying your annoying drones into people's hair?" Emma said. "We should call you Buzz."

"I don't want to be Buzz." Anil folded his arms across his chest. "Don't call me Buzz."

"It's not like you could stop me." She flexed an arm, showing off her inked biceps. I made a mental note to hit the weight area of the gym the next time I was there.

"Are you calling me weak?" Anil's eyes bulged and he dropped his plate of petit fours on the table. "Right here. Right now." He drum-rolled the air with his fists, dancing from side to side in his frayed Converse high-tops. "I'll show you weak." Without waiting for Emma to respond, he took off across the garage and slammed his fists into the aluminum door, making the building shake. "The Butcher will make you bleed."

"You dodged a bullet with that one, babe," Chloe whispered in my ear. "Thank goodness Garcia showed up and put you in handcuffs."

"God, I know."

"You'd better talk him down before he hurts himself."

"No one is calling you weak, Anil." I beckoned him forward. "Come and sit—"

"I am," Gage interjected. "One hint of real danger and that douche is gonna run screaming for his mama. Watch this . . ." He pulled the gun from his holster and fired it into one of the sandbags Rose used when the basement flooded.

Everyone dropped to the floor when the gunshot cracked the air. We'd clearly all been raised in Chicago.

"Did you just fire a gun in my meeting?" I pushed to my knees, barely able to see through the red sheeting my vision. "Are you crazy?" I glared at Jack. "Is he crazy? Did you bring a crazy person into my crew?"

"He's just doing his job," Jack said with a shrug. "He must have decided your people were a danger to themselves."

"So he shot off his gun?" I walked over to Gage and stood toe to toe with him, hands on my hips. "No guns. No violence. If things get out of hand, you have my permission to escort people out the door." I was beyond irritated. Chloe's freedom was at stake, our dreams for a better future. I wasn't going to have it all go wrong because I couldn't control my crew.

"As for the rest of you . . ." I continued. "There will be no nicknames. No interruptions. No name calling. No making people bleed. If anyone has a problem with that, you are welcome to forfeit your $833,333.33 and walk out the door."

Of course, no one left. Who would give up that kind of money?

"The necklace is located at the home of Joseph Angelini, a real estate and casino mogul," Jack continued when everyone had quieted down. "He also dabbles in art, jewelry, and antiquities, acquiring and selling pieces on the black market. He owns a fifteen-thousand-square-foot house in Lake Bluff set on thirteen exclusive acres with nearly seven hundred feet of Lake Michigan frontage."

"That's not a house; that's a mansion," Emma said. "Imagine how long it would take to clean. I have trouble just keeping my car tidy."

"People who own houses like that hire cleaners." Cristian crossed his feet on the chair in front of him. "I don't think any of my clients would even know where to find their vacuum."

Anil frowned. "I thought you sold suits."

"That's my day job. I have a side hustle as a life coach / professional escort. That's where I make the real money."

"Now that is the first interesting thing I've heard since I got here." Emma jumped down from her perch on the tool bench. "Tell me more about being an escort. I briefly considered getting into the business myself."

"Save it for later," I said. "The first thing we need to do is plan the surveillance mission. Chloe found the floor plans, property description, and photographs from a ten-year-old real estate listing. The house has eight bedrooms, ten bathrooms, twenty-two miscellaneous rooms, home theater, game room, gym, library, and a large formal terrace leading down to a swimming pool. There is also a private dock on the Lake Michigan shoreline. It is very secluded and can only be accessed through the forest, lakeshore, or the long private gated driveway. And of course, it has state-of-the-art security."

"How are we supposed to do surveillance?" Cristian asked. "It's not like we can sit in a white van across the road and watch them coming and going."

Jack pushed aside the madeleines, canelés, religieuses, and macarons and spread a topographical map across the table. "Here." He tapped the lakeshore. "They have over seven hundred feet of beachfront and no rights to stop boaters or walkers past the shoreline. We can rent a boat, anchor in the lake, and do some recon as tourists."

"I'm driving," Emma said. "No one can keep up with me on the water."

"We won't be renting a speed boat." I flipped to the search I'd done on my phone when we'd made the tentative plan at the bar. "We'll be renting a slow and steady Bennington pontoon boat that can hold ten people and has a 115-horsepower Yamaha outboard."

"Jesus Christ." Emma snorted in disgust. "That's like giving a Formula One driver a Chevy Spark."

"You get a pontoon boat. Take it or leave it."

"You're no fun." Emma slumped in her seat. "My talents are being wasted."

"I'll book it for tomorrow morning," I said. "They have tubes and water skis available to rent. That should give us good cover. Bring binoculars, and make sure your phones are charged so we can take pictures."

"You'd get better images with a drone," Anil said. "I've just modded up my DJI Air 2S. It's got an operating time of around thirty minutes and the camera capabilities really make it shine. We'll be able to get close-up images while maintaining the fifty-foot distance from people required by law. It's not the best surveillance drone out there, but it was all Santa could afford this year."

"Looks like the heist is a go," I said into the silence. I wasn't sure if everyone was blown away by Anil's expertise or by his reference to the big man in the red suit, but whatever. We had a plan.

Chloe made the sign of the cross. It had been years since she'd prayed.

TEN

◇ ◇ ◇

S itting on a dock waiting for the pontoon boat that would take us to the house of a dirty real estate mogul so we could figure out how to break into his mansion to steal a $25 million necklace wasn't how I usually spent my Sunday mornings, but Chef Pierre had aced his blueberry muffin homework assignment, and his basket of goodies soothed the pain of our early start.

The sky was blue and clear with no hint of the rain that had been forecast for the day. Not that I minded the odd shower. Chicagoans make up for long, harsh winters by embracing the outdoors from the moment the first snowflake melts. After surviving frost quakes, polar vortices, arctic blasts, thermal whiplash, and the almighty bone-chilling Hawk blowing off Lake Michigan every winter, we can handle a summer sprinkle.

"Are you planning to share those?" Jack reached for the basket beside me. Rose had dropped off the muffins at my parents' house on her way into the city for an audition. Chef Pierre had a sauce assignment to complete for class the next day, so she'd left him at home with the stove and a bottle of brandy.

"I'm waiting until we board the boat so we can enjoy them during the ride." I breathed in the scents of pine and fish and fresh lake air. It had been ages since I'd been out on the water, and I was looking forward to our day of sunshine and surveillance.

"Tell Emma to go easy on the throttle," Anil warned. "My drone doesn't like to be rattled." He'd gone extra with the day-on-the-lake theme in colorful Bermuda shorts, rattan flip-flops, a pink shirt printed with pictures of toucans, and a big straw hat.

"That's what I said when Cristian showed up in his bright blue Speedo and nothing else." Emma joined us at the dock. "Paperwork is all done, and I've got the keys. Let's get going."

"You laugh, but who goes on a boat ride without swimwear?" Cristian posed for another Speedo selfie at the edge of the dock.

"Is that what it is?" Gage said. "I thought it was a hammock for mini bananas."

"Look over there." Jack pointed to something in the distance. I looked. He stole a muffin from the basket. I couldn't believe I'd fallen for a trick so lame.

"Would anyone else like a muffin?" I snatched the basket away, glaring at Jack.

"I'll pass." Anil held up his hands in a warding gesture. "I don't eat carbs. I have to keep my body fat down so I can compete in the featherweight division once we get our money and I start my new MMA career. One muffin and I'll get bumped up to welterweight. You should see those guys. Steamrollers. All of them. I have to stick to apples."

"You and Cristian have a lot in common. He doesn't eat carbs, either."

"I'm gluten, dairy, and animal free," Cristian said. "Also, no nightshades, brown rice, or cruciferous vegetables. I'm still working out my IBS triggers."

"So you're vegan?" I asked as we followed Emma down the dock.

"I eat fish."

"Pescetarian?"

"I don't eat farmed fish. They need to be free swimming. I also can't give up bacon."

"I hope to hell the pigs aren't free swimming, too," Gage muttered under his breath. "Must make for one hell of a dinner date."

"Here we are." Emma stopped in front of a sleek and stylish sport boat with a spaceship-like roof over an expansive cockpit. "What do you think? It's a 2018 Luxury Sea Ray 31SLX with a top speed of 53 miles per hour. It's so stable, you can walk around comfortably while cruising at high speeds. Usually, you need to pay for a captain, but I know the guy who runs this place, and I've got my boating license, so . . ."

"It's supposed to be a pontoon boat," I said. "Our cover is a bunch of a crazy kids taking it easy and kicking it back on the lake. A pontoon boat is perfect because it's the kind of thing you park for the day so no one would give it a second glance. This boat is all about speed and attention."

"And fun," Emma said. "You gotta live a little. I took one look at the pontoon boat and threw up my breakfast. I couldn't be seen in something like that. I have a rep to protect."

"I agree." Gage climbed aboard and stretched out on the white leather seating in the cockpit.

"It is pretty cool." Anil gave an apologetic shrug before clambering into the boat. Cristian stretched out on an aft-facing lounger to take another selfie.

"I suppose you think it's awesome, too." I turned to Jack when we were all aboard, only to see him waving from the dock.

"Why aren't you coming?" I shouted when he turned away. "We're supposed to be a team." We'd already lost Chloe to Olivia's dance recital, and Rose and Chef Pierre weren't really part of the crew.

"Not much of a team player, sweetheart." Jack gave me a backward wave. "I'll see you later."

"Leave him," Gage said when I grabbed the railing, fully intending to vault over it and chase Jack down. "He works best on his own."

I spun around to face him, redirecting my anger against the impenetrable shield that was his expressionless face. "He's the one who said I needed a crew."

"You do. He doesn't. If not for the baked goods, he would have left when you all arrived. You're lucky he even showed up to check on you."

"He can take the damn muffins and shove them up his—"

The boat lurched, throwing me off balance and saving me from an uncharacteristic burst of temper. I'd learned to hide my feelings long ago, to bury my anger and frustration. Six hours standing in the rain on the soccer pitch being elbowed in the head by overexcited parents while the twins played yet another game? Fine. A ten-hour car drive to Nikhil's hockey tournament with nothing to do because someone had forgotten to load my Barbie backpack? Fine. Family movie night watching superheroes, gunfights, car chases, and endless violence because no one wanted to watch cartoons or Disney films with me? Fine. But for some reason, I couldn't handle the thought of being abandoned by the muffin man.

"Take a seat," Emma called out. "And get ready to ride. I feel a need for speed."

◇ ◇ ◇

We put Cristian in the inner tube behind the boat when we finally dropped anchor because he was the only person in swimwear.

"Try to look like you're having fun," I called out. We were about five hundred yards offshore from the Angelinis' beach. Gage was on the back deck with a fishing pole in one hand and a pair of binoculars in the other. Anil was in the bow getting the drone ready.

"Just don't drive too fast," Cristian shouted. "Bouncing is bad for my IBS."

"Go fast," I told Emma. "He likes the speed."

"Honey is ready to go," Anil said, patting his drone. "Clear skies. Light breeze. It should be a good flight."

"You named your drone Honey?" Emma snorted a laugh. "It looks more like a spider or one of those spaceships from that show with the aliens."

"Shows that take place in space almost always have aliens." Anil gave an indignant sniff. "They make the perfect antagonists—"

"Bo-ring." Emma held up a dismissive hand. "I like real things that take place in real places with real people who aren't green or puce or have tentacles for mouths or fifteen ears."

"There are no space shows that have creatures with fifteen ears," Anil said, starting up his drone. "I've seen them all."

"And that's why we'll never be friends," she told him.

I watched the drone lift straight up in the air. It was small but sturdy, holding steady when the wind picked up over the water.

"We can see everything on the screen." Anil held up his controller. "We're in their airspace now and officially breaking the law. We're criminals."

"Real property trespass isn't a criminal offense unless we enter after being warned not to, or if we don't leave after being asked," I said. "Then it's a misdemeanor punishable by up to six months in jail or a $1,500 fine. My lawyer explained it to me when I was at the police station after trying to rescue Chloe."

"When you slit a man's throat, stab him in the heart, or shoot him in the head, that's a real criminal offense," Gage offered. "You want to be a criminal, go big or go home."

"Thanks for the advice." I grabbed another muffin because having non-carb-eaters on the boat just meant more for me. "I'll file that one away for when I need it, which will be never."

We crowded around the screen when the Angelinis' mansion came into view. The two-story limestone-clad home resembled an Italian villa, with a clay tile roof, numerous balconies and shutters, and a broad front terrace. A ten-foot fountain dominated the front courtyard, and ornate stone vases bursting with colorful flowers lined the tiered concrete stairway leading to the front door.

Anil flew the drone higher, giving us a full aerial view. The property was surrounded by a ten-foot metal perimeter fence and secured with an electric gate. Acres of thick, lush forest gave way to ornamental gardens and a vast manicured lawn. The shoreline was accessed with steps leading down to a private dock, which was partially hidden by a row of tall trees.

"What's going on out front?" I pointed to a cluster of people standing beside three white vans parked in the circular driveway. "Can you zoom in?"

Anil dropped the drone a few feet. "I can't get closer without breaking the law or drawing attention."

"Keep an eye on those two." Gage pointed to two men in suits standing near the stairs. "They're security."

Two women in dresses and heels emerged from the house. One of them looked to be about my age. She was tall and slim with long, dark hair and supersize sunglasses that hid most of her face. The other woman was older, but shared similar facial features. Likely her mom.

"That guy looks familiar." I stared at a man in coveralls exiting the back of one of the vans. Anil increased the zoom. We gasped as one.

"What is Jack doing there?" I couldn't believe what I was seeing. "He's going to compromise the whole heist."

Jack looked up and waved his hand in the air before disappearing into the bushes beside the house. Was it a friendly hello or a warning wave? Before I could decide, a red light flashed on the screen and the audio picked up a sound like the buzzing of bees.

I didn't know anything about drones, but I did know that red lights meant bad news. "What's going on?"

"Proximity alert," Anil said. "It could be a bird or a plane or . . ." His eyes widened when two tiny yellow drones came into view. "Bees!"

"Do I want to know?" I asked.

"They're very sophisticated fully autonomous surveillance drones that automatically deploy from a Hive in response to vibrations in the air or motion on the property," Anil said. "They know we're here."

"Well, don't just hover. Get out of there."

A third Bee buzzed past our camera, and then a fourth. Moments later we were surrounded.

Anil gave a horrified gasp. "It's an attack."

"Fly!" I grabbed his arm. "Fly!"

Anil flew Honey in a serpentine pattern toward the boat. A gunshot echoed across the water. Honey dropped and tilted to the side. Anil frantically pushed the joystick, his forehead a sheen of sweat. The screen went blank. High above us in the sky, Honey fought to survive, spluttering and spiraling until, finally, the brave little drone plummeted to the ground.

"Noooooooo." Anil jumped to his feet just as three guards came running down the beach. One of them gestured to our boat.

"We need to get out of here," I said to Emma. "I'll pull Cristian in."

Another gunshot cracked the silence.

"Are they shooting at the boat?" Anil was shaking, his gaze on the grass where the drone had fallen. "Why? They took out the drone. We're no longer a threat."

"I'm sure it was just a warning."

Another shot. A bullet pinged off the elegant hull.

"Oh my God." I screamed. "They *are* shooting at us. Who are these people? It was just a drone. Now they're trying to kill us?"

"Emma. Get the lead out." Gage pulled the gun from his holster. I silently rescinded my "no guns" rule and made a mental note to thank him for ignoring me.

Emma started the engine and looked over her shoulder. "What about Cristian?"

"No time." Gage moved to the stern. "They're getting into a speedboat. We gotta go."

"Hang on, Cristian," I shouted. "It's going to be one hell of a ride."

"No. Wait. I'll—"

The rumble of the motor drowned out his words. Emma pushed the throttle and the boat lurched into motion.

"Holy crap," Anil said, watching the inner tube bounce violently over the boat's wake. "Look at Cristian fly."

Between revs of the engine, I thought I heard Cristian scream.

"Here they come," Gage called out. "Everyone down. This isn't the movies. Good shooters don't miss."

"Why couldn't they just have put up a No Trespassing sign?" Anil buried his face in his hands beside me on the deck. "Why couldn't they just shout, 'Hey, guys. This is private property. No trespassing.' And we'd say, 'Sorry. We were just out having a nice afternoon air tubing and fishing and eating muffins and testing our new drone. We'll be on our way.' Why did they have to shoot it down? What is Santa going to think when he shows up at Christmas and Honey is gone?"

"Guys like that don't do a lot of talking," Gage shouted over the roar of the engine.

"Guys like what?" I asked.

"Jack didn't tell you?"

"Tell me what? That they were paranoid about security? Or that the guards would be armed?" I felt a rush of anger at the man who had put us all in danger. If Jack had been here right now, I would have thrown him overboard.

"Uh . . . yeah." He hesitated, frowning. "That they'd be armed."

"Did you hear that, Emma?" I called out. "Jack and Gage knew the security guards would be armed but forgot to mention it."

"Cool."

"It's not cool." I rolled to my side because the floor was hard and wet and smelled like stale beer. "I don't want to die in a speedboat shootout. I want to go home. I want to sleep in a warm bed and wake up to breakfast parathas and warm chai."

"Get . . . meeeeeeee . . . out . . . of . . . heeeeeeeeere," Cristian shouted, white-knuckling the handles on his inner tube as he bounced over the waves.

Multiple gunshots echoed across the water. An engine roared.

"Can't you go any faster?" I asked Emma.

"First, I want to hear an apology for giving me a hard time for ditching the pontoon boat." Her hair whipped across her face, her cheeks wet from the spray of the water.

"I'm sorry," I said. "Do you want me to get on my knees and grovel? Kiss your shoes? Tell me what I have to do so we don't get killed by some overly zealous security guards who take the concept of protecting privacy to a whole new level."

"What do you need?" she asked in a singsong voice.

I tipped my head back and groaned. "I need speed."

"Say it like you mean it."

"*I need speed.*"

◆ ◆ ◆

I was utterly incensed when Jack casually strolled into Rose's garage a few hours later.

"Armed guards? Seriously?" I shoved him in the chest. He had a nice chest, so it wasn't a hardship. "Is that why you bailed at the last minute? You knew they'd come out shooting and you didn't want to be killed? Did it ever occur to you that was information we needed to know?"

"He's an insanely rich property and casino guy." Jack gave a casual shrug, like he hadn't just sent us to die. "He has a fifteen-thousand-square-foot mansion filled with expensive art and a $25 million necklace sitting in a safe. Did you think he wasn't going to protect it?"

"We could have been killed." I moved to shove him again, but he grabbed my hands.

"That's why Gage was there. He told me he shot their gas tank and disabled their boat. That's the job he was hired to do."

"You didn't tell us we were going into a potentially life-threatening situation. You didn't warn us." It was difficult to stay angry and indignant when he was standing so close, I could feel the heat of his body and breathe in the subtle woody fragrance of his woman-wooing cologne.

"And neither did Gage." I glared at Gage, but he wasn't looking at me. Chloe had just walked in, and his lips had tipped at the corners in what I suspected was a smile. And why not? She was wearing a yellow sundress with little white flowers, a big floppy hat, and a pair of white kitten heels. If sunshine could have a human form, it would be my girl.

"Gage?" I repeated. "Care to comment?"

"No."

"Try again."

He sighed and held up his phone. "I've calculated the timetable and routes of the security team. We'll need to do another recon to cover dusk to dawn."

"You did that and caught three fish?" I gestured to the cooler by the door.

"I'm good at multitasking."

"You're also good at withholding vital information. Things like, 'Be careful because this guy is so paranoid about security, he'll shoot down—'"

I cut myself off when I remembered poor Anil would be going home without his drone. He hadn't said a word since we'd docked. Not even when we'd finally pulled in the inner tube and Emma had asked Cristian if he'd enjoyed the enema.

"Everyone is safe." Jack placed my hands on his chest as if the feel of rock-hard muscle under my palms would slow my thundering heart.

"Don't be condescending." I ripped my hands away. "Where were you during all this? Oh wait! I remember. You decided not to follow the plan and just waltz up to their house instead."

"With all due respect," Jack said. "The plan sucked."

"You agreed to the plan."

"When I realized it sucked, I came up with a better plan."

"Maybe you should have shared that with the class."

"You would have gotten in the way." His supercilious tone infuriated me. Adrenaline throbbed through my veins, demanding release. I grabbed the nearest whiteboard pen and threw it across the room.

"Feel better?" Jack asked.

"No."

"How about we cool off with a snack?" Rose suggested. "Chef

Pierre made mousse yesterday for a bedroom game and there's still a lot left. I wouldn't mind trying it with a bowl and spoon."

"That would be a big no for me." I shuddered and looked around the room. "Anyone else want some sex-game mousse leftovers?"

"Is it chocolate?" Emma asked. "I'll take it if it's chocolate."

Rose went to get the mousse for the only taker in the room. I went to sit with Anil and watch the drone footage he'd saved before Honey went down.

"Apple?" He offered me a piece of fruit from the bag beside him.

"Aren't you worried you'll get cyanide poisoning from the seeds? I've never known anyone to eat so many apples."

"I would need to eat anywhere from one hundred and fifty to several thousand crushed seeds to be at risk of cyanide poisoning," he said. "The average apple contains only about five to eight seeds. So unless I'm eating eighteen apple cores a day and have been meticulously chewing all the seeds, I should be fine. I usually limit myself to six."

"Have you ever considered other fruits?"

"Why? Apples are the best." Anil pulled up the video. "We got a good aerial view with shots of the entire property, exits and entrances, guard postings, and perimeter paths. I was just moving in to check out the vans when the . . ." He choked, tears welling in his eyes. "Bees attacked Honey."

"Because of him." I pointed to Jack. "It's his fault. If he hadn't been there, we wouldn't have sent Honey down to check him out."

"To be fair, we needed to get closer to find out what was going on," Anil offered, guaranteeing himself no gift at Christmas.

"They're having a wedding at the property," Jack said. "Their daughter Bella is getting married. The vans were from the catering service, the videographer, and the event company providing the tents. Apparently, Bella just fired her wedding planner, and no one knew what was going on. It was chaos. My favorite thing."

"Bella Angelini." Chloe read off her phone. "Her engagement was big society news last year and she's got lots of wedding stuff on her social. She's marrying Mario D'Amico in three weeks. Looks like she's a bit of a bridezilla. Three of her bridesmaids have been replaced and she's managed to piss off most of the wedding vendors in town."

"There's no chance we'll be able to break in." Anil picked up his third apple. Or maybe it was his fourth. I wished apples were my go-to food for stress eating, but no. I gravitated to candy and fried food. "It's a fortress," he continued. "There are cameras everywhere. The fence is electric, and I saw two dog kennels. The guards are armed and clearly not afraid to shoot."

"What about the day of the wedding?" I suggested. "Security won't be as tight. There will be lots of people there: guests, vendors, staff . . ."

"It's a double-edged sword," Rose said. She'd returned with a tray of mousse in tiny cups. "More people means more eyes watching what's going on."

"We can't just crash the wedding." Chloe took two cups of mousse and offered one to me. "Someone would know we didn't belong."

I had no self-control when it came to desserts so I took the cup and tried not to think about where it might have been. "What if we got invited?"

"Does anyone know the bride or groom or their families?" Rose surveyed the room. "No one? You're a disappointing bunch. Back in the day, I knew everyone who was anyone in Chicago."

"I could find out where her mom hangs out and offer her some life coaching." Cristian had changed out of his Speedo and into a pair of mustard pants and a skin-tight white shirt. He seemed no worse for wear after his ordeal. "I am your inside man, after all."

"What kind of 'inside' are we talking?" Emma asked. "Look how bonkers they went when they saw the drone on their property. What do think will happen if Mr. Angelini finds you in bed with his wife?"

"I don't think it's going to matter." Chloe looked up from her phone. "There might not be a wedding. Bella posted on her social asking for recommendations for a new wedding planner because she had to fire her last one. If she doesn't find someone soon, she's going to postpone the wedding."

An idea niggled at the back of my mind. I'd never planned a wedding on my own, but I'd been dragged into preparations for the weddings of numerous relatives and had attended dozens—maybe even hundreds—more. Wedding season in the South Asian community started in May and went until September. I spent every weekend and most Thursday and Friday nights at welcome dinners, sangeets, mehendi ceremonies, and then Saturdays and the occasional Sunday attending the wedding itself. Granted, they involved South Asian traditions, but at their essence, weren't all weddings the same?

"What about us?" I suggested. "We could plan her wedding."

"I hate weddings," Emma grumbled. "All that fake happiness, drunk dancing, family feuds, cringeworthy speeches, and shoving cake in people's mouths isn't for me. And then after you spend the equivalent of a down payment on a house for one stupid day, he cheats on you with your best friend when you're at the hospital with your mom who has just been injured in a motor vehicle accident, runs up all your credit cards so you can't pay for her medical treatment, and skips town in the car you and your dad built together before he got cancer and died."

"Wow," Cristian said. "Is that what happened to you?"

"No." Emma shrugged. "It's just something that might happen that makes the whole wedding idea a total waste of time."

"I thought we were planning a heist." Gage folded his arms across his chest. "Not a wedding."

"The wedding is the perfect cover for our heist. We can plan both."

"We can't just message her randomly and offer our services," Chloe pointed out. "She's been through some of the biggest event planners in the city. We have no street cred. We don't even have a website or a social media footprint."

"We can set all that up," I said. "The biggest problem is finding a way to meet her. We can't just show up at her door."

"Not unless we want to get attacked by killer Bees." Anil gave a dejected sigh. "Honey never had a chance and neither do we. I say we give up and go home."

"I say we crash the Summer Garden Charity Ball." Chloe looked up from her phone. "Bella is going to be there on Thursday night with her fiancé. She's been posting pictures of dresses."

"You need an invitation for that event," Cristian said. "I have clients who go every year. It's only for the rich and famous."

Gage shot him a sideways glance. "Thought you were an escort. Can't you find some single rich lady who needs a date?"

Cristian stroked his chin. "I could make a few calls."

"I can get an invitation." Jack's gaze dropped to my worn sneakers, then up my torn jeans to my faded white T-shirt and flannel shirt. "Do you have something nice to wear?"

I gave an affronted sniff. "Are you saying my clothes aren't nice?"

By way of answer, he held out a black card with BLOOMING-DALE'S on one side and the name *Clare Richards—Stylist* written in gold script on the back. "Clare will take care of you."

I stared at the card, aghast. "I can buy my own clothes."

"It's black tie and you gotta dress to impress." He tucked the card in my shirt pocket. His fingers may or may not have brushed my breast. My nipples didn't care. They reacted with enthusiasm.

"Is this one of those prank shows where I go to the store and people jump out and laugh at the naive candy store clerk slash suit salesperson who thought she'd met her Daddy Warbucks?"

He patted the card in my pocket. Another touch. Another sizzle of heat through my veins. "You wanna run with the big dogs, sweetheart, you have to look the part."

"What big dogs? Where am I running?" Was he asking me out on a date? If so, shouldn't I be offended that he didn't accept me for who I was? Or that he assumed I didn't have a dress fancy enough to wear to a high-society black tie event? And did I want to go out on a date with a man who kept a stash of "Clare" cards in his pocket, all ready to whip out when he wanted a hookup with someone but didn't like the clothes she wore?

"I thought you wanted to be Bella Angelini's wedding planner," he said.

"I do."

"This is how you'll get the job."

ELEVEN

◇ ◇ ◇

My parents and my grandmother were eating dinner in the kitchen when I returned home after our boat ride from Hell.

"Here she is," Nani called out after spotting me in the hallway. "Were you selling suits or candy today or were you out looking for a proper job?" In her usual dramatic fashion, she pressed a hand to her chest. "What is the world coming to when women have to sell suits to men? It's the end of days."

"I would have picked world wars, climate change, food insecurity, the rise of AI, or the fall of capitalism as indicators of the fall of civilization as we know it." I slipped off my sandals. Suit-selling aside, the world truly would end if I walked into the house wearing shoes. "Or even my arrest as an accessory to burglary."

"I called Riswan's mother." Mom gave an absent wave of the chutney spoon. "She says it's all a misunderstanding and he'll make it go away."

"I'm almost thirty years old. I don't need you calling people's mothers when I get into trouble. I've got a plan to solve my problem." I grabbed a plate and joined them at the table.

"What is your plan?" Mom asked. "Why do you need a plan when you have a cousin who is a criminal lawyer?"

"Lawyers cost money."

"He's family. Your father gave his father a suit for his brother's wedding at a 10 percent discount. The least he could do is waive his fees."

My dad shoved an entire samosa in his mouth as if he knew what was coming.

"Is he going to charge her, Rohan?" Mom glared at my dad. "His own cousin? Should I call his mother again?" She leaned across the table, shaking her finger at Dad. "He's your side of the family. How could you let this happen?"

"I told you," Nani muttered. "If only you'd married that doctor from Detroit . . ."

"His fees are going to be about one thousand times the suit discount if it goes to trial," I said. "I want to pay him for his work. He has to earn a living, too."

"At least *he's* using his degree." Nani smiled as if she hadn't just sliced my heart with her cutting remark. "How is it? Too spicy?"

"I like spice." I didn't like the inquisition, but I needed a proper meal after eating five bowls of sex mousse so it didn't go to waste.

"What are you going to do with your life?" Nani asked in the same casual tone one might use to inquire about the weather.

"I thought you were interested in my plan to stay out of jail," I said, trying to put her off. I knew where this was headed and even my life of crime was a better topic.

"If you had a husband, you wouldn't be worried about going to jail," Nani said. "You'd be too busy looking after him and having babies to run around committing crimes. Even a boyfriend would be useful to keep you out of trouble."

"She was with Anil Kapoor at the Lake Bluff marina at ten A.M. this morning," Mom said. "Satya called me with the news."

My father paused between bites of coconut curry. "Anil? The boy with the drones?"

"Yes, that's him," I said. "We went for a boat ride on Lake Michigan today with some friends."

Mom leaned back in her chair, her plate of food momentarily forgotten. "You said he was a loser. Now you want him? You want a loser?"

"'Loser' doesn't mean the same thing it did in your Boomer times," I said. "It's more lighthearted."

"We can't be picky." Dad patted my mom's hand. "She's going downhill fast. First it was the business degree. Then the entry-level office jobs. The candy store. The apartment that floods. All the failed relationships. We could do worse than a loser."

"He's not a loser," I said. "He's a little immature and naive and a bit of a geek, but he's a nice guy." I pushed my plate away. "I'm not seeing him. We're just friends."

"Men and women can't be friends," Nani said. "Take it from me. Every time I try to be friends with a man, we wind up in bed."

"Please . . ." Dad held up a hand, blocking his view of Nani. "Spare us the personal details."

Nani lifted an eyebrow. "You might learn something."

"I can guarantee you that I will not wind up in bed with Anil," I said. "I'm going to take one of Nikhil's old drones for him. Nikhil hasn't used them in almost ten years and Anil lost his at the lake today."

"Nikhil won't like that." My father speared another samosa. They were his favorite food. Usually my mother put them out of reach because he'd inhale them in a matter of minutes without even thinking to pass them around.

"It's okay," my mother said. "She's a criminal now. Stealing is what she does."

"It's just a phase," Nani assured her. "Next week she might be selling donuts, then she'll join a circus, and who knows, by the end of the month she could be married with three kids of her own."

"That's a physical impossibility," Dad said.

"Times have changed," Nani said. "These young people today do all sorts of things we don't understand."

Dad didn't miss a beat. "I don't think the basics of procreation have changed since the beginning of time."

"Could we not talk about sex at the dinner table?" I filled my plate from the dishes on the table: rogan josh, coconut curry, biryani, dal, and warm roti. I left the rest of the samosas for Dad.

"What do you want to talk about?" Mom asked.

"How about who would be the best person to talk to about planning a wedding?"

"You're getting married!" She clapped her hands together and then frowned. "To Anil?"

"I'm not getting married," I said. "I'm starting my own business. I'm going to be a wedding planner."

◇ ◇ ◇

Detective Garcia was waiting for me outside Dad's shop the next morning.

"If you're here for a suit, I'd recommend the tailor shop on the next block," I told him. "They're having a sale on false accusations and police harassment."

"I just have a few questions, if you don't mind." Garcia looked irritatingly handsome today, dressed in a blue off-the-rack suit and white cotton shirt open at the collar.

"The question is: Will my dad mind? You're taking me away from work."

Garcia followed me into the store and looked around. "There's no one here."

"You never know when people will be struck with a desperate need for a suit." I nodded a greeting at Cristian, who was adjusting the display behind the till. "We might get a stampede any moment."

"Then I'll be quick."

"Give me a moment. I'll need to ask Cristian to cover for me."

"He looks like a cop," Cristian whispered after Garcia had wandered over to check out the ties.

"He is a cop."

"What's he doing here?"

"He wants to talk."

Cristian held up his hands in a placatory gesture. "Look, I didn't know she was married and I thought the cash was legit—"

"It's not about you," I said, cutting him off.

"Did someone overhear us in Rose's garage?" he asked in a hushed tone. "Are we in trouble? Or does this have to do with the boating incident? I'll tell him I wasn't involved. I wasn't even on the boat. You pressured me into it . . ."

"Nice to know how quickly you would throw me under the bus," I said. "Lucky for you, he's not here about that, either. He's working the museum theft and probably has some questions about the night the necklace was stolen."

"I thought I'd have to run out the back. It wouldn't be the first time." Cristian ran his fingers through his thick hair. "He's pretty hot for a cop. Are you two together?"

I shrugged, feigning disinterest. "He's not really my type."

"Can I have him?"

I opened my mouth to tell him to take his best shot, but nothing came out. It made no sense. I didn't like Garcia that way. Or did I? Sure, he was gorgeous, fit, and a decent guy. He had a badge and a gun and handcuffs. His warm eyes and soft smile would have made me a little weak in the knees if he hadn't thought I was a criminal.

"He's not a leftover bagel, Cristian. He's a person with feelings. He probably has his own type—"

"And you're saying it's not me?"

"I thought your type was older women who were unhappy in their marriages, committed to their careers with no time for relationships, or newly divorced and looking for the kind of loving they'd dreamed about while raising three kids with a beta male husband who had erectile dysfunction."

"That's work," he said. "Not play. In my off time, I'll hit on anything warm and willing."

"He's mine so that means off-limits." I couldn't imagine anything worse than Cristian getting it on with the police officer searching for the necklace that we were about to steal.

"Why do you get all the hot guys?" Cristian huffed, turning away. "Didn't your parents teach you how to share?"

"What guys?" I called out. "I have no guys."

◇ ◇ ◇

"What was that all about?" Garcia pulled out his black notebook and flipped through the pages after I'd hunted him down beside the argyle socks.

"He wants to steal you away from me."

Garcia laughed. "I didn't know we had a thing."

"We do if you're going to show up at my place of work and raise questions. I had to think fast, so now you've come to see me hoping to get a date."

"Do I succeed?" He looked up, his dark eyes amused.

"You would be so lucky."

"I really hope you turn out not to be a thief," he said. "I'm due for a suit upgrade and I like what I see."

I couldn't tell if Garcia was flirting or joking or if this was some kind of police trick to throw me off guard. "What's this all about? Do I need to call my lawyer?"

"One question," he said. "And then I'll be out of your hair. Or we can do it at the station in the presence of your lawyer. Your choice."

I had no wish for another trip to the station. "Okay. Go for it."

"How tall was Oliver Twist?"

"Is this a trick question?"

"We have a boot print from the scene, but my crime scene investigators say there is a discrepancy in the weight distribution that suggests that the size of the perp's feet may not have matched his boots."

I remembered the print. When I'd mentioned it to Jack, he told me he'd borrowed the boots from his cousin to throw the police off his tracks.

I tipped my head to the side, considering. Jack was around Garcia's height. If he'd borrowed boots that were too big, Oliver Twist would have to be taller. "How tall are you?"

"Six feet two and a half inches." He straightened his already straight back and puffed out his chest for good measure.

"That's a good height," I said. "That half inch makes the difference. I'll bet your dance card is always full."

His eyes lit up and he laughed. "No time for dancing when there are criminals to catch."

"He was taller than you," I said. "I would guess he had two inches on you from where my head hit his chest when he grabbed me."

"Heavy?"

"That's two questions," I said. "But I'll give it to you since you aren't pulling out the cuffs today. I can't guess his weight, but he was kind of beefy although not enough to stand out in any way. Anything else?"

"That's it." He snapped his notebook closed. "Do you enjoy selling suits?"

"I need to pay the bills while I look for a new job," I said. "I seem to be constantly underemployed. Why did I get a degree when everyone wants someone with two degrees, or they don't need a degree at all? Why did I burden myself with all this debt? I should have gone into something with a guaranteed job like you."

"I have loans to pay, too," Garcia said. "I did a degree in criminology before joining the CPD. I love the work, but I have to admit the pay isn't great."

"You should pick up a side gig. That's what I did. I work a second job at the candy store in Westfield Shopping Mall."

"$25 million would make quite a difference . . ."

"Garciaaaa . . ." I tipped back my head and groaned. "You always ruin things with your baseless accusations just when we're vibing. I'm not going to fall for your underhanded tricks."

"So $25 million wouldn't make a difference?" He tipped his head to the side, a smile tugging at his lips. I could see a real criminal falling for his charm.

"Not if it comes with a jail time price tag. Imagine the interest that would accrue on those loans if I spent the next ten years in prison. I'd get out and have to spend the rest of my life trying to earn enough to pay them off."

He laughed again, a warm rich sound that vibrated through my body. "Give my best to Riswan."

"I will." I waited until he reached the door. "Next time you need a suit, stop by the shop. I'll give you a 10 percent discount."

"In that case," he said, "I'll definitely be back."

◇ ◇ ◇

Chloe and Olivia came to Bloomingdales with me the next day for my high-end dress-shopping experience.

"I hope they turn you away," Chloe said. She'd forced me to go to the designer floor, where the private shoppers were located, even though I'd told her I was buying my own dress. "Then you can come back after you've bought clothes somewhere else and tell them they've made a big mistake."

"This isn't *Pretty Woman*. I can buy my own clothes." I looked around at the racks of designer outfits, most of which were chained to the rails.

"That movie was so lame." Olivia stretched out on a cream velvet chaise. She was in a new Goth phase and had come dressed all in black with a pair of Demonia thick-soled knee-high boots covered with buckles and chains. Her eyes were heavily rimmed in black and her blond hair was now green, framing a face that was the mirror image of Chloe's except for her still-chubby cheeks. "I couldn't believe the underlying misogyny. Edward is a condescending dick. He was rude to the staff, there were no diverse characters, and the movie assumed all sex workers want to be saved."

"Aside from the fact that I'm bursting with pride at your astute sociological and political analysis, I see I haven't raised you right when it comes to traditional rom-coms," Chloe said. "First, that kind of language is unacceptable. Second, rom-coms from the eighties and nineties can still be enjoyed for what they are despite their problematic content. They are light, fluffy entertainment where you can indulge in the willing suspension of disbelief and accept that an insanely rich man can fall in love with a hard-up struggling woman, and they can live happily ever after."

"Is that what Simi is doing?" Olivia crossed her ankles, careful to keep her boots off the couch. I was relieved to see that, despite the attitude and angst, she still had some sense of decorum. "Because it sounds real to me."

"I'm not a sex worker with a heart of gold, Olivia," I pointed out as I flicked through a rack of dresses I couldn't afford. "And how do you know what a sex worker is anyway? When I was your age, I still believed in Santa Claus."

And then, because I was annoyed that I'd agreed to come to this floor instead of going to a department store where normal people with normal amounts of money shop, and Olivia was guilting Chloe over something that brought her mom joy, I said, "I think you're spending too much time on your phone."

"Mom!" Olivia bolted upright at the hint that her life might be imminently ruined. "Don't listen to her."

Chloe's lips rose at the corners. "She has a point."

"I have to be on my phone. It's part of life. This isn't the Dark Ages." Olivia shot me a look of pure desperation. "Okay. I take it back. I'll stream every eighties and nineties rom-com I can find as soon as I get home and I'll love them. I'll tease out my hair, wear blue eyeshadow and leg warmers, and give up my agency as a woman to be pampered by an uptight billionaire as he destroys the world with his capitalist greed."

"Can I help you?" The salesperson who'd been watching us since we'd arrived on the floor must have decided it was time to stop the lowly masses from pawing through the five-digit dresses. She was dressed in head-to-toe pink Chanel and her black-and-gold name tag read CLARE.

"I'm looking for a dress for a charity ball," I said. "But I think these are outside my budget."

"Yes, of course." Her smile didn't reach her eyes. "We have more affordable dresses down on the second floor."

Chloe bristled beside me. "Tell her."

"No." I turned to go. "We shouldn't have come up here. Let's go back down to the swamp, where we belong."

"She has this." Chloe produced Jack's card with a flourish. "Jack sent her and told her to ask for Clare. I assume that's you and you're a personal shopper."

"Where did you get that?" I reached over to grab the card and she went up on her tiptoes to keep it away.

"I stole it from your purse because I knew you wouldn't use it. You're not good at accepting help." Chloe handed it to the salesperson. "You've made a big mistake," she said to the woman. "Massive."

"Mom," Olivia groaned. "You're embarrassing me." She bent over, hiding her face in her hands.

"Me too." I would have hidden my face, but the salesperson was staring right at me.

"Jack sent you?" Clare said his name as if it were a religious experience.

"You know him?"

"We knew each other when I worked in New York," she said. "It was such a surprise when he showed up at my door the other night."

Nice. He'd sent me to one of his old girlfriends. Or maybe she was a current girlfriend. Of course she was stunning—long dark hair, perfectly oval face, big dark eyes with impossibly long lashes, and a body made to model the designer dress that clung to her curves the way Cristian had clung to his inner tube at the lake.

"Same." I gave her a tight smile. It's not like I hadn't had regular hookups, or even the occasional relationship. Last year, I'd spent two whole weeks dating an accountant who suffered from both allergic rhinitis and an obsession with cycling. Chloe almost choked to death on a chicken wing when I invited him to my favorite bar to meet her. It had been a hot day. He'd just come back from a long, sweaty ride in his body-hugging white spandex onesie that left nothing to the imagination. He sneezed. Chloe gagged. I like a little mystery in my men, so I ended it the next day.

"We're going to the Summer Garden Charity Ball on Thursday."

I plastered a fake smile over the glare I was saving for Chloe. "He said you'd be able to help me with a dress."

She gave me a quick once-over and lifted a perfectly manicured brow. "You'll need more than a dress. You'll need shoes, a bag, accessories, and jewelry. And your hair . . ."

"What's wrong with my hair?" Sure, it had a tendency to frizz when it rained, but it was thick and shiny and tended to stay put if I threw in a few handfuls of product on my way out the door.

"I know someone." She gestured to the fitting room. "I'll make a few calls. We'd better get started. We have a lot of work to do. And don't worry about the cost. Jack has it covered."

"Makeovers are one of my favorite tropes in rom-com movies," Chloe said to Olivia. "Especially when someone else is paying."

"I'm not getting made over," I shouted from a dressing room that was almost the same size as my basement suite but much more lavishly decorated. "I'm perfect just the way I am."

"Okay, babe. Whatever you say."

TWELVE

◆ ◆ ◆

Chloe and Olivia showed up at Rose's house on Thursday night just as Rose was putting the finishing touches on my makeup.

"Are you here to drive my pumpkin coach to the ball?" I called out from the kitchen. "My fairy godmother is almost done."

"We'll do you one better than a pumpkin," Chloe said. "There's a limo outside and a man in a uniform waiting by the door."

"Showtime." Rose draped my new black cashmere wrap around my shoulders. Chicago weather being unpredictable, Clare had been concerned I would get cold in my one-shoulder hot pink evening gown. Made from gazar fabric from some obscure designer, the dress featured ruching along the bodice and a cape skirt overlay. It was smooth and sleek, hugging all my curves to perfection. The bill for my outfit—dress, shoes, bag, wrap, and jewelry—had been more than three months' rent. There was no way I could pay Jack back unless we were able to retrieve the necklace and claim the reward.

"Oh. My. God." Chloe slapped a hand over her heart. "You look incredible."

"You look amazing," Olivia said. "And I say this despite the fact you have dressed for the patriarchy you have internalized since birth. I personally choose to reject the restrictive fashions that are designed for the male gaze and are rooted in socially constructed gender norms. When I'm not vibing with the Goth look, I wear gender-free lingerie, pro-women sweatshirts, elastic-waist pants with functional pockets, giant glasses, padded running shoes, and blanket scarves to keep me warm. I dress for comfort, protection, convenience, and ease of movement, and not as a sexualized, idealized object of heteronormative desire."

"Um . . . thank you. I think." I shot a questioning glance at Chloe and she grinned.

"I couldn't be more proud."

"I've never been to anything like this," I said to Rose for the fourth or fifth time that evening. "I don't know how to act."

"Act rich."

"How do rich people act?"

"Like they don't give a damn about what people think about them, although secretly they do. And say 'darling' a lot but pronounce it 'dahling.'"

"She should have a cigarette," Olivia called out from the couch. "It looks cool."

Chloe's head whipped around. "Only if she wants lung cancer. Is that what you want? Lung cancer? You'd better not be smoking."

"Mom. Seriously. Chill. Gen Z's don't smoke cigarettes. It's so old-school."

"That's good to hear," Chloe said. "I thought—"

"We vape."

"What?" Chloe's voice rose a few decibels.

"You're so easy to wind up, Mom. It's not even fun anymore." Olivia gave an exaggerated sigh and went back to staring at her phone. "Have a good time, Simi!"

"Thanks, dahling!"

Jack's driver didn't talk except to call me ma'am, which made me feel like I was past my prime. After a few fruitless attempts at conversation, I helped myself to the mini bottles of champagne in the ice bucket beside me then moved on to the free snacks in case platters of hors d'oeuvres weren't enough to sustain me. By the time we reached the InterContinental Chicago, my tension had ebbed, and I was buzzing and ready to party.

Jack was waiting at the curb. He opened the door and helped me out of the car. Then he stared at me like I'd grown a second head.

"Should I get back in the car? Were you expecting someone else? Clare perhaps?"

"You look . . . lovely," he said. "You take my breath away."

I immediately forgave him his lapse. I'm generous that way.

"Thank you for taking care of the bill. I met Clare. She wants you to give her a call."

"Umm-hmm." He pressed his hand against my lower back and gently urged me forward through the throng of people and cameras. I was getting strange vibes about his relationship with Clare—more ex than current. Or was that just hope?

"You clean up nice." I didn't want to tell him he looked gorgeous in his tailored tux and black bow tie. He'd done something to his hair that made it look almost conventional, and the scent of his cologne was playing havoc with my hormones.

Jack gave me the briefest of nods. He took us on a circuitous path to the front entrance, dodging and weaving when we could have just walked straight ahead. "Did Chloe get your wedding planning website and social media set up?"

"Yes, we're online. Her daughter, Olivia, designed the graphics and made a logo. I had some business cards printed up before I came." I carefully pulled a card from my new gold beaded clutch. I planned to sell the bag if I couldn't pay my rent. "We've called it Simply Elegant Events. Olivia came up with that name. We tried C & S, Chlosim, Simchlo, Simpliteevent . . ."

Jack's fingers dug into my hip, and I trailed off mid-recitation of all the failed names we'd come up with. "What's wrong?"

"Kiss me." He turned to face me, his arm going fully around my waist.

I'd never looked so good that a man was overcome with passion and demanded a kiss in the middle of a crowd, but it was a fabulous dress, and I did look amazing. I licked my lips and leaned in to oblige.

Usually, I'm a pretty good kisser. Chloe and I practiced on our plushies in high school and, a few times, on each other. We watched YouTube videos to learn proper positioning, how to breathe, what to do with your tongue, and how to tilt your head. I put my research into practice when I started dating and I'd never had a complaint. But then I'd never been taken by surprise. Jack went straight in for the kill without even a hint of foreplay.

"Ooooph." Our lips mashed together. Teeth clacked. Tongues smooshed. I tasted blood. Somehow, I'd managed to bite my own lip.

I pulled back for a breather. Jack wasn't even looking at me. His gaze was fixed on someone behind me and slightly to the left.

"Again." His arm tightened, and he pulled me so close, I could feel every inch of his hard body against mine through the thin fabric of my dress. Every button on his shirt. Every edge of his belt buckle. Every. Damn. Thing.

Oh hell.

This time I was prepared. I parted my lips and his mouth grazed mine. Nice. More than nice. His lips were soft, sweet, his tongue skimming past my teeth. My fingers slid into his hair and he groaned, a low rumble that vibrated through my body. I arched into him, tipped back my head, and breathed through my nose the way Kimmie4729 had demonstrated in part 3 of her YouTube *Seduction Education* series. A few more seconds and he would be putty in my hands.

"He's gone." He released me so suddenly, I stumbled back a step, mouth gaping in readiness for Kimmie's trademark "Swoop 'n Slide."

"What . . ." I swallowed hard, blinking to clear the haze of lust from my vision. ". . . just happened?"

"Photographer for the *Chicago Tribune*." He clasped my hand and led me up the steps. "I try to stay out of pictures. I needed you to hide my face."

Not really what a girl wants to hear after a kiss that leaves her knees weak. "Next time give me more warning when you need me to 'hide your face' so I can be better prepared." I couldn't keep the sarcasm from my tone, but if he noticed, he didn't let on.

Instead, he said, "Will do," and led me into the hotel.

Chicago boasts hundreds of world-renowned museums, hospitals, and nonprofit institutions—so it's no surprise that some of the most spectacular galas in the world take place in the Windy City. I had never attended a formal ball, but I had attended weddings at the InterContinental Chicago, so I didn't gape when we walked into the Renaissance Room ballroom. With its frescoed ceilings, massive crystal chandeliers, artistic wood carvings, and ornate interior, the room transported me back in time to the days when men wore wigs and tights and ladies swished around in puffy dresses.

We took a turn around the ballroom. Small groups of couture-clad upper-classers huddled around standing tables covered in gold-and-green brocade. I sampled from the trays proffered by tuxedo-clad waiters and drank too much free champagne while Jack searched for our target.

I excused myself to visit the restroom and stopped on my way out to reapply my new Ruby Red lipstick, which I'd managed to eat off my lips between the vol-au-vents and the Coquilles St. Jacques.

"Love your dress." A woman with a thick Southern accent fluffed her blond hair in front of the mirror. She wore a sparkly gold sheath dress with an emerald tiara and a massive gold-and-emerald necklace.

"Thank you." I beamed at her in the mirror, trying to think of a way to repay the compliment. "I like your necklace."

Her hand went to her throat. "I didn't want to wear this to-night. It's ugly as sin and weighs a ton. We had to get special in-surance just to take it out of the safe, but Wade insisted. It's been in his family for generations. His great-grandfather was an archae-ologist and he excavated it from a dig in Serabit al-Khadim, in southwest Sinai. You know how it is."

I smiled and nodded as if I, too, had a rich husband who in-sisted that I wear a hideous antiquity to a charity gala.

"I'm Simone Du Post," she said, smiling at me in the mirror. She didn't seem to notice the women behind us trying to find a space to touch up their hair.

"Simi."

"We've got the same Judith Leiber clutch." She held up her gold embellished bag, identical to my own. Clare had picked it out along with the wrap and a pair of "internalized patriarchy" gold stilettos. "I've seen three other people with the same bag here to-night," Simone said. "I'll have to get rid of it. If three people have it at this event, thirty will have it at the next. It doesn't even close properly."

My hand tightened on the bag. No way was I casually tossing a

$2,000 clutch in the trash. "There's a little hook that goes over top." I showed her the trick Clare had taught me to get the bag closed.

"Marvelous." She unclasped her necklace and dumped it in her bag. "You've saved me from having to wear that dreadful necklace all night. How can I return the favor?"

"I've just started a wedding planning business." I handed her my card, trying on the pitch for size. "I haven't had any clients yet but—"

"How many cards do you have?" She studied the bright modern design Olivia had created for us.

"Fifty. I just had them printed this morning."

"Fifty?" She gave a light laugh. "For an event with over 800 people?"

"I didn't really come here tonight planning to pitch for work." I gave what I hoped was a modest shrug.

"Whyever not?" She held out her hand. "Come with me. We'll have them all handed out before the charity auction. It will give me something to do. These things are such a bore."

I nodded in feigned sympathy. "Dahling, I couldn't agree more."

◆ ◆ ◆

Simone introduced me to her friends while Jack was off doing mysterious Jack things. Rich people were just like me except they had a lot more money, wore fancier clothes, couldn't get good staff, and shouldn't have bought little Amanda that third horse because she could only stable two horses at her private school. Imagine. Where was all that tuition money going?

Rich people also had a place in the Hamptons, a place in Italy, a place in Florida, and thank God "Jim" finally got a private jet. First class is so congested. Shudder. Like me, they found there were simply just not enough hours in the day. Unlike me, it was because their days were spent with personal trainers, stylists, therapists, and Reiki practitioners, and their nights were spent at galas, balls, banquets, charity events, operas, symphonies, and fundraisers. Then there was the shopping. Honestly. Jim/Richard/David/John just couldn't understand that it was impossible to wear the same dress twice. Everyone was run ragged. Exhausted. What about me time? Who wanted to fly up to New York to spend a day at the spa? Jim's treat.

Me! Me!

I smiled and tried to appear fun and friendly but couldn't score an invitation. Maybe "Jim" didn't like desperate debt-ridden brown girls who were planning a heist. Or maybe his jet couldn't take the extra weight. I'd eaten my way through two plates of hors d'oeuvres and four bowls of bar snacks. No matter. Private jets were such a bore. Shudder.

Jack found me before I found him. "Have you found Bella?"

"No, but I made a new friend." I pointed out Simone talking to two women near the bar. "She was wearing a hideous necklace and I helped her—"

"It's dancing time," he said abruptly, cutting me off. Without so much as a "by-your-leave," he put a hand around my waist and swirled me onto the dance floor.

My God. The man could dance. I didn't know whether to look down at his fancy footwork, a little higher at his swinging hips, or into his eyes as he searched the room, no doubt for someone who didn't have two left feet.

"You're pretty good," I offered. "Where did you learn to dance?"

"Self-taught," he said. "I had foster parents who were fans of old movies. I must have watched *Singin' in the Rain* a dozen times."

Foster parents. I filed that little tidbit about his life away for later.

"I've seen it. Gene Kelly smiled the whole time he was dancing."

"No one can dance like that today. He's a legend." He twirled me around. "I found a pair of tap shoes in a thrift store and saved up my paper route money to buy them. I watched the movie over and over, learned the steps online, and practiced until I had blisters. I was pretty good."

He held me so firmly, moved so fast, I felt like I was floating. "Why didn't you go to a proper dance school? Become a professional?"

"Life had other plans for me." Jack leaned in, his lips pressed against my ear, his breath hot on my skin. For a moment I thought it was "hide my face" time again, or maybe the seduction was real. Instead, he whispered in my ear. "Ten o'clock. The man at the bar holding his jacket over his arm is Angelini. The two dudes with him are his bodyguards. His wife and daughter are beside him talking to the CEO of the Chicagoland Chamber of Commerce and his wife."

Jack spun me around so I could surreptitiously check them out. I recognized Bella and her mother from our botched surveillance mission. Mr. Angelini was just shy of six feet and solidly built. He had a strong jaw, gray-flecked brown hair, and a slightly crooked nose. At first glance, he didn't look much different from most of the other tuxedoed men around him, but something about him sent a shiver down my spine.

"Go get 'em, tiger," Jack said.

Exasperated, I blew out a breath. "I can't just go up to them and ask if they want to hire me because I stalked his daughter on social media and know she just fired her wedding planner."

"You're resourceful. I'm sure you'll think of something." He caressed my cheek, my jaw, a quick slide of his thumb over my lips, and then he released me. "Watch your back."

"I thought that was your job." I looked over my shoulder, only to catch Jack's gaze on my ass.

"It's more of a hobby right now," he said.

I pretended to be searching for someone while considering my approach. Academic life and entry-level jobs don't prepare you for the real world. They don't teach you how to hobnob with Chicago's elite or convince the daughter of a rich real estate dude slash fence to hire you to plan her wedding. They teach you about late nights and deadlines, partying until dawn, and writing exams when you're hungover. They teach you about staving off boredom when you're inputting endless streams of data into spreadsheets and how to calculate the number of seconds before lunch. I needed help.

Help came in the form of Simone, who must have seen me standing alone.

"I've given out the rest of your cards," she said, joining me at the edge of the dance floor. "Do you have more?"

"Just a few." I lifted my chin toward the Angelinis. "I was hoping to give one to them. I heard their daughter is looking for a wedding planner."

"You don't want that gig." She sipped her drink, something pink and fruity with a cherry on the bottom. "She puts the zilla in bridezilla. She started planning her wedding two years ago and they've been through all the top event planners in the city. No one wants to work with her."

"I grew up with three brothers," I said. "I'm up for the challenge."

Her face brightened. "I've never had a chance to speak to the Angelinis. They aren't in my circle. How exciting. Moira is going to die. Dead. It will kill her that she wasn't here."

I didn't know who Moira was, but I sent her a silent thank-you for not showing up so Simone could be my guide. Without a moment of hesitation, she walked up to the group and started a round of introductions. She knew the CEO and his wife, and within moments I was shaking Bella's hand.

I guessed Bella to be around twenty-five years old. Up close, she looked like she'd just stepped off the runway in Milan. Tall and willowy with long dark hair that reached her waist, and wearing a simple white dress, she looked out of place among the middle-aged mavens in their ostentatious sequined bodycon gowns.

"Simi is new to the gala circuit," Simone said. "I've been introducing her around. She's a wedding planner. One of the best. I've recommended her to just about everyone."

"Thank you, dahling." I offered a card to Bella. "Simply Elegant Events. We're all about effortlessness and authenticity. Whether it's an iconic twenties-style ballroom in a historic hotel, a rustic barn on the Apple River, a romantic fairy-tale hideaway in a reclaimed courtyard, an enchanting tropical paradise in the heart of the city, or a beautiful lakeside garden, we help clients find the most talented vendors to bring their visions to life." I'd never been to any of those places, but I'd trawled the Internet for a marketing pitch that I thought sounded pretty good.

"I thought I knew all the wedding planners in the city." Bella frowned at my card. "Why haven't I heard of you?"

"She's private," Simone said, touching her gently on the arm. "Very exclusive. She doesn't need to advertise. It's all word of mouth."

Bella's parents shared a look that sent my pulse kicking up a notch.

"My daughter is getting married in three weeks," Mrs. Angelini said. "Our wedding planner left us unexpectedly and we've been trying to manage everything ourselves. It's a shambles."

"We can just postpone the wedding," Bella said. "It's no big deal."

"No big deal?" Her father turned on her, his face creased in a scowl. "It is a big deal; not just for our family but for the D'Amico family as well. This wedding is going ahead as planned. For two years you have dragged it out with your bad behavior and outrageous demands. But no more." He was shaking now, his fury evident in every line of his hard body. Simone clasped my elbow and gently pulled me back a step.

Mr. Angelini turned his stormy gaze on me. "Can you get an elephant?"

Not how I had expected the conversation to go, but when you have a big family, you're used to thinking on your feet.

"Yes, I can." Elephants were not uncommon in South Asian weddings. I'd been to several baraats over the years where the groom had ridden an elephant to the ceremony, and I was pretty sure my aunties would know where they'd been sourced.

Mr. Angelini looked over at his burliest bodyguard, a six-and-a-half-foot mammoth of a man with a prison haircut and a gold tooth. "She can get a fucking elephant."

"Oh my. Language." Simone fanned her face. I grabbed her arm and braced myself in case she collapsed in a swoon.

"How much?" Mr. Angelini demanded.

"For the elephant?"

"For everything," he said. "The wedding is on June twenty-fifth."

Even if I'd been a professional event planner with dozens of weddings under my belt, I wouldn't have wanted to take the gig. The dude legit scared me. His bodyguards scared me. The prospect of failing a man who clearly had no patience and little time for incompetence and failure scared me.

But . . . Chloe.

"I can check the calendar—"

His face darkened. Gold Tooth folded his arms across his massive chest. "Give me a number," Mr. Angelini said. "The last one wanted ninety thousand, which was 15 percent of her estimated total costs. What about one hundred thousand? Can you clear your schedule for that?"

I would have kissed his shoe—both shoes—for ninety thousand dollars, but I was supposedly a professional and had to remind myself not to scream and jump with joy. Instead, I needed to act as if it were every day that people offered me one hundred thousand dollars for three weeks' work for which I was not remotely qualified. "I'll have to check with my business partner. It's a lot of work in a short time. And we haven't heard if Bella even wants us—"

"One hundred fifty thousand. Bella will do what she's told. I'm the one footing the bill."

Bella's face had gone blank. She didn't even meet my gaze.

Simone indiscreetly poked me in the back. I took that to mean I should accept the offer, but it was so much money, and I had no experience, and he was such a scary dude, I could barely breathe. "If you could give me a minute—"

"Two hundred fifty thousand plus a bonus if everything goes well, and I'm not taking no for an answer." He nodded at Gold Tooth. "Get her card and put her in touch with my assistant to handle the payment."

"You've got yourself a wedding planner." I held out my hand like they taught in interview courses. He grabbed it and squeezed so hard I thought the bones would break.

"I'm a fair man," he said. "Do well and you'll be rewarded. Fail and—"

"So serious." Simone laughed lightly and tapped his hand, gesturing for him to release me. "I'm sure Simi will do a wonderful job."

"Saturday. Noon. My assistant will send you the address." He looked over at his daughter. "That's how you get things done. You've got a new wedding planner. You got your elephant. There is no reason now why the wedding can't go ahead."

"Yes, Papa," she said quietly.

"How did I do?" I whispered to Simone after they walked away.

"Dahling." Simone gave me a squeeze. "You're fucked."

THIRTEEN

◆ ◆ ◆

closed the door to Rose's garage and looked around at my crew. I still couldn't believe everyone except Jack had shown up on a Friday night. It was no big deal for me to be here—my Friday nights were usually spent watching crime shows with Rose or kicking back with Chloe and Olivia—but I'd assumed everyone else would have had plans.

"Thank you for attending this emergency meeting," I said. "I'm sure you all have better things to do with your Friday night." I used a red marker to write our company name on my new whiteboard. "Our new business is up and running. We are now officially Simply Elegant Events. Chloe will be handing out packets of business cards. You can use the QR code to check out our website and familiarize yourself with what we do."

"What do we do?" Anil asked.

"We organize events—in particular, weddings—and in this case, the wedding of Bella Angelini. I spoke to her dad last night and we cut a deal. We are now her official wedding planners."

"Cut is right," Gage muttered. "You piss him off and you're gonna lose a limb or two."

"I could do without the negativity."

Chloe patted my arm. "Don't mind him. He's been grumpy since he got here. I don't think he's been sleeping well."

"How would you know? He hardly ever talks."

"Just a feeling."

"What kind of deal?" Cristian asked. He was dressed in his uniform of cargo pants, pastel shirt, Sperrys, and a backward ball cap. As usual, he looked like he'd just stepped off a fashion runway.

"He's going to pay us two hundred and fifty thousand dollars to organize his daughter's wedding."

Cristian whistled. "Fuck me."

"I thought no one fucked you unless they paid," Emma quipped.

"Fuck you." Cristian dropped his feet and sat up like he was about to start a fight, which I knew would never happen because he was anti-violence as well as being anti-everything-else.

"How about no one fucks anyone and we listen to Simi's plan." Chloe shot me a worried glance. "You do have a plan."

"Yes. I have a plan." I wrote four headings on the whiteboard. "Tomorrow we're going to the Angelinis' mansion to meet with the bride. I'll introduce you as my team. Everyone will have a different wedding-related job that will give you access to an area of the house that needs to be searched or a system that we need to understand to pull off the heist."

"What do you mean by 'job'?" Anil asked.

"We do actually have to step in to save the wedding," Chloe said. "That's what the money is for."

"I don't know about the work part." Cristian sat back in his chair. "I was down for a quick snatch and grab but—"

"This is how we're doing it," I told him. "If you don't like it, you can leave. That just means an extra . . ." I trailed off because math had never been my strong suit. Luckily, Anil jumped in for the save.

"We would each get $833,333.33 plus $41,666.67 for the wedding planning fee, for a total of $875,000 per person."

"Did you just do all that math in your head?" Emma asked.

"Numbers make more sense to me than people."

"Damn, dude," she said. "That's impressive. We should give you Cristian's share just for working all that out."

"I didn't say I was leaving," Cristian protested. "I'm still in."

I was disappointed to hear it. I still didn't trust Cristian, especially not after he'd blackmailed his way into the heist. Nothing about him screamed loyal, reliable, or valuable member of the crew. "You can handle—"

"Schmoozing and keeping the mama bears occupied while they suffer through the existential angst of realizing no one will ever look at them the way everyone is looking at the young twenty-somethings in their strapless dresses and stiletto heels?" Cristian offered. "I'm in."

"Um. No. I thought you could manage the catering staff— snacks for the bridal party while they get ready, chocolate strawberries and nibbles while pictures are being taken, the banquet, the late supper . . ."

"Food?" He folded his arms over his chest. "That's not an important job."

"Italian weddings are all about the food," I said. "I went to an Italian wedding that had a fourteen-course meal, followed by cake, a mobile espresso cart, pastries, a candy buffet, and then, just before midnight, they served a second meal."

"But it's a behind-the-scenes job," Cristian whined. "I'll be stuck in the kitchen. I want to be part of the action, meeting and greeting all the horny drunk people who'll be looking for some love." He grabbed a rusty pipe, jumped up on the table, and crooned Elvis Presley's "Can't Help Falling in Love."

He didn't look like Elvis. He didn't sound like Elvis. Even his hips—and Cristian could move his hips—didn't move the way Elvis's hips moved. I refrained from clapping to avoid another painful repeat performance.

"We're going to have to keep an eye on him," Chloe whispered.

Cristian grabbed his crotch and did a pelvic thrust.

"Honestly," I said. "I'd rather not."

"What have you got for me?" Emma called over the crooning.

"You can handle the transportation and parking," I said. "That gives you a chance to walk around the property. We'll need room for a huge trailer. An elephant will be involved."

Emma's eyes lit up. "Will I get to drive this elephant?"

"People ride elephants; they don't drive them. And no. It will have a handler."

"What about me?" Anil moved to the edge of his chair, one leg shaking in nervous anticipation.

"You're in charge of entertainment—I'm thinking string quartet while pictures are being taken, maybe a jazz band after the ceremony, and a DJ for the dance floor. You'll ask to see the electrical box and the breakers ostensibly to ensure there is enough power outside for the sound system, but really in case we need to cut power during the heist—all things in a mechanical engineer's wheelhouse."

Anil's delight was almost palpable. "We won't need to hire a DJ. I can drop my own sick beats."

"You're in charge," I said. "Just make sure Mr. Angelini is happy with the music. He's not the kind of dude you want to disappoint."

"I'll be the security liaison," Chloe said. "That will give me access to the IT and security systems. I'll be able to get the information I need to hack the system and find out the number and positions of the cameras, drones, and any other security they might have."

"What about Gage?" Anil asked. "He should have a job, too. Or is he just here to shoot at people?"

"Gage? Do you have any wedding-related skills?" I tried to make out his expression, but he was standing in the shadows.

"I used to be a priest."

Silence filled the room.

"You're joking," Emma said. "Tell me you're joking."

"I don't joke."

Of course, Emma couldn't let it go. "Have you performed any actual weddings?"

"One."

"Were they conscious?"

"Bella was wearing a cross around her neck," I said. "I wouldn't be surprised if they're planning to hold the ceremony in a church. Gage, can you do a church ceremony?"

"The key words were 'used to be,'" he said. "I was released from my sacred duties. I can no longer represent myself as clergy."

"What made you give it up?" Anil asked. "That would have been a serious commitment involving many years of study. Did you lose faith?"

"It had to be the celibacy." Cristian pumped his fists and rocked his hips in a lewd gesture. "I'll tell you right now, I could never be a priest. I can't go more than a day, much less forever."

"Was it a woman?" Emma joined in the speculation. "Did you fall in love?"

"I'll bet he never had any trouble filling his church on a Sunday morning," Chloe whispered, digging her fingers into my arm. "I read an erotic romance series about a sadistic priest and the woman he fell in love with . . ." She shoved her fist in her mouth and groaned. "It was the hottest thing ever. And now my deepest, darkest naughty priest fantasy is coming to life."

"He's an ex-priest," I murmured. "And it's Gage, not some sexy sadist. He spends most of his time hiding in the shadows glaring at people."

Chloe fanned herself with her hand. "He had robes, babe. Oh God. I'm not going to be able to sleep tonight."

"Does anyone else have a secret past they want to share?" I asked. "Hand up if you are an undercover agent or in witness protection. Do you have the ability to shoot lasers from your eyes? Are you the secret heir to the throne of some European country? Are you an expert in ancient languages because you had to research them for a secret *New York Times* bestseller that you published under a pen name? Any members of the Illuminati? Ninja warriors or alien princes, please step forward."

"Jack's got that weird thing for plants," Gage offered. "He knows everything about them. You should get him to handle the flowers."

Where was Jack? Why was he never around when we were planning things, only to show up at the most inopportune moments, make my blood boil, and disappear again? He'd put me in the limo last night after the ball with only the barest brush of his lips on my cheek as a good-bye.

"We're all weird," I said. "If we weren't, we'd be out living normal lives, earning minimum wage in a nine-to-five job before moving on to an evening side hustle just to pay rent as we dream of houses we'll never be able to buy and lives we'll never be able to live. Instead, we're huddled in Rose's garage on a Friday night, eating stale petit fours and planning a heist and a wedding."

"Emma seems kind of normal," Anil said.

Emma flipped a pen across her knuckles, feet up on the chair where Jack should have been sitting. "I have a side gig as a clown."

"Fuck." Gage shuddered. "I hate clowns."

"And I hate priests." Her eyes glazed over for a moment and then she shook herself and smiled. "Just wait until you see me in costume."

"You show up here dressed as a clown and I'll lose my shit," Gage said. "I won't be responsible for what might happen."

Emma leaned back and laughed. "Now, that is something I'd like to see. Next time we meet, I'm going full Pennywise on you."

"Emma . . ." I shook my head. "Let's try not to send any of our fellow crew members into years of therapy. Maybe he had a bad experience with a clown when he was younger. It's not good to dredge up those old memories."

"I had a bad experience with a dog," Anil said. "It waited at the end of the road and chased me home every day. My mother couldn't understand why I was coming home with wet pants. She thought I was afraid to use the university toilets."

"How old were you?" Emma asked, frowning.

"Twenty-one."

Her lips quivered at the corners. "And now?"

"Twenty-five."

"That was only four years ago," she said. "Is the dog . . . ?"

"He was hit by a car." Anil sucked in his lips. "I'm ashamed to admit I didn't go to his funeral."

"But not ashamed about . . . ?" She waved her hands vaguely in the air, as if words had failed her.

"My mother says lots of people have accidents when they're scared," he retorted. "Even Gage just admitted he would lose control of his bowels if you dressed up as a clown."

Gage muttered something under his breath that didn't sound very priest-like. "That's not the kind of shit I'd lose."

I rapped my knuckles on the whiteboard. "If you're done

pretending you're still in middle school, we need a van to carry supplies. I also thought it might be a nice bonding experience if we travel to the mansion together."

"Not riding the fucking party bus," Gage said.

"I didn't think you would." I looked around the room. "Anyone else have togetherness issues?"

As it turned out, it was a moot question. No one had a car. Who could afford one? Traffic was always bad in Chicago. There was nowhere to park. Between gas and expenses, it was a disaster waiting to happen.

"I know someone with a van," Emma said. "I'll work something out with him and meet everyone here tomorrow morning."

"You're all free to go." I gave the crew a magnanimous wave. "Enjoy your Friday night. Don't party too hard. We're meeting the Angelinis at ten A.M. If you're riding the 'party bus,' be here at nine A.M."

No one moved.

"I usually spend my Fridays gaming online in my parents' basement with a bunch of fourteen-year-old kids," Anil said, tossing an apple in the air.

"I drive my Uber to places I wish I could go if I had the money." Emma folded her hands behind her head.

"I go to the gym." Cristian shrugged when I frowned. "It's always quiet on Friday nights. Most of my clients are busy with their husbands or family."

I don't think anything could have surprised me more. Cristian was always talking about his crazy nights out at bars and parties. It hadn't occurred to me that there were nights he might be alone.

"Olivia and I play games or watch rom-coms," Chloe said.

"Rose and I were planning to watch crime shows and drink

every time the killer leaves an accidental clue." I looked around the room at my merry band of misfits. "There's always room for a few more."

◇ ◇ ◇

Rose knew a lot of drinking games.

We were still going strong when Chef Pierre returned from his evening deep dish pizza class with five boxes of leftovers. He joined in the fun until Rose dragged him off to bed.

After that, things really got crazy. Cristian was one of those guys who became hyper when he drank too much. Gage took him outside to work it off with a wrestling match on the back lawn. Chloe couldn't take her eyes off Gage. She was a happy, giggly drunk and her running commentary on their match had me in stitches.

We called it a draw even though Gage was the clear winner and went back inside for more refreshments. At some point we started singing. Chloe had an incredible voice. Toneless Cristian almost broke my eardrums. Anil could sing harmony. Emma drummed on Rose's pots and pans. And even Gage joined in.

It was a good night. So good I didn't know how I wound up on my bed in the basement suite with Jack beside me, his face illuminated only by the faint warm glow of streetlights through the curtains.

"Where were you?" I rolled to my side and propped my head up with my elbow, mimicking Jack's pose. He was wearing a black T-shirt and jeans and his jaw was rough with a five-o'clock shadow. "You missed our emergency meeting."

"I had to visit my cousin. He owns a greenhouse. I figured you'd need someone to handle the flowers." He ran a finger down my arm, sending a wave of goose bumps across my skin.

"You figured right, mister." I poked his chest with my free

hand; at least I tried to poke his chest, but my hand wasn't going where my brain was telling it to go.

"I thought you said you could outdrink anybody." He caught my hand, wound his fingers through mine. "Looks to me like you might have pushed your limit."

"I did outdrink them. I was the last one standing."

"Actually, you were lying on the floor when I walked in," he said. "I thought you'd be more comfortable in your bed. I didn't realize your room wasn't habitable until the water soaked through my shoes."

"You carried me?" I flushed with pleasure even though I should have been concerned that I'd been so drunk, he'd picked me up and I hadn't even noticed.

"You didn't seem to want to be vertical." He brought our joined hands to his cheek, pressed his lips to my palm.

I didn't know where this was going, but I wanted more—more gentle touches, more quiet talking, more sexy Jack without the armor.

"I wish I'd been awake," I said. "I haven't been carried since I was a child."

"I'm happy to carry you around whenever you want." His voice caught as if he was holding himself back, as if there was more he wanted to do. *Yes, please!*

"You smell good." I leaned closer and sniffed his neck, breathing in his scent of flowers and earth and the cool evening breeze.

"Freesia and a bit of peony. I helped my cousin with some transplanting. Too much damp and peonies suffer botrytis blight." He released my hand and traced his finger along the edge of my jaw.

I tilted my head to give him better access to my lips. Touching was nice but kissing was better. I would have made a move, but I didn't trust my aim. Everything was still a little fuzzy.

"You missed a good party," I said. "I can't remember the last time I had so much fun. Did you know that Anil has a photographic memory? Or that he can multiply six-digit numbers in his head? He was also a spelling bee champion."

"Useful skills in a heist." He brushed my hair back, tucking it behind my ear, his fingers so gentle a soft shudder worked its way through my body. If he'd asked me at that moment to take off my clothes, I would have done it without hesitation.

"Emma knows a lot of people who've done a lot of interesting things." I talked so I didn't have to think, so I could live in this quiet intimate moment and just feel. "She told us she spent some time in prison. It wasn't her crime, but she took the fall for her sister, and then her sister turned around and stabbed her in the back."

"People are who they are." His fingertip skimmed lightly along my throat and down the vee of my shirt to stroke the crescents of my breasts. My skin rippled with shivers.

"Who are *you*?" I shifted closer, pressing my body against his. "I don't know much about you. Not even your last name. I'm pretty sure it isn't really Danger."

"There's not much to tell."

We lay with our foreheads touching, breathing as one. Jack put his hand on my hip, slowly traced the curve of my waist.

"I know you like literature," I offered, gently prodding. "You also love plants. You've got underworld connections. You had a thing with Clare. You're a great dancer, and you look sexy both in a tux and a leather jacket."

"You think I'm sexy?" His jaw tightened, fingers digging deeper into my hip as if he were willing himself to hold back.

"I just said so." I ran my fingers over his cheek, the rough stubble on his jaw.

Jack caught my hand and brought it down to rest on his chest. "How sexy?" His lips moved along my jaw, feathering kisses to my ear. My body melted into his until I couldn't tell where I ended, and he began.

"Kiss me and I'll tell you."

Jack leaned in and kissed me softly on the lips, going from teasing to demanding so quickly, it was like a dam had broken inside him. Everything fell away except the crush of his lips against mine, the heat of his body, and his firm hand holding me still as he ravished my mouth.

Yes, ravished. There was no other word for it. His tongue slid between my teeth, and he stroked every inch of my mouth, tasted the full swell of my lips, drank me down like he was dying of thirst.

My hands went to his head, holding him still as he moved above me. Bracing himself on his forearms, he spread my legs wide with his knees and settled his hips against mine, his hard length a delicious pressure where I needed him most.

I slid my hands through his hair and kissed him until I could barely breathe.

"God, I want you," he whispered against my mouth.

"You can have me." I slid my hand beneath his shirt, palm against his heated skin. "What part of this suggests I want to stop?"

He pulled away, breaking our connection with a groan. "Not now. Not like this."

"This isn't the time to start being a gentleman."

"I've never been a gentleman," he said, rolling onto his back. "But you deserve more, and I can't destroy everything I've worked for. It would end me."

I'd never had a man declare that sex with me would end him. I'd also never been left in such a state of painful desire that I wanted to scream. My skin burned and I ached all over.

"Now I am become Death, the destroyer of worlds," I said, desperate for a distraction from the throbbing between my legs.

"Oppenheimer?"

"That's what most people think, but it's actually from the Hindu sacred text the Bhagavad Gita. It's a conversation between a great warrior prince called Arjuna and his charioteer Lord Krishna, an incarnation of Vishnu."

"Am I the great warrior prince in this story?" He stared at the ceiling, hands clenched at his sides, teeth gritted. I was pretty sure it wasn't because he hoped he was the prince.

"Do you need absolution for doing your duty even if it goes against your personal moral code?"

"Yes." One word. Heavy with emotion. It hung there between us, a tiny beacon to the darkness inside him.

"Then you can be Arjuna." I edged over to him, lay my head on his shoulder. He wrapped his arm around me, his fingers settling into the curve of my waist. I sighed and snuggled closer.

"I think I'd make a good warrior prince," he said. "I'm strong, brave, loyal, and I can ride a horse. I'd look good in armor, and I already steal from the rich and give to the people."

"You're confusing warrior princes with Robin Hood," I pointed out. "But Robin Hood did have a band of Merry Men and an evil foe, the Sheriff of Nottingham." I lifted my head to look at him. "Do you have an evil foe?"

His body tensed beneath me, his hand curling into a fist on my waist. "Yes."

"He also had a lover, Maid Marian," I said, trying to lighten the mood.

"That's you." He relaxed, muscles softening, hand back to stroking, lips pressing a soft kiss to my forehead.

"Maid Marian wasn't denied a good time when Robin Hood came to lie with her in Sherwood Forest," I pointed out, still hoping for a miracle.

"Maid Marian didn't get so drunk, she passed out on the floor," he retorted. "What kind of noble hero takes advantage of a woman whose ability to consent is dubious at best?"

"I know what I want." I buried my face into his chest. His shirt was soft, his body warm, his arm heavy against my back.

"I want to give it to you, sweetheart. But not like this."

He stroked my back, my hair, my cheek. My tension eased and I relaxed into his embrace. "Give me a minute." I closed my eyes. "I just need a quick nap."

When I opened them again, he was gone.

FOURTEEN

◆ ◆ ◆

Thanks to a friend of a friend, Emma showed up at Rose's house the next morning in an unmarked white van.

"Why are all the windows blacked out?" Cristian didn't look like a man who had been jumping on tables and rolling on the grass a mere twelve hours ago. He was perfectly groomed, immaculately dressed, and he didn't even look like he was suffering the kind of hangover that was making my head pound like it was caught in a middle school drum. His T-shirt cause for the day was *Save the Animals* and his tan shirt had a cute pawprint on the chest.

"Privacy." Emma pushed the door aside, showing off the interior as if it were a prize in a game show. "The seats can be removed to carry heavy goods."

"Or bodies," I offered. "If we wanted to get into the serial killer business, this is exactly the kind of van they use."

"Also preferred by kidnappers and sexual predators," Cristian said. "Maybe we should write *Free Candy* on the side in red paint before we set off to destroy the environment with this gas-guzzling beast."

Rose poked her head into the van. "It reminds me of a road trip I took across the country with my Christian youth group in '65 to protest the Vietnam War. I was high on LSD for three straight weeks. We robbed a few banks, set fire to a school, destroyed a few monuments, and I think I slept with the pastor. It was quite the trip."

Anil climbed inside, his nose wrinkling. "What's that smell? Is it sauerkraut?"

"That's the smell a dead body makes after three days," Rose said. "It starts to bloat and blood-containing foam leaks from the nose and mouth. That could account for the dark stain on the floor."

My tender stomach recoiled, and I dry heaved over the bushes. "Please tell me that isn't blood."

Emma gave an exasperated sigh. "I'm 56 percent sure its food based. The friend who lent it to me did do some time in prison, but it was for assault and arson. No murder—at least not back then. He hasn't used it for months because he's driving an ice cream truck now."

"I can't tell if Emma is joking," Anil said.

"Just do what I do when anyone tells a crazy story." Cristian put an arm around Anil's shoulders. "Pretend it isn't real."

Chloe arrived before I finished cleaning the stain off the carpet. She was wearing a big pair of sunglasses even though it was a cloudy day. I hadn't seen those glasses in years, but I knew what they meant.

"Babe." I grabbed her arm and led her over to the garage, where there was no risk we'd be overheard. "What happened?"

"Kyle didn't pay his child support again," she said. "It's been three months and DCSS isn't doing anything because he's smart enough to keep the amount owing below the threshold that would make it a misdemeanor. I couldn't make my rent again this month and my landlord is threatening to evict us so I went to see Kyle this morning."

"Please tell me you didn't go alone."

"I was desperate." Chloe took off her glasses. Her left eye was swollen, her cheek was bruised, and she had a cut above her eyebrow.

"Oh no." I pulled her into a hug. Kyle hadn't changed. He was a violent man with a hair-trigger temper, and he still blamed Chloe for the mess he'd made of his life.

"Of course, he didn't give me the money," she said. "He said he didn't have it, but he just bought a new car, he's renting a huge apartment in a fancy building, and his place is full of expensive electronics. I think he's finally got a steady job and he wants to hide it from the DCSS."

"I know you don't want to go to the police," I said. "But Detective Garcia is a good guy. I know he'd do something even though he thinks we're thieves."

She wrapped her arms around her body, hugging herself. "I can't take the risk that they'll arrest him and then let him out on bail and he'll come after me and Olivia. He feels in control when I visit. He likes me to beg."

Bile rose in my stomach. It wasn't enough that he refused to acknowledge Olivia and withheld child support; he had to demean and abuse Chloe to feel like a man.

"Mr. Angelini's assistant called me yesterday and I negotiated an upfront payment of fifty thousand dollars," I said. "You can have my share. That will be more than enough to cover your rent arrears. You aren't going to lose your home on my watch."

"Thank you," she said. "You know I'll pay you—"

"What the fuck?" Gage was standing a few feet away, his gaze fixed on Chloe.

"I'll get everyone ready to go." Chloe put on her glasses and walked toward the van.

"It's not nice to eavesdrop," I told him.

Gage wasn't in a chatty mood. "Who did that to her? And don't tell me she walked into a door."

"Her ex. The guy's a piece of shit. She was trying to get him to pay his child support so she could pay her rent."

A dark shadow crossed Gage's face. In that moment, I saw who he really was, and I was glad he was on our side. "Name."

"I'm not giving you his name," I said. "I have a pretty good idea what you plan to do, and I need you to not be incarcerated so you can help with this heist."

His jaw clenched, eyes darkening like twin black holes. "Bastard is going to pay."

"I won't stop you," I said. "After the heist, I will gladly give you all the information I have on him, and I'll feed those flames of hate by telling you in detail all the things he did to Chloe when they were together. But right now, we have a bride to meet and a heist to plan so pack away the avenging angel superhero costume and get your ass in the van."

Gage folded his arms across his chest. "I thought I didn't have to do any wedding shit."

"You thought wrong."

◇ ◇ ◇

Jack was deep in conversation with a man in blue coveralls when we pulled up in front of the mansion. Instead of waiting for us as we'd agreed, he'd gone rogue again and it grated on my already unsettled nerves. What had happened between us last night? Had I pushed too hard? Was he already regretting kissing me for real and not in a "hide my face" kind of way? Had he turned me down because he was a gentleman, or because I wasn't his type?

"Is there a reason you didn't come with the rest of the team?" I asked after he deigned to join us.

"I wanted to have a word with the head gardener before everyone arrived. When I was here the other week, I noticed some twig blight on their azaleas. I wanted to make sure he knew to prune and dispose of the diseased branches before it causes wilting and defoliation."

I didn't know what to say. On the one hand, it made sense; on the other hand, we were supposed to be working together. And then there was the fact he was talking to me as if it were just an ordinary day, and we hadn't kissed and shared secrets and spent a few hours wrapped in each other's arms. My disappointment threatened to distract me from the task at hand, so I gave him a curt nod and walked away.

Bella was waiting for us in the doorway. She was wearing a yellow sheath dress that I recognized from my trip to the upper floor of Bloomingdale's. Did rich people dress up all day long? Would I have to give up whipping off my bra and pulling on a pair of sweats and an oversized T-shirt when I got home from work after I became an almost-millionaire? Would I even have to work?

"I guess you might as well come in," she said with a sigh after I made the introductions. "My mother will want to talk to you."

We followed her through a cavernous marble hallway featuring an enormous crystal chandelier and a grand central staircase lined by wrought-iron railings. We passed rooms larger than my basement suite, with marble and hardwood floors, high ceilings, custom moldings, French doors opening to outdoor terraces, and wood-burning fireplaces. Outside, a large back patio led down to a swimming pool and grassy lawn. In the distance I could see the private dock, where Honey had met a cold and brutal end.

We arrived at a glass-walled conservatory. Five women around Bella's age were drinking fruity drinks from coconut shells, decorated with paper umbrellas and straws.

"These are my bridesmaids." She introduced them so quickly,

I didn't catch their names. Except for their clothing in varying shades of expensive, they looked almost identical, with long brown hair, brown eyes, and twiglike arms.

I reciprocated by introducing everyone again: Jack: flowers; Chloe: security; Anil: entertainment; Emma: transport; Cristian . . . AWOL.

Where was Cristian?

"What does he do?" One of the women pointed at Gage, who had found a nice shadowy corner in which to hide.

What was he going to do? I'd been so wrapped up in thoughts of Jack, I hadn't come up with a job for Gage.

"He used to be a priest," Anil blurted out.

The women all gasped at once. One of the bridesmaids handed the other a twenty-dollar bill. I wished I'd been part of that action.

"We can get him recertified or whatever has to happen to get his priest qualifications back if you don't have someone lined up for the ceremony." I ignored Gage's glare and vigorous headshaking. "I'm sure it can all be done online," I continued. "It's not like we're back in the Middle Ages, where the Pope had to get involved with every little administrative detail."

"We're getting married by the priest who married my parents," Bella said. "My parents got special permission from the Archdiocese to hold the wedding in our back garden instead of in church. I doubt my father would agree to a new officiant this close to the ceremony."

"No problem," I said, thinking quickly. "Gage is great with kids. He can handle the children's activity area and give the elephant rides."

"Jesus fucking Christ," Gage muttered, making no effort to lower his voice.

"Is he single?" one of the bridesmaids asked.

"Do you want him to be?" I'd pimp anyone out to make this gig a success.

"Fuck yes."

I liked her instantly, because anyone who could swear while wearing a pair of $4,000 Christian Louboutin heels was my kind of woman.

"Unfortunately, we have a strict nonfraternization policy. We want everyone to feel safe and respected while we handle the event. However, after the wedding is over, he's fair game."

"Does that mean you really are going to get the elephant?" Bella asked.

"Yes." I'd already been in touch with Annika Auntie, who had put me in touch with another auntie, who knew an uncle who knew the father of the groom who had ordered the elephant for his son's baraat.

I caught a curious silent exchange between Bella and her dirty-mouthed bridesmaid. More dismay than excitement. I was getting a strange vibe from the bride. Not so much bridezilla but something else.

"Have you changed your mind about the elephant? Was there another animal you wanted? A tiger, perhaps? Panther? Or are you not into jungle cats? My cousin has a monkey and a boa constrictor, but they can't be in the same room together. The monkey is a terrible tease."

"The elephant is fine." She sucked in her lips. "I just never imagined anyone could do it."

Bella and her mother took us for a quick walk around the grounds to finalize the locations for the ceremony and the tent. I couldn't imagine owning so much land. What would you do with it? Aside from the tennis court, swimming pool, running track, and riding trail, was there really any reason to have so much grass, you had to hire someone whose sole job was to keep it trimmed in summer?

"You can get a good view of the house from here," Bella said, turning around when we reached the summit of a small hill. "Family bedrooms are on the top level left, along with another sitting room, meditation room, and a reading room. Guest bedrooms are on the right. My dad's office, the library, and the conservatory are on the ground floor in the south wing. Kitchen and various sitting rooms all on the right. We've also got a finished basement with another sitting room, home theater, yoga studio, games room, gym, wet bar . . . you know . . . all the stuff."

"Sure." I nodded like I knew "all the stuff" rich people had in their multiwing mansions. God forbid they only had one sitting room or no dedicated space to do a Downward Dog.

I excused myself from the pool/boathouse part of the tour to look for Cristian. I found him in the van, hiding between the seats. He'd stripped off his jacket and had his head down between his knees.

"What's going on? Are you okay?"

"Her mom . . ." He shook his head. "I ran out of the house the second I saw her. I just hope . . ." He groaned, dug his hands through his hair. "You'll have to replace me."

"I don't understand," I said. "Do you know her?"

"She was a client." His voice was raw, hoarse. "She told me her name was Sophia Jones."

"A client of your life coaching business? That's not . . ." I trailed off when he shook his head. "Ah. That kind of client."

"I slept with her." His voice rose in pitch. "Can you imagine what her husband would do to me if he found out? They destroyed that drone. There was nothing left but little pieces."

"We're not going to replace you," I said. "You're part of the team and the team sticks together."

"I could get you all killed," he moaned. "I don't want to put you in danger. You're the first real friends I've ever had."

Cristian was the most sociable guy I knew. He was Dad's best salesman. Whenever I was in the store, it was all about the parties he'd attended, the celebrities he'd met, the crazy nights . . . It was hard to believe Cristian had no friends. Or maybe it wasn't. We all wear masks. Sometimes they become such a part of us that we forget who we really are.

"It's not like she's going to tell him," I said. "She didn't strike me as a woman with a death wish."

"She told me things. About him. He can't . . ." He waved his hand in a circular motion. "You know . . . perform."

Some things you don't want to know so I didn't ask for details.

"I get it, but she has as much to lose as you. Look at this house. The life these people lead. No offense, but do you think she's going to give it all up to be with you?"

Cristian bristled. "I'm not that bad. I care about the environment, endangered species, food security, and climate change. I recycle and I'm an ethical consumer. I take public transportation, only drink craft beer, and I don't eat meat. Just look at my social media. People love me."

"Of course you're not awful." I leaned over the seat to give him an awkward pat on the shoulder. "But you're also not an insanely wealthy real estate magnate with a 15,000-square-foot mansion and acres of lakeshore property. If she even notices you—which is unlikely because you'll be 'the help'—she'll pretend she's never met you before. You were a fling, an exciting diversion before she went back to her regular humdrum *'Wherever are we going to park the new Ferrari?'* life. I'm pretty sure she isn't going to jump you and drag you up to her bedroom."

"You don't know her." Cristian shook his head. "It's not beyond the realm of possibility."

I tried to keep things light with a shrug. "Then you'll have the perfect excuse to search the bedroom for a safe."

"You've become a hard woman." His lips curled in a smile. "Criminal life suits you."

"It suits all of us," I said. "Now get up and straighten your clothes. I've got five bridesmaids for you to meet."

◇ ◇ ◇

I was filling bags with jellybeans and mentally planning the heist on Monday afternoon when Garcia walked into the candy store at Westfield Shopping Mall. It had been a slow day, so I didn't mind the distraction. My only customers had been a shoplifting toddler and his law-abiding mother, who dragged him back to return a handful of melted chocolate raisins and three dirty hard candies.

"What do you recommend?" Garcia walked along the aisle, inspecting the plastic bins full of treats. We had the tiniest shop in the mall with only two aisles separated by a wall of candy bins and a counter flanked by two barrels filled with toys. Plushies filled shelves along the walls, and boxes with sweet-smelling candies were stacked six feet high behind the counter.

"The peach penguins are my favorite," I said. "But I also like the cola bottles. If you're into sours . . ."

"If it's sour, it's not candy," he said. "It defeats the purpose." He took a small bag of peach penguins from the bin.

"An excellent selection." I rang up his purchase and added a bonus package of Life Savers to his bag. "I don't suppose you just happened to be in the shopping mall and by coincidence just wandered into my store . . ." I trailed off, half hoping.

"I have to buy gifts for my twin nieces," he said. "They're turning six next weekend. Since I had to shop anyway, I thought it might as well be here where I could drop in and see you."

"If you keep this up, I might start getting ideas."

"You and me both." He smiled. I smiled. We smiled at each other. Damn him for his charm. Double damn him for his power of arrest.

"What can I do for you other than offer you penguins?" I said when the muscles in my cheeks protested the extended joy.

His smile faded. "There was an incident at the InterContinental Chicago the other night. A necklace was stolen at the Summer Garden Charity Ball. I was going through security footage, and I saw you." He cleared his throat. "You looked stunning, by the way. Breathtaking."

My smile came back, unwanted and unbidden, and along with it a pair of very heated cheeks. "Thank you."

"It was hard to process—"

"Because I usually look slovenly and unkempt?" My free hand found my hip. Why did he have to ruin a good compliment by being unable to process the fact that I could look amazing? "Are you used to seeing me in rags and covered in cinders from the fireplace where I have to sleep while my wicked stepmother and stepsisters bounce in their feather beds upstairs?"

A bark of laughter burst from his throat. "I just wasn't expecting to see you at that type of event."

"Maybe I go to events like that all the time," I said, bristling. "Maybe I have a closet full of designer dresses that I only wear once, and when I see someone else with my clutch, I toss it in the trash."

His voice was quiet, gentle. "That doesn't sound like you."

"You don't know me."

"I know people," he said. "You're one of the good ones, Simi. Not many people would do what you did for your friend."

My head jerked up, hope filling my heart. "So you believe me?"

"It doesn't matter what I believe. It's all about the evidence."

I stared at the scratches in the glass counter and heaved a sigh.

"I got an invitation from a friend. I've never been to an event like that before, so you were right on that count."

The spell broke. His eyes shuttered. He transformed from sweet guy to grumpy cop in a heartbeat. I hadn't even heard the clock chime twelve.

"Does your friend happen to wear size thirteen boots and go by the name 'Oliver Twist'?"

I picked up a mini gumball machine and fiddled with the plastic dial. "That's an oddly specific question, but the answer to both parts is 'no.'"

Garcia flipped through his phone and held up a picture of a green-and-gold necklace. "Do you recognize this?"

For a heartbeat I considered lying, but if he had security footage of the event, he would have seen me talking to Simone.

"Yes, it belongs to Simone Du Pont." My smile faded with his frown. "I met her in the restroom. She took it off and put it in her clutch. She said it was heavy and difficult to wear."

"You had the same bag." A statement, not a question. I was beginning to realize that Garcia didn't ask questions if he didn't already know the answers.

"Yes, she said there were three other people besides us who had one, and after the event she was going to toss it in the trash because it was too common. Can you imagine?"

"Is it possible you took hers by mistake?" His question was deceptively casual, but I heard the accusation beneath his words.

"No, because I cleaned it out the other day so I could sell it on Craigslist to help Chloe make rent. Her ex isn't paying his child support and she was worried she'd have to move out of her place." I hadn't received the money from Mr. Angelini, and I didn't want to take any chances.

His face softened and he shook his head and sighed. "Of course you did."

"It was a gift," I said quickly. "I'm not in a habit of selling gifts but she's in a difficult situation."

"As am I," he said. "Two valuable necklaces have gone missing in the last few weeks, and you happened to be at both crime scenes. I don't believe in coincidences."

"Well, prepare to have your mind blown," I said. "I was there because I've started a new wedding planning business. I thought the ball would be the perfect place to get clients, and Simone made it happen. I got my first client that night."

"Maybe you should give me the client's name so I can warn her to keep her jewels locked up."

Ouch. Burn. Garcia had to be worked up because sarcasm wasn't really his style. It was that, more than the frighteningly accurate assessment or the subtle accusation, that made my bottom lip tremble. I liked Garcia. Too much. He'd even appeared in my bath time fantasies, but that was when I thought we had an understanding. He knew I was innocent, but he had a job to do. Now something had changed.

"That's unkind, Garcia. My client is in her twenties. People our age don't often have expensive jewelry, and if they do, I can't imagine they'd have many places to wear it. There were only a handful of people at that ball under the age of fifty. What would be the point?"

"I don't know why anyone wears authentic pieces anymore when 3D printing technology is so sophisticated, no one would be able to tell a replica from the real thing," he mused, fiddling with a candy pen on the counter. "If people were sensible about these things, I wouldn't be here questioning you again."

"I didn't steal anything," I said firmly. "Not from Simone and not from the museum."

His eyes filled with earnest concern. "I want to believe you. I've been doing this a long time and I know a thief when I see one.

But you are hiding something from me, and I need to know what it is or this situation is just going to get worse. Is someone else involved?"

My mind jumped back to Friday night when I'd fallen asleep in Jack's arms.

I've never been a gentleman.

"No. There's no one else. I seem to be able to screw up my life perfectly fine on my own."

He tucked his phone away and picked up his bag of candy. "You may find this hard to believe, but I care about what happens to you."

His gentle voice and kind words gave me all the feels. "I appreciate the sentiment, but what I'd appreciate more is not being suspected of things I didn't do."

Garcia was a good cop, and a nice guy. But what about Jack? He'd offered to hold my clutch—a clutch that had been picked out by someone he knew—at least twice during the evening when I needed my hands free. Had I been used? Had one of his many disappearances been to perform an old "switcheroo"? I wanted to trust him, but like Garcia, I didn't believe in coincidences.

FIFTEEN

◇ ◇ ◇

With the wedding coming up fast, I gathered the crew together on Friday night. Between contacting all the vendors and suppliers, organizing the big day, working my two jobs, and planning the heist with Chloe in the evenings, I was on an energy high.

"Breathe." Rose set down her tray of munchies and helped me put up the whiteboard in her garage.

"I am breathing." I flipped through the notes I'd made on my phone. "There's just a lot to cover. I still have to make arrangements for the reception table, pick up the wedding favors, buy coloring books for the kids, finalize the menus, and tomorrow I'm meeting Bella and her mother at the bridal shop for the final fitting of her wedding dress. And then there's the heist to think about. Dad needs me at the tailor shop tomorrow. I have an afternoon shift at the candy store on Sunday, and my parents have invited Anil's family over for Sunday dinner because they think we're getting married."

"You and Anil?" Rose chuckled. "That would never work. You're both too excitable. You'd drive each other crazy. You need someone more laid back, someone calm."

Garcia was calm. Jack was laid back. Garcia was trustworthy but thought I was a thief. Jack was a thief and might be using me to help him steal necklaces in Chicago. I was better off alone.

"Where's Chef Pierre?" I asked to take her attention off my nonexistent love life that involved three entirely unsuitable men.

"He's got a meat exam today: barbecue ribs, Italian beef, and hot dogs. It gives me time to visit Stan. Juggling three men isn't easy."

"Three? I thought you had two."

She gave a dramatic wave. "I had drinks with the director of my new play the other night and one thing led to another. You know how it goes."

"Actually, I don't but I wish I did." I kissed her cheek. "You're such an inspiration."

"I keep Fridays open for our crime show binge nights," she continued. "Tuesdays for drinks with the girls, and Wednesdays and Sundays are rehearsal days and evenings out with the cast. I slot the men in where I can."

"I thought *I* was busy."

"We both shine when we have too much to do," Rose said. "That's why we get along."

◆ ◆ ◆

Jack didn't show so we started the meeting without him.

"Our best chance of getting into the house undetected will be the night of the rehearsal dinner when everyone will be out." I spread a blueprint of the Angelinis' mansion over the table. Chloe had hacked into the city property database to retrieve it. She was awesome that way.

"Everyone except the security guards," Gage added. "They have two armed guards. One walks the perimeter and the other stays near the house. Angelini brought them on when he secured the necklace. The perimeter guy does a quick walk-around every hour and then hangs out with the other guard, smoking and shooting the shit."

"You got all that from our day on the boat?" Emma had brought a six-pack of Coors Light and drank her beer straight out of the bottle. She hadn't wanted to dirty a glass.

"I did a little solo recon because boat day was a fucking disaster," Gage said. "Except for Cristian in the inner tube. That was comedy gold."

"Could we not mention the inner tube?" Cristian huffed. "I'm sensitive about it."

"I'm sure you are."

Emma and Gage laughed together until I motioned for them to stop. They'd formed some kind of bond that involved cackling at other people's expense.

"Don't forget about the dogs," Anil said. "There were kennels outside."

"You'll be fine." Gage waved a dismissive hand. "They're Rottweilers."

"Are those nice dogs?"

"The best. Very friendly."

I shot Gage what I hoped was a withering look. "You won't have to worry about dogs because you'll be inside," I said to Anil. "Gage will be our outside man."

Anil's face brightened. "Does this mean I have a key role in the heist?"

"You have a supporting role," Gage said. "Expendable crew member. I suggest you wear a red shirt."

Emma snorted a laugh and the two of them started chuckling again.

"Leave him alone," Chloe said gently. "He just wants to help."

"I've booked the rehearsal dinner for the Thursday before the wedding at a restaurant in the Loop," I said. "We'll have three hours plus the forty-five-minute drive each way, which should give us more than enough time to get in, crack the safe, and get out with the necklace. Cristian will be our point man at the dinner. He's good with the social stuff, so if there are problems and we need to keep them at the restaurant, he can sort it out."

"I could even do a little entertaining." Cristian did a little tap dance and finished with a flourish.

"You've missed your calling," Chloe said. "You're very good. Maybe after we get the money, you should consider a career on-stage."

"My big dream was to develop an educational kids' show after I finished my animal science degree," he said. "I wanted kids to see all the amazing things animals can do so they understood why wildlife needs to be protected. I got some serious interest in the project and even had a director, screenwriter, and producer lined up so I could focus on the acting side, but I couldn't get the financing together."

"That's amazing, Cristian," Chloe said, breaking the stunned silence in the room. "If we pull this off, you could make that dream a reality."

Gage shared an irritated glance with Emma. "We can't give him a hard time now."

"Sure we can." She clinked bottles with him. "Just picture him bouncing away on that inner tube and you'll forget he's a hooker with a heart of gold."

"I'm not getting paid for sex," Cristian retorted. "It's just one aspect of my life coaching service. Intimacy is part of the human condition. I give my clients a holistic experience."

"Moving on," I said, fighting the quiver of my lips. "The wedding rehearsal will be at the Angelinis' house on Thursday afternoon. Chloe and I will arrive at the mansion in the van. I'll tell

Bella that we're storing wedding decorations in it and we'll need to leave it parked outside her house overnight. After the rehearsal, Emma will pick us up and take us to Rose's house to rendezvous with Jack, Gage, and Anil." I checked to make sure Emma was paying attention and not still whispering with Gage in the corner. "Emma, we'll need your friend's limo for the evening, and also for the day of the wedding."

"No problem," she said. "I'll even wear the uniform and the fancy hat."

"At six P.M.," I continued, "Emma will return to the house in the limo to drive the family to the restaurant and wait there until they want to come home. If we haven't cracked the safe by then, she can buy us some time with engine troubles or wrong turns." I shot Emma a warning look. "No exceeding the speed limit."

"You're no fun." She leaned back in her chair. "There's a sweet stretch of road that I'm just itching to drive in the dark."

"How are we getting past the ground security?" Anil asked. "There was a gate out front and cameras everywhere. Not to mention the guards."

"We don't have to worry because we'll already be inside." This was the best part of the plan, inspired by a Trojan horse toy my brothers had when they were young. "When Emma arrives to pick the family up, we'll be inside the limo. She'll park beside the van, and when no one is looking, we'll slip out of the limo and into the van undetected."

"Very elegant." Gage gave me a curt nod. "What's your plan for getting inside the house?"

"Their security system doesn't connect with the police, fire station, or any private security service," Chloe said. "It sends notifications and video feeds directly to the family phones. Bella told us her dad didn't want the police or fire trucks showing up if an alarm went off when they weren't around."

"Makes sense if he's involved in fencing high-end jewelry," Emma said. "I'll bet that's not his only criminal activity. He's probably got weapons inside, maybe even bodies in the walls." She shot a questioning glance at Rose. "What do you think? You're the crime expert."

"Bodies start to smell after only a few days," Rose said. "It's not feasible to store them in the walls of a building where people are living, especially once they start to decompose. The smell is so bad, most people will throw up."

"I'll throw up if the alarms go off," Anil said. "Loud ringing noises make me nauseous."

Emma leaned back in her chair and stretched. "Too much sex made my ex four-times-removed nauseous. Seriously. Every fucking time it was the same thing." She raised her voice to a mocking tone. "'It's too much. I need to rest.' I was, like, 'Man up.' Who can't do eight hours of sex? I've had hookups that went on for days. And the work I had to do just to get him going . . . it was exhausting. My hands were constantly covered in callouses. That relationship was doomed to fail."

"You are an interesting woman," Gage said. "Terrifying, but interesting."

"We're getting off topic," I said, ignoring Anil's hand in the air. I suspected there was a lot Emma had said that he wanted to ask about.

"Their reluctance to use a monitored system works in our favor. It means they've had to use a DIY wireless home security system. Chloe had a chance to study it when she met with one of the guards to discuss security for the wedding, and she's confident she can hack it using a laptop and a portable radio frequency transceiver. She'll jam the signals from the cameras and motion sensors so we can enter the house without triggering the alarm."

"It's hard to believe they have a system that's so easy to hack when they have so many things to steal," Emma said. "If my mother's second cousin ever heard about this place—"

"It's not easy," Chloe said. "I'm just very good at what I do."

"We do have one problem," I said. "An alert goes out if the system has been jammed, so Cristian will need to get his hands on the Angelinis' phones long enough for us to get inside and find the safe. Chloe can then unjam the system and they'll hopefully think it was just an RF glitch. She'll have to jam it again for us to get out, but by the time they're back to investigate, we'll be safely back in the van."

"They aren't just going to hand over their phones because I ask," Cristian said. "I can definitely get them from the women, but not from Mr. Angelini."

"You're our inside man," I said. "You understand these people and how they work. I need suggestions, not problems."

Cristian twisted his lips to the side, considering. "I played a trivia game at a party one time, and we all had to put our phones in a basket on the table so we couldn't look up the answers. I think that might work. Mr. Angelini could see his phone so he wouldn't be worried that someone is trying to get into it, and he'd look like a bad sport if he refused to participate at his own daughter's rehearsal dinner."

"That sounds like a plan," I said. "You'll need to play the game again when we leave the house because the system will send out another jam alert. After we're out, we'll wait in the van for Emma to bring everyone home then slip back into the limo when they are inside, and bingo! They'll never know we were there."

"Except they'll be a missing a $25 million necklace," Emma said.

"They won't know it's missing because Anil is going to make a fake."

Anil's head jerked up from his phone. "I am?"

"Yes, you are," I said. "I'd never really thought about the bracelet you gave me in the context of the heist, but I was talking to Detective Garcia, and he said you can't tell a 3D-printed fake from an original. If I give you a picture, can you make a 3D replica?"

Anil grimaced. "I might lose my job."

"You don't like your job," Chloe reminded him. "You said you wanted to move out of your parents' home and pursue an MMA career far, far away. What would The Butcher do to win?"

"Anything."

"Go, Butcher!" Chloe pumped a fist in the air.

Anil pumped his fist, too. "It's 'The Butcher.'"

"It sounds better the other way," she said. "You might want to reconsider your ring name so people don't get confused."

"What do we do after we get the necklace and claim our reward?" Cristian asked. "We'll need to disappear in case they suspect us. I vote for a tropical island until the heat dies down." He raised his beer bottle in a mock toast. "Bikinis are on me."

"No bikinis. No tropical getaway." I folded my arms across my chest, hoping Cristian didn't get the wrong message from my "stern teacher" pose. "It will look suspicious if we all suddenly disappear. Also, I can't do that to Bella. The wedding goes ahead as planned two days later on Saturday."

"And DJ Ka-Poor is ready to rock!" Anil pulled a stack of business cards from his pocket. "I thought I should have a name and proper brand so people who love my musical stylings know who to call for their weddings." He handed the cards around. "There's a hyphen between Ka and Poor so when you say it, leave a pause. Ka Poor."

"Jesus Christ." Gage stared at the card with *DJ Ka-Poor* written in gold script on a background of colorful music notes.

"I've got the playlist all ready to go." Anil was not put off in the least by Gage's muttering. "Lots of highs and upbeat tunes, but then every ten to twelve songs, I'll throw in a slower one to keep the flow going. People want them . . . just not as much as the fast ones. I'm starting with 'Yeah!' by Usher, then 'Can't Feel My Face' by The Weeknd, 'Shut Up and Dance' by Walk the Moon—"

"Are earplugs part of our heist comp package?" Gage asked.

"Gage." Chloe put a gentle warning hand on his arm. "We're lucky to have Anil. He sacrificed his drone to get some amazing surveillance pictures. He's risking his job to get us a replica necklace, and he's putting in a lot of effort to make sure Bella is going to have a great wedding. I think a little support and gratitude are warranted."

Gage stared at Chloe's hand. She flushed and moved to pull it away, but he covered it with his own, holding it in place. I made a mental note to have a serious conversation with her about former priests who carried guns and hid in the shadows.

"What's Jack doing in all this?" Rose asked. She'd been so quiet, I'd almost forgotten she was there.

"Having a good time," he said from the doorway.

"How long have you been there?" I'd been so caught up in the plan, I hadn't even noticed he'd arrived.

"Long enough," he said. "I'm your man for opening the safe and picking locks. I also know a guy who can get the equipment you need to hack the security system. He might also be able to find us a place for a dry run to make sure there are no problems with the plan."

"My plan is solid." I gave an affronted sniff. "Chloe and I have run through it dozens of times."

"You should probably take him up on the offer," Rose said. "In the movies, the crew always practices before the big day. It's the most important part of the heist."

I looked to Chloe, and she gave an apologetic shrug. "It can't hurt."

"Fine. We'll do the run-through. Meeting dismissed." I crossed the room to join Chloe by the table of snacks. I didn't want to talk to Jack, not after my conversation with Garcia. I would have to ask him if he knew anything about Simone's necklace, and I didn't know if I wanted the answer.

"It's all coming together." She squeezed my hand as the room descended into chaos. "I can't believe it's actually going to happen."

"I know. A few weeks ago, we were just living our normal lives, struggling to keep our heads above water, and now we're planning a heist and a high-society wedding with our very own crew. The thought of sitting at another desk typing numbers into a spreadsheet gives me hives. I don't think I could go back to my regular life. We've been arrested and shot at. We've done a surveillance mission and shopped for a dress on the top floor of Bloomingdale's. I've been to a charity ball, hobnobbed with Chicago's elite, and met a real estate magnate who oozes evil. Our dreams are finally in reach. I feel like someone has opened my eyes to a whole new exciting world of possibilities and interesting people. We've broken rules, Chloe. We've broken the law and it's exhilarating."

"Right back at you, babe." She slid her arm around my waist, and we watched Cristian chase Emma around the room with an apple core while Anil tried to goad Gage into wrestling with him on the concrete floor. Only Jack was still. He leaned against the wall, his focus not on the mayhem around him but on me.

The intensity of his gaze sent a delicious shiver straight down my spine. A shiver that felt way too good. Everything faded away except the heat in his eyes, the thud of my heart, and the soul-deep certainty that I had finally been seen. Even if none of this worked out, even if I never saw Jack again, I knew in my bones, I would never be the same.

SIXTEEN

◇ ◇ ◇

After the meeting, Jack took me to see his "guy who can get things."

"It's safer than ordering from Amazon," he said after Chloe mentioned it was going to take five days to get an RF transceiver to hack the system because she didn't have Prime.

I was excited to meet the kind of guy who sold stuff out of the back of his truck. I'd let a sheltered life in the suburbs. Even when I'd moved out in a big show of independence, I'd stayed in Evanston and rented a suite in a house with a responsible adult—at least that's what I told my parents. As it turned out, between me and Rose, I was the responsible one.

"What do you think of our plan?" I asked after a full three minutes of silence in his black Toyota 4Runner. It had rental plates and a small tree-shaped air freshener hanging from the rearview mirror that filled the car with a fresh pine scent.

"It's not bad."

"Not bad could get us all thrown in jail," I said. "It has to be perfect."

"There is no perfect plan. Something always goes wrong." He whipped around the Dempster Street cloverleaf and onto the expressway without putting his foot on the brake to slow to the recommended speed.

"What's going to go wrong?"

"That's the question you need to ask yourself about every step," he said. "If it can go wrong, it will. You need to plan for contingencies. What if someone gets sick and doesn't go to the dinner? What if Angelini doesn't give up his phone? What if he sees the notification and sends his security guys to check it out? What if the jamming doesn't work and you're stuck inside with a bunch of cameras live-streaming your face to a shoot-first-ask-questions-later kind of dude?"

"Why didn't you mention any of this at the meeting?" My plan suddenly seemed foolish and naive. With cold clarity, I could see at least a dozen things that could go wrong.

"You didn't ask."

"I didn't ask? You weren't there until the end." I struggled against the urge to give him a smack. "Don't you know what it's like to be part of a team? You show up on time. You share your skills, experience, and knowledge and point out problems that may result in our team being tortured or killed. You support us, and in return, we support you. We have your back. You walk in the world knowing you aren't alone. Your casual, laid-back, laissez-faire attitude to this heist isn't going to cut it any longer. You're a team player or you're out. I covered for you at the ball and when Garcia came to my store, but—"

"Garcia?" His jaw tightened. "Is that the cop you're seeing?"

"I'm not seeing him," I said. "He keeps showing up looking for extra information. He said someone stole Simone's necklace at the charity ball, and since I was already a suspected jewel thief, he thought it might be me. So now I'm the go-to gal every time there's a crime."

I thought he'd at least smile at the rhyme, but for the first time since I'd met him, he had nothing to say.

"Was it you?" I asked into the uncomfortable silence. "You were also at both crime scenes. I'm not accusing you, but—"

"You are accusing me."

I thought back to the night at the museum, our meeting in the dark, the conversation that lit me up inside, and the curious sensation of feeling safe in a stranger's arms. We had some kind of chemistry, a bond that told me not to delve any deeper. The irony of feeling ashamed that I'd accused him of theft wasn't lost on me, but since he was driving and needed to keep his focus on the road, I let it go.

Ten minutes of awkward silence later, he stopped the car in a deserted parking lot in East Garfield, one of the most crime-ridden community areas in Chicago. Jack motioned me out of the vehicle and opened the hatch. I leaned against the bumper while he made a call.

"Dog's running late. He'll be here in ten." They were the first words he'd spoken since our discussion in the car, and I was desperate to move past the hurt I'd caused him.

"So this guy . . . Dog . . . Is he a friend of yours?"

"My cousin knows him."

"Is he . . . legit?"

"We're meeting him in an empty parking lot at night. What do you think?"

His uncharacteristically cold manner and harsh tone put me on edge. "Right. Of course. I didn't want to assume. Or label. I mean, he could have spent time in jail, but that doesn't make him a bad person. Maybe he's got kids and he's hard up for cash or maybe he has a warehouse full of stuff from his past life, and he needs to get rid of it . . ." I knew I should stop talking, but my mind was racing, spinning out of control. I'd broken something between us. Jack made me feel calm. He eased the discomfort that took up space in my mind. I could breathe when I was with him, but he'd withdrawn and I couldn't feel him anymore.

"Simi . . ." He closed the distance between us, trapping me between his body and the back of the car. "Stop," he said quietly. "You don't need to—"

"I watch crime shows with Rose," I continued, my words tripping over my tongue. "She likes the old shows and I like the new shows, so one week it will be *Murder, She Wrote* and the next it will be *Criminal Minds*. Some of the shows have reformed criminals who just want a better life, but they need money, so they do one last heist. That's okay, too. I'm not judging. I wasn't judging you. Or accusing. I didn't mean to offend you or—"

"It's okay." He slid his hand beneath my hair, his thumb stroking my nape. "We're good."

A wave of relief washed over me, followed by a ripple of desire. I didn't care if he was a thief. I closed my eyes, focused on his gentle strokes, the connection I could feel again.

"Have you ever wanted to disappear?" he asked. "Just run away and start your life all over again as someone else?"

I couldn't tell him what I knew he wanted to hear. "Honestly, no. I couldn't imagine leaving Chloe and Olivia. Or Rose. Or my family, even though they ignored me for most of my childhood and are now trying to make up for it by meddling in my life. If we get this money, it won't mean anything unless I have someone to share it with, the people I love."

"I had that once." He drew back, and I could see the pain in his eyes.

"Love?"

"And family."

His eyes never left mine as he lowered his mouth. His kiss

started soft but deepened toward delirium. He backed me right up against the vehicle, pressing me against the cold, hard door. Then he was everywhere. Strong hands roamed up my arms, over my shoulders, and down to my rear. His hips pinned me in place, hard length pressed tight against my belly.

"Jack . . ." I turned my head, drew in a ragged breath. "Maybe we should take this to the back of your vehicle. Did you know it's built for more than just profiling at Target? It's got a very spacious cargo hold. If you fold down the seats, it's big enough for two."

"You deserve more than the back of a rental vehicle in a parking lot in East Garfield," he said. "If we do this, it will be a whole night—soft bed, silk sheets. It's going to be slow. I want to take my time with you, strip off your clothes piece by piece, kiss every inch of your skin—"

I didn't get to find out what else he was going to do or when "this" would happen. Dog interrupted our intimate moment by trying to hit us with his truck.

"That was close." Jack carefully slid away from Dog's bumper. "He almost didn't make it this time."

Dog was a balding middle-aged man with more beard than face. "Got your equipment," he said, holding out a cardboard box. "You can have it all for 15 percent off the retail price."

I checked the box against the list Chloe and Gage had made in Rose's garage—burner laptop, burner phones, RF transceiver, assorted gadgets I didn't understand . . . "Why are these ropes and pulleys here? And this glass cutting tool? And this other stuff?" I pulled a few things out of the box at random.

"I added it to the order," Jack said. "Just in case."

"How do I know the electronic equipment isn't faulty?" I asked Dog. "Do you give a money-back guarantee?"

"You get what you get, and you don't get upset." Dog smirked. At least I thought it was a smirk, but between the mustache and the beard, a whole lot of things could have been going on with those lips.

"That worked when I was twelve and got the smallest piece of birthday cake," I said. "But a 15 percent discount with no guarantee doesn't do it for me."

"17 percent," Dog said.

"Let's test it out right now. That way, if anything doesn't work, I can call all your contacts and let them know to be wary of electronics in cardboard boxes." Nani had taught me to negotiate, and she was a master of the art.

"20 percent and that's my final offer." Dog folded his arms across his chest in a move that I assumed was meant to intimidate. He had sizable muscles, but the effect was watered down by his My Little Pony tattoos. I could swear I saw Fluttershy wink.

"Don't give me that 20 percent bullshit," I said. "I work in retail. I know the margins and I know you didn't buy these goods so everything is profit for you."

"You didn't tell me she was a hard-ass." Dog glared at Jack.

"I like to keep the good stuff to myself."

"Give me the Boxing Day special," I said. "Six A.M. door crasher."

His eyes widened. "40 percent?"

I shook my head. "First five people in the door."

"*Sixty?*"

"Take it or leave it." I pulled out a wad of cash. We'd all chipped in to cover the costs in hopeful anticipation of a bigger return at the end.

Dog took the money, but not before registering a complaint with customer service.

"You said she was a newb," he said to Jack.

"She's a smart and savvy newb." Jack grinned. "Gotta say, it's pretty damn hot."

He told Dog he also needed a large, vacant mansion in an iso-lated area for an afternoon. Unlike most normal people, Dog didn't ask why. He pulled out his phone, made a few calls, and within five minutes Jack had an address.

"Hold on a second," I interjected. "How much?"

"$1,000," Dog said. "It's up for sale and the owners are out of the country. Half goes to the agent, who could lose her license if anyone finds out. Other half is a finder's fee. And the final half is my danger pay."

Dog wasn't smiling anymore so I refrained from sharing that there were only two halves in a whole. In the end, it didn't matter how he divided it up. The cost to us would be the same.

"We'll take it." I figured $1,000 was cheap for an afternoon at a mansion, considering how much I paid in rent for the privilege of living in a damp basement suite, and the fact we would be commit-ting a crime.

"I already said we'd take it," Jack mumbled. "You're just say-ing what I said."

"I said it after eliciting some useful information that you forgot, like how much it was going to cost."

After I handed over the money, Dog scrawled a phone number on the flap of a cigarette package. "Here's my card," he said to me. "You need anything else; you call me. Ask for Wren."

"So . . . Dog is your . . ." I trailed off, hoping he'd fill in the blanks.

"Middle name," he said. "I didn't vibe with 'Wren' when I got into this line of work, but that's my mom's number and she doesn't like it when people call me Dog."

"I'll definitely call if I need anything else." I could hardly wait to see Chloe and share every detail of this crazy night. Just imag-ining her reaction when I told her about Wren Dog made me smile.

There was an awkward moment when we got back into Jack's vehicle. I leaned toward him, fully expecting him to show me just how hot he was for my retail negotiation skills, but he just turned the key and hit the gas, his only interest seemingly to be getting the hell out of Dodge. To be honest, I didn't mind. I needed time to process our encounter. I'd hash it out later with Chloe over drinks in her kitchen as I always did.

"Dog doesn't give his number to just anyone," Jack said. "He liked you. Respected you."

"He's an interesting person." I sucked in my lips and took the plunge even though I could sense his withdrawal. "Should we . . . ?"

"Rain check?" Jack asked, bursting my bubble of hope.

"You good for it?"

"I've never let a customer down."

◇ ◇ ◇

I made Jack stop at Buffalo Joe's for Chloe's favorite wings and cheddar chips on our way home. He pulled up outside her house and helped me sort through the box to take out the equipment Chloe would need.

"Thanks for connecting me with Dog." I gave a farewell nod instead of a wave because my hands were full.

"Pleasure."

Chloe pulled open the door before I had a chance to knock. Her face was flushed, and her eyes had a sparkle to them that I hadn't seen before.

"Are you on something?" I moved to step forward and she blocked the door. My skin prickled in warning. I put down the box and my Buffalo Joe's bag and reached into my purse for my pepper spray. "Is Kyle here?"

"No." She swallowed hard, her gaze drifting down to the box

and then up again. "He *was* here," she said. "He was drunk. Angry. Someone garnished his wages and he thought it was me trying to get the child support payments. I didn't want to call the police because it would just inflame the situation."

"Did he hurt you? Why didn't you call me? I would have come right over." I was getting a weird vibe from Chloe, like she was holding something back. "Is he still here?" I whispered. "Is he threatening you? Should I call 911."

"Babe . . ." She sighed. "He kept banging on the door, so I called Gage."

"Gage?" My voice rose in pitch. "You called Gage and not me? He's a stranger."

She gave a half shrug. "The day I had to wear the sunglasses, he took me aside, and he made me promise that if Kyle ever showed up at the house, I'd call him. I told him it wasn't his concern, but you know how he gets . . ."

"Actually, I don't 'know how he gets' because I don't know anything about him and neither do you." My head was spinning again. My girl was in danger and hadn't even sent me a text. We had a plan for when Kyle showed up—and his visits had become more frequent over the last few months—she called me; I called my brothers; we all showed up at the house and Kyle went away.

"He's very protective," she said. "And he's gentle with animals. When we were at the Angelinis' mansion, he was lying on the grass playing with the Rottweilers."

"I don't care if he's gentle with tigers." I shook my head. "Babe, he isn't safe. He carries a gun."

Her face brightened. I knew then it was already too late.

"He disabled the boat during our recon mission without harming anyone," she said. "Wasn't that amazing? He's got a permit for a concealed carry. He says in his line of business, he always needs to be armed."

"And that doesn't worry you?" I was shaking, my lungs so tight, I could barely breathe. Chloe was my everything. It was *my* job to keep her safe. *My* job to be there when she was in danger. "What if his business follows him home? Or to your home, where your child sleeps. Where is Olivia anyway? What does she think of all this?"

"She's with Gage on the couch. We're watching a show about lions on Animal Planet."

"He's inside your apartment?" I couldn't picture Gage in Chloe's place with all the frilly cushions, soft furnishings, and feminine decor.

"You should have seen him, Simi! He came here so fast. Olivia and I watched from the window. He flew out of his truck, grabbed Kyle by the back of the neck, and threw him down the stairs. Kyle took a swing at him, and in two seconds he had Kyle on his stomach, face down in the grass. I don't know what he said, but the second he let go, Kyle ran to his car and drove away. I invited Gage in for a drink after Kyle left. It was the least I could do." She bent down and picked up the box. "He says he can help me test the equipment so you don't have to stay. I know you have to work in the morning."

Have to stay? Chloe was the other half of my heart, and Olivia was like my own daughter. Spending time with them was a joy; not an obligation.

"Take the food." I handed her the bag, my heart in my throat making it difficult to swallow. "There's more than enough for three. Let me know if there's a problem with any of the equipment."

I pulled out my phone to call an Uber, but when I turned around, Jack was there, leaning against his vehicle, arms folded across his chest.

"I saw his car," was all he said when I joined him on the sidewalk.

"Her ex was here. She's never not called me." I rubbed my chest. "It hurts."

"Where do you want to go?"

My head was spinning. There was too much going on, too many changes, too many emotions to process. Despite my big speech about people needing people, I desperately wanted to be alone.

"Just take me to my parents' house. I'll sneak in the back."

SEVENTEEN

◇ ◇ ◇

In heist movies, there's always a montage of scenes where the caper crew rehearses for the big day. The grease person practices maneuvering through a mock laser beam field made up of string. The driver races through obstacle courses, back alleys, and dark city streets. The hacker pounds on her keyboard, staring at screens full of code. The gadget person demonstrates all their clever toys. The key master practices opening a safe. The muscle finds a few security guards to knock unconscious and wrestles guard dogs to the ground. The inside person seduces or befriends the target and gets them to spill their secrets. And the leader organizes it all with the help of her second-in-command.

At least, that's the way it works in the movies. In real life, with a bunch of newbs who are scraping by with low-paying jobs, inflexible hours, difficult bosses, and a bunch of side gigs to make ends meet, just organizing a rehearsal heist was one hell of a task. And on top of it all, we had a wedding to plan.

We met at Rose's house on Saturday morning for the drive to the vacant mansion in Englewood where we were going to do our dry run. Jack had gone ahead in the van to collect the keys from the real estate agent. The rest of us traveled in the limo Emma had borrowed from her friend.

"Chloe got the floor plan off the real estate listing," I said, trying to balance the plan, my phone, and my list of tasks on my lap while sipping a glass of complimentary champagne. "The layout is similar to the Angelinis' mansion. Is everyone clear about what they'll be doing?"

"Aye, aye, Captain." Anil had shown up with my brother's old drone, a pirate hat, and a velvet jewelry box containing the fake necklace he'd made at work. In response to my query about the hat, he'd simply said, "Dead men tell no tales."

Gage pulled a weapon from the holster under his jacket and another from his boot. "Lock and load."

"Put those away," I snapped. "This is a no-shooting heist."

"Not even one shot? Just to scare the guards away?"

"No." I polished off my glass of champagne and poured another.

"What about a Taser?" Emma looked back over her shoulder instead of keeping her eyes on the road.

"Do you have a Taser?"

She cut her gaze to Gage, who was following the conversation with obvious interest. "Maybe."

"Do I want to know why you have a Taser?" I checked out the champagne supply. It was becoming clear that I would need a substantial amount of alcohol to get through this day.

"I do." Anil lifted his hand. "I'm a curious beast."

"Yes, you are, sweetheart." Chloe patted his knee.

"Do you want the good answer about how a nonlethal legal weapon is always a highly preferred choice for self-protection . . ." Emma asked as she turned off the highway and onto a gravel road. ". . . or the bad answer about my last boyfriend who was into electric—"

"Oh look!" I cut her off with a shout. "We're here."

Jack arrived a few minutes later and parked the van beside us. We practiced the switch from limo to van. Cristian was going to be entertaining the family at the rehearsal dinner, so we got him to time us. Mostly, he just laughed.

"Anil, the idea is to move quickly from the limo to the van," I said. "You should have the seat belt off well before go time. And no apples. We don't want to have to deal with the cores or the smell when we're in close quarters."

"Safety is important," Anil said. "What if the limo is hit from behind? I'll go through the window. My parents spent a fortune on orthodontics to straighten my teeth. Imagine how they'd feel."

"I'd hope they were more concerned with the damage to your face than the money they spent on your teeth if you went flying through a window," I said. "Or are they not that kind of people?"

"They're very frugal," Anil said. "Two squares of toilet paper for a number one and five squares of toilet paper for a number two."

"Jesus Christ," Gage said. "You still call them number one and number two? Man the fuck up."

Emma stretched out on the floor of the van. "How many for a number three?"

Anil tipped his head to the side, frowning. "What's a number three?"

"Explosive diarrhea."

I automatically looked to Chloe to share my silent exasperation but her attention was on Gage. I was happy that she'd finally met someone who lit her up inside, but at the same time I missed our connection.

"Please don't tell us—" I made a desperate attempt to divert the conversation, but Emma cut me off.

"Los Cabos, 2004. Meatball sub on the way to the airport. I'll tell you right now . . . bring your own toilet roll when you fly because they don't have enough."

"I think in a situation like that, my father would approve the use of a few extra squares," Anil said.

"Remind me never to come to your place for dinner." Gage opened the van door. "I'm done with this shit. Let's get to the fun part and practice breaking into the house. I'm giving up my Saturday golf game for this. Tomorrow would have worked better for my schedule."

"Chloe and I are meeting Bella and her mom at the bridal shop tomorrow," I reminded him. "And what schedule are you talking about? I still have no idea what you do during the day. I find it hard to believe you spend it playing golf. You're not a shorts and polo shirt kind of guy."

"You're right about that. Last time I wore shorts was never," Gage said. "You can't stop bullets with bare legs."

Housebreaking was surprisingly easy. Emma stretched out in the back seat for a nap. Cristian pretended to send a text to my burner telling us he had started the party games and had secured the Angelinis' phones. Chloe tapped on her keyboard and did the mysterious things that would supposedly jam the signal. Jack attached one of the devices Dog had given us to the front door and pressed buttons until the door unlocked.

"I thought the real estate agent left it open," Anil said.

Jack tucked the device away in his pocket. "I wanted to make sure it worked. Dog's stuff isn't always reliable."

"Are you kidding me?" I grabbed the edges of his leather jacket and pulled him toward me. "Everything hinges on that equipment. If Chloe can't jam the signal or hack the system, we'll be sitting ducks for armed guards and Rottweilers."

"You're very sexy when you're riled," Jack murmured, studying me with hooded eyes. "There's a guest room on the main floor with a four-poster bed. Maybe we should—"

"If that equipment doesn't work, you won't be able to get out of bed for months," I warned, cutting him off. "And not in a good way."

Gage wandered through the house pretending to be keeping watch. The rest of us made our way upstairs. The house had been staged for viewing, with high-end furniture and luxury decor. I wasn't expecting to find an actual safe in the master bedroom.

"This is staging to a whole new level," I said.

"Dog told his real estate contact we wanted a safe for our private viewing so we could see how it looked," Jack said.

"If I had enough money to need a safe, I would be concerned with security and not aesthetics, but now we have a safe to crack." I stood aside to give Jack access. "Did you bring your tools?"

Jack pulled out a notebook, pen, and stethoscope. "Let's get started."

"That's it?"

"That's it." He knelt in front of the safe and turned the dial.

"My dad has a safe almost identical to that one," Anil said, flopping backward on the bed. "He uses it for his paratha recipe. My paternal grandmother kept trying to steal it so he has to lock it up."

Jack looked over his shoulder. "Seriously?"

"They're the best parathas in the state," Anil said. "Probably even the country. The recipe has two special ingredients and was handed down from father to son for over a century. My grandfather wouldn't give it to her, and when he passed, she tried to get it from my dad. Every time she came to visit, she would search for it. We caught her crawling under tables, wiggling under beds, and climbing on the counters in the kitchen to reach the high cupboards. Once she got stuck on the roof trying to get into the master bedroom because my father had locked the door. We had to call the firefighters to get her down."

"I really hope this works out so Anil can get the fuck out of that batshit crazy house." Gage leaned against the doorjamb, one foot crossed over the other, instead of being outside pretending to watch for guards like he was supposed to be doing. Managing a heist, I'd discovered, was much like trying to organize a Chopra family dinner.

"You're supposed to be on watch downstairs," I said.

"I got bored."

"We've only been in here for five minutes. What's going to happen during the real heist?"

"Hopefully, I'll get to shoot someone," Gage said. "Otherwise, what's the point?"

"I've got it." Jack opened the safe and moved to the side to show us the empty interior.

"That was fast. I thought cracking safes was hard."

"It wasn't locked," he said. "I just spun the dials for show. Were you impressed?"

"For half a second, then I was disappointed. Now I'm worried about how long it will take in real life. We don't even know what kind of safe they have. Maybe it's one of those super-duper ones you see in banks with a spinning dial on the front and three locks." I held out my hand to Anil. "I need the fake necklace to put in the fake safe."

Anil handed me the large velvet box. I lifted the lid and felt my heart leap. Inside was an exact replica of the necklace I had only ever seen in police photographs. The diamonds sparkled, the emeralds glowed, and the pink heart glittered in the sunlight streaming through the window. I lifted it carefully from the box, feeling the substantial weight in my hand. It was hard to believe it wasn't real.

"This is amazing," I said. "Garcia was right. Why would anyone spend insane money on real jewelry when they can have the same look for a fraction of the cost and without any risk?"

"For the same reason people buy NFTs," Anil said. "If you have the money, why not buy the real thing?"

I put the fake necklace in the safe and then removed it and gave it to Anil. "Fake in. Real out," I said.

"Why are you giving the necklace to Anil?" Jack frowned. "Don't you trust me?"

"Not entirely. Plus, no one's going to mess with The Butcher."

Truth was, I still didn't trust Jack. How could I? From skulking behind the museum to dragging me into the bushes and from ditching the crew on the boat recon to disappearing for most of the evening at the charity ball where another necklace was stolen, he hadn't left me much choice. On a personal level, I didn't care anymore. I was desperate to jump into bed with him and explore our crazy chemistry. But professionally—and I counted the heist as a professional venture—I wasn't taking any risks.

"I accept this important task and the responsibility you have given me," Anil said, his tone formal, face serious. And then he ruined it by pumping his fist in the air and grinning so wide, I could see every one of his teeth. "The Butcher won't let you down."

It was almost worth trusting him with the necklace to see all that joy.

EIGHTEEN

◇ ◇ ◇

t was almost ten A.M. on Sunday morning, and Chloe and I were sitting in the bridal shop, sipping mimosas in a fantasyland of white organza. Chloe was our official photographer for the pre-wedding events. She'd taken photography courses in high school and had planned to pursue it as a career until her unexpected pregnancy changed the trajectory of her life.

"I don't usually start drinking until eleven," I told the elegantly dressed sales associate as she refilled my glass.

"If you worked here," she said, "you'd start at nine."

"I always imagined the day we'd come to a bridal salon together," Chloe said after our high couture barkeep had returned to the front desk. "But it didn't involve committing a crime."

"Some of these dresses are a crime." I pointed to three giant meringue-like gowns suspended from the ceiling beside an elevated carpeted dais. "A little necklace theft pales in comparison to the travesty of someone dressed as a marshmallow to start the next stage of their life."

Bella and her mother arrived a few minutes later. They sipped herbal tea—*oh, we couldn't possibly drink alcohol in the morning*—and talked about the weather while Chloe and I got tipsy waiting for the sales associate to bring out the dress.

"Are we good?" Chloe asked after Bella had gone to change. "I know I hurt you last night, and don't say you're fine because I saw your face and I know you too well."

"I'm fine, really. I'm glad Gage was there." I still had mixed feelings about Gage. On the one hand, he scared me with his quiet intensity and deadly shooting accuracy. On the other hand, he'd stepped up for Chloe. He'd protected her and made her feel safe. For that, I could forgive him for almost anything, even getting between me and my girl.

"He's installing a high-tech security system at my place this afternoon," she said. "I might actually be able to sleep through the night without waking at every sound."

We didn't get a chance to continue our conversation because Bella came out of the fitting room and twirled in front of us in a strapless floral sequined mermaid gown with an enormous layered lace skirt and a low-cut bodice embellished with crystals.

"What do you think?" she asked mid-twirl.

I thought I shouldn't tell her about my friend Val, who had tripped on the sidewalk in her mermaid meringue and rolled into traffic. I'd signed both her casts with pink hearts and held her crutches when she hopped up the aisle.

"It's beautiful. Very you."

"I've never seen a wedding dress plunge that low," Chloe whispered. "I think I can see her navel."

I made a mental note to bring a few rolls of double-sided tape to the wedding. There was no way those demi cups were staying up on their own. I wished I could pull off a dress like that, but my girls required some serious scaffolding, and at best, those demi cups would give me nipple coverage.

"It's my dream dress." Bella shared a glance with her mother. "It's the only thing in this wedding that's really mine."

"Why don't we get Chloe to take some candid pictures of you and your mom before they do the final fitting? Just pretend she isn't there." I gave Chloe a nudge to put down her mimosa. The sales associate had grown tired of asking if we wanted refills and had positioned herself beside us so she could continually top up our glasses.

Bella's mom joined her daughter in front of the mirrors, and they had the traditional rom-com movie moment. Mom, all teary-eyed at seeing her little girl in her wedding dress. Daughter beaming as her childhood fantasy of being a princess for a day came true. Wedding planner hoping for a few more minutes of crying so she could finish the rest of her booze.

Chloe had only just positioned her camera when the front door flew open and a tall, dark-haired man stormed into the store. He wore a black suit and a white shirt, open at the collar to reveal a thick gold chain around his neck. His hair was slicked tight over a slightly oversized head, which tapered down to a narrow jaw, thin lips, and a receding chin. Two heavyset men accompanied him, both in dark glasses, black T-shirts, gold chains, and jeans.

"What the hell?" He stalked up to Bella, his thin lips twisted into a snarl. "My father said you'd need to be watched and it turns out he was right." He lifted his chin toward the window and gave a thumbs-up to a man in a T-shirt and jeans standing outside. I hadn't even noticed him when we walked in.

"Mario." Bella stared at him in horror. "What are you doing here? You're not supposed to see the dress before our wedding."

You know that moment in the movies when the villain first appears? There's always something about him that seems a little off. It could be as innocuous as a sneer, or as obvious as blood dripping down his chin. Your skin prickles. A shiver goes down your spine.

You munch your buttered popcorn and wonder how the good guy could possibly win. That's how I felt the first time I met Kyle. This guy was Kyle times ten.

"Take it off," Mario snapped. "You aren't wearing that to our wedding. You look like a whore." He raised a hand. My breath left me in a rush. I hadn't expected Hell to open and spew out a monster when I'd come for the dress fitting, but I'd handled monsters like him before.

"Dude." I interposed myself between Mario and Bella, acutely aware I was within striking distance of his hand. "You're killing the vibe. A bride likes a little privacy before the big reveal."

He cut his dark gaze to me. "Who the fuck are you?"

"Simi. I'm the wedding planner." I didn't offer my hand because I liked having a matching set.

"Get lost, wedding planner. This doesn't involve you."

I wanted to get lost. Hell, if I hadn't grown up with three brothers and just downed three mimosas, I would have been out of there the minute those soulless eyes fixed on me.

"Firstly," I said, poking him in the chest. "This is a happy place. You may not have noticed the soft lighting, pretty flowers, frothy dresses, frills, and lace when you barged in. We don't swear in happy places so fudge the bad language. Secondly, the bride wears what she wants to wear." I shot a pointed glare at Bella's mother. How could she just sit there? Why didn't she step in and put the dude in his place?

"It's okay, Simi," Bella said quietly. "I'll find another dress."

"Damn right you will." He puffed out his chest like a bullfrog. "You do what your man tells you to do."

"Damn wrong you won't. You do what you like." I would have puffed out my chest, but my shirt was already tight, and I didn't want to pop a button and give him a peek at something only select people were allowed to see.

We faced off. Me high on liquid confidence, heart pounding

like I'd run a mile, knees only seconds away from turning to jelly. Him with a sneer and breath so bad, I couldn't even imagine what horrors he'd eaten for breakfast.

"Bella's father paid me to make sure the wedding goes as planned," I said to Mario. "If you have a problem, you'll need to take it up with him."

"I sure as h—"

"Uh-uh." I shook my finger in his face. "Not here. Say 'sugar.'"

The look he gave me was pure poison. He lifted his hand. My brain screamed a warning, and I threw up my arm, bracing for impact.

"*Raaaaaaah.*" Chloe came out of nowhere, kicking and punching like she was high on radioactive spider juice. Mario struck back, his fist glancing over her eye. My vision sheeted red, and I head-butted him, driving my forehead into his solar plexus—a trick that had always brought my brothers down. His goons sprang into action. One used his body as a shield, trying to protect the groom-to-be from the flying kitten heels of my fighting-machine best friend. The other grabbed Chloe by the shoulders and pushed her away. She stumbled into me. I fell into Bella, and we all went down in a flurry of crystals and lace.

"What the fuck?" Mario shouted, cowering behind the wall of muscle. "What. The. Fuck? Your father is going to hear about this." He stormed out of the shop, taking his goons with him. Bella's mother collapsed on the nearest chair, grabbed a mimosa from the refreshment table, and drank it in one gulp.

Struggling to extricate myself from Bella's skirt, I didn't realize the police had arrived until I heard a familiar laugh.

"Simi? Is that you in there?"

"Detective Garcia." I pushed back a clump of lace and stared up at his smiling face. "Did you happen to be in the neighborhood and thought you'd stop in to ask me some questions?" I kept my voice low. "Or was there a jewelry theft nearby and I'm always first on your list of suspects?"

"I was having coffee across the street, so I responded to the ten-forty at a wedding shop. And here you are."

"You could give me a hand instead of just standing there laughing," I said. "The bride needs this dress for her wedding."

"Of course."

I took the hand he offered while his partner helped Chloe and Bella off the ground. Then it was half an hour of statements while the bridal shop owner tried to salvage the dress.

"You were awesome," I whispered to Chloe while we waited for our turn. "Where did you learn to fight like that?"

"I told Gage I wanted to be the one who tosses Kyle down the stairs, so he showed Olivia and me some Krav Maga moves. He's teaching us how to defend ourselves."

"You were always a fast learner," I said.

"I wasn't even thinking about what he taught us." She squeezed my hand. "My bestie was in danger. I did what I had to do."

"I'll have to tell Anil there's a new 'The Butcher' in town."

"It felt so good," Chloe said. "I felt powerful for the first time in my life."

Chloe went to find another mimosa. Detective Garcia sat on the pink velvet couch beside me. "So your client is Bella Angelini?"

"Yes, that's right."

"She says it was all a minor understanding and she doesn't want us to press charges."

I couldn't imagine Mr. Angelini would be happy if his future son-in-law was thrown in jail one week before the wedding, so I nodded. "The groom got upset about the dress and things got a little out of hand. You know how anxious people get as they approach a big life milestone. Except for a few scrapes and bruises, no one got hurt and we're sorting it all out."

"I don't know if you're aware," he said, "but your client's family allegedly has ties to organized crime. Her father is rumored to be a high-profile boss in the Chicago Outfit. These aren't the kind of people you want to get mixed up with. They are dangerous, Simi, in every sense of the word."

As soon as the words dropped from his lips, everything made sense. The isolated mansion. The crazy security. The guards shooting at our boat. And then there were the bodyguards who looked like they'd walked straight out of *Goodfellas* and Mr. Angelini, giving off evil *Godfather* vibes left, right, and center. I'd known we were dealing with criminals—law-abiding citizens didn't act as fences for stolen jewelry—but the Mafia? Jack was so dead. I made a mental note to ask Emma if I could borrow her Taser.

"No. I can't believe it." I covered my mouth in mock horror. How much worse would things get for Chloe and me if Garcia thought we had knowingly jumped into bed with the mob? "Bella's so nice. Her mom is nice. They have a nice house. She's having a lovely wedding to a not nice man."

"She's getting married to man whose family is also connected to organized crime," he said. "His father is a boss in a New York crime family." He shook his head and sighed. "You didn't know."

"Do I look like I knew?" I drew an air circle around my face. "Does anything in this expression suggest prior knowledge? Do you think I would have taken the job if I thought I would end up with a horse head in my bed? Or swimming with the fishes? I don't even like fish. And I just got new shoes. I don't need concrete ones." My brain was still trying to take it all in, so I let my mouth run wild.

"You seem to attract trouble," Garcia said.

"Maybe trouble attracts me." I grimaced and shut down the runaway train of my free-form thoughts. "That didn't really make sense."

"Very little you do makes sense, and yet every time I see you, I leave with a smile."

Was Garcia flirting with me? Or was he trying to lighten the mood after telling me I was in bed with the mob and likely to die a horrible death if the wedding didn't go as planned? I typed myself a reminder to find my earmuffs as soon as I got home. I'd seen *Reservoir Dogs*. How would I tuck my hair back if I only had one ear?

"I can't bail on her now," I said. "The wedding is in one week. It's not her fault who her father is. I'll do the job I was paid to do and hope for the best."

"You have my number," Garcia said. "Call me if you ever need me. I promise no questions."

"I'll try not to call because I know that will be a strain for you."

Garcia smiled and brushed his lips over my cheek. "Watch your back," he whispered. And then he was gone.

◆ ◆ ◆

"You shouldn't have made Mario angry," Bella said after the police had cleared out. We were sipping a calming tea in the lounge while her mother talked to the seamstress about the new set of alterations that would be necessary after the scuffle.

"I have a feeling angry is his natural state of being." Just like "mob" was his family and Sicilian neckties were probably what he gave to people he didn't like at Christmas.

I had a strong feeling that Chloe and I had just earned a spot on Mario's necktie list. We'd headbutted, kicked, and punched him. We'd sent him running out of the bridal shop covered in kitten heel scratches and without a shred of dignity. He was probably waiting outside right now with ten machine-gun-wielding mafiosos in trench coats and fedoras who were going to give us a bullet sandwich when we left the building.

My lungs seized and I bent over, struggling to breathe.

"Simi." Chloe bent over beside me, her forehead creased in a frown. "What's wrong?"

"Maaaaaaa. . . ."

"What?"

"Maaaaaaaaafffffffeeeee . . ." My throat was closing like it did when I ate poppy seeds. Maybe I was allergic to violence.

"Mafee? Coffee? Do you need coffee? Something stronger than tea?"

"I'll go ask the shop assistant to bring her a coffee," Bella said. "I could use one myself."

"Maaafia," I managed to spit out after Bella was out of earshot, and then I managed to tell Chloe the rest.

"We attacked a mob boss's son." Chloe covered her mouth with her hand, but her shock was real.

"Hence my inability to breathe." Bile rose in my throat. "He's probably a made man. Made men have guns. He could have shot us right here in the middle of the meringues. I cut him off when he was trying to swear at me. I told him to say 'sugar.' I disrespected him, Chloe. 'Sugar' is going to kill me, just like Dad said. My dad was right about sugar."

Chloe gave my arm a squeeze. "You're not going to die because of sugar."

"What if he shows up at my house to teach me a lesson?" My lungs tightened again. "What if he gives me a Sicilian necktie? My neck is my best feature, and it will have to be covered up at my funeral. My mom will be so upset."

"Put your head between your legs." She pushed me down

gently. "He's not going to off you because then the wedding won't happen. He needs you alive."

"For now." I sat up and dropped my head in my hands. "What about after the wedding when he decides to clean up some loose ends? We're loose ends. His men won't respect him if he doesn't deal with the women who beat him up and told him 'sugar.' We've robbed him of his dignity."

"We're also going to rob his father-in-law of a $25 million necklace," she said. "We're going to rob a mob boss. Think what would happen if we were caught. Why didn't Jack tell us?"

"I can't think. My brain is replaying every mob movie I've ever seen. Every type of torture. Every death . . ."

"We need to tell everyone," Chloe said. "They have a right to know what we're walking into. It was one thing when we thought they were just ordinary criminals. This takes it to a whole new level."

"I'm more worried about what's going to happen when we leave the shop," I said. "What if they're waiting outside?"

"I'll text Gage," she said. "He's supposed to be the muscle in our heist / wedding planning gig."

Gage. For a moment I'd forgotten about the night she'd blown me off for him, and the pain came rushing back.

"Your eye is swollen," I said. "If he threw Kyle down the stairs just for knocking on your door, who knows what he's going to do if he sees you like that? We can't have him running around in a protective frenzy trying to find Mario so he can toss him down the stairs. It will compromise the mission."

"He's got a gun," Chloe said. "He can keep us safe."

"We kept ourselves safe," I retorted. "We beat up a mob boss's son. We don't need Gage. We've always been fine on our own."

"Babe." Her face softened. "What's wrong? And I don't mean what happened this morning."

"I don't know." My voice wavered. "I don't know anything about Gage and neither do you, and yet you let him into your house when Olivia was there. You put her in danger instead of calling me." I didn't know if it was the fight or the adrenaline or the shock or if it really had anything to do with Gage, but I couldn't think, couldn't breathe, couldn't stop my hands from shaking. "It's always been you and me," I said. "Ride or die. I was nothing at home growing up. No one had time. No one cared. I was a nuisance, a burden. I had to be good. I had to be quiet. I had to disappear. But you saw me."

"I still see you," she said. "It's still you and me."

"And Gage."

"I don't understand why you're being like this." She knelt on the floor in front of me, taking my hands. "You've never had a problem with any of my boyfriends, and I'm not even seeing Gage. He's been over a few times—"

"Not just that once? A few times? And you didn't tell me?" I studied her face. The answer was right there. "You like him," I said.

"I do like him."

"And he likes you. I see it every time we get together. He looks at you like he's never seen anything more beautiful in his life, which of course you are, but only I'm supposed to see it."

"Aw, babe." She gave me a half smile.

"It feels different than when you've been with other guys."

"You aren't going to lose me," Chloe said, understanding. "Look what you've done for me. The crew, the heist, the danger, the wedding . . ."

"The Mafia," I added. "Don't forget them."

Chloe wrapped me in a hug. "If it's going to be a concrete coffin, we'll be in it together. You and me."

"I tasked Gage with elephant rides and entertaining the kids,"

I said, "but now it seems we do need his fighting chops and maybe even his guns."

Bella returned a few moments later with a cup of coffee and a plate of macarons. "I'll need to find another dress." She cast a wistful glance at the counter, where the sales associate was deep in conversation with the dressmaker. "I thought at the very least I'd be able to have the dress I wanted."

"You *can* have the dress you want," Chloe said. "If you really don't want to push back, you can wear a cloak or a half jacket to cover your shoulders, or we can ask the store to add some lace to the bodice. If they can't do it on short notice, Simi has relatives who can. The bigger question is, do you want this relationship? My ex was like Mario, and I can tell you from experience, it doesn't get better."

"I don't have a choice." She looked around, lowered her voice. "Our dads arranged the wedding to unite our families. There is no backing out. Ever."

My heart went out to her. Even though my dad was a tailor and not an evil mob boss with armed bodyguards and a stolen necklace in his safe, I knew just how difficult parents could be when it came to marriage.

Something clicked in the back of my mind. "Is that why you've had five wedding planners? You were trying to stall?"

"There's someone else," Chloe blurted out. "You've got a secret boyfriend."

"Bennito DeLuca." Bella's bottom lip quivered. "I love him."

"Why don't you just run away?" I'd effectively run away when I left home and moved into Rose's basement suite, although I kept going home for Sunday dinner. Nani's cooking was just that good.

"My dad has had me followed since the day he told me about the match because he knows I don't want to marry Mario," Bella said. "I've only been able to see Ben when I go to public places, and then we have to pretend we don't know each other. I managed to sneak out at night a few times by climbing out the window, but someone saw me leaving the boathouse in the morning and my dad got security drones to patrol the grounds."

"Did you ever talk to your parents about him?" Chloe asked. "Did you tell them how you feel? Simi's parents are constantly trying to set her up, but when she says no, they respect her decision."

"My father only cares about my older brother," she said. "He's being groomed to take over the family business. I'm a piece of property to my father, a pawn in his game. He ignored me for most of my life until he needed a way to unite our families. I tried to drag out the wedding with unreasonable requests, firing the wedding planners . . ."

I could feel her pain. I'd also been overlooked as a child, but I didn't share her hatred, anger, or bitterness. Therapy and my parents' belated interest in my life were helping me forgive and move on. I wanted Bella to be free to do the same.

"I didn't think you were really a bridezilla type," I said.

"It was working until you said you could get an elephant."

That was the downside to having a large family. There was no problem that couldn't be solved.

She squeezed my hand, her dark eyes beseeching. "You have to help me. Please. I can't marry Mario. You have to quit. My father won't let me fire you."

I didn't have to look at Chloe to know what she was thinking. She was everything that was good in the world. There was no way she'd agree to continue our wedding planner charade.

Not with the Mafia involved.

Not when Bella loved someone else.

Not even if it meant she'd go to jail.

NINETEEN

◇ ◇ ◇

By the time I got home that evening, the gossip mill had done its work. My parents were still up and waiting for me at the kitchen table with Nikhil. I knew right then it was going to be bad. They only trotted my older brother out when I was really in trouble because they knew he would always back them up.

Usually, I'd sit quietly and endure the tirade, but after what had happened at the wedding dress shop, I wasn't in the mood. I had more important things to worry about than family drama.

"This is what happens when you wait too long to get married," my mother shouted only seconds after I'd walked in the door. "You start working for the mob."

"I don't think that necessarily follows." I knew I shouldn't have gone to Satya Auntie's store with Bella's wedding dress, but the bridal shop couldn't accommodate the extensive alterations necessary to make the dress less revealing in the short time before the wedding. I knew Satya Auntie could do it, but I had to give Bella's name, and of course, she'd looked the family up. That meant no stone had been left unturned.

"Of course it does." Dad let out a long breath. "If you were married, you would have a house and a mortgage and a steady office job to help pay for it. You would be coming home every night to cook a nice dinner for your husband. And you would be having babies to keep you busy instead of running around working for criminals."

"To be fair, I haven't seen any criminal behavior," I said. "They haven't done anything that made me think they were anything other than a nice, normal family."

"Satya Auntie said they were going to throw you into the ocean to be eaten by fish." Dad couldn't get an idiom right to save his life. He'd come to America when he was twelve years old, and it was the only aspect of the English language he couldn't grasp. He was a literal thinker. Rain was water, not cats and dogs. Nothing was rocket science except rocket science itself.

"She's overdramatizing." I put my bag on the counter near the door in case I had to make a quick getaway.

"You will stop this at once," he said. "Tell them your father said you can't work there anymore. If they give you a hard time, I will speak to them. I won't have my daughter getting involved with organized crime."

Wouldn't that be special. My dad driving up to a mob boss's mansion to tell him he didn't want his daughter working with his family. At least the fishes and I wouldn't be alone.

"I'm almost thirty, Dad. I can handle my own affairs. Why don't you trust me to make my own decisions? You were never involved in my life growing up. Why do you care now?"

"He always cared," Nikhil said in the faux sympathetic voice that always made my skin crawl. He was the spitting image of my dad but younger and with my mother's thick hair. He'd taken to wearing a hideous mustache and beard that looked like something had died on his face, but I kept that to myself.

"I don't recall asking your opinion." I couldn't look at him. He just *loved* coming home to see me squirm.

"You haven't been yourself lately." Nikhil shook his head and sighed. "You've gone off the rails. We just want you to go back to being who you were—sweet, good, quiet, respectful. Listen to the people who know what's best for you."

"Shut up, Nick." I was sick of him and his officious, condescending attitude, sick of him thinking he knew anything about me. Where was he when I was struggling at school? Where was he when I needed a big brother, or even a friend? "Why are you here anyway?"

"To make sure you do the right thing."

"And that would be what? Telling the head of a Mafia family I'm going to bail on his daughter's wedding? Do you know how much money he's paying me to see it through? You can't even count that high."

Nikhil swallowed hard. He couldn't stand being bested in any way. "We've found a perfect match for you. He's a dermatologist and he's looking for a wife. The family all agrees this is the best thing for you."

"Single and has a job. That's a pretty low bar," I said. "Personality. Interests. Political views. Sense of humor. Pets. Hobbies. Character. Intelligence. Values. None of those matter?"

"Not when you've lost all sense of who you are." Nikhil leaned forward. "Not when the family honor is at stake."

"Oh, I'm sorry." My voice dripped with sarcasm. "Did I go to sleep and wake up in the wrong century? The family honor? Since when does our family have honor? And in what universe did you ever think I would agree to something like this?"

It struck me at that moment that Bella and I were in the same position. I wasn't going to marry a man I didn't love, and I couldn't let her do it, either.

"I'm leaving." I grabbed my bag. "Don't wait up because I won't be back."

"Simi, wait," Mom called out. "Nikhil went too far. He'll apologize."

"Why would I apologize?" Nikhil spat out. "I've done nothing wrong."

I left them to what would inevitably turn into yet another fight, and stormed out of the house. I was frustrated and furious and had nowhere to go. My basement suite was basically uninhabitable because Rose had thrown a few buckets of water on the floor to make it look extra damaged for the insurance adjuster's upcoming visit. Gage was at Chloe's place and I didn't want to disturb them. I couldn't stay with relatives without becoming the subject of the gossip mill yet again, and in my current mood I wouldn't be good company for any of my friends. I needed a couch to crash on and an outlet for my anger. Who could weather my storm?

◆ ◆ ◆

I held it together until Jack opened his hotel room door.

Whack. My hands thudded against his chest, fingers curling into thick, hard muscle as I pushed him back. He was wearing pajama pants and nothing else. I could see every ripple of his six-pack abs, the deep lines of his V cuts, and the soft trail of hair leading from his navel below his waistband. Damn him for being so fine. "You knew who they were."

To his credit, he didn't even pretend not to understand. "Does it matter? It's your only way to save Chloe." He reached over and pushed the door closed behind me.

"I suspected Mr. Angelini wasn't on the up-and-up," I continued to rant. "Good guys don't act as fences for stolen jewelry or show up at a charity ball with gold-toothed bodyguards and radiating evilness. But the Chicago Outfit? Seriously? No wonder they shot at us in the boat. And of course they have killer Bee drones and two layers of security at their house. They're not worried about theft; they're worried about other mobsters or the FBI showing up and taking them all out in a hail of bullets, just like they're going to do to us."

"That only happens in the movies," he said.

"Movies are based on real life."

"In real life, ponies aren't pink and can't fly," he pointed out.

"You didn't give us all the information." I shoved him again, but he didn't move. "No one would have signed up if they knew we were going to steal from the mob."

"Then it's a good thing they don't know."

"They will know," I said. "Because I'm going to tell them. I won't keep secrets and I won't put anyone at risk. We could have been killed today. Bella is being forced into the marriage, and her psycho fiancé showed up at the bridal dress shop. Chloe and I attacked him, something we would never have done if we'd known he was in the Mafia."

A smile spread across his face. "I would have loved to see that."

"It's not funny." I slapped my hands against his bare chest, more for dramatic effect than anything else. Except when my bestie was being attacked by a mob boss's son, I wasn't the violent type. "We were in danger."

"Mario's not a made man. He's a lightweight. And besides, it sounds like he was the one in danger." He stroked my cheek, his gentle caress soothing my savage inner beast.

"I did get in a few pretty good kicks and punches . . ."

"I can imagine." His hand circled my waist, pulling me roughly toward him.

My knees buckled. My mouth went dry. His eyes stayed on mine as he trailed a finger down my throat, sending a rush of white-hot heat through my veins. How could I go from fury to fire in the space of a heartbeat?

"Are you just saying nice things so I don't cancel the heist? Because you need me to get the necklace?"

"I'm saying them because they're true." He nuzzled my neck, feathered kisses along my jaw.

I could feel the steady thud of his heart in his chest, the whisper of his breath on my skin, the soft slide of his knee between my legs as he drew me closer. I was tempted to just let myself go, to fall into those arms, drown in the warmth of his kisses. But Jack hadn't been honest with me. He'd put my crew at risk. I wasn't prepared to take this any further until he told me the truth about who he was, why he was really here, and what he knew about the Angelinis.

Drawing in a deep calming breath, I pulled away and walked over to the floor-to-ceiling windows, putting some distance between us. His suite was larger than the main floor of Rose's house, the living area decorated in varying shades of beige and brown with dark wood furniture and nondescript decor.

"I can't do this if there is no honesty between us," I said. "I know you have some secret agenda. I should have asked that at the beginning but you . . . you bedazzled me with your charm."

"What do you want to know?" He came up behind me as I took in the incredible skyline view and wrapped his arms loosely around my waist.

"What are you going to do with the necklace?"

"Exactly what I said." He turned me away from the window to face him. "I plan to return it to its rightful owner. The reward is yours to keep. That in itself should be evidence of my goodwill. I didn't mention the Mafia angle because it didn't matter. You knew he was a bad guy. Bad guys do bad things."

"Mafia guys do worse things." I didn't see any deception on his face. His gaze was clear and true.

"The risk doesn't change. Neither does the reward."

"Is there any other information I need to know that would put me or the crew at risk? Were you in a relationship with Bella? Did you have some kind of failed business dealing with Mr. Angelini or his wife? Is there some bigger personal issue in play?"

I felt a brush of heat against my upper lip, a soft touch at the corner of my mouth, and then the rough graze of bristles against my throat. "No. Nothing like that."

"Who are you? Really?" My breath shuddered through me as he teased my mouth open. I'd been kissed before—many times, if you were wondering—but I hadn't known there was so much to feel, so many sensations to be discovered by the simple joining of lips.

"Jack," he murmured thickly against my mouth. "I can't tell you any more."

And then there was nothing but the rapid beat of his heart, the scent of his skin, the taste of whiskey on his tongue, the strong fingers caressing my breast in a constant quiet motion that turned me to jelly.

"Jack." His name was a groan on my lips. "What else are you keeping from me?"

"Nothing that could hurt you. I would never let anything happen to you. If you trust anything, trust that."

My mind went blank, the last of my thoughts fading away to be replaced by the desperate need to lose myself in this man, to drop all my defenses and surrender to the electric passion that sparked and crackled between us.

I lifted myself up on my toes, threaded my hands through his hair, and kissed him hard, trying to calm the storm raging inside me. The pressure of emotion, of frustration, of fear and loneliness and longing that had been building inside me all day—my whole life—demanded release, raw, hot, and wild.

Our mouths clashed, tongues tangled. I didn't care who he was—cop or criminal, good or bad, dangerous or just a man of mystery. I wanted him with every inch of my being, every part of my soul.

He broke our kiss to push my hands above my head, bracketing my wrists, holding them firm against the window, and then he was everywhere. Warm. Solid. His lips on my skin. His hand on my body. His fervent, urgent need mirrored by my own.

"I want to touch you," he said, his voice low and gruff. "I've imagined taking off your clothes, running my hands over every inch of your naked body . . ."

I lifted my eyes to his. He was breathing hard, longing etched in every angle of his face. "Do it. Touch me."

Before I could draw in a breath, he kissed me again. Hard and fast. Rough and demanding. I gasped and arched back, and as I did, his hand slid into my shirt, unhooking my bra, then moving to cup my breast. I moaned as his tongue roughly explored my mouth, his hand gently squeezing.

"So soft," he said as he pulled my shirt and bra over my head. Arms released, I sank my fingers into his thick hair and pulled him down. He brushed his mouth over my nipples, teasing one then the other into tight peaks. "So beautiful," he whispered.

My blood pulsed between my legs. I wanted him—desperately—in a way I'd never wanted any other man before. If someone interrupted us this time, what I'd done to Mario would be nothing compared to what I would do to them.

His fingers skimmed around the waistband of my skirt, then he slowly unzipped it, letting it drop to the floor. I trembled as he knelt in front of me, trailing featherlight kisses between my breasts, over my belly, to the elastic edging of my faded, blue-striped cotton briefs.

"I didn't come here expecting . . . this," I said when he hesitated.

"I didn't expect you to come at all." He eased my underwear over my hips, looked up, and caught my gaze. "But I hoped."

We had sex for hours—against the door, on the couch, in the

shower, and on the thick shag rug in front of the gas fireplace under the glow of the city lights. When we ran out of furniture, Jack wanted to have sex against the floor-to-ceiling window. At first, I demurred. With my luck, one of my relatives would happen to be in the building across the way with a telescope, and two days later I'd be walking down the aisle of shame with the desperate dermatologist.

Jack changed my mind. He changed my mind about a lot of things.

After the window—10/10, by the way; highly recommend—we staggered up to his palatial bed. I allowed Jack to have his way with me since he promised he'd do all the work and I could have all the orgasms. It was a kind gesture and very much appreciated since my failure to commit to a morning workout routine had left me lacking in the stamina department.

Many orgasms later, I lay across his chest and lightly traced the scars that marred his tanned skin. "What are these?" There were circular scars, long thin scars, white scars, and scars with nasty red edges.

"Took a few shots," Jack said. "Couple of stab wounds. No big deal."

"You're in a dangerous business."

"Life is a dangerous business." He leaned down to kiss me, and then slid his hand under the sheet. "You know what's really dangerous?"

"Wolves?" I teased.

"You."

He clearly didn't want to talk. He wanted to touch. Everywhere. Until he brought me to the brink again and again and again.

TWENTY

◇ ◇ ◇

Later, languid and completely spent, we lay in the dark listening to the steady hum of traffic.

"Your chest makes a good pillow," I said, snuggling up beside him.

Jack idly traced the curve of my hip. "I aim to please."

"I wasn't pleased when I came here," I said. "I was the opposite of pleased. My parents think I'm out of control and were trying to convince me that marriage would solve all my problems. They still don't see me or respect me as a person."

"I see you," Jack said.

I leaned up to kiss his jaw. "I was so angry with them. Angry at a world that makes it so difficult to get ahead. Angry for Bella, who is being forced into a marriage when she loves someone else. Angry that our heist won't happen once everyone finds out that we'd be stealing from the mob. Angry with you for keeping that information from us."

His fingers moved to my shoulder, a cool caress over my heated skin. "If you were so angry at me, why did you come?"

"I don't know. One minute I was storming out of the house and the next I found myself here. Something about you calms the chaos inside me."

"Something about you is distracting me from what I'm here to do."

"It's not just about the necklace, is it?" I pushed myself up to study his face. "There's something more."

Jack pressed a kiss to my forehead. "A man has to have his secrets."

"You're all secrets," I said. "Everyone has opened up over the last few weeks. They've shared things about their past, their hopes for the future, personal details . . ."

"I just shared something very personal with you." Jack lifted a suggestive brow.

"I'm not the only person you've shared it with," I said, thinking of the black card with *Clare* written in gold script.

"Are you jealous?" He eased me up, so I was lying flat on top of him and well positioned to see his self-satisfied smirk.

Yes. No. I didn't care. I'd had hookups before and enjoyed them for what they were. A fleeting moment of pleasure. I'd always been happy to walk away the next day and not look back. So why did the idea of never seeing Jack again make me ache inside?

"Of course not," I said. "This was fun, but I have absolutely no expectations. You have your man-of-mystery life and I have my ordinary-woman life, and since the heist is likely over, we'll go our separate ways and—"

"You're giving up?" His hand slid down my body, cupping my ass. "That doesn't sound like you."

"I don't have a choice. I can't do the heist alone, and who's going to want to stay involved once they hear the truth?"

"You might be surprised." He lifted my hand and pressed a kiss to my knuckles, making my insides curl with longing. "I don't think your friends will abandon you so quickly."

"They're not friends. They're a heist crew. After it's over, we'll probably never see each other again." My heart twisted at the thought of never hearing Emma's crazy stories or watching Anil wrestle with Gage in the grass. Even Cristian, who I saw only occasionally at Dad's store, made me laugh with some of his outfits and his indignant sniff when anyone mentioned the boat ride. And Jack. Would I ever see him again? I closed my eyes and tried to memorize the feel of his body beneath me, his warmth, his strength, his scent, and the sparkle in his eyes.

"I have to get everyone together to break the news," I said. "I suppose I could give them the option."

"Your hand is bruised." He held it up, frowning.

"That's what happens when you punch a Mafia boss's son."

"Every time I think I've figured you out, you serve up a new set of skills," he said. "You are hands down the most intriguing woman I have ever met. Even now I'm wondering, 'What is she going to do next?'"

"No one has ever wondered what I'm going to do next," I said. "It was always 'what are we going to do with her?' or 'how can we keep her quiet?'" I told him about my childhood and how hard I struggled to be good and stay out of trouble when my brain didn't seem to work the same as everyone else's. I thought sideways instead of straight, was easily distracted, and my insatiable curiosity was rewarded with discipline and exasperation. I told him about the time my parents left me behind at a gas station on their way to a hockey game and how it was hours before anyone even realized I was gone.

Abandonment. My therapist had named it the first time we met, along with issues of self-worth, an inability to trust, and a fear of intimacy. Moving away from home had been a big step in helping me heal those wounds.

"I know what it's like to feel alone," he said, cupping my head and running his fingers gently through my hair. "To feel like you don't fit in."

"Things got better after I met Chloe," I said. "She was lonely, too. Her dad left when she was young, and her mother was an alcoholic. We were paired up in gym class, and it was like finding the other half of my soul. She loves me for who I am. When I'm with her, I don't feel the chaos. I can see the straight path."

"That's how I feel when I'm with you," he murmured. And then he pushed up so quickly, I almost rolled off the bed.

"Are you ready to go again?" I was ready. I had not, in fact, stopped being ready since the moment I'd walked through the door.

"I've got something I want you to see," he said, pushing off the sheet to reveal I wasn't alone in my state of readiness. But when I reached for him, he gently moved my hand away.

"You wanted to know more about me. I'll show you. Get dressed. We're going on an adventure."

◇ ◇ ◇

Jack made a call, and half an hour later, the concierge delivered a set of motorcycle leathers to his room as well as a helmet and boots, all in my size.

"Are you a secret billionaire?" I asked in the underground garage where he'd parked his Harley-Davidson Roadster, over six hundred pounds of badass black steel and chrome. "Or a spy or secret agent? Are you part of an off-the-books organization that steals necklaces and seduces candy store clerks?"

"Were you seduced?" He pulled on his helmet and buckled the strap beneath his chin.

"I will be once I feel the thrum of the motor between my thighs." I put on the helmet and his voice faded to a dull muffle.

"I thought that had already happened."

"Are you cracking jokes at such a serious moment?" I asked. "This is my first time."

"I promise to be gentle." He helped me on the bike and showed me where to put my feet. I wrapped my arms around his waist and he peeled out of the parking garage, tires screaming when we turned onto the street.

Riding a motorcycle was a thrill of adrenaline-fueled excitement coupled with a layer of fear and anxiety. All my senses were heightened. I noticed the rapid change of smells as we left the city center and drove along the lake. I heard the roar of the engine and felt the motorcycle vibrate between my thighs. I watched the world hurtle past while the noise in my head faded away, leaving me feeling exhilarated and free.

After thirty minutes, we turned into Bridgeport and drove down a dimly lit street of boarded-up houses. Jack parked in front of a small run-down bungalow, and we pulled off our helmets, clipping them to a hook under the seat. It was clear no one had lived in the house for a very long time. The wooden staircase leading to the front door had rotted away and the picture window was covered in boards and graffiti. Garbage littered the small front garden, and a tall cedar had fallen into a broken trellis fence.

"Who lives here?"

"I did for a few years," he said. "It was my grandmother's house."

He grabbed the saddlebags from the back of the bike and led me through the broken gate to an overgrown garden lush with plants and flowers, and fragrant with a mix of rich earth and floral perfume. A crumbling flagstone patio, partially hidden by ground cover, gradually transitioned to a grassy lawn. Tall trees and bushes along the worn wooden fence hid us from the outside world.

"This is amazing," I said, trying to capture every detail through the soft glow of the streetlights. "It's like a hidden oasis."

"My grandmother planted probably seventy or eighty species of plants." Jack put down his bags. "She taught me how to nurture them and help them grow. I believed her when she said there was magic in the garden. I'd come out here when I had a problem, and after a few hours with my hands in the dirt, I'd find the answer. I was more myself here than anywhere else."

Jack walked me through the garden, naming plants and flowers with dizzying speed: blue spruce, hydrangea, and boxwood gave winter interest to the garden. Quaking aspen and Boston ivy grew along the fence. Pink Spike and Crimson Queen Japanese maple added colorful purple foliage along with First Love speedwell and panicled hydrangea. "These plants are fighters," he said. "Even without any nurturing, they've managed to flourish. They do what it takes to survive. My grandmother would have been proud that her garden has endured."

"Where is she now?" I asked when he knelt beside one of the flower beds.

"Gone." His voice tightened and he carefully dug up a bunch of pink flowers. "A developer bought all the houses on this street. They're going to be torn down and replaced with condos. I asked my cousin to set up a small greenhouse for me at his nursery so I could save her plants. One day, I'll re-create her garden."

I worked with him for the next half hour, digging up the plants and putting them in plastic bags with damp paper towels around the roots. I'd never been a plant person. My parents didn't have time for a garden, and even if they did, it would have been destroyed by my brothers, who loved to play ball and wrestle on the back lawn.

"It must have been hard for her to leave this," I said into the silence.

"She didn't have a choice." Jack's hand tightened around the trowel. "She was a librarian at the local high school, struggling to make ends meet, especially after I came to live with her. She was worried she'd lose the house, so she borrowed money from a man she thought was a legitimate lender. He took a lien on the house and then charged her an exorbitant rate of interest. She couldn't keep up with the payments, and one day two of his guys showed up and told us to get out."

My heart squeezed in my chest. Chloe had almost faced a similar situation before she found her white hat hacking side hustle. "How old were you?"

"Thirteen," he said. "Old enough to think I could do something. Too young to understand the danger." He dropped the trowel and bent his head. "I tried to kick them out. My grandmother intervened and one of the men pushed her down the front steps. She hit her head on a paving stone and never woke up. His voice caught, broke. "If I hadn't picked a fight . . ."

I felt an ache in my throat and wrapped my arms around his bent shoulders. "It's not your fault. You were just a kid."

Jack shook me off and returned to his digging. "I found out later the man who loaned her the money was a shady real estate developer," he continued. "He'd started the loan business for the sole purpose of doing what he did to my grandmother so he could acquire the huge blocks of land he needed for his developments at a low cost. She wasn't the only person on the block who lost her home, but she was the only one who died."

My heart went out to the boy he'd been and the burden of guilt he'd been carrying all these years. "Did you tell the police?"

"A neighbor called them when she saw my grandmother lying on the ground. The two men told the paramedics it was an accident and she'd fallen down the stairs. No one believed me when I said she'd been pushed. I'm pretty sure the developer paid someone off to make it all go away. He had a lot of power and was owed a lot of favors." He ran his hand through his hair, leaving a little streak of dirt on his forehead. "The last time I visited her grave was fifteen years ago. I made her a promise then that I would avenge her, and I still intend to make that happen."

"What happened to you after she died?" I asked. "Where were your parents?"

"I lost them when I was eight years old, which is why I was staying with her. I had no other family, so it was foster care for me, and when that didn't work out, I wound up on the street."

"She's why you know *Oliver Twist*," I said, putting the pieces together.

"I went to the library every day after school to wait until she finished work. She thought it was better if I was surrounded in books than sitting at home alone in front of the TV."

"She sounds like a wonderful person," I said. "She must have loved you very much."

Jack picked up his bags and looked around the garden. "I won't have time to save them all. I've taken pictures to re-create her design, but it won't be the same."

"How about this one?" I pointed to a graceful, feathery vine with small, delicate, star-shaped red blooms.

"That's a cypress vine," he said. "*Ipomoea quamoclit*. It's an escapee and not native to her garden. People think it's an annual, but with a little help from nature, its self-seeding ability means it can pop up in new places year after year and thrive far away from its original home."

Something niggled at the back of my mind. If the vine could escape and start over again somewhere new, why couldn't a person? If Jack's grandmother's plants were strong enough to survive neglect, why couldn't I? Maybe there was a way to save both Bella and Chloe. Maybe the heist wasn't over after all.

Jack put an arm around me, and we walked to his bike. "Now you know more about me than anyone else."

"Now you're just semi-mysterious and a little bit human."

"Little?" He lifted an eyebrow. "That's not what you said earlier when you were being a wicked girl."

Wicked. I liked it. Much better than "good."

"Take me back to your hotel and I'll show you wicked." I grabbed my helmet and yanked it over my head.

"I like this new you," Jack said.

I liked this new me, too. I didn't give up and I didn't give in. I was a fighter. I was in control. When bad things happened, I found a way around them. And now I had a plan.

I just had to find a way to convince the crew to steal a $25 million necklace from the mob and kidnap a mob boss's daughter.

TWENTY-ONE

◇ ◇ ◇

Here's a helpful tip. If you're planning a heist involving the Mafia, make sure you find a crew who are heavily in debt.

"How much was the reward?" Emma asked after I'd shared the big reveal—Mafia, forced marriage, sadistic groom—and my new plan—steal the necklace and help Bella escape—over beer and wings in Rose's garage the next night.

"That would be $833,333.33 each," Anil said. "We were also offered $250,000 to plan the wedding divided by six, which is another $41,666.67 each, for a grand total of $875,000 per person."

"You scare me when you do that math-in-your-head thing," Emma said. "It's not natural."

"I totally understand if anyone wants to drop out," I said. "The Mafia aspect adds another level of danger, and helping Bella escape raises it up another notch. I still don't have a concrete plan for Bella, but I'm thinking of fake kidnapping her during the wedding." I hesitated, waiting for the thunder of feet as everyone ran for the door. When that didn't happen, I said, "I'm still willing to go ahead and so is Jack but—"

"I'm in," Chloe said. "You started this for me, and now we're going to help Bella, too. I can't believe it's even a question."

"What about Olivia?" I countered. "You've seen the movies, read the news. These guys go after families when they're pissed off. I don't think you should take the risk."

"If I don't take the risk, I might wind up in jail," she said. "If I don't wind up in jail, we might wind up on the street. Some days I try to breathe, and I can't get the air in. I'm almost thirty, and I'm still in the place I was when I earned minimum wage. At the very worst, I know Kyle's parents would look after her, or even my mom if it doesn't work out with them, but this is a chance at a better life for us. I have to take it."

"I'm in," Gage said. "Nothing has changed for me except it just got more interesting."

"What's a little danger between friends?" Emma grabbed another wing. "Seriously, it's worth the risk for a chance to get my life started. I've been waiting for adulthood to kick in for the last decade. My rent takes over half my income. I haven't had a steady job in forever and I've never seen a positive number in my savings account. I don't know why I even opened one. Plus, you need a driver, and no one is better than me."

I fist-bumped her across the table, still trying to process the fact that we still had over half our crew.

"You trusted me with the most important job of carrying the necklace," Anil said. "My mom doesn't even trust me to do the laundry. My parents don't think I can find my own wife. Even at work, they won't promote me even though I'm more qualified than many of the upper-level managers because they think I'm too young. At the rate I'm going, I'll still be living at home, trying to pay off my loans, twenty years from now and The Butcher will still be a dream. I won't let you down. I'm in."

"Dude." Gage ruffled Anil's hair. It was the most affection I'd ever seen him show, except around Chloe.

"I'm out," Cristian said when we all looked to him. "It was bad enough when I found out I'd slept with Angelini's wife—and before you judge me, she told me she was divorced. But now I find out I've slept with the wife of a Mafia boss. Those guys don't play games. I have to look out for myself. I can't take the risk she'll expose me." He folded his arms over his *There is no Planet B* T-shirt. "I'm not strong like you. I couldn't even handle six months of rejection after college when I tried to find work. I went back to my high school job at Pizza Plus to pay off my debt and then tried a bunch of side gigs before I started life coaching and working at Simi's dad's store. Now my degree is almost eight years old, and I have no relevant experience. That money would be a game changer, but not if I'm dead."

"It won't be the same without you," I said, and I meant it.

"I wasn't even supposed to be here." Cristian pushed his chair back. "I scammed my way in. You won't even notice I'm gone."

"I'll notice." Emma stood and held out her hand. "You'll be missed, especially if we go boating again."

His face crumpled—half laughter, half pain—but he shook her hand. "Good luck, everyone. I hope it all works out."

After Cristian had gone, I went to tell Rose the news. Of course, a little mob boss danger didn't put her off.

"I'm still available as a grease woman if you need me." She poured a cup of tea and added two biscuits to the saucer. "Who's going to take over his job at the rehearsal dinner? Your plan won't work if someone doesn't take away the Angelinis' phones."

"I was thinking of asking Emma. She'll be there anyway."

"You're going to let Emma loose on that crowd?" Rose chuckled. "You won't need anyone to tell you when they're leaving because it'll be about five minutes after she opens her mouth."

"We don't have any options. I need everyone else doing the job I've set them to do."

"Then use me," she said. "Theater has been my life. I'm sure I can keep some mafiosos entertained."

"It's too dangerous," I said. "I couldn't let you take the risk."

"Sweetheart, I'm eighty years old." Rose sipped her tea. "I've done a lot of living. Now it's all about finding new experiences, and nothing can top pulling off a heist to rob a Mafia boss. If I have to go, then it might as well be in a blaze of glory and a story that will be passed down through the generations. I don't want my obituary to read, 'She passed away peacefully in a rest home.' I want it to say, 'She was gunned down trying to escape from a bloodthirsty mob boss,' or 'She was found in Lake Michigan encased in cement.'"

"How about 'She pulled off the heist of the century netting an eight-hundred-seventy-five-thousand-dollar windfall that she used to decorate her basement suite for her long-term tenant?'"

When her eyes widened, I said, "You'll get Cristian's cut if we succeed, and I won't take 'no' for an answer. You may have enough to get by, but it's always nice to have more."

Rose grinned. "I'll take those odds."

"You'd also have to manage the caterers at the wedding," I said. "That was also part of Cristian's job."

"I'll bring Chef Pierre," Rose said. "I'm sure he won't mind switching days with Stan."

"Then welcome to the crew." I gave her a hug. "Officially."

◇ ◇ ◇

I pulled Gage aside after we'd all finished a round of whiskey to officially welcome Rose to her new role.

"Do you have a minute?"

His gaze flicked to Chloe, who was catching a ride in Emma's Uber.

"No."

"We both know you're going to follow her home," I said. "There are only two reasons why you would do so. First, you're stalking her. If that's the case, you'll have to deal with me, and I am well versed in the punching arts, thanks to my brothers. I hit Kyle in the face so hard, he had a black eye for weeks. He had to take time off his IT job because he couldn't see the tiny numbers on the screen. I also head-butted and kicked a mob boss's son yesterday morning. So there's also that."

Gage gave me blank stare, but I knew my words were getting through from the twitch of his lips. "Not a stalker," he said. "Also not scared of your weak-ass punches."

"Well then, the second reason you'd be following her is that you like her. If that's the case, you should tell her. She's not a mind reader. I know you've been over there a few times already, but she still doesn't know how you feel. Friday night is spaghetti night, and there is always more than enough to go round. If you show up at her door, I'm sure she would be happy to feed you, and then you can have a heartfelt conversation."

"Again, noted," he said. "But I'm not going in. I'm just there to keep her safe."

"You gave her a top-of-the-line security system," I protested. "You know she'll be safe."

"He's been there three times in the last week," Gage said. "I caught him on the security camera. He doesn't park or get out, just does a slow drive-by and then he's gone."

My breath left me in a rush. "Kyle was there? Is he still angry with Chloe about the child support? Or about you beating his ass? We should call the police."

"The police will just warn him and let him go," Gage said. "They're not gonna look after her and Olivia the way I can."

I stared at Gage for a long time. I knew exactly how he would keep her safe. I'd seen his guns, watched him in action, heard about the way he'd bounced Kyle down the stairs. A few weeks ago, I would have been appalled at what I was hearing. But now, after all we'd been through, it didn't seem so bad. I wasn't afraid now to break a few rules, especially when it came to Chloe and Olivia.

"Make him suffer."

"I will."

His fierce determination to protect Chloe jogged my memory about another bad dude who deserved a taste of what was coming to Kyle. "What about the guy who is responsible for this whole mess? The online contractor who set her up? Do you think you could find him and hurt him, too?"

Gage gave me a curt nod. I liked that about him. There were no wasted words. No questions. No shock or horror that good girl Simi was now setting guys up to pay for their crimes in pain.

"Do you need me to get any information? Chloe remembers his handle, but I think the real thief is your best lead. He was in the museum, and he took the necklace to Angelini. He'd be easier to find than an online ghost. If we could identify him . . ."

"I know a guy."

"Of course you do." I hesitated, then said, "When you find the dude who set her up, could I have five minutes in a room with him before you do what you do?"

"No problem."

"You're good people, Gage. Go have some spaghetti."

He grunted a response that I couldn't decipher. Not that it mattered. Chloe was safe. And by the end of the week, if all went well, she'd be free.

◇ ◇ ◇

"I saw you talking to Gage. What was that all about?" Jack asked, following me to my basement suite, whiskey bottle in hand. I'd left some clothes and personal items behind, and I wanted to take them home before the construction started.

"I threatened him. I told him he'd better not hurt Chloe, or he'd have to answer to me."

"I always knew you had a violent streak." He sat on my bed, the only place left to sit now that the furniture had been removed and the floor stripped down to bare concrete. "It turns me on."

"Everything turns you on." Wicked and violent. Jack liked his girls bad.

"Only when it comes to you."

I pulled open the closet and grabbed a sports bag from the top shelf. "I'm pretty sure he likes her," I said. "What do you think?"

"I can't even begin to try and understand the inner workings of Gage's mind."

"But you're friends."

"Of a sort." He shrugged. "We've worked a few jobs together. Gage and I have a 'don't ask, don't tell' kind of relationship." He leaned back and folded his arms behind his head. "Let's talk about it some more after you've taken off your clothes and seduced me."

"Seduction is the last thing on my mind now that you've told me you don't know much about Gage." My voice rose in pitch. "I thought you two were friends. I just told Gage to tell Chloe how he feels." My words tumbled out of my mouth, unstoppable, unfiltered as my anxiety turned to fear. "What if he's not a good guy? What if they hook up and she gets hurt? Chloe can't go through that. Not again."

Jack got up and wrapped his arms around me, pulling me into his chest. "Gage would never let anything happen to Chloe. She is 100 percent safe with him."

"You said you didn't know how he felt," I mumbled into his chest. His arms were warm and firm, his heartbeat strong and steady.

"I know he protects the people he loves." His voice deepened, his arm tightening around me. "I know when a man meets a beautiful, smart, capable woman, especially one who dazzles him with her wedding/heist organizing chops, fierce loyalty, and mad fighting skills, he would do anything to keep her safe."

"Humph." My pulse kicked up a notch, but this time it wasn't anxiety making my heart pound.

"Are we done talking about other men?" His lips eased mine apart for the slow, sensual sweep of his tongue.

"Maybe. If I were lying down, I'd be able to think more clearly."

With a chuckle, Jack lifted me against his hips and carried me to the bed. "There's only one name I want to hear on your lips."

"Carsen? Oscar? Trey? Bryce? Nathan?" I should have known better than to tease when he was laser-focused on the task at hand. The look he gave me, carnal and intense, made me shiver.

"Jack. Say it." He ripped open my blouse, sending buttons pattering across the floor like raindrops.

"You ruined my blouse, Jack." I tried to feign annoyance, but I was almost vibrating with excitement. No man had ever wanted me so badly he'd torn off my clothes.

His dark eyes smoldered. "I want to ruin you in every way a woman can be ruined."

"Does that mean you've been seduced?" I reached for his shirt and pulled him down.

"You didn't have to seduce me," Jack said. "I was yours the moment we met."

◇ ◇ ◇

I woke in the middle of the night to the sound of gravel crunching outside the window of the basement suite, the low murmur of voices, and then a thud on the door.

"Jack, you bastard. Open up." The man outside didn't sound very happy. Other words came to mind: angry, sinister, menacing, terrifying. Not the kind of words you want associated with a man who is trying to break down your door.

Jack moved with almost preternatural speed. He leaped off the bed, yanked on his jeans and T-shirt, and stepped into his shoes. By the time my body had caught up with my brain, the front door was splintering, and Jack was flying past me.

"Gotta run, sweetheart." He shoved my jeans into my hand, kissed me hard, and sprinted for the bathroom.

"Wait for me." I instantly regretted my lack of attire. When canoodling with a thief, always wear pants. "What happened to doing anything to keep your beautiful, smart, and capable woman safe?"

He slammed the bathroom door, shouting through the wood, "They won't hurt you. They're after me."

"Seriously?" I yanked on my clothes, anger washing away my fear as I stumbled after him. "You're going to leave me alone while you hide?" I pulled on the handle to the bathroom door just as the lock clicked into place. *Bastard*.

I had just enough time to grab my phone before the front door gave way with a loud crack. Two men in hotel uniforms rushed into the room. One tall and ginger haired. The other short with an extremely unflattering beard and a slightly less unflattering mustache.

"Where's Jack?" Ginger asked.

I was tempted—so, so tempted—to tell them where he was. My mouth watered with desire, the word just dancing on my tongue. But he was part of my crew and I needed him alive for the heist. Besides, if anyone was going to kill the selfish jerk, it was me.

"I don't know any Jack," I snapped. "If you take one step closer, I'm calling the police. You'll spend the next few years in prison. You may want to run back to the hotel and grab a few bars of soap so you're ready when they catch you."

"Whoa." Mr. Mustache held up his hands, palms forward. "No need to involve the cops. We just want to talk to him."

"When I want to talk to someone, I don't break down their door." I took a few steps back, putting some distance between us. "What's this all about anyway? Is this a new thing? The hotel sends out a couple of dudes to break your legs if you forget to pay for the Pringles from the mini bar?"

I was seething now, any concern for my safety totally subsumed by utter rage. Why did Chloe get the ex-military dude who installed a freaking security system in her house, and I got the coward who ran and hid at the first sign of trouble?

"Where's the necklace?" Ginger's gaze swept over the bare room, lingered on the bag I'd filled with clothes.

"What necklace?"

His expression darkened. "You really want to play that game?"

I didn't want to play any game. I wanted Jack to come out of the bathroom and tell these dudes to get the hell out of my apartment. I wanted Gage and his guns or Chloe and her bottle of bleach. But it was just me. Alone. Abandoned. Like always.

"The only necklaces I have are from Etsy," I said. "There's a great designer from San Diego who can do incredible things with metals. Feel free to search around. You'll notice there's almost nothing here." I curled my fingers around my phone, ready to press the buttons that would automatically call 911.

"What's Etsy?" Mr. Mustache shot Ginger a questioning look. I decided he wasn't the brightest light bulb in the box, and I should focus my attention on his red-haired friend.

"She's messing with you," Ginger said. "Search the place. If it's not here, then he's got it on him, he doesn't have it yet, or he's

246 ◇ SARA DESAI

already given it to his fence. We might have to go to New York to track it down."

"New York?" Mr. Mustache and I asked at once.

"That's where the best fences are," Ginger said. "Jack's not gonna give a high-ticket item to a fence in Chicago."

"Are you kidding me?" My hands found my hips. I didn't care if we were talking baseball, basketball, pizza, hot dogs, rivers, rappers, or fences. Chicago and New York were age-old rivals, and I would defend my city to the death. "We have the best stuff in Chicago, and because we have the best stuff, we also have the best criminals, and the best criminals need the best fences. The criminals in New York come here looking for fences. Our fences don't need to travel. New Yorkers come to them."

"I think she's saying he got a local fence," Mr. Mustache said to Ginger.

"I'm standing right the fuck here," Ginger said. "We're all speaking the same language. I don't need a translator." He pulled out a gun and motioned me away from the bathroom. "Get away from the door."

Maybe that kind of thing works in New York, but we are born tough in Chicago. Floods, snowpocalypses, killer waves, heat waves, frigid temperatures, tornadoes, twenty-four-hour traffic jams, gunfights, fistfights, and one hundred eight years without winning a world series. Nothing can rattle us. If only one city is left standing in a postapocalyptic world, it will be Chicago.

"Why are you pointing a gun at me?" I shouted again so Jack would know that my life was now at risk. "Have you even thought it through? He's such a coward, he's probably already gone, so you're gonna shoot me for nothing and spend the rest of your lives in jail, and that's only if my bestie's new boyfriend doesn't find you first. And he will come looking because she'll be devastated that I'm dead and he protects the people he loves, even from sadness. This guy is so scary, there is no line he won't cross. He does the work other people don't want to do, and I'm not talking about working retail."

"He's gotta be back there," Ginger said, ignoring my outburst. "Get out of the way."

"Come any closer and I'll call 911," I warned, bending down to pick up a warped floorboard. I was done with these morons. Done with trusting people to have my back. Done with even hoping someone would actually stick around when I needed them.

Ginger let out a string of curse words and snapped at Mr. Mustache. "Check behind the fucking door."

I held out my free hand and motioned them forward like I'd seen in the movies. Of course, in the movies the good guy is "the One" or has some secret martial arts or military fight skills. I had a floorboard with nails sticking out of it, and it wasn't even straight.

"Are you fucking kidding me?" Mr. Mustache said. "I'm not going near her. She's crazy."

Crazy? I'd show them crazy.

"Rah." I lifted my floorboard and charged at them, screaming my frustration. Ginger stumbled back and tripped over the broken door. Mr. Mustache bolted. I ran after them until they jumped into a black Chrysler 300C and roared down the street.

I was still heaving in my breaths when I noticed Jack's motorcycle was gone. He'd climbed out the window like the cowardly slug he was. I texted Gage and told him to add Jack to the list of people who deserved to suffer, then I grabbed my bag and went to see Rose.

◆ ◆ ◆

"It was too much," I said over tea and Chef Pierre's peanut-free twist on peanut butter brownies. "Not just the men breaking into my apartment and pointing a gun at me, but Jack running away and leaving me. My whole life I've been overlooked or left behind. I thought he was different. I thought I'd found someone who would have my back, someone who cared, someone who would protect me the way Gage looks out for Chloe. But he left. Just like everyone else."

I was lucky to have caught Rose on one of her rare nights in, and even more lucky that she'd been up watching *Columbo* because she'd had a double espresso after lunch.

"Not everyone needs protecting," Rose said. "It sounds to me like you were quite capable of handling those goons on your own. When you are that competent and self-sufficient, people don't realize you want or even need their help. It's not easy, but sometimes you need to speak up. You have to ask for what you want and tell people how you feel."

"You are very wise," I said to Rose.

"If I were wise, I wouldn't have eaten an entire plate of peanut-free peanut butter brownies right before bed." She patted my hand. "Even at my age, people make mistakes."

"I seem to make more than most, especially when it comes to men."

"That means you're taking risks, and taking risks means you're finally out there living your life. You've been so busy trying to make other people happy, you've never really had a chance to figure out who you really are. Tonight you learned something about yourself. You chased those men away. You don't need the stability and security someone like Gage offers. His overprotective nature would be too much. You need . . ."

"Chaos?"

"Adventure," she said. "Challenge. Independence. If you're looking for a partner, find someone who isn't afraid to break the rules, someone who is fun and exciting and just as curious about the world as you are. You need a partner, not a protector. Someone who will embrace all the things that make you the unique and beautiful soul you are."

"Too bad I don't know anyone like that." I dabbed at my eyes with a napkin. I'd forgotten how insightful Rose could be. "I only know people who run away at the first sign of danger."

"It is too bad," she said. "Because it would be very entertaining to hear him grovel."

I liked the idea of Jack groveling. I liked it so much I fell asleep on Rose's couch mentally listing all the things I would make him do to earn my forgiveness.

Lucky for Jack, I was so exhausted I didn't make it past ten.

Unlucky for me, Jack wasn't the groveling type.

TWENTY-TWO

❖ ❖ ❖

Despite the fact that I was running on only a few hours' sleep, the wedding rehearsal at the Angelinis' mansion went as smoothly as a wedding rehearsal could go when the bride was being forced into marriage with a cruel and sinister groom who happened to be the son of a New York crime boss. Beefy bodyguards wearing menacing scowls and ill-fitting suits wandered around pretending they weren't packing some serious firepower and just itching to stick someone's head in a vice or grab an ice pick and skewer a couple of eyeballs. I dealt with a bridesmaid and groomsman who kept sneaking off to practice their "horizontal tango," a flower girl who threw a tantrum every five minutes, a priest who kept falling asleep, a crying bride, a glaring groom, unfriendly Rottweilers, overly friendly "uncles," warm champagne, cold pasta, and a swarm of bees—real ones, not drones. It was pretty tame compared to the drama of a South Asian wedding rehearsal, so I chalked it up as a win before giving the wedding party directions to the post-rehearsal dinner in Chicago's city center.

After that, everything went according to plan. Bella was fine with us leaving the van parked out front. Emma picked us up in the limo and drove around for forty minutes, then we all hid on the floor when she returned to the house to pick up Bella and her family for the rehearsal dinner.

"I'm half an hour early," Emma said, leaning over the seat. "I've parked three feet from the van in the camera blind spot. The guards are shooting the shit on the steps. I'll let you know as soon as they're gone, and you can make the switch."

It seemed to me, squeezed between Gage and Anil on the limo floor, that this part of the heist could have used a little more thought.

"What's that lump?" I arched my back, trying to put some distance between Anil's hips and my ass.

"Ski masks," Anil said, leaving me both disappointed and relieved at once. "I brought one for each of us. I also brought surgical gloves, so we don't leave fingerprints."

"The gloves are a good idea, but Chloe will be shutting off the cameras. We don't need ski masks."

"It's better to take precautions," he said. "What if Chloe's hack fails? What if they have a secret battery-operated camera in the room? What if the security guards get past Gage and find—"

"Not going to happen." Gage rolled to his back and pulled out his gun. "No one is getting past me."

"What part of 'this is a no-weapon heist' did you not understand?" I asked him.

"The part where we got shot at on the lake." He holstered his gun. "If it makes you feel better, it's for self-defense."

"As opposed to what?" I couldn't keep the sarcasm from my tone. "Cold-blooded murder?"

"I vote 'yes' for ski masks," Jack said. He was stretched out on the seat above me. I didn't trust myself anywhere near him. Just the sight of his handsome face made my blood boil. Between work and finalizing all the details for the wedding on Saturday, I hadn't had time for anyone over the last four days, and especially not the man who had abandoned me and then didn't even have the decency to call.

"Tell that person beside you no one cares what he thinks," I told Chloe.

She cut her gaze to Jack. "Simi doesn't care what you think."

"Ask him who were the two men in hotel uniforms who broke into my apartment and threatened me with a gun while he hid in the bathroom like the pathetic coward he is."

"Simi wants to know—"

"I heard her," Jack said, his voice laced with amusement. "They were after the necklace, which means we can't fail today."

"Tell him the only reason he's alive right now is because we need him to open the safe, but the minute we've got the necklace, all bets are off," I said. "And tell him he'll have to beg for my forgiveness and do a lot of groveling because he didn't even bother to contact me to see if I was okay."

Chloe leaned over the seat. "Simi says—"

"I heard her." Jack sighed. "I had to get out of town and couldn't risk any communication."

"Christ," Gage muttered. "Are we going to have to deal with your lovers' squabble for the entire heist?"

"We aren't lovers," I spat out. "We aren't friends. We're temporary coworkers. As soon as this is done, I hope never to see him again."

"But first he's going to pay," Chloe said. "I bought zip ties, a bucket, a hunting knife, pliers, bleach, and a mop this morning. No one hurts my girl—emotionally or physically—and gets away with it."

"Bleach?" Gage pushed himself up on one elbow, his forehead creased in a frown.

"It's multipurpose," Chloe said. "It can clean, sanitize, take out stains, blind you, and it's toxic if consumed."

"You two scare me." Gage lay down again. "Remind me never to piss you off."

"You won't need a reminder," I said. "You can remember the sound of Jack's screams and see his shriveled corpse before I bury him in a shallow grave." I looked over at Chloe. "We'll need a shovel."

"I decided to get Prime since we're going to be rich," she said. "We'll have it tomorrow."

"I have a rule about getting involved with coworkers," Emma said. "Too many complications. I was the utility person in a NAS-CAR pit crew a few years back. We went for drinks after a big race. One thing led to another and there I was in bed with four race car drivers. That led to a lot of drama on race day. Fights broke out. Someone lost a leg. You know how it goes."

"How does it go?" Anil asked. "Was it a super king or California king? Or did you all fit in a normal king-size bed? That wouldn't work for me because I'm an active sleeper. Last week my mom came to wake me for work and my pillows were on the floor and I was sleeping upside down."

"Bats sleep upside down," Gage said. "So do sloths and manatees."

"Gage watches a lot of Animal Planet," Chloe said, her eyes going soft.

Jack shifted beside me. "I'm interested in Emma's orgy."

"The point wasn't the sex," Emma said. "It was the bladder infection I got the next day. I was pissing fire. I had to go to the hospital, and I couldn't be there to take the protective film off the windshield, and the driver spun out and crashed. Dude suffered a temporary loss of hearing, so I didn't bother apologizing when I went to see him in the hospital. I mean, what was the point? It's not like he could read lips with his eyes all bandaged from the burns. And really, he should have been apologizing to me. Someone didn't wash their junk before playing monkeys in the bed and I was pretty sure it was him. That's what we call karma."

"I learn so much from you," Anil said. "I've made a mental note to shower before having relations with my future wife."

"The guards are gone." Emma looked back at Chloe. "Can you use your fancy setup to see where they are?"

"I've piggybacked on to the outdoor camera feed," Chloe said. "They're around the back of the house starting their circuit. It's go time."

We scrambled to transfer vehicles. Only moments after Gage had closed the van door, I heard Emma call out, "Hello, everyone. Don't you all look lovely tonight."

"Damn," Gage said. "That was close."

Our serial killer wedding van had no windows in the back, but still my heart pounded until doors had slammed, the limo engine had roared, and the crunch of wheels on gravel had faded into the distance.

"Breathe," Jack murmured beside me. "They're gone."

"Chloe, tell this dude that any communication with me should be limited solely to heist operations."

"Don't speak to Simi about anything other than the heist." Chloe pushed to sit and opened the laptop on her knees. "One guard is walking the perimeter. The other one is still near the house. Rose is on her way to the restaurant to set up the phone-stealing trivia game. She'll be ready to go when everyone arrives."

Rose had practiced the trivia party game several times with a group of friends. She figured we would only have about twenty minutes to find the safe before people got bored and started asking for their phones.

"Since we have some time, can we talk about what happened the other night?" Jack asked.

"No." I would have preferred not to talk to him directly, but I didn't want to distract Chloe from her work.

"I knew they wouldn't hurt you," he said. "They're professionals."

I didn't want to ask, but curiosity is an insatiable beast. "Professional what? Enforcers? Bellhops? I think one of them had a name tag that said CONCIERGE. I didn't know debt collection was part of the job description. Or holding an innocent person at gunpoint."

He had the good grace to look somewhat discomfited. "Gage was on his way. I texted him from the bathroom. You weren't unprotected."

"Gage." I spat out the name. "Not you." Desperate for a distraction from Jack and his sexy cowardly weasel voice, I turned to Anil. "Do you have the replica?"

"Right here." Anil patted the canvas bag he'd slung over his shoulder. "I researched the real necklace after our practice heist. Did you know it has no published provenance, but the Indian government claims it was a gift to a queen from her lover and stolen from a temple in Rajasthan? It's been off the grid since it was bought at auction."

We spent the rest of our time in the van listening to Anil recount the story of the young queen who had fallen in love with her bodyguard but had been forced into a political marriage to save her realm. It made me even more determined to save Bella from the same fate.

My phone finally dinged with a message from Rose. "She's got the phones," I said to Chloe. "Everyone put on your gloves and masks. It's heist time."

◇ ◇ ◇

"I read all about safes and how to hide them in preparation for our venture. We should check the office and the master bedroom first." Anil followed me up the front steps, chattering away. I could barely hear him over the pounding of my heart. It just felt wrong to brazenly walk through the front door even though Chloe had deactivated the cameras and the alarm. I would have been more comfortable crawling in a window.

We took off our masks once we were inside. Gage went to make sure no one was in the house, while Jack searched the lower floor. Anil and I headed upstairs and went straight to the master bedroom. Unlike the rest of the house, which was light and bright and decorated in white and cream, the master was all dark wood and heavy fabrics in shades of navy and gold.

"Safes are usually hidden behind paintings, mirrors, air vents, and in floors—places easily accessible to owners, but also hidden from view," Anil said. "You can also build a secret room in your house behind a bookshelf. I saw a YouTube video about it. When I get my money, I'm going to buy a house and install a secret room like that."

"What are you going to put in it?" I tugged on the air vent and peered inside. "I can't imagine owning anything so expensive that I'd need to keep it in a safe or secret room."

"My most valuable possession is a USB stick containing my first Minecraft skin," he said. "Then the sky's the limit. I've got my eye on an ultra-rare Black Lotus *Magic: The Gathering* card that gives more mana, allowing for more summons and spells."

"Dude, you gotta up your game if you want a wife." Gage walked into the bedroom, all cool and casual like he had nothing better to do. "How about some jewels, bonds, and suitcases full of cash?"

"I take it your unwelcome presence means your first task is completed," I said. "You are now supposed to be keeping watch outside."

"Chloe has access to the external cameras. She'll let us know if anyone approaches the house. I thought I'd be more help inside, and I was right. Anil has no idea about what people keep in a safe."

"Maybe not, but I know how to find one." Anil lifted a painting of a seaside town from the wall to reveal a small, gray wall safe. "Just like on YouTube. It's disappointing they didn't put in more effort."

I sent Gage to find Jack, and as soon as they were both upstairs, Chloe unjammed the system and texted Rose to let her know she could return the phones. Then it was one full hour of watching Jack turn the dial back and forth while Anil gave us a running commentary.

"He's using the stethoscope to listen for the sound the drive cam notch makes when it slides under the lever arm," Anil whispered. "I've watched lots of lock-picking and safecracking YouTube videos, but it's fascinating to see it in real life. I can't believe I get to watch a master at work."

"Don't say things like that," I warned. "His ego is already so big I have to step around it."

"Three." Jack wrote something on the notepad he'd placed on the side table in front of him.

"That's a good thing," Anil said. "A three-digit combination will only require a maximum of 162 attempts. If there were four numbers, we'd be looking at a maximum of 1,944. Jack will have to map the dial in increments of three. Once he has the numbers, he can try different combinations."

"Good thing Emma's not here or your math genius skills

would freak her out." Gage walked around the room, opening drawers and cupboards.

"What are you doing?" I closed all the drawers he'd left open.

"Seeing how the other half lives."

I grabbed Gage's hand when he reached for the nightstand drawer. "How about we don't invade their privacy more than we have to?"

"I'm bored."

"Why don't you shoot the safe so we can get out of here faster?"

"He can't shoot it," Anil said. "It's a Gardall 3018-2 with a four-and-a-quarter-inch anti-pry door and two-and-a-half-inch safe walls, furnace-tested up to 1850 degrees."

"You got all that from looking at the door?"

"The name is on the front. I looked up the rest on my phone. And I have an eidetic memory. Line two of the marriage résumé. Didn't you read it?"

"No. You were sprung on me as a surprise," I said. "But for future reference, I'd move that . . . um . . . selling feature further down the list. No one wants to get into an argument with a partner who can repeat back what they said word for word."

"I hope you're not referring to me." Jack made a mark on the graph he'd drawn in his notebook. "I didn't make any promises."

"Of course not," I snapped. "You didn't have time for promises. You were too busy running out the door with your ass hanging out of your pants."

I checked in with Rose. She'd returned the phones after the game, and no one appeared to have received any alarming notifications. I hoped that meant they'd bought the idea that there had been a system glitch.

"I've got the numbers." Jack nodded at Anil. "Start giving me possible combinations."

Forty-five painful minutes went by with Anil giving numbers

and Jack twisting the dial. I jumped up and down, fiddled with the zipper on my jacket, tied and untied my shoes, counted the number of flowers on the heavy brocade curtains, and pulled out pieces of my hair to inspect for split ends.

"You gotta chill." Gage sprawled on an armchair, feet up on the footstool, arms folded behind his head.

"I am chilled," I snapped. "This is me chilled. I am so chilled, I could be ice. No one is as chilled as me."

"Take a break, Frosty. Go for a walk. We'll call you if something happens."

"I'm the boss. Don't tell me what to do." I looked at the open door. A walk was just what I needed. "I've decided to go for a walk," I announced. "Call me the second something happens."

I walked up and down the hallway, checking out the ultra-posh bedrooms, library, and sitting room. A small stairway at the end of the hall led down behind the kitchen to a side exit. An idea cut through the noise in my anxiety-riddled brain and I raced back to the bedroom.

"I know how we'll help Bella escape!"

Before I could share my idea, my phone dinged with a message from Rose. "They've finished eating," I told the crew. "Mr. Angelini is getting antsy to leave. Rose says he's in the hallway on his phone. I've told her to do something to keep them entertained."

"One hundred eleven numbers to go," Anil said. "It could be any one now."

"One hundred eleven?" My body vibrated with tension. Jack turned the dial. My phone dinged again.

"Chloe says someone is walking outside the van," I reported. "The guards aren't supposed to be there for at least ten more minutes. Do you think Angelini called them about the glitch?"

Ding.

"Rose is going to give a speech celebrating the marriage."

Ding.

"They didn't want to hear her speech. She's going to try singing a song from *West Side Story*. She was Maria's second under-
study in the 1980 Broadway revival."

Ding.

"Chloe hears two sets of footsteps near the van. She says she's
got her gun ready." My breath caught in my throat. "Wait. What
gun? Where did she get a gun?"

"I gave it to her," Gage said. "I couldn't leave her alone in the
van unprotected."

I stared at him aghast. "How many guns did you bring?"

By way of answer, Gage just grinned.

"One hundred three combinations left to try," Anil said. "Or
we could get lucky, and it might be the next one."

Ding.

"They didn't seem to like show tunes so now she's going to
sing Massive Attack's 'Teardrop.'" My fingers flew over my
screen. "How does she know the words to that song? It's not appropriate for a rehearsal dinner."

Ding.

"Chloe says the two guards are talking beside the van. They
didn't get a message, but one of them is having marital problems.
His wife caught him cheating and wants a divorce."

Ding.

"Rose is going to sing 112's 'Anywhere.' Why is she singing
these songs? She's eighty years old. Did someone give her a list of
the raunchiest songs of all time?"

Ding.

"There's a pole in the restaurant. She's going to sing and pole
dance like in the video. Someone shoot me now. Gage . . ."

Ding.

"Chloe said the guard's wife was cheating with the other

guard. He says he loves her and the other guy can't give her what she needs."

Ding.

"Rose's arthritis is acting up so she couldn't finish the pole dance. She's going to sing The Weeknd's 'What You Need' instead. Just what they don't need to hear. A dirty song about infidelity right before the wedding."

Ding.

"The guards are fighting right beside the van. One of them slammed the other into the door. The dogs are there. They're sniffing at the van."

Ding.

Ding.

Ding.

"Someone do something," I pleaded. "My brain is going to explode."

"Got it!" Jack grabbed the handle of the safe and we all rushed over as he pulled open the door.

"It's empty." My heart sank in my chest. "Why is it empty? Who has an empty safe in their bedroom? Is there a false bottom?" I ran my hand over the carpeted shelf. "Is it an illusion? What about their passports? Mrs. Angelini was wearing a diamond necklace the other day and a diamond tennis bracelet. Where are they?" I ran over to the dresser and pulled open a drawer. "Did we miss something?"

"I already checked the drawers," Gage said from his chair. "Also, the nightstands when you were marathon training in the hallway. Three vibrators on her side. No wonder she needed a 'life coach.'"

"There must be another safe," Anil said. "This one must be a diversion in case the police or FBI show up. That's why it was so easy to find."

"Are you kidding me?" My voice rose in pitch. "We don't have time to look for another safe. Rose is planning to sing 50 Cent's 'Candy Shop' next and then Salt-n-Pepa's 'Push It.' She'll get thrown out of the restaurant and we'll be going to jail for nothing."

"If she can buy us ten minutes with another trivia game, we can get Chloe to shut down the system again," Jack said. "She has to do it anyway for us to get out. It just means a longer delay before the system goes back on. At the very least, we should be able to locate the real safe, and then we can make a new plan."

His calm demeanor set my teeth on edge. This was a total disaster. There was a serious risk Chloe might go to jail. If ever there was a time for screaming and shouting and pounding fists on the walls, this was it.

"I can't make a new plan," I snapped. "The wedding is in two days. Do you know how much work I have to do? I wasn't planning to sleep, and that was before we botched this heist."

"You got us this far," Jack said. "Don't give up just yet."

"Fine." I kicked the wall and instantly regretted it when pain shot through my foot. "Ten minutes. Not a second more."

I quickly mobilized my crew. Rose initiated a new trivia game. Chloe jammed the system. Anil went to search the ground floor areas Jack had missed. Gage ran down to the walkout basement so he could get outside quickly if the guards caused any problems. That left Jack and me to search the upper floor again.

"I'm surprised you didn't run away as soon as you saw the safe was empty." I opened one dresser drawer and then another, sweeping my hands through piles of socks, underwear, and shirts. "You seem to have a strong sense of self-preservation and little ability to be part of a team."

"I told you who had the necklace," Jack said with a huff. "I brought Gage to keep you all safe. I set you up to get the wedding planning gig, and I gave you six orgasms in four hours." He lay on the floor and peered under the bed.

"Don't flatter yourself. I've had more orgasms in less time." By myself. But he didn't need to know that.

Nine minutes and no safe later, a gunshot cracked the silence. My breath caught in my lungs and I prayed it was Gage shooting and not the other way around.

Ding.

Through sheer force of will, I managed to lift my phone and read the message from Rose.

"We have to go." I shook myself, forcing my body into action. "Mr. Angelini lost his patience and abruptly ended the rehearsal dinner. They're already in the limo and on their way home. Emma's going to take a detour, but she won't be able to stall for long."

We met Anil in the front hallway. "I have good news and bad news," he said. "The good news is that I found the safe. It was in Mr. Angelini's office behind a false bookshelf just like I saw on YouTube. If I hadn't seen the video, I—"

"We don't have time." I yanked open the front door. "They're already on their way home. Tell me the bad news later."

Gage was waiting by the van. "I fired a shot over the water to distract the guards. They're both on their way to the beach, and they took the dogs with them." He opened his jacket to show his holstered weapon. "It's been a good night."

"What are you talking about?" I climbed into the van. "We failed. There's nothing good about that. All the work, all the planning, all the stress. It was all for nothing."

"We'll get $250,000 for the wedding." Chloe shifted in her seat to make room for Gage, Anil, and Jack. "And you texted that you'd figured out how to help Bella escape. That's not nothing."

"$41,666.66 each plus good karma," Anil said. "If he pays us under the table and we don't have to pay tax, it's worth even more. Ask for cash, preferably unmarked bills."

"The system is back on," Chloe said when we were all safely inside. "I'm sure he'll send the guards to check the house. Two jam alerts would worry anyone."

We lay on the floor of the van side by side in silence. Gage beside Chloe, Jack beside me, and Anil at the end.

"I'm sorry." My throat tightened, disappointment welling up in my chest. "I thought I'd anticipated all the possible outcomes."

"It's not your fault," Chloe said. "You couldn't have known Cristian would bail on us, or that Rose wouldn't be able to keep them entertained, or that Mr. Angelini would insist on leaving early, or that he would have a decoy safe. We did our best. And if I have to go to prison—"

"You will never go to prison," I told her. I would confess to the theft if I had to, although I couldn't tell her because she'd never agree.

Jack's hand slipped around my waist, and he hugged me from behind, as if he knew what I was thinking. I should have been annoyed since I still hadn't forgiven him, but we were lying on the floor of a van with two security guards running around outside, a Mafia family on the way home, no necklace, and a failed heist under our belts. Sometimes you just have to be gentle with yourself.

The atmosphere in the van was thick with disappointment and unfulfilled promise. No one spoke until the limo returned forty minutes later.

"It's over," I said into the silence.

Doors slammed, followed by the low murmur of conversation. I caught a few words, uttered by two male voices.

"Gunshot over the water . . . probably from the other side of the lake . . . boater . . . nothing out of the ordinary . . . glitch in the system."

The voices disappeared. Steps faded into the distance. Emma knocked on the door to let us know the coast was clear. Chloe did a last check of the outdoor cameras, and a few minutes later we were all in the limo and on the road.

"We didn't get it," I said when she lifted an eyebrow.

"No big surprise."

"Why is it not a surprise?" I leaned forward over the seat. "If you thought we'd missed something, why didn't you speak up?"

"The odds were against us," she said. "Too many variables. Too many things to go wrong. In my experience, things like that are doomed to fail."

"I like surprises," Anil said. "One year my family pretended they'd forgotten my birthday. I felt sad all day, but then I walked in the door and 'Surprise!' They'd invited my friends and our family for a party. It was so amazing, it made up for the bad day."

"I'd hate that," Emma said. "A whole day of feeling like shit just for ten seconds of happiness? No thank you."

Anil's smile faded so I said, "I think it sounds fun. I've always liked surprise parties."

"Why don't we have a party after the wedding to celebrate a job well done?" Anil suggested. "It may be the last time we see each other."

"I don't know if I'm going to feel like partying." I slumped in my seat. "We had one chance and we blew it. The house will be filled with people for the next two days. We'll give Bella the best wedding ever, help her escape, and then . . . I don't know. Chloe and I might have to take Olivia and disappear."

"I thought you'd have a plan," Emma said. "You always have a plan."

"Why does everyone always expect me to have a plan?" I

stared out the window, watching the trees rush by. "I don't have any special skills. I can't even hold a steady job. I'm living in my parents' basement, drowning in debt, and working for my dad. Are those the kind of qualities you need in a leader? I don't think so. No wonder it failed."

"Babe . . ." Chloe reached out, but I pulled away.

"Don't. I want to wallow in my misery. Alone."

That was how it was supposed to be. None of this—the crew, the heist, the wedding, the dreams of getting out of debt and following my passion—was real. It had been a stupid fantasy. If I closed my eyes, I'd probably wake up in Kansas.

TWENTY-THREE

◆ ◆ ◆

couldn't even look at Cristian the next morning at the store. Every time I heard his voice, I couldn't help but wonder what would have happened if he'd been at the restaurant instead of Rose. Would he have been able to convince the wedding party to stay long enough for us to open the second safe?

"Hey, baby." He sidled up to me when I was in the staff kitchen pouring my fourth cup of coffee. "Let Cristian turn that frown upside down. Why don't we sneak away at lunch for a little Netflix and chill?"

"Are you serious?" I spun around to face him. "Do you really think I'd sleep with you after you abandoned us?"

"Wow." He jerked back, hands up in a defensive gesture. "I thought you were cool with it, but my bad. I should have told you what was going on. My girlfriend blew me off for one of my closest friends. It really triggered me. I had to deal with a lot of rejection as a kid and I just wasn't in the right headspace to handle the risks of the heist. That's on her. She destroyed my life and ruined everything for you. I hope you can forgive me for falling for someone like that. I'm sure it was a huge success, and now that you're rich, could you lend me a twenty?"

I was tempted to lie and tell him we'd found the necklace and I was now rolling in cash, but I felt so defeated, I couldn't make the effort. "It all went to hell."

His brow furrowed. If I didn't know Cristian was all about Cristian, I would have almost believed his concern was real. "What happened?"

"There were two safes. It wasn't in the one we cracked. We didn't have time to try the second one because Rose couldn't keep the wedding party at the restaurant. She decided to sing the world's dirtiest songs. I'm surprised they didn't call the cops."

Cristian leaned against the counter, sipping his kombucha green tea. "So what's the plan?"

"Why does everyone think I've got a plan?" I grumbled. "I haven't even had a chance to process what happened. Anil must have texted me a dozen times since last night and I ignored him. Emma called me a quitter and told me to go reset. Chloe set up a crew meeting for tonight, but for what? I've got nothing. No solutions. The wedding is tomorrow, and I've got a million things to do. I had to ask my dad for the afternoon off and I really can't afford to lose those hours."

Cristian backed away with a grimace. "I'd offer to help, but—"

"I know," I snapped. "You've got six dates lined up. You need to buy your aunt's dog a new sweater. You're going to see some strippers. I don't need to hear your excuses."

I pulled out my phone to let Chloe know Cristian had gone full "fuckboy" on me, but before I could send my text, my phone dinged with a message from Bella.

My father wants to see you at the house this afternoon.

"What's wrong?" Cristian asked. "You look like you're about to pass out."

"Mr. Angelini wants to see me." I swallowed hard. "What if he knows we were there last night? What if Chloe missed a camera?"

"I knew I made the right call backing out." Cristian slapped a hand to his chest. "Can you imagine what he'd do if he found out I was boning his wife? What if he called the police? Guys like me don't do well in jail." He pulled a pack of cigarettes from his pocket. "I need a smoke."

"It's not always about you, Cristian." My fingers were flying across my phone, letting everyone know they should prepare to leave the city if it turned out we'd been seen.

Cristian made strange eye contact with me. For a moment, I thought he was going to cry. "That's what my mother used to say."

◇　◇　◇

At the end of my shift, I joined Dad in the break room. He'd made a pot of chai and I poured myself a cup and pulled up a chair at the table.

"What's wrong?" Dad asked.

"Why do you think something's wrong? Maybe I just want to have a cup of chai with my dad before I leave for the day."

"You never have chai with me at work," he said. "Are you sick?"

"No, I'm not sick." I sipped my tea, breathing in the soothing scents of vanilla cream, cardamom, nutmeg, and cloves.

"Did you lose your job at the candy store? Is your new business not doing well? Did Annika Auntie not get the elephant? Did you break up with Anil? Did Rose get a new tenant?" Dad was good at pointing out all the things that could go wrong with my life.

"What if I did something really bad? Would you still love me?" There was one thing I could do to salvage this situation, assuming I got out of the meeting with Mr. Angelini alive. It was drastic and involved going away, likely for five to ten years, but it would ensure Chloe and Olivia would always be safe. It made my heart hurt to think about it, and part of me needed to know if I would still have a place to land when it was over.

"You've already been in trouble with the law, and here you are drinking chai with me and working in my store. I think that answers your question," Dad said. "What do you need? Do you have to flee the country? Do you need a new passport? A place to hide?"

"No, nothing like that." It warmed me to know the efforts my dad would go to if I needed to escape.

"We're here for you," he said. "Whatever you need."

"I would have liked to hear that when I was young."

"That was a difficult time," he said with a sigh. "Your brothers took up all our attention and we know you got lost in the shuffle. It has been a constant source of guilt for your mother and me. If you'd been difficult or loud or noisy, it might have been different. But you were just so good, so quiet, so willing to please. You didn't make any waves. You didn't ask for anything. You entertained yourself and that just made it too easy for us to focus on the boys, but we didn't love you any less."

"It was hard for me, Dad. I felt lonely and abandoned." I'd never said those words out loud and it felt good to put them out there. "I just wanted some attention, to feel like I had a place in the family and that I was as important as everyone else. I wanted to feel loved."

"I'm sorry, beta." He ruffled my hair. "We know it wasn't fair to you. We weren't perfect parents. That's why we're trying so hard to find you a match. We can't make up for the past, but we want to help you build a good future. We want you to be happy. We don't want you to wind up alone."

◆ ◆ ◆

Jack picked me up outside the shop after I'd finished talking with my dad. After I'd shared the news of the meeting in our group chat, he had insisted on driving me to the Angelinis' mansion, and to be honest, I didn't want to go with anyone else. I was tired of being angry with him. Tired of hiding my feelings. Tired of not taking what I wanted.

"No motorcycle?" I climbed into the white serial killer van. With all the stress, I'd been looking forward to the chance to clear my mind with the focus that came with riding on the back of his bike.

"I thought this would make us look more professional." He pulled away from the curb with a hard jerk of the wheel.

"Us?"

"I'm going in with you," he said. "It's not safe."

"It's a little too late to pretend you care." I couldn't keep the bitterness out of my voice. "Not that it matters. I have to go in alone. It's my company. I'm the boss." I pulled a bag of mixed candies from my purse. I always had one on hand for dire emergencies. If this was my last day on earth, I wanted to go stuffed with sweets.

"It's a fake company," he pointed out. "You're a fake wedding planner. It's not like you've got a reputation to protect. You've got no other clients."

"Simone handed out my business cards at the gala," I said. "Maybe someone will call me. Maybe this wedding will be a success, and everyone will ask Bella who she hired to plan the wedding, and next week my phone will be ringing off the hook."

"I thought you were going to help Bella escape. She's not going to be telling her friends what a great wedding planner you are if she's hiding in a small villa in the middle of Tuscany."

"Do you have a negative comment ready for everything I say?" I bit into a sour key and my mouth watered.

"Would it stop you from going into the mansion alone?"

"No. I like being a wedding planner." I felt the truth of the words as soon as they dropped from my lips. "It's the first thing I've ever done in my life that makes me feel alive. I'm good at it. I'm good at juggling all the vendors and the schedules, traveling around the city, meeting people, making plans, and exercising my creativity. Organizing the heist on top of it just made it even better. Someday, I'll have enough money to make this business real, and I want to be ready for when that happens. I have to be able to deal with clients on my own—whether they're bridezillas or Mafia bosses."

"I still don't like it," he grumbled.

"You don't get a choice," I said. "But I like knowing that if I wanted, I wouldn't have to do it alone."

◇ ◇ ◇

Even seated behind his giant mahogany desk, Mr. Angelini was an imposing man, especially when he spent the first few moments of our meeting staring at me in silence.

"Close the door." He lifted his chin and gestured to one of the two bodyguards in the room.

I was flattered he thought I was such a threat, but two massive armed guards seemed a bit extreme.

After the door clicked shut, I focused on my breathing, but the cloying scent of cigar smoke made me choke on my second inhale.

"Any problems with the wedding plans?" he asked in a conversational tone that did nothing to relieve the tension that had frozen me in place.

"No problems," I said with a conviction I didn't feel in the least. "We're all set for tomorrow."

"Good." He drummed his thick fingers on the desk. "The wedding must go ahead. You understand that."

"I see no reason why it wouldn't," I said. "I've checked in with all the vendors, the priest, the musicians . . . Even the elephant will be here."

"Excellent."

"If that's all you need . . ." I moved to stand, and he waved me down.

"There's something else we need to discuss."

Bile rose in my throat. Maybe the two guards were here to kill me and chop me into pieces and spirit me out of the house in the gym bag in the corner. Although I hadn't seen a hatchet . . .

"I understand you had an altercation with my future son-in-law at the bridal dress shop." His voice was cool, but his coal-black eyes burned with hellfire. "And that you spoke to the police."

"Someone else called them," I said quickly, in case he thought I'd ratted him out. "I told the detective in charge that it was just a misunderstanding. I didn't want anything to spoil the wedding and I thought you'd prefer to handle the matter in-house."

Had I misjudged Mr. Angelini? Maybe he'd been horrified when he found out what had happened. Maybe the gym bag was for Mario. Maybe Mario was already in there.

"Indeed I do." He pulled a white envelope from the desk drawer and pushed it toward me.

What the hell? Was he terminating my contract? It wasn't my fault Mario had stormed into the shop. And what was I supposed to do when he threatened my bestie?

"I thought he was going to hurt Bella," I said, thinking fast. "He was violent and I was trying to protect her. I'm worried for her after they get married."

"The marriage is my concern," he said. "What happens between them is not."

I couldn't imagine my father ever saying anything like that. When he'd found out about Kyle, I had to hold him back from hunting Kyle down. But what did I expect of a Mafia boss who was forcing his daughter into marriage? He wasn't a normal dad. This wasn't a normal life. She deserved better. She deserved to be loved.

"I'm sorry it didn't work out." I reached for my bag, and he gave an irritated grunt that froze me in my seat.

"I appreciate your discretion." He nodded at the envelope.

Taking the hint, I opened the envelope and thumbed through the wad of bills inside, wishing I had Anil's gift for math. This wasn't a send-off; it was a pay-off.

"Is that enough?"

I stared at him openmouthed while my brain went into overdrive. How much was in the envelope? Was it polite to take it out, or should I count it in the envelope? Should I use the calculator app on my phone, or would he think I couldn't count by twenties and fire me on the spot? What did normal people do in this situation? Did normal people ever get into this situation? Was this legal? Would I have to declare it on my taxes? What should I say? Would I be underselling myself if I said yes?

"No? You want more?" Misunderstanding my silence, he gestured to one of the guards. "Gino, open the safe."

I hadn't paid much attention to Mr. Angelini's bodyguards, but Gino was the kind of guy who sucked all the light out of a room. Well over six feet tall, his arms and chest thick with muscle, Gino was dressed in all black, his dark hair shorn to a fuzz. His face was hard, cold, and chiseled with menace. If anyone was going to chop me up and stuff me in a gym bag, it was him.

"Gino's the head of my private security team," Mr. Angelini said when he caught me staring.

I suspected Gino also headed the Assassination Squad, the Body Disposal Team, and he probably enjoyed mixing different types of concrete the way Chloe and I liked to mix different types of cocktails on a Saturday night.

Gino slid his hand over the top of the bookcase behind the desk. I heard a click, and the bookcase swung open to reveal a safe embedded in the wall, just as Anil had described. Gino spun the dial and the door swung open to reveal a bundle of papers, a stack of white envelopes stuffed with cash, and a large blue velvet jewelry box, the perfect size to hold the Wild Heart.

I stifled a gasp. There it was. Only five feet away. The key to Chloe's salvation and our financial freedom.

Gino's head snapped to the side, his narrowed gaze locked on my face. Without missing a beat, he shoved the jewelry box to the back of the safe before taking out an envelope and handing it to Mr. Angelini.

"Another five thousand for your continued discretion." Mr. Angelini slid the envelope across the desk and my brain finally clicked into focus mode.

"Thank you." I stuffed the envelopes in my purse like I accepted bribes every day. "I won't say anything." Had he paid off the staff at the bridal shop, too? What was the going price of silence these days?

"I know you won't." He folded his arms and leaned back in his chair. "Gino checked you out. You sell suits and candy and live with your parents. You're a good girl, nice and squeaky clean as they come."

"You investigated me?" Did he know about the heist? The meetings in Rose's garage? Was he toying with me? I glanced over at the bag in the corner, wondering if I would fit, considering I'd already gained a few pounds since I'd moved back home. And then there was my candy addiction . . .

"I like to know who I'm doing business with," he said. "If I'm happy with your work, things will go well for you."

"And if you're not happy?"

"You don't want me to be unhappy."

"No," I said. "I don't suppose I do."

◇ ◇ ◇

"How was it?" Jack asked as we drove away from the mansion.

"I'm alive. I'd call that a win." I pulled out the envelopes and showed him the cash. "He paid me to keep my mouth shut about what happened at the wedding dress shop. I've never been bribed before. It was a surreal experience. I was so shocked that I didn't answer when he asked if it was enough, so he had his bodyguard open the safe to give me more. You'll never guess what I saw."

"The necklace."

I gave him the side-eye. "Way to ruin the surprise."

"It was kind of obvious," Jack said. "The only surprising thing is that he let you see it."

"I saw a box; not the actual necklace. But what else could it be?"

Jack stopped at the intersection leading back to the highway. "Where to next?"

Right would take us back to Evanston—Rose, Chloe, my apartment, my family, and the garage that had become a second home for my crew. Left would take us back into the city, where I could walk into the police station and confess to the crime so Chloe could be free. She wouldn't have to worry about lawyer's fees or trials or prison, and she'd get my share of the wedding planning money to keep her going over the next little while. But did I really want to go to jail for something I didn't do? Six weeks ago, I wouldn't have hesitated. I'd spent most of my life struggling to prioritize my needs, thinking so little of myself that I would always give up what I wanted for the greater good.

You didn't want anything.

My father's voice echoed in my ears. I *had* wanted things, but I'd been afraid to ask—love, attention, time, even small things like age-appropriate movies on family movie nights or five minutes at dinnertime to share my day at school. I wanted things now—a wedding planning company that made me excited to get out of bed in the morning, a bestie who showed up with bleach, a bunch of oddballs who had suddenly become friends, my flawed family who loved me and was desperately trying to make up for the past, and Jack, who was so wrong for me and yet so right.

I wasn't going to get what I wanted if I went to jail. I loved Chloe, but there had to be another way to save her besides throwing my life away. And that had to start with speaking my truth.

"You're thinking too hard," Jack said. "I can hear it all the way over here. Whatever you're trying to decide, follow your heart. That's what my grandmother always told me."

"You hurt me when you left me to face those strangers alone," I said, speaking up for the first time in my life. "I trusted you. I felt safe with you. I have issues with abandonment and that was pretty much the worst thing you could do. You made me feel like I wasn't important, that I wasn't worth protecting. I've been trying to fight that feeling of worthlessness all my life."

I expected Jack's usual evasiveness. He gave me honesty instead. "I'm sorry. I knew you could take care of yourself, and I knew they wouldn't hurt you, but there was no excuse for leaving the way I did. You were scared, helpless, and alone—"

"I wasn't scared," I interjected. "They were idiots. They didn't take my phone. I could have called 911 at any time."

"I stand corrected," Jack said. "Not scared, but helpless and alone, and I—"

"I wasn't helpless, either," I cut in. "I grabbed a rotten floorboard. It had nails in it. I could have caused them some serious damage, and as you know, I also have mad fight skills. I can take care of myself, but sometimes I would like someone to have my back."

"Of course." Jack nodded. "Not scared or helpless, but alone."

"Very alone." I gave him a stern look. "Abandoned."

"I never meant to make you feel that way," he said. "I'll do what it takes to prove that to you in the hopes one day you will forgive me."

"I forgave you when you said 'sorry,' but I enjoyed hearing you grovel." I leaned over for a kiss. He was most obliging.

"You told me to listen to my heart," I said. "My heart says I want more kisses. I want to live my life outside four cement walls. I want Olivia to have her mom and Chloe to have her freedom and Bella to marry the man she loves. I want us all to have a chance to really live our lives without struggling to keep our heads above water. I want to take risks. I want to be wild. And I want to be wicked . . . with you."

His lips tipped up at the corners. "Sounds like you need a plan."

"We know the necklace is in the safe," I mused. "The safe is in the office. Chloe said the office has no cameras . . ." I was on a roll now. With the mental block down that had been holding me back, I could finally see a world of possibilities open up before me. "Only Mr. Angelini uses the office. He won't be there during the wedding ceremony or afterward during dinner. I have to be at the ceremony, but at dinner, I'll just be walking around making sure everything is okay." I wrapped my hands around his neck and pulled him down for another kiss. "I think I have a plan."

"Glad to hear it, and so will the three cars waiting behind us. Which way?"

"Right," I said. "I need to talk to Chloe. And then we've got a meeting to get to. We're going to save Bella, steal the necklace, and have our happy ending after all."

TWENTY-FOUR

◆ ◆ ◆

P lan B. We're going to steal the necklace during the wedding dinner."

I steadied the whiteboard in Rose's garage and looked over the sea of smiling faces. I hadn't shared the details of my meeting with Mr. Angelini except to divvy up the ten thousand dollars among the crew. Cash always made people smile.

"$1,666.66 each," Anil had said when I fanned it out on the table. "But since there's no change, we'll round down, and you can have the extra four dollars as danger pay."

I forced a laugh, but after my meeting with Mr. Angelini, I knew that the danger was all too real.

"She had a plan all along," Chloe said. "She just needed time."

"Thanks, babe." Chloe and I had worked through the details at her place. She'd assured me nothing had changed between us. She was and would always be my ride or die and no man would get between us. I'd given myself a mental kick in the ass for letting my fears and insecurity affect our friendship. I was worth being loved and I wasn't going to be afraid to ask for what I wanted.

"Although the lower floor of the house will be open for guests, everyone will be in the tent for dinner," I said. "The outdoor sensors and drone Bees will be turned off, but the indoor cameras will still be on. We can't risk jamming the system again, so we're going to put helium balloon arrangements in front of the cameras."

"Simple but elegant," Gage said. "Why hack a system when you can just use balloons?"

"If you need them in animal shapes, just let me know. I have lots left over from my last clown gig." Emma pulled a balloon from her pocket and blew it into a long, thin tube. She quickly twisted it into the shape of an elephant and placed it on the table.

"Why an elephant?" Anil asked.

"Because if we can get an elephant for a wedding, there is nothing we can't do."

"We're assuming the office door will be locked," I said, my heart even lighter than it had been since I walked in. "Rose will be supervising the caterers in the kitchen, so she can watch the hallway while Jack picks the lock. Chloe will liaise with the servers to make sure Mr. Angelini's drinks are always topped up so he is less inclined to leave the tent, and she'll try to intervene if he does look like he's making a move."

"I'll only need ten, maybe fifteen seconds to pick the lock," Jack said. "Getting into the office won't be the problem, but getting into the safe . . ."

"The safe I saw was exactly the same as the one upstairs so we already know it will have a three-digit code," I said. "That means . . ."

"One hundred sixty-two possible combinations," Anil offered, biting into an apple. "But if I were you, I'd try the same combination as the safe upstairs. I follow a professional safecracker on YouTube. He said people don't like to remember lots of numbers, so they use the same passwords and the same combinations for everything."

"Don't tell me you have a different password for every app and website you use, or I might have to throw up," Emma said. "I have one password and it's password1234. Makes things simple."

Anil reached down for the wastepaper basket he'd been using for his apple cores and held it out to Emma. Laughter bubbled in my chest at the burn. Anil wasn't quite so innocent anymore and he'd developed a wicked sense of humor.

"I have a different twelve-digit password made up of a combination of uppercase and lowercase letters, numbers, and symbols for every site I use and they are all committed to memory," he said. "I don't know why people think it's so hard."

Gage and Emma shared a look and snickered in the corner. Some things changed; others stayed the same.

"We should have a two-and-a-half-hour window to open the safe," I continued. "The meal is fourteen courses and then there are the speeches, first dance, and the cake cutting ceremony. I can't imagine Mr. Angelini is going to run to his office when it's all done with all his friends and family around. I personally would not be able to move after eating fourteen courses and Bella mentioned he's a heavy drinker."

"We could put something in his drink to knock him out," Gage said. "Then we'd have as much time as we needed."

"No drugs." I waggled my finger at him. "No guns. No fights. This might be a fake wedding, but I won't have it ruined with a big spectacle. I want everyone to have a great time. This might be our only wedding event, but I want people to remember our name."

"Assuming you get the necklace," Emma said. "What happens next?"

"I hand it out the window to Anil. He hands it off to Chloe. She takes it to the van. I'll buy a mini safe and she can put it in there and hide it in the ice cooler."

"Ice on ice." Gage snorted a laugh.

"You can be sure the necklace will be safe with me." Anil pumped an arm in the air. "No one will get past The Butcher."

I scribbled another line on the whiteboard. My drawings looked like the football plays my brothers used to sketch on the family whiteboard when I was trying to watch *My Little Pony* on TV.

"What about me?" Emma asked. "After I've helped with parking all the cars, I'll have nothing to do except sit in the limo and wait to take the unhappy couple to the airport for their honeymoon."

"You're the key to Part 2 of Plan B," I said. "Saving Bella. I haven't talked to her yet because I wanted to run through it with everyone first. After Emma has sorted out the parking, she'll drive the limo to the boat rental place and rent a small . . . and I repeat, small . . . motorboat, which she'll drive across the lake to the shore of the Angelinis' property. Meantime, after the dinner and necklace stealing and while DJ Ka-Poor is dropping his sick beats, Bella will go upstairs ostensibly to get ready to leave for her honeymoon. Instead, she's going to change out of her dress, sneak out the back stairs, and run through the forest to the beach. Chloe and I will meet her at the boathouse. Emma will then take Bella in the boat down to a secluded boat launch where Ben will be waiting in a cab. They'll go straight to the airport and fly off to start their new life. While we're gone, Rose, Jack, and Gage will take turns guarding the necklace in case mysterious bellhops show up with guns."

"That is curiously specific," Emma said. "Care to elaborate?"

"Ask Jack." I'd avoided asking more questions about the intruders during Jack's grovel in the car because I didn't want to hear the answers. I still wanted Jack to be a good guy and not part of the criminal underworld.

"We're not the only people who want the necklace," Jack said, leaning forward, knees on his elbows. "There is a particular individual with whom I have a long history. He shares my interest in acquiring certain objects but for different reasons. He has a larger team at his disposal, and they are more than willing to use violence to achieve their ends, although they rarely hurt innocent people."

"What?" Emma's brow creased in a frown. "Did anyone understand what he just said?"

"In gaming speak, he's got an evil nemesis who sends out his hench people to steal things Jack wants to steal, using force if necessary." Anil looked over at Jack. "Or did I misunderstand?"

"I wouldn't use the word 'steal,'" Jack said. "But the rest is fairly accurate."

I didn't care about an evil nemesis or hench people. I had fixated on one word. "'Rarely'?" I glared at him. "They *rarely* hurt innocent people? You said you *knew* they wouldn't hurt me. Every time I think I can trust you, I get a big fat slap in the face."

"You were never at risk," Jack said. "Some things are a matter of professional courtesy."

"What profession? What if they thought you had the necklace? If I hadn't chased them away, would they have tortured me to force you to bring it to them? What if they peeled off my skin to make a dress?"

"Why would they do that?" Jack's brow creased in a puzzled frown. "They had their own clothes."

"I put on lotion this morning." I was in full-blown panic mode. "I rubbed it on my skin."

"This is on you," Chloe said to Rose. "You made her watch all those old-school serial killer shows. She still hasn't gotten over *Silence of the Lambs*."

Rose gave an apologetic shrug. "I thought she liked them."

"I think the bigger question is, are they going to steal the necklace out from under us?" Chloe asked, patting my hand to calm me down. "Does your evil nemesis have a name? Who should we be watching out for?"

"Mr. X."

Emma threw back her head and laughed. "This is like a B-list crime show, the kind you stream at two A.M. when you've watched everything on Netflix and you can't afford HBO."

"Mr. X won't send anyone else after the necklace because he knows we're after it and he'll let us do the heavy lifting," Jack said. "Our most difficult task will be keeping the necklace safe once we get it. That's why I hired Gage. He's the best."

"Well then, he's going to have a new job that involves staying near the van when you or Rose are inside guarding the necklace." I was irritated with Jack all over again. Why didn't he tell me about Mr. X? What profession required the courtesy of not hurting people after breaking into their home with a gun?

"What about the elephant?" Gage asked. "What's it going to do while I'm watching the van?"

"Show of hands," I called out. "Who wants the elephant to join the crew?"

Every hand went up. My crew was nothing if not accepting.

"There you go," I said to Gage. "Problem solved. It can be your backup."

TWENTY-FIVE

◇ ◇ ◇

Everything went perfectly the morning of the wedding until it didn't.

"Where's the priest?"

Jack tied a swath of white chiffon to the delicate curved wedding arch on the Angelinis' back lawn, where the ceremony would take place. He'd decorated the aisle with lilies, hydrangeas, and sprays of pink roses, and sprinkled rose petals between the seats. With so much natural beauty already packed into the setting, it was truly magical.

"I haven't seen him." Jack added a sprig of greenery to the arch. "But the organist mentioned he wasn't happy you'd made him come so early. Maybe she knows where he went."

As if on cue, the organist played the first few chords of the theme song to *The Phantom of the Opera*. I'd dreamed of playing Christine in our middle school production of the play, but the school didn't want a Christine who was always off-key.

"I wasn't leaving anything to chance," I said. "This day has to be perfect. I'll go talk to her and find out what's going on."

I went in search of the organist. She knew the priest well. He was old and tired easily, so maybe he'd gone to find somewhere to rest. We walked through the main floor of the house, knocking on doors.

"Maybe he's still asleep," I said. "He might have gone on an all-night prayer bender and now he's hungover after one too many Hail Marys."

My sacrilegious joke failed to amuse.

We found the priest unconscious in a puddle of soup on the kitchen floor. I called an ambulance and the paramedics whisked him away to the hospital. I assured a horrified Mrs. Angelini that we would find a replacement, but after a valiant effort and many phone calls to church administrators, I was unable to find a priest available on short notice. I checked online but there were no "Dial a Priest" services that could deliver.

"We can't have a wedding without a priest." I sank into one of the outdoor chairs while Jack fluffed organza beside me. My first wedding was going to be over before it began, and with it our heist, Bella's escape, and my chance at saving Chloe.

"Gage used to be a priest," Jack reminded me. "He's out front waiting for the elephant."

"Thank God." I looked up at the sky. "No offense."

Gage was sitting on the steps beside Chloe. No words were being shared. I didn't understand a relationship that seemed to be silence only.

"Gage!" I ran up to join them. "I need a priest. You used to be a priest. Can you do the ceremony?"

"As I told you before . . ." He lifted an eyebrow in censure. "I was released from my sacred duties. I cannot defile a sacred sacrament with my unholy presence in the sight of God."

"Not really where I saw this one going," I said, catching the negativity vibe. "If you can run around shooting people, why can't you pretend to be a priest? I can't follow your logic."

"That's religion for you."

"If he were an ordained minister," Chloe said, "he could perform the ceremony." She scrolled through her phone. "He can register online. A few clicks and he can be legally ordained to perform weddings. It's fast, free, and easy, and registration gives him access to training materials and a wedding ceremony script generator. He even gets a certificate. It says here this is one of Earth's largest and most active religious organizations."

"What about Mars?" Gage asked. "Are they big on Mars, too?"

"Don't be grumpy," Chloe said. "You'll also be able to do baptisms and funerals. Just think of it as a new skill set that will open you up to a world of new possibilities."

"Only you could see this as a good thing," Gage murmured under his breath, but not before his dark eyes softened.

"I see a bad thing, too." Chloe scrolled through her phone. "You have to wait forty-eight hours to get your certificate." She checked her phone again. "Or we can pay an extra fifty dollars for expedited four-hour processing."

"That's perfect," I said. "Gage could even do a minister-priest wedding mash-up." My mind was racing, my heart was pounding, and I felt totally and utterly alive.

"Your irreverence is killing me," Gage said. "I have a feeling that deities of all cultures will be lined up to kick your ass into Hell when the day comes."

"Are you going to wear robes?" Chloe flushed, her voice dropping to a husky rasp. I'd almost forgotten she had a thing for books about kinky priests.

Gage studied her with interest. "Do you want me to wear robes?"

"Yes." She swallowed hard and licked her lips.

"I'll wear robes."

For a moment I was torn between throwing a bucket of water

over them and calling the hospital to check up on the priest. Since I was a professional, I made the call, and immediately wished I hadn't.

"The priest was poisoned," I told Mr. Angelini in his office after I got off the phone. "They think it was the soup. I checked in the kitchen for the pot to send them a sample for the lab, but I couldn't find it." I'd already talked to Rose when I searched the kitchen. She was busy managing the catering staff, but she assured me she was all over the case of the poisoned priest.

"Who's going to officiate at the wedding?" Mr. Angelini didn't seem shocked or surprised to hear that someone had tried to poison one of God's representatives on Earth in his home and then disposed of the evidence, but then I suppose if you're used to chopping off hands and slitting throats on a daily basis, a little poisoning is pretty tame.

"One of the members of my team used to be a priest," I said. "He was released from his sacred duties some time ago and now handles elephants for us, but he is also an ordained minister and can perform the ceremony. If you like the priest look, he still has his robes, but he can't do a Catholic ceremony. I think he's afraid God might smite him or hit him with a bolt of lightning or send him to a bad place."

Mr. Angelini blew a smoke ring in my face. "I don't care how he does it so long as it's legally binding. As I told you before, you don't want to disappoint me."

"Of course." I stifled a cough as the acrid smoke filled my lungs. "The ceremony will go ahead as planned."

After stopping by the bathroom to throw up my breakfast after my unsettling meeting with Mr. Angelini, I went to see Bella to explain what had happened. She was having a few quiet moments alone in her room between hair and makeup.

"Poisoned?" Bella gasped and staggered back, clutching her

chest, her reaction as dramatic as her father's had been understated. "We should cancel the wedding. Out of respect."

"I've come up with a solution," I said. "Gage used to be a priest and in four hours he will be an ordained minister. Your dad wants to see his certificate, but if we can get you married before it arrives, your marriage will technically be invalid. You won't even need to get an annulment for lack of consummation. I can give the certificate to your father after the ceremony, and by the time he finds out the marriage was invalid, you'll be long gone. Chloe will be able to fake some kind of computer glitch that will absolve us of blame. I hate to say it, because I feel terrible for the priest, but this makes things even easier for you. Now you won't even be legally married. No trying to get an annulment while you're in hiding. You'll be free."

Far from being excited about the plan, Bella sighed. "Do you have to solve every damn problem?"

"I thought you'd be pleased." I fought back my disappointment. "It's one less thing for you to worry about. If we don't have the wedding, how will you escape? Everyone is distracted. The outdoor security system is off. The security guards are busy watching the guests. This is still your best chance to get away."

"No wedding would have made me more pleased." She tightened the belt on her robe and walked over to the window. "If by some chance the marriage turns out to be valid, Mario will never stop hunting for me. Your minister cannot be ordained when we say 'I do.'" She turned to face me, her eyes cold and hard. "Do you understand?"

"Of course." I didn't appreciate her condescending attitude after I'd come up with such an amazing solution to the problem of the poisoned priest on short notice. I'd also arranged to help her escape, putting my crew at risk. A simple thank-you would have been nice. A "you're incredible" would have been even better. I chalked it up to wedding nerves.

After I checked the kitchen again for the missing soup pot, I grabbed Chloe, Jack, and Gage for a huddle.

"Someone poisoned the priest. Bella isn't the only one who doesn't want this wedding to go ahead. Maybe it's another Mafia family who would be threatened by the merger."

"Maybe it was just bad soup," Gage said.

"The hospital is certain it was poison. They identified the drug and said it cannot accidentally find its way into soup."

"You gotta have balls to poison a priest," Gage said. "We've got a stone-cold killer in the house."

"I don't care who is in the house so long as the wedding goes ahead. We've all got jobs to do. Keep your eyes open and don't eat any soup."

"You are so fucking sexy when you're bossing people around," Jack said, nuzzling my neck as he pulled me behind an azalea bush. "Have you ever done it outdoors?"

"Didn't last night count?" We'd sneaked up to the roof of Jack's hotel for a little loving beneath the stars.

"There were no trees or bushes, no flowers or grass. I want you naked in the hellebore moaning my name." He pulled me into his chest, squeezing me so hard, my breath came out in a huff.

"Jack, you know how much I love sexy times with you. But I've got a minister to ordain, a wedding to run, a heist to plan, a necklace to steal, and a bride to kidnap. I can't juggle any more balls."

◇ ◇ ◇

The first guest arrived five minutes after we'd finished setting up for the ceremony. I alerted the crew and then took a short breather with Chloe.

"If not for us, she'd be marching to her doom," I said. "Did you see the groom? In that tux, with his hair slicked down, he looks like every movie mafioso. He's got the scowl, the swagger, the arrogance, the cruel slash of a mouth, the hard beady eyes, and I'm pretty sure he's packing."

"I just remember him cowering behind his bodyguard after we beat him up," she said. "But if he gives us any trouble today, Gage will deal with him. I already ruined one pair of heels on his sorry ass; I'm not ruining another."

"I don't want our first wedding event to turn into a bloodbath." I searched the huge grassy lawn and spotted Gage beside the elephant. He was wearing all black—shirt, jeans, boots, sunglasses, and a long leather coat. "I thought you were getting him into priestly robes."

"Are you kidding? We're saving those for the bedroom." She adjusted the button on her shirt. Chloe had dressed to match the Angelinis' security guards in a white shirt, dark jacket, and dark pants. Her hair was swept back into a ponytail, and she was wearing dark glasses and one of the earpieces I'd bought for the crew. She and Anil had devised something that ensured we were on a closed circuit so we could talk to one another without being overheard.

"Babe, he looks like he just stepped out of *The Matrix*. He's supposed to be officiating the ceremony. He needs to look official."

"He said this was his Sunday best."

"I'll talk to him," I said, watching him help a kid feed the elephant a handful of hay. "I'll tell him it's my way or the highway."

"Be gentle," Chloe said. "We need him to protect us from Mr. X." She squinted into the sunshine. "Who is that walking toward us? He looks familiar."

My eyes narrowed in on the man in the blue Italian wool silk herringbone suit, frat vest, pink shirt open at the collar, and cuffs an inch above the tan Italian loafers to show off a pair of whimsically patterned socks.

"Cristian." I spat out his name like the priest should have spat out his poisoned soup. "What the hell is he doing here?"

"You talk to Gage," she said. "I'll go and find out."

◇ ◇ ◇

Chloe found me in the foyer while I was adjusting Bella's train a few minutes before the ceremony.

"He managed to get an invitation as the plus-one of a bridesmaid," she whispered. "He says he slept with them all, but this one is his special baby girl."

"Of course she is, but by the end of the night he'll have forgotten her name and tomorrow he'll ghost her."

Chloe helped me smooth out the lace edging. "You're being pretty hard on the guy. He gave up over eight hundred thousand dollars because he was afraid of being recognized. Now he says he's here to help."

"He must have realized just how big a mistake he made and now he thinks he can cash in on our hard work."

"Actually, he just found out that the two huskies he's been visiting at a local shelter are going to be put down and he wants to save them," she said. "They're a bonded pair and no one will take them together. He needs the money to rent a place with a yard so he can adopt them, and he came here hoping for a second chance despite the risk."

I snorted a laugh. "And you believed him?"

"Not at first, but I checked out his story," she said. "I asked him for the details and then I called the shelter. Everything he said is true."

"Even if it is, we don't need him. We have Rose." I sent a text to Anil to make sure everyone was ready for the bride and then did a last check of Bella's ensemble. Satya Auntie had added delicate lace shoulders and sleeves as well as a lace front panel to make the dress more modest. Despite the fact she was being forced into marriage, Bella was a beautiful bride.

"Are you sure it won't be real?" Bella murmured.

"We didn't get the certificate yet," I said. "Your officiant is an ex-priest and soon-to-be minister of the largest online church on Earth. You won't be married in the eyes of God, the city of Chicago, or the Earth church."

"And everything else . . . ?"

"I've booked a cab to pick up Ben and take him to a boat launch a few miles away on this side of the lake. He's got your suitcase and your plane tickets."

Bella squeezed my hand. "I'm sorry I was abrupt earlier. I can't thank you enough. I wish I could recommend your company to all my friends, but—"

"You'll be gone," I said. "Don't worry about that. You go and wear your dream dress, have your fake ceremony, and then enjoy your party. I'll let you know when it's time to—" I cut myself off when I saw Bella's father coming toward us, all ready to walk her down the aisle.

"You're loving this, aren't you?" Chloe asked after we left them to get ready.

I couldn't stop a grin from spreading across my face. "It's been the most fun I've had since college. I'm solving problems. I'm organizing like a queen. I'm telling people what to do and they're doing it because they believe in me. Not only that, but I'm also actually using my business degree. PR, marketing, law, accounts—I need it all to run the company. And we haven't even done the heist."

"Heists aren't supposed to be fun," Chloe reminded me as she followed me outside.

"We've had our ups and downs. But every morning I wake up

excited for the day. I've never felt that before, and part of me is sad it's going to be over. Just think. Tomorrow we'll be rich, the necklace will be back where it belongs, Garcia won't be knocking on my door, Bella will be free, and we'll have successfully planned the only Italian wedding in Chicago with an elephant."

"Don't get ahead of yourself," Chloe warned. "It's not over until it's over. In fact, it's only just begun."

TWENTY-SIX

◇ ◇ ◇

dragged everyone out to watch the ceremony. We'd worked hard for this moment, and I wanted the crew to share in our moment of success.

"How long is this going to take?" Anil scrolled through his phone. "The demographic is ten years older than I anticipated and I need to rejig my playlist."

"I need to get back to the kitchen," Rose said. "It's crazy in there. The Italian nonnas are all up in everyone's business. Apparently, the food isn't the way they make it in Italy, and they threw away an entire bowl of dijonnaise. Chef Pierre almost got into a fight with one of them over the tiramisu."

"I had a bad dijonnaise once." Emma leaned against a low stone retaining wall. "I was on a cruise with my mom and twelve of her best friends. I should have known when I saw it untouched at breakfast, lunch, and dinner. Some things should not be left unrefrigerated. Thank God I had my own cabin because I owned that toilet for the next three days, and the smell . . . it was so bad, they thought they had a sewage leak."

Anil looked up from his phone. "Why do your stories always end up with you on a toilet?"

"Why don't I take you to the nearest portable and stick your head down it so you can see?"

"How about we have a conversation that doesn't involve things that should stay on the inside coming outside," Chloe said gently. "This is a wedding. We should be thinking light, happy, beautiful thoughts."

"I'm thinking about how the bride's Mafia boss father is forcing her into marriage with a cruel, controlling psycho so their families don't whack each other," Cristian said. "There is nothing fun, beautiful, or light about that."

I had explained to Cristian that Rose had taken his place in the heist, but for old times' sake he could hang with the crew. I'd updated him on the recent developments and enjoyed watching his face when I told him how we were going to help Bella escape. I hated to admit it because I was still annoyed that he'd blown us off, but it was nice to have him back.

"Bella's mom is over there," I said, pointing to the front row of the nearest aisle. "Make sure she doesn't see you. I still can't believe you're even here. I thought you were afraid of her."

"That's because I was single," he said. "Now I'm in a committed relationship with . . ." He trailed off, circling his hand as if we would know the name of his latest conquest.

"You don't know the bridesmaid's name," I sighed. "Do you?"

"It doesn't matter," he said. "I'm with her. There's no risk of temptation."

Emma stared at him, her eyes wide. "Are you saying you gave up over eight hundred grand because you were afraid you couldn't keep your dick in your pants?"

"Women are attracted to me," Cristian said, adjusting the cuffs on his shirt. "It's a gift and a curse. Sometimes I wish I didn't have this gorgeous face and hot body."

"Uh-oh. She's looking this way." Rose grabbed Cristian's arm, pulling him back. "Hide in the shadows."

"Too late. She saw me." Cristian lifted his hand in a weak wave, his voice rising to a shaky pitch. "I shouldn't have come. I just felt bad things didn't work out the first time and I wanted to help. What if she wants a session? I can't bone a Mafia boss's wife in his own house."

"I thought you already boned her," Emma said. "And from the way her two friends are looking at you, I'm guessing you boned them as well."

"Could we use a different word?" Chloe asked. "Bone is so . . . well . . . hard."

Emma snickered, her gaze flicking to Gage, who was standing under the flower bower with Mario, waiting for the bride. She clearly missed her partner in crime.

"I thought you were a life coach," Anil said.

Cristian tried to pull his front tuft of hair down over his face as if it would make a difference. "Most women want coaching in one particular aspect of life."

"What aspect?"

"Coitus." Emma pumped her fists and rocked her hips. "Also known as fornication, doing it, getting laid, knocking boots, doing the Devil's dance, shagging, screwing, nailing, banging, or doing squat thrusts in the cucumber patch."

Jack swept my hair away and pressed a kiss to the nape of my neck, sending a wave of heat rippling across my skin. "I have another word," he whispered. "We can try it out tonight."

"Stop it. Bad." I turned to admonish him, and he caught me with a kiss.

"You teach women how to have relations," Anil said, studiously ignoring us. "It's a noble and useful profession."

"Actually, my clients—all women of a certain age—don't really need lessons," Cristian said. "They have experience, and they know what they like. It's very refreshing. There's no guesswork involved."

"That's what all my men say." Rose gave Chef Pierre an exaggerated wink.

"Shh." I glared at them. "You're attracting attention. We're supposed to be professionals."

Sunlight sparkled on the water and danced over the freshly mowed grass. The string quartet played the wedding march and Bella's father nodded curtly as he walked his daughter down the aisle.

"Why is the elephant standing behind the arch?" Jack whispered. "And what's with all the head-patting?"

"She bonded with Gage," I said. "Now she won't leave him alone. She wasn't happy when Chloe helped him change out of his leather jacket into a suit. Chloe got a trunk swat to the head."

"He can't perform a wedding ceremony with an elephant patting his hair."

"Tell that to the elephant."

"What happened to the handler?" Jack asked.

"He's inside having a snooze. He said the elephant doesn't want him there and that his presence would agitate her. Apparently, you don't want to get on an elephant's bad side."

To his credit, Gage didn't seem perturbed by the amorous elephant behind him during the ceremony. He followed the script I'd printed for him off the Internet without even a hitch in his voice, seemingly unaffected by the elephant stroking his hair. The bride and groom exchanged vows, rings, and a perfunctory kiss. I called it a win.

Emma took the bridal party for pictures. The guests drank champagne and ate chocolate-covered strawberries to the dulcet tones of the string quartet. The elephant became a TikTok sensation. I left discreet piles of business cards on every table.

◇ ◇ ◇

When dinner was finally served, I put my heist crew into play. Chloe hid in the bathroom with her laptop, ready to jam the system if we tripped any alarms. Anil hovered in the bushes near the office window, pretending to be on an important call. Jack joined me in the office hallway with a bunch of helium balloons.

"I've put balloons in front of the back entrance camera and at various places around the house, so the placement doesn't look deliberate," he said, tying five pink and white balloons to the small table under the hallway camera. "If anyone is checking the cameras, they won't see anything."

With Rose keeping a lookout at the entrance near the kitchen, Jack picked the office lock with some nifty gadgets in a black leather case. Once inside, we closed the door, leaving Rose to stand guard. Jack had no trouble finding the catch for the hidden bookcase. Moments later, it swung forward to reveal the safe.

"It's definitely the same safe as upstairs," I said. "I was worried I'd misremembered."

"Maybe they got a two-for-one discount."

I left Jack to his safecracking work, and crossed the room to open the window for Anil, letting the fresh air in and the tobacco-infused air out. I'd been too terrified to look around the last time I'd been here, but I hadn't missed much. Mafia bosses, it seemed, had a fondness for dark wood furnishings, boring paintings, stone figurines, and marble statues.

"If I were rich, I wouldn't buy a painting of a bowl of fruit," I said, studying one of the pictures on the wall. "I'd go for bright colors, bold designs, or something that makes you think."

"That's Monet's *Prunes et abricots*, painted between 1882 and 1885," Jack said without even turning his head. "The waterside scene on the other wall is also by Monet. *Glaçons, environs de Bennecourt* depicts the Seine in the winter. Together they're worth over fifteen million dollars."

Gah. Cringe. No wonder I'd only scored 52 percent on my final art history exam in college. But what did the teacher expect when he scheduled the class for Friday nights? Fridays were for partying, not sitting in a stuffy classroom looking at pictures of fruit.

"The statues are more interesting." He pressed his stethoscope against the metal door. "The basalt falcon is from Thirtieth-Dynasty Egypt during the reign of Nectanebo the Second to the Ptolemaic period. It's worth about five million and subject to a claim for repatriation by the Egyptian government."

"And the statue of the naked woman?"

"That naked woman is Venus, carved in the Medici style. It's a second century AD Roman copy of a Hellenistic original from the second century BC worth around eight million. It belongs in the National Archaeological Museum in Greece."

"I never imagined a Mafia boss would be an art collector." Or that Jack would be so knowledgeable about art. I'd thought his expertise was limited to jewelry of the stolen kind.

"He had to do something with all the money he stole through his loan sharking, money laundering, and illegal real estate transactions." He turned the dial, then opened the safe with a flourish.

"You got it."

"Anil was right," he said. "It was the same combination. I'll need to spend more time on YouTube." He handed me the jewelry box and then turned back to rifle through the safe.

"What are you doing? This is just about the necklace."

"Just curious," he said, pulling out a brown manila envelope. "Do the switch so we can get out of here."

I opened the box and stared at an empty sea of blue velvet. My heart sank and a wave of despair washed over me, making my knees buckle.

Jack looked up from the sheaf of papers in his hand. "What's wrong?"

"It's empty." I felt like a black hole had swallowed me up. How could two heists fail?

Jack took the box and ran his fingers over the blue velvet interior. He pried up the plastic mount and felt inside. "Let's check the safe. Maybe it fell out."

We emptied the safe. Aside from the cash, some papers, and the envelope Jack had found, there was no sign of the necklace.

I racked my brain, trying to come up with an explanation. I wasn't giving up. Not this time. "Could he have given it to his wife to wear for the wedding? Or maybe he's planning to give it to Bella as a wedding gift because he feels bad about forcing her to marry a jerk."

"People don't wear jewelry that valuable and with that kind of history for a backyard wedding," Jack said. "Pieces like that are displayed in museums and private collections. Occasionally a big star will ask to wear one to the Met Gala or the Academy Awards and then the insurance company will only release it subject to strict rules and top-level security including a detail of bodyguards that must accompany the star everywhere. When that kind of piece is sold, it's done through an auction house or a broker who handles private sales."

"Do you think he sold it? He is a fence, after all. Isn't that what was supposed to happen? Maybe we were just too late. Or could Mr. X have beaten us to it?"

"It hasn't hit the black market, and I'd know if it was on the move," Jack said. "The two guys who broke into your place aren't known for keeping their mouths shut."

I messaged Anil to let him know he could stand down from his post outside the window. I was about to put my phone away when I got a message from Chloe.

"Jack . . ." My heart raced, almost exploding. "Chloe says Mrs. Angelini is on her way to the office. She overheard Mr. Angelini asking her to get something from his desk. Rose couldn't stop her, not even with a tray of eclairs."

Jack had spread all the papers from the envelope across the desk. He pulled out his phone and took a picture. "I just need one minute."

"We don't have one minute." A wave of dizziness caught me, making my legs and knees weak. "She's coming right now."

"Climb out the window. I'll be right behind you."

I ran to the window. A group of people had gathered outside, drinking and talking like they didn't realize there were two people twenty feet away who needed to escape before they were caught by a Mafia boss's wife.

I heard voices in the hallway, the rattle of a handle, the scratch of a key.

"Jack . . ." My pulse roared in my ears. "We can't get out. We'll be seen."

Jack closed the safe and pushed the secret bookcase back in place. "We need a distraction. Find something heavy to throw."

"You want me to throw something heavy at them? What if I hit someone?"

"Then the plan will be a success. They'll be distracted."

"Sophia," a male voice said loudly. "How nice to see you again."

"Cristian, I thought that was you on the patio." Mrs. Angelini's voice was crystal clear through the door.

"It's Cristian," I whispered, incredulous. "He's come to save us."

"I was invited by one of the bridesmaids as her plus-one," he said, his voice dropping, husky and low.

"Which one?"

Silence.

"He still can't remember which bridesmaid he's with," I muttered. "He probably doesn't know any of their names."

"Don't tell me you're jealous, Sophia. You know how special you are to me. You're the only woman who can . . ." Cristian's voice dropped to a low murmur. Unable to resist, I leaned toward the door. What could only Mrs. Angelini do?

"Simi." Jack grabbed my arm. "Stop eavesdropping when we're trying to escape."

Mrs. Angelini responded to Cristian's whispers with a flirtatious laugh. "You naughty boy. I think we should talk about it some more in my husband's office. I just came to get his cigars."

"Cigar smoke triggers my asthma," he said, mimicking Anil's words. "Is there somewhere else we can go? Somewhere we can be alone?"

I texted frantic messages to the team, asking them to get the crowd away from the window.

"He has cameras all over the lower floor," Mrs. Angelini said. "And we can't be seen going upstairs. This is the only room where we can talk privately. If he checks the cameras, I can always tell him I wanted to show you his art."

I heard the key in the lock, the thunk of a deadbolt sliding back. We dove under the desk, huddled together, knees and foreheads touching.

"Oh, here we are," Cristian said loudly, his tone so forced, I was amazed Mrs. Angelini wasn't suspicious. "In the office. Together."

"Don't worry," she said. "We're perfectly alone."

The door clicked shut, bolt sliding into place. I jammed my hands into my armpits, my breath bursting in and out.

"I can book you in for a coaching session next week," Cristian said.

I could see his feet as he walked around the room. He was looking for us. When he came to the desk, I tapped his shoe. He lifted his toe in acknowledgment.

"We can talk about your goals for the future—"

"Silly boy." Mrs. Angelini laughed. "You know that's not the kind of coaching I want."

From my vantage point under the desk, I saw her shawl drop to the floor.

Cristian coughed, choked. "Why don't we get a drink at the bar and we can discuss your needs—"

"Now. Sit."

"Your husband . . . oof."

I peered under the desk. Cristian was sitting on the couch with Mrs. Angelini straddling his lap, dress hiked up her thighs, back to the window.

"My husband doesn't need to know," she said.

Oh God. Oh God. The last thing I wanted was to listen to Cristian having sexy times with a Mafia boss's wife.

Window, I mouthed.

Cover, Jack mouthed back.

I sent a text to Gage. I need your elephant.

◇ ◇ ◇

To be perfectly honest, I did not have "crawl out of Mafia boss's office window under cover of large elephant while friend sexes up boss's wife" on my bingo card for the day of the wedding. But when you're a wedding planner / heist crew organizer, you have to expect the unexpected.

Cristian kept Mrs. Angelini busy on his lap while Jack and I crawled across the floor.

"What's that noise?" she said when we were halfway across the room.

"Focus on me, baby." Cristian cupped her face, fingers covering her ears, and pulled her closer. "Just on me."

Gage arrived with the elephant following behind him. He stopped when the elephant's body blocked the outside crowd from the window and glared at us as she stroked his head with her trunk.

Jack went out the window first, then helped me over the ledge. Once we were down, we walked beside the elephant, using her massive body as a shield until we were clear of the house.

"You owe me big-time for this." Gage pushed the elephant's trunk off his shoulder. "Anil told me you didn't get the necklace. What happened? I thought you saw it in the safe."

"I saw a jewelry box. I assumed the necklace was in it. Apparently, I was wrong."

"Fuck."

The elephant slapped Gage lightly on the head. She clearly didn't like bad language.

"Cristian is in there with Mr. Angelini's wife," I said. "Do you think he needs us to save him?"

We shared a look, laughed, and then returned to the wedding empty-handed.

TWENTY-SEVEN

◆ ◆ ◆

For the next few hours, we focused on the wedding. Dinner went off without a hitch in the huge tent, followed by speeches, toasts, the dreaded garter removal, the first dance, and the cake cutting. I'd turned Bella's fairy-tale wedding dream into a reality with a classic, modern motif of glass, mirrors, and acrylic accents. Lavender softened the brilliance of the white orchids, hydrangeas, peonies, and roses Jack had selected to decorate the tent. After the young people hit the dance floor and the older people hit the bar, the catering staff set up a dessert trolley to tide people over until the second meal, which would be served after the happy couple bade their farewell.

As soon as the trolley rolled in, I gave Bella the signal to leave. She excused herself to get ready for her honeymoon departure, ran upstairs to change, and then slipped out of the house through the back stairs to the side exit. From there she skirted around the tent and through the trees to meet Chloe, Emma, and me at the beach.

"You made it!" Chloe gave her a hug. "Our crew didn't spot anyone following you so you're in the clear."

I helped Bella into the motorboat Emma had moored at the far end of the beach and out of sight of the house.

"I can't believe this is really happening." She tightened the scarf around her neck. "It's a dream come true."

"What are your plans?" I handed over her small travel bag. We'd decided a suitcase might draw unwanted attention, so Ben had been tasked with buying everything she would need to travel.

"We decided to charter a private jet because my father has connections everywhere and the risk of being caught at one of the main airports is too high." She set her bag down and settled in her seat. "We'll fly from a private airstrip to Miami and then down to Rio. After that . . . who knows."

Even if we pulled off the heist, I wouldn't have enough money to charter a private jet on a whim. Either Ben was very wealthy, or Bella had some money stashed away to finance her life on the run.

"I'm so happy for you," I said. I know what it's like to be overlooked by your family and how it feels to meet someone who actually sees you. "You're very brave to follow your heart, especially because your dad is a . . ." I bit back the words on the tip of my tongue. "Formidable man."

"The irony is that I'm more like him than my brother," Bella said. "He just refused to accept it because I'm a woman. If he'd given me a chance, I could have made him proud."

"We need to get going." Emma dipped her oars. She was going to row until they were far enough away that the sound of the motor wouldn't attract any attention.

We said our final farewells and watched Emma row until they disappeared into the darkness.

"I'm sorry, babe." I sank down on the sand, dropping my head between my hands.

Chloe sat beside me and put her arm around my shoulders. "It's okay. You went above and beyond. I couldn't have asked for a better friend. And on a positive note, we saved Bella from a terrible marriage."

"We still have our lawyers," I said. "They're from one of the top criminal law firms in the city. If anyone can get you off—"

"My lawyer told me to prepare for the worst." Chloe pulled out her phone and tapped the screen. "I've just sent you all the legal documents the firm prepared for Olivia's custody. I know I had originally named Kyle's parents as her legal guardians, but I can't take the risk that they'll let Kyle back into their life."

"You won't go—" My throat thickened, and the night sky blurred.

"I might and this is important to me," she said. "I don't trust anyone else to look after her, and I know no one will fight for her the way you will. It has to be you."

Nausea roiled in my belly at the thought of Olivia alone without her mom. But it wasn't going to happen. I'd prepared my own document—a letter—to be delivered to Chloe after I turned myself in.

"We'd better get back." I helped Chloe to her feet. "We'll need to stall so Bella has time to get away."

"Gage might be able to help," Jack said quietly from behind us.

I spun around at the sound of Jack's voice, my eyes making contact with his broad chest before I tilted my head back to meet his cool gaze. "How long have you been there?"

"From the moment you left the house. Gage is busy with the elephant. I wanted to make sure you were safe."

My heart swelled in my chest. We'd been extra careful. There was no way we could have been seen, but it made me happy that he'd come.

"How can Gage help us stall?" Chloe asked.

Jack smiled, but I saw a glint of mischief in his eyes. "We could ask him to arrange an elephant stampede."

◆ ◆ ◆

We didn't get our stampede, because the handler had taken the elephant home by the time we returned to the party. Instead, we got

DJ Ka-Poor filling the dance floor with his upbeat high-energy playlist.

"Where the fuck is Bella?" Mario accosted me beside the enormous working ice sculpture of a family of swans—another of Bella's extravagant demands.

I smoothed my face into a mask of bewildered innocence. "She went to get changed into her going-away outfit."

"She'd better hurry up or we'll miss our flight." He stabbed at his phone, an overt dismissal.

"Where are you going for your honeymoon?" I tried to keep my tone light although everything about this dude made me seethe inside. "Bella said it was supposed to be a surprise. I promise I won't tell."

"Berlin."

"Berlin?" I struggled to hide my shock. "It's not really a traditional honeymoon destination but it's good to be different. I would have picked somewhere warm and tropical—Hawaii, Jamaica, or maybe somewhere new and exciting—a cruise down the Nile, or a hike up to Machu Picchu. Or Morocco. I've always wanted to see Fez."

"Just go get her," he snapped. "I'm tired of waiting."

I took a long walk around the house and checked in on Rose, who was still playing referee between the caterer and the nonnas. Emma texted that she was back and ready to ride. Upstairs, I lingered in Bella's room and then walked up and down the hallway calling her name. After a suitably long time, I made my way back to the main floor and asked everyone I met if they'd seen her.

"Mr. Angelini wants to know where his daughter is." Gino cornered me in the grand hallway, a scowl on his menacing face. "The happy couple are supposed to be on their way to the airport." His voice was rough and gravelly, like he gargled with stones.

"I don't know where she is," I said honestly. "She left to get changed over an hour ago. I was just upstairs, and her suitcase is packed and on the bed. She must have come down to say good-bye to her friends. I was just about to check the kitchen."

"Mr. Angelini isn't happy. He wants her in the car in ten minutes. The guards are already searching the property."

"I don't know why she'd be anywhere except right here at the house," I said brightly. "We still have to do the petal parade, throwing the bouquet . . ."

"Ten minutes."

"I'll get my crew on it right away, and I'll check the bathrooms again," I said. "It might just be a case of bridal jitters."

Ten minutes later, Gino escorted me to Mr. Angelini's office, his thick hand heavy on my shoulder. There was no evidence of our visit or of Cristian's clandestine meeting with Mrs. Angelini on the brown leather couch.

"Where is she?" Mr. Angelini drummed his fingers on the desk.

"We're still looking for her." I wrung my hands and furrowed my brow for effect. "The last time I saw her, she was going upstairs to change."

I was tempted to feign shock at the very notion that she would run from her marriage to such a wonderful man, but he knew I knew Mario was an abusive bastard. Her disappearance couldn't have been a huge surprise.

Mr. Angelini leaned forward, dark eyes intense. "Did she ever share any plans with you about running away? Did she have a boyfriend?"

"We didn't really have any personal conversations. There was a lot to do and not much time, so we mostly talked about her dress, the flowers, music—wedding stuff."

"Work with Gino," he barked. "Find her."

I didn't want to work with Gino, but Gino said, "Come," and I went because Gino wasn't the kind of guy any sane person would refuse.

"Someone put balloons in front of the cameras at the back exit," Gino said. "We had no visibility at the back door."

"That's unfortunate." I met Gino's fierce gaze with one of my own. After everything I'd been through in the lead-up to the wedding slash heist, nothing and no one could scare me.

"It's convenient," Gino said. "Not unfortunate. I don't believe in fortune—good, bad, un, or mis."

"I don't think that take on prefixes really works," I pointed out. "My mom is an English professor. I thought about being an English major, but it would have been a huge disappointment to my family. They wanted me to be a doctor. What did you study? Or did you go straight into intimidation?"

Gino wasn't up for a conversation. "Where were your people when Bella went upstairs?"

"Running the wedding," I said. "Rose was in the kitchen overseeing the food. DJ Ka-Poor was rocking the dance floor. Emma was taking a nap in the limo while she waited to drive the bride and groom to the airport. Gage was helping with the elephant. Chloe was doing a security sweep. And Jack was spritzing the flower arrangements to keep them fresh for the second meal. I have to say we've done an excellent job." I also gave myself an A+ for excellent lying and quick thinking on the spot.

Gino folded his arms over his massive chest. "Didn't do such a good job if you lost the bride."

"Didn't do such a good job as head of security if she managed to leave without being detected," I countered with the same level of snark.

His eyes narrowed. "Are you saying she left?"

"Are you saying she didn't?"

Who was this woman burning a terrifying armed Mafia guard without a trace of fear, and what had she done with Simi? I wasn't scared of Gino. I was just annoyed that he didn't seem to believe my lies.

"Are you mocking me?" His voice rose in incredulity, and really, it was incredulous. I was waving a red flag in front of a bull, heedless of the consequences.

"What do you think?" I folded my arms, mimicking his pose. "A bride goes missing, and instead of thinking wedding jitters, or maybe she needed some alone time, you're treating me like I did something wrong. I'm the one who made this wedding happen. Why would I help her run away? Disappearing brides are bad for business. Not only would that worry potential clients, but it would also mean I'd have no one to give me a five-star review. Are you a contractor or an employee?" I didn't wait for him to answer, because I didn't really care how Gino made his living. I just wanted to keep him busy to give Bella the time she needed to get away. "If you're a contractor, you'll understand the importance of reviews. Instead of pointing the finger at me, you should really be looking for Bella or you might get a one-star review for losing the bride. You'll never get another security gig. This could be the end of your career."

"You're a mouthy one," Gino said. "I don't like mouthy."

"It's unfortunate that we have to work together because I'm all mouth all the time."

In retrospect, my clever comeback wasn't quite so clever because Gino's dark eyes smoldered, and not in a come-hither kind of way.

"It's not just about Bella," Gino gritted out. "She took something of value from Mr. Angelini."

"What did she take? His honor? We both know she was being forced into the marriage. Is it really such a surprise that she might need more than a few moments to collect her thoughts before she leaves her family home with the man who called her a whore and attacked her wedding planners in a dress shop?"

A pained expression crossed his face and for a moment I thought he might actually care. "There is a price to pay for betrayal."

My leg muscles tightened; my body ready to run. Would breaking into Mr. Angelini's office be considered a betrayal? How about spiriting the bride away?

"Simi." Jack stepped out of the shadows and draped his arm over my shoulders. "You're needed in the kitchen. Who's your new friend?"

"This is Gino." I straightened, buoyed by his support. "He thinks Bella ran away from her own wedding. As if she could go anywhere on the property without being seen. She's the bride, for goodness' sake!"

Jack bellowed a laugh as if I'd said the funniest thing in the world. "I thought I saw her dancing in the tent. Was she wearing a green dress?"

Damn, Jack was quick with the lies.

"Yes, that's her going-away outfit. She couldn't decide between that and a pink Chanel." I gave Gino my best fake smile. "Sounds like you just need to check the tent. Let me know when you find her. Maybe check the ice sculpture, too. She might have turned into a swan."

Gino made a V with his fingers, pointed to his eyes and then at me before walking away.

"Did you see that?" I whispered to Jack. "Did he seriously do the 'I'm watching you' gesture with his fingers?" I looked up and shouted, "I see you, too."

"Don't goad him," Jack warned. "You don't want to mess with a guy like that."

"He should be more worried about messing with me. I beat up a mob boss's son. I chased away armed intruders with a floorboard. Who knows what I'd do to him? I'm not the simpering Simi you met at the museum. I organized a successful wedding, an escape, and two failed heists. I just broke into a Mafia boss's office and went through his safe. I'm just surprised he wasn't quaking in his boots."

Jack leaned over to kiss my temple. "You were never simpering. You just didn't know your own strengths."

We walked through the house to the kitchen. The catering staff had finished cleaning. Rose was shooing the last of the nonnas away, and Gage was leaning against the counter pouring Chloe a glass of what looked to be cooking sherry.

"Simi!" Cristian ran into the kitchen, narrowly missing one of the servers. He grabbed the counter to slow his momentum and heaved in a breath. "Bella . . ."

"Christ," Gage said. "You did her, too?"

Cristian shook his head. He looked around to ensure we were alone and said in lowered voice, "Bella has the necklace."

"*The* necklace?" My heart leaped into my throat. "Our necklace?"

"Sophia . . . er . . . Mrs. Angelini pulled me off the dance floor about half an hour ago," Cristian said. "She said she'd walked in on Bella when she was packing upstairs and saw her put a necklace in her bag. Bella told her that her father had given it to her as a wedding gift. I asked Sophia what it looked like, and she described the Wild Heart. She went on and on about how her husband had never given her anything so beautiful, how he didn't really love her." He shook his head. "She was so distraught. I had to take her somewhere quiet and do what I could to calm her down so she didn't run to her husband and confront him before we had a chance to find Bella."

"I'm sure you did . . . calm her down," Gage muttered. "You're a model of altruism."

"Gino said she'd taken something of value," I said. "That must be it. And now Bella's on her way to Rio. We have to catch her before she gets on the airplane or Gino gets to her first." I stared at the shocked faces around me. "Well, come on. Move. Everyone to the van. We'll get Emma on the way. We can't take the limo or they'll know something is up. Where's Anil?"

"He's still DJing," Chloe said. "We can't pull him away without drawing attention."

"I'll stay and pass on the message," Rose offered. "You'll need someone here in case there are any problems."

"What about Jack?" I hadn't even seen him leave. Why did he always disappear when we needed him most?

"Don't worry about him." Rose pushed me gently in the direction of the door. "I'll find him. You need to go before you lose your chance."

We dodged and weaved through the crowd toward the parking lot, grabbing Emma on our way to the van. Heaving our breaths, we piled inside while Emma climbed into the driver's seat.

"Where to, boss?"

"I'm not sure. I can't think." I dropped my head between my knees and made a mental note to start jogging again. "She's taking a private jet and she didn't tell me which airfield they were using. I can't call because she and Ben both dumped their phones in case her father could track her."

"Didn't you book their cab?" Chloe asked. "You could call the company and ask them where they dropped her off."

I made the call. The cab company gave me the address of a warehouse in Hanover Park that was nowhere near any airstrip that I could see online.

"What's she doing there?" I stared at the map on my phone, trying to figure out why they'd made a stop when they were supposed to be on their way to Rio.

"Maybe Gino had men nearby and they caught her," Gage suggested.

"Then she'll definitely need our help. The warehouse is in an industrial park forty minutes away. We can't wait for Anil and Jack. I'll text them the address. This is our last chance to get the necklace."

"What if she won't give it back?" Chloe pulled the door closed.

"Don't worry," I said. "I'll come up with a plan."

TWENTY-EIGHT

◆ ◆ ◆

Pull over and let me drive," Gage shouted from the back seat. "You're going to get us all killed."

"Poor baby." Emma swerved around a car, and we all braced ourselves against the seats. "Can't take the speed?"

"I don't have a fucking death wish."

"You're perfectly safe with me," Emma said. "There isn't a vehicle I can't drive, and I haven't been in an accident since I got my license back."

"Back?" Chloe knocked on the wood paneling inside the van. She'd always been superstitious.

"Reckless driving. It was a bogus charge," Emma said. "If I'd had a better lawyer, they would never have made it stick. That road was made specifically for drag racing."

"Why does it smell like tacos in here?" I sniffed and my stomach rumbled, reminding me that I hadn't eaten since breakfast.

"Elephants don't like chili peppers," Gage said. "I got some tacos delivered when her handler took her for a snack. I thought the smell might put her off."

We followed the map to a small auto parts warehouse in the middle of a vast industrial park. Gage made us sit in the van while he checked the place out. He returned to report that the building was about 25,000 square feet and had only one entrance or exit. Through the windows, he'd seen a labyrinth of engine parts, crates, and fifty-five-gallon drums. Bella was inside with three men and didn't appear to be in any danger.

"Was one of them about five-ten, thick brown hair with two widow's peaks, baby blues, four-finger forehead, kinda average but kinda cute?" I asked. "That would be her boyfriend, Ben."

Gage stared at me as if I were speaking a second language. "They were looking the other way and I couldn't see their faces, but what the hell kind of description is that?"

"Andrew Garfield. *Spider-Man* 2012," Cristian said.

"Why the fuck didn't she just say that?"

"How was I to know you were a *Spider-Man* stan?" I said. "You rarely talk during meetings. We don't know much about you. Not even your favorite snack."

"Tacos."

"Thanks for the share." I peered out the side window. "What do you think they're doing in there?"

"Looks like they're waiting for someone. They weren't making themselves comfortable and they didn't have any stuff with them. One of them kept checking his phone."

"Maybe they're waiting for a fence," I suggested. "She can't risk taking the necklace on a plane to a foreign country, and it's very unlikely she has the connections to sell it directly. A necklace like that is usually sold in underground channels on the black market."

"Look at you, babe." Chloe gave me a nudge. "You know just as much as a real criminal. I couldn't be prouder."

"I still can't believe she took it." I slumped back in my seat. "She seemed so sweet."

"She was willing to defy her mob boss father and flee the country with the man she loved," Chloe said. "I'm not surprised she would steal from him, although my guess is that she's doing it out of spite. The question is, how are we going to convince her to give it to us?"

"You can't." Emma turned in her seat. "That's the kind of money people kill for. She may appear sweet, but she's a tough-ass bitch and she knows her daddy's goons will be coming for her. She needs that money to disappear. There's nothing you can offer her that she won't be able to buy once she sells the necklace."

I caught movement in the rearview mirror. A man walked out of the warehouse and lit a cigarette. I would have recognized his four-finger forehead even if Bella hadn't shown me pictures of her secret boyfriend when we were preparing for the wedding.

"There's our answer," Gage said. "We'll kidnap Ben and offer to trade him for the necklace."

"Kidnap?" Chloe stared at him aghast. "What do you know about kidnapping people?"

"I wouldn't give up twenty-five million for that dude," Emma said. "Timothée Chalamet or Tom Holland? Maybe. But him? He reminds me of my cousin Joe. Painfully average. Only differences are the hair and this dude's got all his fingers. Cousin Joe liked to experiment with chemicals and one time it all went wrong. He set himself on fire and lost three fingers. He's into woodworking now. Much safer."

"She loves him," I said. "She was willing to risk everything to be with him. People will do crazy things for love. I'm sure if I explain the situation, she'll understand."

"You ever loved anyone like that?" Emma asked.

"No."

"Me neither. If I ever come to you and tell you I'm about to hand over twenty-five million dollars in the name of love, please hit me over the head with something hard and bury me alive until I come to my senses."

"That's very touching," Cristian said. "I always knew you had no heart."

Emma turned and gave him a withering look. "Look who's talking. Which bridesmaid brought you as her plus-one? Ten dollars says you still don't know her name."

"I spent time with all of them." Cristian gave an irritated huff. "I like to share myself around."

"Twenty bucks if you can name even one."

"We don't have time for this," I said. "He's not going to be out there for long. I wish Rose were here. She knows everything about kidnapping."

"I saw rope and duct tape in the back of the van," Emma said. "Also, a tarp, some zip ties, a shovel, bleach, garbage bags, and a bone saw. I call dibs on the tire iron. I've taken up golf and I want to practice my drive."

"Why use a tire iron when we have a .22?" Chloe pulled a gun from her purse.

"Babe!" I held up my hands in a warding gesture. "I thought Gage was joking when he said you'd brought a gun to our last heist. Since when do you own a weapon, much less know how to use one?"

"Gage took me out to the shooting range last weekend," she said. "I want to be able to defend myself. What if Kyle attacks me on the street? Or in a parking lot? What if he gets past my security system? I'm not going to be a victim anymore. I'm taking charge of my life."

"Why didn't you tell me?" We'd never kept secrets from each other. I wasn't as shocked about the gun as I was about the fact that she hadn't shared any of this with me.

Chloe gave an apologetic shrug. "I guess I didn't know what you'd think. I've changed since we started this heist. I've done things I would never have imagined doing. I'm badass now, Simi.

I don't need to be protected by you or Gage or anyone, and I wasn't sure if you'd still love the new me."

"I can't believe you'd even think that after everything we've been through together. You'll always be my ride or die." I patted her purse. "Now, how about you put that away so we can get to planning our kidnapping?"

As soon as she took her attention off me, I leaned over and whispered in Gage's ear, "After we've kidnapped the boyfriend and recovered the necklace, we're going to have words."

Gage gave me a curt nod. "Noted."

"I'm anti-violence," Cristian said. "I can't be an active participant in a violent crime. I can, however, watch the van and be ready to drive if we need to get out of here in a hurry."

Emma shook her head and sighed. "Were you born anti-everything, or did the world make you that way?"

"There's enough violence in the world," Cristian said. "Someone has to take a stand."

"Or in your case, hide while the rest of your crew puts their lives on the line." Her voice was as bitter as I'd ever heard it. "At least you're consistent. And this time you're not running away, so yay to your personal growth."

"We're not putting our lives on the line," I said. "It's just a simple kidnapping for ransom. What could possibly go wrong?"

◇ ◇ ◇

As it turned out, we didn't need the tire iron. Gage knocked Ben out with the handle of his gun.

"What did you do?" I shrieked when he returned to the van with an unconscious Ben over his shoulders.

"What if it doesn't go the way you planned?" Gage said, dumping Ben on the floor. "He'll be able to identify us. Kidnapping is a felony. I thought you were trying to stay out of jail."

"Okaaaay." I sucked in a sharp breath. "Not how I thought the plan would go, but I can work with that. Everyone grab a weapon and let's get going."

"What should I do?" Cristian helped Gage lift Ben back onto his shoulders.

"You need to text Jack and Anil again and update them. Tell them we've kidnapped Ben for leverage and we're going in. Then you should keep a lookout for suspicious activity. I've watched enough crime shows with Rose to know that nothing good happens in industrial parks at night."

"This should be a quick in-and-out operation," Gage said. "Once we control the exit, we control the room. We make the trade. And we're gone."

◆ ◆ ◆

With Gage carrying an unconscious Ben over his shoulders, we walked into the warehouse. Bright fluorescent lights hung from the ceiling, casting shadows on the grease-stained cement floor. I could smell diesel and sawdust and the lingering scent of perfume. A woman's laugh echoed through the cavernous space. A hush. Silence. The slide of a clip in a gun. By the time we had navigated the labyrinth of wooden crates, metal drums, and plastic barrels, we knew they knew we were in the building.

I don't know why it hadn't occurred to me that a mob boss's daughter might be armed, but the way the day was going, I wasn't surprised to be staring down the barrels of three guns when we reached the center of the warehouse.

"Simi?" Bella's eyes widened. "What are you doing here? If my father sent you . . ."

"He doesn't know I'm here." I gestured to Gage to put Ben down. If things went bad, I wanted him to have both hands free.

"So you've come to solve another problem." She tipped her

head back and groaned. "You're the most irritatingly efficient event coordinator I've ever known. I successfully got rid of five wedding planners before you. I'd finally put myself in a position where the wedding would never happen. But no. There is nothing you can't do. Plan a wedding in a few weeks? Sure. Find an elephant? Sure. Six-foot ice sculpture of swans in flight? Sure. Alter a dress in two days to meet the demands of an insufferable monster? Sure."

"I thought my aunt did a good job with the lace."

"If I wanted to get married in the eighteenth century." She got steely-eyed and glared at me. "I had to poison a priest because of you and not even that was enough. Somehow you managed to fix that, too."

I struggled to process what was happening. "Why did you need to poison the priest? We had everything ready for your escape, and it all went according to plan."

"Mario came to see me last night," she spat out. "I don't know if he knew about our plan, but he put a knife to my throat and told me that once we were legally married, there was nowhere on earth I could run that he wouldn't find me. It was a matter of honor, and honor is everything for our families. I'd never really be free. And then it occurred to me: there would be no wedding if the priest was dead. It would be seen as a bad omen."

I stared at her aghast. There was cold, and then there was liquid nitrogen cold, and then there was Bella. "But how did you plan to escape?"

"I was going to hide in your van," she said. "I figured it would be chaos when we had to shut it all down. I was going to get you to take me to the boat launch to meet Ben, and the rest would go as planned. But you solved that damn problem like everything else. Why didn't you just give up when the priest was out of the picture? Or, more to the point, why did you have to go looking for him in the first place? If you'd just been a little less competent, he would have been dead."

"But it all worked out in the end," I pointed out. "In fact, it was even better. No murder. No real marriage. And you got away to be with Ben."

It occurred to me at that moment that she hadn't reacted to seeing the love of her life lying unconscious on the floor. No gasps. No tears. No shrieks of "Ben, are you okay?" or "What did you do to him?" or even "He's not part of this. Let him go." It was almost like she didn't care.

"Is that why you're here?" Her face twisted in a sneer. "You want me to thank you?"

"I want the necklace you took from your father, and I'm willing to trade Ben for it," I blurted out.

Emma gave an exasperated sigh. "She means give us the necklace or Ben's gonna shake hands with Elvis."

Gage pulled out his gun and made a show of positioning it near Ben's forehead, as if there was an optimum place to shoot out someone's brains.

Bella's lips curled at the corners. I'd never noticed before, but her lips were narrow and thin. Even the makeup artist had struggled to plump them up. "And who are you? The jewelry police?"

"Just think of us as a repo team," I said. "You give us the necklace. We give you Ben. No one has to get hurt."

"A chauffeur, an ex-priest slash elephant trainer, and a weakass security gal who doesn't even have a gun." She snorted a laugh. "That's who you brought as backup?"

"It's a gig economy," I said. "They have many skills."

My phone buzzed in my pocket. Once. Twice. Thrice. Four times. Whatever the caller wanted couldn't be good, but there was no way I could check my messages now.

I heard a door slam. The thunder of feet. Before anyone could react, Gino burst into the clearing and greeted us all with a menacing scowl. "What the fuck is going on?"

For the first time since I'd met her, Bella almost lost her composure. "Gino . . ." Her voice wavered. "You found us."

"Of course I found you. I just had to follow her." He pointed at me. "She knew more than she was letting on. I could see it all over her face. Were you trying to run from me?"

"Of course not, baby." She rallied quickly, and her honeyed voice turned sickly sweet. "I found a buyer for the necklace and he wanted to meet right away. I was going to surprise you."

"Bella? Sweetheart?" Ben pushed to his knees, rubbing the back of his head where Gage had hit him. I motioned for my crew to take a step back so he didn't see our faces. "What happened? I was standing outside and . . ." He shook his head, scrubbed a hand over his face. "Why did you call him 'baby'?"

"Who the hell is this?" Gino demanded. "Are you fucking him? Because I swear—"

"He's no one." Bella waved a dismissive hand. "I was using him to help us get out of the country. He's rich and had access to a private plane. I was going to call you to meet us at the airfield after I got the money, and then we'd ditch him and head to Rio. He doesn't mean anything to me."

And right at that moment, our simple kidnapping didn't seem as simple anymore.

"Bella?" Ben got to his feet and took an unsteady step forward. "I don't understand. I love you. I thought we were going to make a life together."

"This is better drama than I ever saw in prison," Emma whispered.

"He loves you?" Gino was almost vibrating with rage. He

seemed more concerned that she was cheating on him than the fact that she was clearly planning to run off with the money. "Do you love him?"

"No, baby. I love you." Bella held her ground. I had to hand it to her: I couldn't handle one man, much less three, and mine wasn't in the mob. "We're going to get the money, jump on the plane, and live the life we dreamed about. Just like we planned."

"Then we don't need him?" Gino stared pointedly at Bella, and something passed between them that made the hair on the back of my neck prickle in warning.

"Not anymore. The plane's been chartered and it's all ready to go." She gave the briefest of nods. Without a second of hesitation, Gino drew his weapon and shot Ben in the chest.

"No." My hands rushed to cover my mouth. Chloe let out a sharp scream.

Ben staggered back into Gage, knocking him off balance. Emma moved to catch Gage and fell with them, their bodies toppling like dominoes to the floor.

I couldn't move, couldn't breathe. My ears were ringing from the echo of the gunshot, my heart pounding so hard I thought it would break a rib.

"Oh dear." Bella walked past me to pick up the gun that had fallen from Gage's hand. "Now you have nothing to bargain with. Solve that fucking problem."

TWENTY-NINE

❖ ❖ ❖

I hate to say I told you so . . ."

"Then don't say it." I glared at Emma, tied to a barrel across from me, hands duct-taped behind her, feet bound in front. After rounding us up and forcing us to our knees at gunpoint, Bella had sent one of the non-Ginos out to the van. He'd come back with Cristian, our rope, and the roll of duct tape. Ten minutes later we were all tied to barrels like Emma and spaced far enough apart that we couldn't help each other escape.

"What wouldn't you do for twenty-five million dollars?" Emma said. "It's a life-changing amount of money."

"I wouldn't poison a priest, steal from my Mafia boss father, shoot my boyfriend, or tie up my wedding planners and hide them behind a pile of barrels in a warehouse in the middle of nowhere on my wedding day." I looked over at Gage, tied up and unconscious on the floor. After extricating himself from the pile of bodies, he had proven to be more than Bella and her companions could handle. Gino had finally hit him over the head with Emma's tire iron, just to keep him still.

"I would."

"That's because you have no morals," Cristian said. "I'm anti-violence for this very reason."

"What reason? So you can scream and put up your hands when a dude with a gun comes to the van instead of driving away and calling for help?" Emma was in prime fighting form. Fear seemed to bring out the worst of her snark.

"I texted Anil after you left," he said. "He didn't respond, but he has the update. He knows what's going on."

My gaze cut to Cristian. "I told you to text Jack, too."

"I thought they'd be together," Cristian said. "Why send two texts when you can send only one?"

"They'd better be together or we'll have to rely on Anil to rescue us." Emma banged her head against the barrel. "Shoot me now."

"He might surprise you." Chloe shifted her weight, pulling at the rope they'd used to tie us to the barrels. "He's proven to be very resourceful and we all know he's seriously smart."

"He's young, naive, and lacks common sense," Emma said. "It won't occur to him to call the police if he sees the van empty. He'll probably knock on the door and walk right in."

I caught a soft moan and saw Ben move his head. He was still unconscious, his shirt soaked with blood, his skin sheet white. "What are we going to do about Ben? He's going to die if we don't get some help. This is on us. He wouldn't be here if we hadn't brought him into this."

"She would have shot him anyway," Emma said. "That bitch is made of ice. Why share twenty-five million when you can keep it for yourself? The only thing I don't understand is why she needed Gino. He clearly has feelings for her, but I'm pretty sure she doesn't give a damn about him."

"He could get into the safe," I said, working it out as we talked. "He knew where it was, and he knew the combination. She was using him, just like she used Ben."

"Maybe she does love him," Chloe said. "You don't know what's in people's hearts."

Emma snorted a laugh. "Who needs love when you can have cash?"

"I still believe in love," Chloe said firmly. "I believe that there is someone out there for each of us. Someone who will take your breath away and make your heart pound. Someone who would give up everything just to be with you."

"Someone who lives in La La Land," Emma spat out. "In the real world, the people you love most betray you, so you stop believing in love or even friendship. You learn to be alone. You learn to watch your own back because no one will do it for you."

"Leave her alone," I said. "You don't know anything about her life."

"It's okay." Chloe's gentle voice took my anxiety down one notch. "She's scared. I'm scared, too. I think we all are. And I do know about the real world. But I won't let anyone take away all the things that make life beautiful. I'm going to keep believing until it becomes real."

"You won't be believing anything for long," Cristian said. "They're not going to leave any witnesses if Ben dies."

Ben was still breathing. I didn't need my mirror to see his chest rise. I may not have done well in my first aid course, but I still remembered a few things. "We need to put pressure on his wound. Who can reach him with their feet?"

Cristian angled his body and placed his legs on Ben's chest. "You're lucky I have abs of steel and an excellent cleaner who can get blood out of anything."

Gage groaned and raised his head. Gino had used extra rope and extra tape to secure him to one of the barrels. "Stop yapping. You're giving me a headache."

"I think it was the tire iron," Emma said. "They got you from behind."

"What's the plan?" He pushed himself to an unsteady seat and immediately began sawing his legs, stretching the tape around his ankles.

"Anil's coming to save us," Emma said.

"Christ. Someone knock me out again."

"I have faith in Anil," I said. "I think he just may surprise us."

"We're dead." Gage shook his head. "We are so fucking dead."

◇ ◇ ◇

Time goes slowly when you're tied up in a warehouse. It could have been ten minutes, or it could have been an hour before we heard a door slam. Then footsteps. Two sets. Raised voices came from the main warehouse floor. I couldn't make out their words, but the tone was one of frustration.

"The buyers must be here," I whispered. "That means our time is running out."

"Where's Anil?" Gage was still working away at the duct tape around his ankles. He'd managed to loosen it almost enough that he'd be able to free one foot if he took off his shoe.

"Maybe he's tied up this evening," Cristian said.

Emma's gaze snapped to him. "You've just been waiting to use that one, haven't you?"

"I can find humor in any situation."

What happened next is something I'll never forget. I heard a faint noise coming from overhead. At first, I thought it was just buzzing from the lights, but as the sound got louder, I looked up, trying to track it.

I spotted the small drone just before it flew overhead. It dropped down, hovering just above us. Tiny lights flickered on its wings.

"It's Anil." I couldn't help the smile that spread across my face. "I told you he'd come."

The drone rose higher and higher and then disappeared through a hole in the ceiling that I hadn't noticed before.

I tensed in hopeful anticipation. Who would be coming through the door? Police? Fire? Jack? Or would Anil try to pull off the rescue on his own?

"What the fuck?" Gage's gaze was fixed on the ceiling. The hole was actually an access hatch, and someone was looking down.

"Is that . . . ?" I squinted through the glare of the fluorescent lights, trying to identify the figure now climbing through the hatch. "Rose?"

"It is Rose." Chloe's face was a mix of happiness and horror. "But what is she . . . ? No. No. Nope. She didn't. She can't."

But she did, and she could. Spread-eagled and dressed entirely in black, Rose dropped slowly from the ceiling, supported only by a thin wire tied to some contraption around her waist.

"It's our grease woman come to rescue us à la *Mission: Impossible*," Emma whispered in delight. "Look at Rose go."

Rose descended at a slow, steady pace. She was wearing a backpack over a formfitting spandex bodysuit, running shoes, a pair of cat ears, and a long tail.

"I think I might have a concussion," Gage said. "I'm seeing an eighty-year-old cat woman dropping from the ceiling."

"It's real. It's Rose to the rescue."

"I can't watch." Chloe ducked her head. "She's going to get hurt."

"She's done it before," I assured her. "Although I think it was quite a few years ago."

Rose stopped a few inches from the floor. "Did someone call for a grease woman?"

"You can put your feet down," I said, keeping my voice low. "There are no booby traps, pressure plates, or lasers. You're good."

"I wanted to see how close I could get." She dropped to her feet and detached the cable around her waist. Above in the opening, Chef Pierre gave her a thumbs-up.

"You're amazing, Rose," I whispered, my senses alert for any hint that we'd been heard.

"You're lucky I kept my rigging, ears, and tail," she said. "I wore the bodysuit because Chef Pierre wasn't comfortable with me going nude the way I did in the original show. He doesn't like to share, so don't tell him about Stan."

I made a mental note to thank Chef Pierre for his discretion.

"I've got chocolate croissants, madeleines, macarons, and tools to cut you loose." Rose removed her backpack and pulled out a plastic food container, sewing scissors, and a handful of kitchen knives.

"It's all I had," she said when Gage gave her a quizzical look. "We'd just returned home from the wedding when Anil called to say he couldn't get in touch with you and he thought you might need a rescue. I told him he couldn't go alone, so he came and picked us up. I was still in the garage packing my rigging when he arrived, so I just grabbed what I could from the kitchen on my way out."

I looked up at the opening, but all I could see was Chef Pierre. "Where is Anil?"

"Hi, guys!" Anil squeezed between two barrels and into the circle. He was dressed in black, his face covered in a ski mask.

Chloe shot Anil a puzzled look. "How did you get in?"

"Through the door." He pulled out a meat cleaver and sawed at the tape around Gage's feet. "There were two guys in suits outside when we got here so we went up to the roof on the rear access ladder to launch the drone. Rose volunteered to go down, so we rigged her up, but by the time we finished, the two guys were inside. Rose wanted to drop down anyway, just in case I had a problem getting in."

"Best five minutes of my life." Rose ran her bread knife over the tape on my ankles. "If anyone wants a go . . ."

I updated Rose and Anil while they cut us loose. As soon as I was free, I went over to Ben and lifted Cristian's feet so I could check the damage. I didn't have any experience with bullet wounds, but a chest covered with blood and a gaping hole seemed pretty bad to me.

"Someone give me a shirt. We need to put pressure on his wound. Who's got a phone? They took all our stuff when they tied us up. We need an ambulance right away. Where's Jack?" My brain was going at full tilt. I was determined to get everyone out alive.

Anil handed me his shirt. "Rose has a phone. I can create a distraction so everyone can get out and she can make the call. Jack isn't here." He grimaced. "The situation is . . . complicated."

I wanted to ask what he meant by complicated, but the blood was coming faster and we were running out of time. "Everyone go," I said. "I'll stay with Ben."

Anil picked up his drone and pulled a handful of foam pellets from his pocket. "I modded my drone to shoot Nerf darts. I can cause a little chaos while everyone slips out the door."

"Sounds good. Rose, as soon as you're out, call for an ambulance and then call the 18th Precinct and ask for Detective Garcia. Tell him I'm here and there are people with guns, but don't give any other details."

"I'm not leaving you." Chloe knelt down beside me. "Four hands are better than two."

"You are leaving, because Olivia needs her mom and someone needs to get Rose to the van before she does something even crazier than dropping from a warehouse ceiling." I gave a hollow laugh. "She's seen too many crime shows. She might forget the bullets are real."

"I'll come back for Simi," Gage said to Chloe, pulling her up.

"No, you won't." I met his gaze with a shake of my head. "Your job is to keep everyone safe. There are people out there with guns, and they are not afraid to use them." I swallowed hard, reached for the strength inside me. "I'll be fine. Bella's not going to stick around when things start to go wrong. She's a survivor."

And so was I.

Anil started up his drone and sent it into the middle of the warehouse. I heard an "ow," a shriek, a grunt of pain.

"What's going on?" Bella shouted. "Where is it coming from?"

"Go." I tipped my chin toward the door. "Now."

Chloe shot me a last desperate look before following the rest of the crew into the shadows.

Gunshots echoed in the warehouse; a bullet pinged off the ceiling. Sweat beaded on Anil's forehead as he made the drone swoop and dive.

"You have to leave," I insisted. "The van needs to be gone before the police arrive."

"They might come for you," Anil said. "I think it's time to let The Butcher out to play."

"Anil . . . no."

In the distance, sirens wailed.

◇ ◇ ◇

"Hi, Garcia."

"Simi." Garcia moved off the sidewalk while the paramedics

lifted Ben onto the gurney. "Fancy meeting you here at a crime scene."

"It's a funny story." I glanced behind me, caught the back of the van hurtling down the road.

"I look forward to hearing it." He shrugged off his jacket and wrapped it around my bloodstained dress. "I think you know the drill by now."

"I'll call Riswan and ask him to meet us at the station."

◇ ◇ ◇

"Let me see if I've got this right." Garcia leaned back in his steel chair across from me and Riswan. We were in the same interrogation room as the night we'd first met. If I hadn't been so worried that I'd forget our cover story, I would have been touched.

"You started a wedding planning business and got a last-minute gig salvaging the wedding of Mr. Angelini's daughter. She told you she was being forced into the marriage, so you and your friends decided to help her escape so she could be with her boyfriend."

"We're a full-service business," I said. "There isn't anything I won't do for my clients."

"Escaping from the mob?"

"My client has no knowledge of whether or not her client's family is involved in organized crime," Riswan said.

"She does because I told her." Garcia tried to stare down Riswan. A normal mortal would have crumbled, but Riswan had a core of steel that made even the sternest prosecutor tremble.

"I believe you used the words 'allegedly' and 'rumored' in that conversation." Riswan flipped through the notes he'd made in our pre-Garcia meeting. "Your speculation does not constitute actual knowledge on the part of my client."

"Um. Hmm." Garcia tapped his fingers on the table. "You said

Mr. Angelini called you to his office to ask if you'd seen his daughter. Subsequently, you spoke to Mr. Angelini's head of security, a man named Gino. He told you that Bella had taken something valuable from her father. Do you know what it was?"

"Bella mentioned a necklace when we were in the warehouse."

Garcia lifted an eyebrow. My lips quivered with a smile. Riswan cleared his throat and we got back down to business.

"Gino issued a threat, saying there was a price for betrayal, so you took it upon yourself to track Bella down to warn her after already having helped her escape from a forced marriage."

"I'm sure you've watched a Mafia movie or two." I drew a line across my throat. "Although I had no direct knowledge of any Mafia connections, your comments did raise some red flags that made me concerned for my client's safety. I couldn't let her get killed by the mob." I caught Riswan shaking his head and made a quick correction. "Alleged mob."

"I see." His face suggested he didn't see at all, but I wasn't going to do all the work for him.

"It would destroy my reputation," I continued. "Event planning is a cutthroat business, Garcia. No pun intended. Reviews are everything."

"Indeed."

"And I believe in true love," I said quickly. "She wanted to be with Ben. I wanted her to have love and life and all the happiness in the world."

"Ben," he said dryly. "The man she shot in the chest."

"Gino shot him in the chest, but she approved the hit by nodding." I wasn't above breaching client confidentiality after what she'd done to Ben. If there had been a bus nearby, I would have thrown her under that, too. "Gino is a nasty piece of work. I hope you find him and lock him up for a long time." Somehow Gino had managed to escape before the police rounded up Bella and her accomplices.

"How is Ben?" I asked while Garcia wrote in his notebook.

"In surgery," he said. "I've been told he'll make it."

"It's kind of symbolic if you think about it. Maybe true love doesn't exist after all."

Garcia didn't seem to be interested in philosophizing about the meaning of love. Instead, he continued in the same monotone he'd been using since he'd joined us in the interrogation room. "Did you see the necklace that was allegedly stolen?"

"No." I'd seen Anil's replica but never the real thing.

Garcia stared at me. I stared at him. How had I forgotten how gorgeous he was? He had a dimple at the corner of his mouth that only appeared when he smiled. I was pretty sure he didn't run away when bad guys showed up or disappear when you needed him most. I tried to imagine him without any clothes, but my mind kept going back to Jack, who was still MIA.

He picked up his black notebook and continued his recap of my story. "You tracked Bella to the warehouse alone in a vehicle that has since disappeared . . ."

"It's not a safe neighborhood," I said. "You might want to ask the uniforms to add a foot patrol. I was there only a few hours and now my van is gone. A serial killer probably has it. You might want to check your database for serial killers in the area."

Garcia lifted an eyebrow. "Mmm-hmm."

I shifted in my chair, trying to get comfortable. It was basic interrogation room issue—cold, hard metal with a slightly slanted seat. I wondered if he would oblige if I asked for a pillow.

Garcia poured himself a glass of water and took a long, slow sip. "You walked into the warehouse and warned Bella that her father had sent someone after her," he continued. "You were surprised when that very person—Gino—suddenly showed up. There was an altercation. Gino shot her boyfriend. Her associates captured you and tied you up with five sets of duct tape and five sets of rope."

"What can I say? They must have sensed I would be a formidable opponent. You learn a lot when you have three brothers. Menace must have oozed from my pores."

He hesitated, frowning. "Not the kind of gratitude one would expect for the incredible service you'd done for her."

"I witnessed an attempted murder," I said. "I suspect she didn't want to take the risk I might tell someone about her nod of approval."

"Why not just ask Gino to shoot you, too?"

"Maybe she had friends who were getting married, and she wanted them to have the best damn wedding planner in Chicago. I got her an elephant, a family of ice swans, a last-minute dress alteration, an escape plan, and an expedited ordained minister after she poisoned her priest."

"She poisoned a priest?"

I glanced over at Riswan to make sure it was okay to tell this part of the story. He gave me a brief nod to continue.

"Father McCormack. He's at Mount Sinai Hospital. You can check it out. She poisoned him so he couldn't perform the ceremony, but unlucky for her, I'm good at my job and I found a replacement."

"I'll add 'priest poisoning' to the report," he said. "And I thought this was going to be a quiet night."

I wasn't getting a good vibe from Garcia. Usually, he shook his head in feigned exasperation, laughed at my jokes, and gave me warm, tender looks that made me feel melty inside.

"Two people arrived to buy the necklace," he continued, reading from his book. "But before they could finish the transaction, a mysterious person in a ski mask arrived. He used a drone with

Nerf darts to distract Bella and her associates and then cut you free." Garcia paused. "Why was he wearing a ski mask?"

"Why does anyone wear a ski mask?" I retorted. "He didn't want to be recognized."

"I thought ski masks were for skiing in the cold."

"That's because you lack imagination, Garcia, but I won't hold it against you."

Riswan coughed a warning, and I gave myself a mental kick. Garcia wasn't in a playful mood tonight.

"Instead of leaving the warehouse and running to safety, the masked man engaged Bella and her associates in a fight during which time Gino and the buyers disappeared. You stayed behind to try and save Ben. The masked man managed to single-handedly subdue your captors and disappeared before the paramedics arrived." He put down his book. "Like Spider-Man."

"I didn't see any webs and he wasn't wearing spandex. I'd say he was more like a butcher, pounding his meat."

Garcia leaned forward, his weight on his elbows. "Here's the problem. Bella's associates have a different story. One involving multiple assailants."

My eyes watered and I swallowed past the lump in my throat. After getting Rose and Chef Pierre back to the van to make the emergency calls, Cristian, Gage, Chloe, and Emma had returned to the warehouse. When they realized The Butcher was battling the evil villains alone, they'd run to help him. I'd caught glimpses of them through the barrels. It had been one hell of a fight.

"Well, of course they'd say that. They must have been humiliated. And if it were true, you should be thanking the multiple assailants for handing the bad guys to you on a silver platter. It means less paperwork for you."

"There are a lot of holes in your story," Garcia said. "A lot of holes."

"There were a lot of holes in Ben, but it sounds like he's going to pull through."

"If you've got evidence that counters my client's story . . ." Riswan began.

Garcia shook his head and sighed. "I honestly don't know what to do here."

"Garcia," I said quietly. "I didn't commit any crimes. I didn't steal the necklace. I didn't shoot Ben. All I did was salvage a wedding and try to help a poor girl from being forced into a marriage to a man she didn't love. I'm not a bad person. I started this business as a side hustle to help pay off my debts, and even that didn't work out."

"That is the only part of your story I believe," he said.

"What's going to happen to Bella? Did she confess? Did you recover the necklace?"

"Her story makes even less sense," Garcia said. "She said Gino held a grudge against her father and decided to kidnap her and Ben and hold them for ransom. He intercepted them on their way to the airfield and brought them to the warehouse, where they were held at gunpoint by his two associates. Ben tried to save her, and Gino shot him. Then you showed up because apparently there is no problem you can't solve and nothing you won't do for your clients. After Gino tied you up, the masked man arrived, took everyone down, and tied her up by mistake."

"That's really sweet of her," I said, smug in the knowledge that I had told a much better story. "Did she mention if she was going to give me a five-star review?"

Garcia reached into the box beside him and pulled out a plastic evidence bag containing a necklace. "We found this at the scene. On a hunch, before talking to you, I called Mr. Angelini. He said he didn't know anything about a necklace, nothing had been stolen from his home, and as far as he was concerned, no crime had been committed. By an incredible coincidence, this necklace is a replica of the necklace that Chloe allegedly stole from the museum."

"Replica?" There was no hiding my shock. We'd risked everything for a fake?

"As in not real." Garcia pointed to the pink heart-shaped diamond pendant. "You can see here that it's cracked. If it were real, that couldn't happen, or so I've been told. I'm not really a diamond man."

"Where is the real one?"

"I was hoping you'd tell me."

"If I had it, do you think I'd be hiding it? That necklace is the key to Chloe's freedom." A shiver ran down my spine. "Did you ask Bella? Maybe she took it to pay for her escape and she was trying to sell a duplicate to the buyer. Or maybe she had it and lost it. Or maybe Gino took it."

"We caught Gino," Garcia said. "He was trying to hitch a ride out of town. He had a gun on him that matched the caliber of the bullet that the surgeon pulled out of Ben but no necklace. Bella is lawyered up now. I asked her about the necklace, seeing as how I knew it would be important to you, but she had nothing to say."

That small concession, the hint of understanding, made my heart squeeze in my chest. "Thank you."

"Are you going to charge my client with anything?" Riswan asked. "You've heard her story, and so far, it sounds to me in any version of the events that the only thing she is guilty of is trying to help people."

I gave Garcia my best pleading look. I needed to get out of here. I had to find Jack. I wanted him to look me in the face and tell me I wasn't wrong to trust him, that I hadn't repeated the worst mistake of my life. I wanted him to tell me he hadn't betrayed me and that at no point in time had he switched the real necklace for the fake.

Garcia studied me for a long moment before he closed his little black book. "I'm not laying any charges," he said. "You're free to go."

THIRTY

◆ ◆ ◆

We met the next morning in Rose's garage. She and Chef Pierre had made it safely home. Chef Pierre was resting. Rose had worn him out after the excitement of the day. It was more information than I needed to know.

"Where's Anil?" Cristian asked. "He's the one who called for an urgent meeting."

"I don't know. He didn't answer my text, and when I called him, he sounded really down." I shot a look at Gage. "Did you hear from Jack?"

"Nope."

"Anyone?" I knew it was stupid, but I couldn't stop hoping. How could he have just walked away?

"We kicked ass in that warehouse," Emma said. "Chloe took Bella down with just one punch."

Chloe held up her fist. "I bruised my knuckles."

Gage took her hand and pressed his lips to her bruises. Chloe melted in front of my eyes. This time, the only thing I felt when I saw them together was joy. Nothing would come between me and my bestie, but now two people would have her back.

Anil walked in, his coat dripping from the rain. He had none of his usual enthusiasm. No funny hat or gamer T-shirt. No bounce to his step. No sparkle in his eyes. He didn't even have an apple in his pocket.

I'd had a bad feeling all night, and Anil's face confirmed it. "What's wrong?"

"I had the real necklace and I lost it." He slumped down in the nearest chair.

Everyone in the room seemed only mildly surprised. I shared the feeling. After what we'd been through, I felt like nothing could shock me anymore.

"The night we did the first heist, I went downstairs to check for another safe and found the one in the office," he said. "I opened it with the same combination. I saw the necklace and replaced it with the replica I had in my pocket. Simi said she didn't trust Jack so I didn't say anything in front of him." His gaze slid to me. "You didn't answer my texts that night, and then you were always with him and I didn't know what to do. I didn't want him to know I had it, and I was worried that if I gave it to you, he might steal it when you were in bed . . . together . . ." He cleared his throat. "Asleep."

I was tempted to slap myself across the face, but then I would have had a sore face and there would be more than enough time to beat myself up when he was done.

"You said you liked surprise parties," he continued. "I thought I'd wait until after the wedding and we could have a surprise party and not invite Jack, and the necklace would be the surprise. Meantime, we'd have fun pulling off a second heist." He gave a weak smile. "You always made it sound so easy. I didn't think any danger would be involved."

I had no words. No words.

"But then everything went wrong." His voice wavered. "After the dance was over, Rose came to tell me what had happened. I checked my phone and saw all the texts. I didn't want to text you that I had the necklace in case Jack saw your phone. I tried to call but you didn't answer. Finally, I went looking for Jack. When I found him . . ."

My heart sank into my stomach. "You told him."

"I had to," he said. "I was in a total panic. I couldn't get in touch and you were chasing after a fake. I was going to text you then, but Jack was worried when I told him no one was answering their phone. He said someone might have your phones and it wasn't safe. I wanted to go and find you guys right away, but Jack said the necklace wasn't secure in my house and that my parents were in danger. He said we needed to get it out of there and I couldn't go alone." He heaved a sob. "I'm sorry. I chose my parents over you."

"It's okay, Anil." I patted his leg. "Parents are parents. We all understand."

"We went to my house, and I got the necklace from my book safe—it's a safe that looks like a book." He bent over, shoved his hands through his hair. "My mother is always going through my room and there aren't many places to hide things."

"Dude," Gage said. "We need to get you out of there."

"She insisted that we have something to eat. I don't usually bring friends over and she was so excited. I left the book with Jack and followed her into the kitchen to try and explain that my work colleagues might be in danger, and I had to go, but she just shoved a bowl of pakoras in my hand, and when I went back to the living room, Jack was gone."

"He took the necklace," Emma gritted out. "The bastard."

"I don't know how he got away because the van was still there," Anil said. "I drove around the streets trying to find him. I tried everyone's phone again and then I called Rose."

"He was utterly distraught," Rose said. "He was going to go and find you alone. Can you imagine? A young boy in an industrial park at midnight."

"I'm twenty-five," Anil said stiffly.

"You're young to me," Rose said, not unkindly. "I told him to come right over and we'd all go together. That's when I knew I had to dig out my rigging and my old cat costume."

"I am so sorry," Anil said. "You told me not to trust him. Now Chloe will go to jail, and we won't have any money, and . . ."

Emma stood so quickly that her chair toppled backward. In three big strides she was across the room.

"Emma . . ." I moved to intercept, but before I could reach her, she wrapped her arms around Anil in a big hug.

"Dude. No apologies. You saved us in that warehouse. I'm pretty sure that bitch was going to off us, too. You fucking rocked."

Anil shuddered in her arms. "I did?"

"Sending Rose down from the ceiling? Genius. The Nerf dart shooting drone? Also, genius. I even liked the ski mask. It gave you a real badass vibe. When I saw The Butcher in action, I was damn impressed. You got in some good punches. Your left hook could use some work, and you need to turn your body more so you're not a target, but you did good, Anil." She released him and gripped his shoulders. "We wouldn't be alive without you."

"But what about the necklace?" He dabbed at his eyes with his sleeve. "What about Chloe?"

"Do you have surveillance at your house?" Gage was still holding Chloe's hand. Why did he need to hold her hand all the time? What if she needed to use it?

"My parents are paranoid. We have cameras everywhere." Anil slapped his forehead with his hand. "I can't believe I didn't even think to look at the recording. I can access it from my phone."

"We can start there," I said. "Let's see where Jack went and then we can make a plan."

Anil pulled up the surveillance video. We watched him and

Jack go into the house. A few minutes later a black SUV parked across the street. Ginger and Mr. Mustache got out.

"I know them!" I looked over at Rose. "They're the guys who broke into my apartment. They were after Jack, and they knew about the necklace."

Ginger stood watch while Mr. Mustache broke into our van. A few minutes later he got out, shaking his head. Mr. Mustache pulled out a gun and motioned toward the SUV. Two other men got out, one thick and sturdy, the other skinny, tatted, and wearing a string vest. They walked across the lawn to the house.

"My parents." Anil stared at the screen in horror. "Jack was right. They were in danger."

Moments later, Jack came barreling out the door. He was fast, but not fast enough. The big dude caught him and knocked him to the ground. Jack fought hard but it was four against one. They dragged him to the SUV. Moments later, they were gone.

"He didn't abandon us," Chloe said. "He was taken."

Something niggled at the back of my mind. "Can you go back to the moment Jack came out of the house?"

Anil scrolled back and I stared at the screen. "Enlarge it frame by frame until they catch him."

"What are you looking for?"

"The book."

"He doesn't have it." Anil sucked in a sharp breath. "That means . . ."

"The necklace is still at your house."

❖ ❖ ❖

"Anil!" Anil's mother greeted us at the door of his family's modest townhome in Naperville. "You've brought friends. You'll need food." She ran down the hall. "Salim! Salim! Anil has friends. He brought friends to the house. Get them drinks. Quickly before they run away."

"Mom." Anil coughed, choked. "We're just here to pick something up."

"Nonsense. Into the kitchen. All of you. We had a big family dinner last night and there are lots of leftovers."

"I do like Indian food," Emma said. "What have you got?"

Everyone followed Emma into the kitchen. Anil and I ran to the living room.

"What book is it?" I asked. "What does it look like?"

"*The Exorcist*. It's black and red." He held up his hands in a helpless gesture. "My mother doesn't like horror. I knew she'd never open it."

We checked the entire room. No book on the couch. No book on the tables, floor, or bookshelf. Anil pulled all the cushions off the furniture and tossed them on the floor.

"He wouldn't have had much time," I said. "It has to be here."

"Anil! What are you doing to the couch? Where will your friends sit?" His mother stared in shock at the mess.

"I left a book here the other day," he said. "Did you see it?"

"Horrible book." She shuddered. "I couldn't even touch it when I saw the cover. I told your father to put it downstairs."

Anil raced out of the room and I followed him into the basement. His bedroom was filled with drones, robots, models, and computer equipment. He grabbed a book from the shelf and flipped it open. It was, as he'd said, a miniature safe complete with a combination dial. He turned the knob and the door clicked open.

"It's here." He held up the necklace, his face creased in delight. "We've got it."

My knees gave out and I sank down on his bed. "Now we just need to find Jack."

THIRTY-ONE

◇ ◇ ◇

JACK

They say your life flashes before your eyes in your last moments. There are actual scientific reasons for this. Something to do with a secret trapdoor in the memory center of the brain that is triggered when the body shuts down. For some people, this venture into the past is a gift—all puppies and rainbows, hugs and kisses, and piles of presents at Christmas. But imagine if the idea of reliving your childhood all over again is something to be avoided at all costs. You've already experienced the pain of watching your parents die in a house fire, and then the loss of your grandmother to a developer's greed. You suffered abuse and neglect in foster care followed by a hard life on the streets under the thumb of a cruel and brutal man. You don't dwell on these things, of course, because you've learned to move on, but when Mr. X's hench people grab you and throw you into their SUV, you are resolved to survive simply so you don't have to relive the nightmare again.

You hold to your resolution through a bumpy ride with a sports bag over your head. The smell of old sweat is nauseating but not as bad as the sharp scent of blood and offal that assails your nose when the sports bag comes off and you find yourself in a butcher shop, complete with chopping table, a full complement of cleavers and knives, and a giant walk-in freezer. Hog-tied and beaten on the floor, you realize you finally might have run out of lives.

"Where's the necklace?" Virgil kicks you in the ribs. After so many years of chase-catch-beat-shoot and chase again, you and your thickly mustached friend are on a first-name basis. After all, his bullets have been inside you.

"Angelini's daughter took it." You try to breathe through the pain but your lungs aren't obeying commands. "She's at a warehouse in Hanover Park with a buyer on the way. You'd better hurry or you're going to lose out. If you'd just asked me instead of throwing a bag over my head, we could have been there by now." You have always believed the best defense is offense.

"What the fuck were you doing in Naperville if the necklace was in Hanover Park?" Virgil kicks you again. He's bought some new steel-toed boots and he's trying to break them in.

"My friend's mother invited me for dinner. I thought it would be impolite to refuse. She makes wonderful pakoras." You wish you'd had a chance to taste them because they smelled amazing, but when you saw the hench people through the window, you had to act quickly to save Anil's family. Henches don't care who they hurt when they are doing Mr. X's bidding, unless of course it's someone you love. You and Mr. X have a professional understanding. Family, partners, even pets are off-limits. Break that rule and there will be hell to pay.

Virgil wraps a chain around his fist and punches you in the gut. The chain is new for Virgil. Usually, he uses his bare hands. He throws a few more practice punches, hitting your ribs and kidneys before he tires of his new toy and grabs a thick metal pole to beat you with instead. Over and over again, until the world becomes a haze of pain.

"Don't kill him yet," Rusty says. You don't call this henchman

"Rusty" to his face because he's sensitive about his red hair. His real name is Andrew.

"Too bad, Virgil." You heave in a breath. Some part of your brain screams at you to shut your big mouth, but you have a habit of not listening. "I know it's how you get your kicks."

Virgil gets his kicks with a well-aimed blow to your head.

You black out.

◇ ◇ ◇

A bang. A blaze of light. Footsteps. You feel fire on your cheek and cold deep in your bones. Your hands are chained over your head and your feet dangle, barely touching the floor. You open your eyes and wish you hadn't.

"I thought you'd be dead by now," Mr. X says from the door of the meat freezer.

"Give me a little credit," you say. "I grew up in Chicago. Have you lived through a Chicago winter? My grandmother made me play outside when it was so cold my eyelashes froze together."

"And you had to walk uphill both ways in a snowstorm to get to school?"

"I didn't go to school. I couldn't see."

"Funny. You're a funny guy." Mr. X walks into the freezer flanked by two extra hench people. You are flattered that he needs four henches to protect himself from you, considering you've been badly beaten and you are chained up in a meat freezer, well on your way to hypothermia.

Mr. X has a cane, but no limp. A head, but no hair. He is tall enough not to be short, but too short to be considered tall. His face is as round and red as an overripe plum, and his lips are so thin, they beg for Botox. Taking a page from the Villains-R-Us manual, he has a thin mustache and a thick goatee. The last time you met, he had a thick mustache and a thin goatee. The new look is an improvement.

"Funny enough for you to let me off the hook?" Mr. X hates it when you joke around. Torture time is supposed to be serious.

"Where's the necklace?" He leans so close, you can smell his fetid breath. Someone didn't brush his teeth this morning—maybe ever. If you purse your lips, you could spit in his face. Not that you ever would. Your grandmother taught you that a gentleman never spits.

"I told your hench people, Angelini's daughter took it." You study the face that has haunted your dreams for over ten years—the face of an enemy who was once a mentor and friend. Over the years he's had you beaten, whipped, buried—that's another story—and shot. And then there was that time in the desert with the honey and the ants, and the night he caught you in bed with his sister . . . although to be fair, you'd just pushed him over a waterfall and thought he was dead. But you digress. There is a word for men like Mr. X: nemesis.

Mr. X has aged since your last encounter. His facial hair is graying and he has crow's feet at the corners of his soulless black eyes. His gray suit has lost the fight against business casual, with a baggy eighties silhouette minus a sense of purpose. His pants are pleated for comfort and wide down the leg, pooling around box-toed shoes. A double-width Mickey Mouse tie is attached to a billowing silky mauve dress shirt, and his belt has a shiny gold buckle engraved with a big *X* to mark the spot. Villainy might pay, but it can't buy a sense of fashion.

"That necklace was a fake," Mr. X says.

"No. Really?" You feign as much shock and surprise as your frozen face can muster, although your primary concern is down below. Your balls are so cold, you can't feel them. Your only chance of continuing the family line is soon going to be limited to special snowflakes and talking snowmen in funny hats.

"You knew that." Mr. X sips coffee from a cup with the name *Susan* scrawled across it in black pen. He's never told you his real name, and you are excited at the little glimpse into his true self. He doesn't look like a "Susan" to you, but you don't like to judge.

"How's that trenta double-blended extra-hot mocha . . ." You read off the cup. "Twelve pumps sugar-free pumpkin spice, twelve pumps sugar-free hazelnut, twelve pumps sugar-free caramel, twelve pumps sugar-free vanilla, five pumps toffee nut, two heaping scoops of matcha, a splash of soy, coffee to the star on the siren's head, two raw sugars, extra whip, a sprinkle of cinnamon, a drizzle of caramel, and . . . just move your thumb so I can read the rest . . ."

"No foam," he offers.

"I'll bet that's what all the girls say."

Mr. X isn't amused. "This is entirely unnecessary."

"I must agree. Why do you need fifty-three pumps when it only takes one if you do it right? I'll bet the girls say that, too."

"I think he needs an incentive." Mr. X gestures over his shoulder, and one of his hench people—every good villain needs a solid half dozen—walks into the freezer. He is nondescript as hench people usually are. Medium height. Medium build. Brown hair of medium length cut into a cringeworthy eighties mullet, although he is slightly better dressed than his boss. Skinny black jeans and a black mesh tank never go out of style if you weigh barely 130 pounds and are covered in ink from your high school rocker days. His straight nose and unscarred skin tell you everything you need to know even before he slaps you across the face. Were you ever that green?

"Your newb doesn't seem to understand how an incentive

works." You explain slowly and simply so everyone can understand. Also, you are so cold, it's hard to talk. "I would have to know where the necklace is to be incentivized to give up its location. Torture me all you want. I can't give you information I don't have."

Mr. X shrugs. "Torture it is."

The newb is wearing brass knuckles a few sizes too big for his skinny little fingers. Still, he has a good right for someone so small and thin. Pain explodes through your body. You double over, struggling to keep your feet.

"To be honest, I'd call that a disincentive . . ."

He throws three more punches, aiming not for your stomach but for the crown jewels. Nausea rises in your gut and blackness claws at your vision. Forget the snowflakes. You'll be lucky if it rains.

You lift your legs and awkwardly kick at his chest. Not your finest moment but you can't give up the fight.

Another hench person joins the party. He moves in with a length of rope, grabbing your feet and tying them together. He is blond and built like a linebacker with muscles so thick he has to wear a shirt with the sleeves torn off and shorts with an elastic waist.

"That's not playing fair," you say. "Four against one? I'm not even using my hands."

"Give me that chain." Mr. X holds his hand out and the newb scurries to do his bidding. You've always wanted a henchman or two. It would make the work that much easier.

"I've never been into the whole whips and chains thing," you say. "But to each his own."

"Where's the fucking necklace?"

"Can I be blindfolded for this part?"

Mr. X raises the chain and swings with all his might.

You black out. Again. You have to stop making it a habit.

◇ ◇ ◇

Cold seeps through your skin and into your bones. Your eyes close and your mind flickers in and out of consciousness. You are outside in the snow banging on a door that won't open. Fire sears your skin as your home explodes into flames. Then you are in a garden pruning the lavender before the first frost. Your grandmother gives you a quarter for every bundle. She sews them into sachets for the Christmas craft fair and always splits the money with you. Your dog, Bob, licks your face. A bee buzzes overhead. You try to swat it away, but your hands won't move. You look for the light and see Simi in a garden of hellebore, crushing the delicate leaves with her huge feet. She smiles and your heart pounds, sending a rush of warmth through your frozen body. There is something you need to tell her—a feeling you have whenever you see her that doesn't go away.

Thunder roars in the distance. A storm, bringing with it a rush of warm air. Simi fades into the distance. Water trickles down your face.

"Jack! Jack! Get him down!"

You are drawn to the woman's voice. It pulls you out of the mist and back into the light. You see shadowy figures around you, sense panic in the air. Bob keeps licking your face, your lips. For once he doesn't have horrendous doggy breath. His tongue is soft, and he smells like tacos.

You are flying, drifting. You wake to the most horrible sight a man could see. Two eyes in a black wooly ski mask. You ask the obvious question through swollen lips. "Are you the Grim Reaper?"

"It's me. Simi." She pulls off the mask and her beautiful face warms you inside. Too bad she's frowning. "You have hypo-thermia," she says. "I'll get some blankets to warm you."

"Best cure for hypothermia is skin-to-skin contact." Your words come stronger now because Simi is here, and she's real and her tears are deliciously hot and they remind you of other places that can be hot and hopefully she'll take you to bed so you can hold her and make the cold go away. "I think you should take off our clothes and lie on top of me."

"Have you seen yourself?" Her voice has a slightly hysterical edge that you've never heard before. Even when she's wound up or anxious and her words spill out so fast, you can barely keep up, she always maintains a core of calm.

"I'm afraid to touch you." Her bottom lip quivers.

"Not something a woman has ever said to me before." You see boxes stacked beside you, each bearing a picture of a smiling cow. You smell blood and something sickly sweet. If you are at all squeamish and don't like lying in blood and offal, the floor of a working butcher shop is not a great place to be.

"He's fine." Another ski-masked man with Gage's voice is leaning against the counter with Virgil in a headlock. Next to him is a woman in leather pants holding a .22 to Rusty's head. Maybe she is Chloe's evil twin because you've never seen Chloe wear anything other than pastels and flowers.

"I didn't feel much because they tried to freeze me first," you explain. "Let that be a lesson to you. Torture first. Freeze later. That way they can feel more pain."

"I usually just go for the fingernails." A masked person with Emma's voice nods. "The brute force beating just makes them pass out or shit themselves."

"Another toilet story." The man behind that mask sounds like Anil but his tone is curiously jaded.

"Is this Heaven? Or is it Hell?" You try to sit but your arms aren't obeying commands. Everything seems to be topsy-turvy. "Why is everyone wearing ski masks?"

"It was Anil's idea," Emma says. "He thought it would be better if we weren't recognized."

"And people on the street wouldn't be suspicious of a bunch of masked people storming into a butcher shop in the middle of the day?"

"It's night." Emma has one foot on the newb's neck. She has a meat cleaver in her hand. It suits her.

"It took us a while to find you." The masked man standing in the doorway in a *Ban Fossil Fuels* T-shirt has to be Cristian. "Sorry I can't come in," he says. "I'm vegan."

"Chloe had to find special software to get a clear read on the license plate of the SUV." Anil randomly punches Virgil in the head. "Then Simi had to call in a favor from her police boyfriend to track the vehicle . . ."

Police boyfriend? Your brain sticks on those two words, and you don't hear anything else.

"What police boyfriend?"

"Shhh." Simi strokes your forehead. "The ambulance is coming."

You shake your head, concentrate on not passing out from the pain of the damage to your rapidly thawing body. "How long?"

"About twenty-four hours," she says.

"That's it?" You try to push yourself up, but your arms still aren't listening to the messages from your brain. "You moved on in less than a day?"

"It's not what you think," she says. "Garcia and I . . ."

"Garcia? Not *Detective* Garcia? You're now on a last-name basis?" You don't care about your broken body or the necklace or the hench people. You don't even care if they've captured Mr. X or killed him. You care about Simi in a way you've never cared about anyone before. You love her.

You love her and she dumped you in less than a day for someone far more worthy than you. A good guy. A man in uniform who doesn't live a life of secrets and lies.

Pain washes over you. You close your eyes and let the words settle in your heart.

Police boyfriend.

Death. Come for me now.

THIRTY-TWO

◇ ◇ ◇

Are you going to sulk, or do you want to hear what happened?"

I'd been visiting Jack in the hospital for two weeks. He'd drifted in and out of consciousness while his body healed, occasionally murmuring nonsensical things like the Latin names of flowers and something about police and boyfriends. Now that he was fully awake and on the mend, I was excited to catch him up but he wouldn't even look in my direction.

"Fine," he said. "Tell me."

"Why are you staring at the ceiling?"

"Given the age of the hospital, those ceiling tiles probably contained asbestos," he said. "The fibers are likely falling on me right now. Given my run of bad luck, I'll get lung disease and be dead in three years. That is, if Mr. X doesn't find me first."

"Jack." I reached over to pat his hand. "Don't be morose. You survived. The doctors said it was a miracle, given how low your body temperature was and how badly you'd been beaten."

"You wouldn't lie on top of me," he grumbled. "My body temperature would have gone up faster if I'd had skin-to-skin contact."

"You were covered in blood and bruises and you had broken

bones. I wasn't about to make things worse, but if you cheer up and get out of here quickly, I promise you can have all the skin-to-skin contact you want." I kissed his forehead, then his nose and one cheek.

"What about here?" Still pouty, he touched his lips.

"We'll save those kisses for when you get out. Now, do you want to know what happened?"

"Hold my hand."

I wrapped my hand around his and settled in my chair. "Anything else?"

"How did you find me?"

"We reviewed the security tapes at Anil's house and realized you'd purposely left the necklace behind when you ran outside." I squeezed his fingers. "You did that to lure them away and keep Anil's family safe, didn't you?"

"They're good people. They wanted to feed me."

"They want to feed everyone," she said. "After we found the book, they made us stay for lunch."

Jack sat up straight and shook off my hand. "You had a big celebratory lunch and left me to be tortured and die in a meat freezer while you stuffed your faces with pakoras and vindaloo?"

"My, aren't we testy today." I stroked his forehead and eased him back on the pillow. "You were foremost in our minds. We made a plan to rescue you while we were eating, knowing we'd need that energy if it came to a fight. It also took Chloe some time to get a clear reading of the license plate on the SUV. And I had to call Garcia and ask him to track it."

"Garcia." He spat out the name, his gaze on the ceiling again. "Your police boyfriend."

"He's a detective and a friend." I gently turned his face to mine. "That's all."

"You and Garcia aren't——"

"No. I'm a one-man kind of woman."

"And this one man . . ." His eyes lit up. Hopeful. Intent. "What's he like?"

"He's brave." I pressed a kiss to his forehead. "He's strong." Another kiss, this one on his cheek. "Funny and sarcastic." Kisses down his jaw despite the bristles. "Selfless." A kiss on the corner of his lips. "Loyal and honorable." Another kiss on the cheek. "A team player."

Jack gave a satisfied rumble. "He's always worked alone."

"Not anymore." I brushed his hair back from his face. "No one wanted to be left behind when it came time to save him. Everyone wanted to help. He was part of a team, and the team looks after each other."

"How is he in bed?" His voice dropped to a sensual rumble.

"Incredible."

"The best you ever had?"

"I wouldn't want him to get too cocky."

Jack laughed. "He's cocky now."

"Maybe I should go," I teased, pulling away. "You are in a hospital, after all, and I'm not the only person who wants to visit."

"No." He lay back on his pillow. "Tell me more. What happened to the necklace?"

"Chloe got the information for claiming the reward from the Dark Web. We did the exchange behind the museum at night. Everyone wore a mask so there was no chance we'd be able to identify each other. Chloe set up a Swiss bank account and we handed the necklace over as soon as she verified the money was there. The next day Garcia called me to let me know the necklace had been found in a storage drawer in the museum and all charges against Chloe and me had been dropped."

"Did you give everyone their share?"

"Yes, we did. Rose gave Cristian part of her money because he did save us when we were in the office, and he was the first to volunteer to come and find you. We also got paid for the wedding gig. I was terrified when Mr. Angelini called me to the house, but he just wanted to pay me and thank me for our service. He said we'd done a good job despite the fact someone had stolen some priceless statues from his office, and his daughter had poisoned the priest, betrayed him by having secret affairs with both Gino and Ben, run away with something valuable, and was now being charged with attempted murder, accessory to murder, and various firearms offenses. I think he was actually proud of her. He said she was her father's daughter."

Jack's laughter filled me with joy. There had been moments in the last two weeks when I'd thought I would never hear it again.

"Mr. Angelini wasn't even angry when I told him the marriage wasn't valid," I continued. "He said it saved the groom from having to get an annulment. And do you know the best part?"

"What was the best part?"

"He said he'd give us a five-star review and recommend us to his friends!"

Jack brought my hand to his lips and kissed each one of my knuckles. "I thought the wedding planning gig was a one-off for the heist."

"Chloe and I are going to give it a go for real," I said. "I loved being in charge. I loved sourcing things and talking to the vendors. I loved organizing everything and working with the team. I loved dealing with last-minute emergencies, and I loved seeing it all come together at the end. This is what I've been looking for since I started college. This is my passion. I'm going to take it on full time. Chloe is coming in part time. She decided to be brave and find her passion, too. She sent out some résumés and within days she got a fantastic job as a white hat hacker. Everyone else in the crew said they'd be happy to pitch in with my business as a side hustle while they follow their own dreams."

"I had dreams," Jack said, his voice quiet, his gaze drifting to the window. "I used to dream about a normal life—a house with a garden, a job in a museum, friends without criminal records, someone to love—but then there was a night when everything went wrong. I had to make a terrible choice and Mr. X will never forgive me."

My mouth opened and closed again. I'd given up my expectations of Jack sharing anything about his mysterious past. "Jack . . . I'm so—"

"How about the others? Are they still around?" He was getting tired now. His eyes were beginning to droop, and his face had softened.

"Cristian got his rental with the big backyard and adopted his rescue huskies. He's already started getting things set up for his new wildlife show, and his first episode is going to be about elephants."

"No more life coaching?"

"He still does his coaching. I think he enjoys it more than he lets on." I wasn't the only person who'd gotten a few referrals after the wedding.

"What about Emma?"

"She's still driving her Uber because she likes meeting interesting people, but she's decided to get into Formula One like her dad. It's an expensive sport but she's excited to get started. She and Anil have been spending a lot of time together."

"Is he still living at home?" He laced his fingers through mine. I'd missed our connection, our easy banter, the way he looked at me like I was the only person in the world.

"He moved in with Emma the day after we got our money.

They're both mechanically minded and they're inventing a new kind of drone together. She promised she wouldn't try to set him up with anyone although she seems to have a lot of cousins his age who come to visit. He sent you a bag of apples." I gestured to the bag on the table beside a vase filled with peonies. No one knew where they'd come from, and they'd started to wilt after only a few days.

"And Rose?"

"She enjoyed her drop from the ceiling so much, she signed up for a course in aerial arts for seniors. She's doing it all: aerial, cirque, trapeze, and pole dancing. She's talking about leaving the theater and joining a circus. Chef Pierre finished his course and went back to France. She dumped Stan because he couldn't keep up—her words, not mine—and now she's with some guy she met in her new play. We're going to see her perform next week. You should come."

"I can't stay," he said. "I've got another job."

"How long?"

"A week. Maybe two. As soon as I can travel."

His words hit me like a blow to the chest. I hadn't realized how much I had hoped he would stay, but now that I knew it was over, my heart felt like it was cracking in two.

I leaned over and kissed him firmly on the lips. "Then we'd better make the most of the time we have."

THIRTY-THREE

◆ ◆ ◆

Chloe and I sprawled on the bed in Rose's partly renovated suite in a state of semi-inebriation. We'd spent the day moving my stuff from my parents' house to my new apartment and had come to check in on Rose and say good-bye to my old place.

"Babe?"

"Yeah?" She twisted the knob at the end of the bed. It had been Rose's bed when she was a girl, and even though it was badly water damaged, she refused to give it away.

"I found the perfect office space," I said.

"Here?" She giggled. Chloe always giggles when she's drunk.

"It's only a few blocks from Olivia's new school. You won't have to worry about child care. She can come and hang with us after she's done."

Chloe turned to face me, resting her head on her elbow. "You didn't need to do that."

"I wanted to do that."

"Cristian thinks we should change our name," Chloe said. "He said Simply Elegant doesn't fit a bunch of misfits."

"What did he suggest?"

"Nothing."

"Typical Cristian."

"Yeah."

"Anil had an idea," she said. "It works for both heists and weddings. He suggested The Wedding Crew."

"It's perfect." I typed it into my phone because I'd had so much to drink, I didn't think I'd remember it in the morning. "He's good with the ideas. I hope he finds a wife who appreciates his creativity."

"Not you."

"Not me. I'm taken." I was stronger now. I'd made peace with my past. I didn't have to sacrifice who I was or what I wanted to make other people happy. I didn't always have to be good. I was brave enough to go after what I wanted, and strong enough to stay standing if I failed. I was worthy, and I had opened myself to love.

"What if he doesn't come back?"

I gave her a wicked grin. "As Gino said, there's a price to be paid for betrayal."

I heard the crunch of footsteps outside. For the briefest of seconds, my breath caught, and then I heard Gage say, "I've got something for you."

"Come on in."

Gage slammed open the door and pushed a hooded man into the room, forcing him to his knees. "Your favor," he said to me.

"What's going on?" Chloe looked from Gage to me and back to Gage. "I thought you said you had to leave town for a job."

"This is it." He kicked the man at his feet. "A job for Simi."

"I asked him to find the man who set you up," I said. "I didn't like the idea that he was still out there doing the same thing to someone else, and I thought you deserved some revenge. It was a loose end that begged to be tied." I waved a hand in the man's direction. "My gift to you."

"Take off his hood." Chloe's voice was firm and hard.

Gage obliged, and Chloe and I gasped as one.

"Kyle." She spat out his name. "You set me up? Why?"

"Because you're a fucking thorn in my side," he growled. "A constant reminder that I fucked up. My parents have never forgiven me. I lost my trust fund because of you. I was supposed to inherit the family business and they gave it to my brother."

"That's hardly my fault." I'd never seen Chloe so angry. Her body shook, hands clenched into fists at her sides. "You made your choices. The consequences are on you."

"Fuck that." He twisted, struggled to get to his feet, but Gage pushed him down. "I'm in debt, working entry-level jobs, living in a shit rental apartment, and you still come after my fucking money for a kid I never wanted."

"You took advantage of me," Chloe shouted, face red, nostrils flared. "I was barely sixteen. I had no one to look out for me. You wouldn't leave me alone. Day after day you harassed me, until I agreed just so you would stop. We both knew the risks. We are both responsible for that decision, although I wouldn't change it for the world. Olivia is the best thing that ever happened in my life."

"How did you do it?" I asked him. "Why did you do it? Was it just about the money?"

"She destroyed my life." He turned his furious gaze on me. "I wanted her to pay and I got the perfect opportunity when I met a guy who was looking for someone to hack a museum security system. I couldn't do it, but I knew Chloe could, so I told him I'd give him her details if he made sure she took the fall."

"But then you'd get custody of Olivia," I said. "I thought you didn't want her."

"I wanted the fucking money," he said. "I was going to tell my parents I needed the trust fund to look after the little brat, and boom, I'd be back in business. I'd play the good son for year, get my inheritance back, then dump her off with them and live the life I deserved."

Chloe crossed the room and slapped him across the face. "Never speak about my daughter like that again."

"You think you're so tough 'cause you got your friends here," he spluttered, "but we both know who's the boss when we're alone."

Chloe nodded at Gage and then at me. "Leave us."

I grabbed a half-empty bottle of vodka and dragged Gage out of the room. "I'll get the bleach."

"Don't like leaving her inside with that piece of shit," Gage muttered on our way out.

"She'll be okay. She's not the same woman you met all those weeks ago. None of us are." I took a swig from the bottle and handed it to Gage.

"Never much liked change," Gage said, taking a sip. "But if it means she can send that prick a message that will keep her and her daughter safe, then I'm all for it. He's a fucking cowardly weasel."

"Strong words."

"He framed the mother of his child for cash and didn't even do the deed himself." His face hardened and I hoped Kyle appreciated that Chloe was doing him a favor by sending Gage outside. "I already got the story from him and taped his confession. He doesn't have much pain tolerance."

"Too bad. I would have liked him to suffer a little bit longer."

"I wasn't done with him," Gage said. "But you asked for five minutes, and I thought you'd want him conscious."

"If Kyle wasn't in the museum, who took the necklace and locked her in?" I took another sip from the bottle. After the adrenaline rush, I wasn't getting my usual buzz.

"A couple of mid-level jewel thieves," he said. "The guy who organized the whole thing has computer skills, but he couldn't handle a job that complex. He got a tip that the necklace would be at the museum and went looking for a hacker. He lucked out when he found Kyle, who gave him Chloe's details. I found that guy, too. Got the rest of the story from him." Gage tipped his head from side to side, cracking his neck. "You didn't ask me to bring him to you, so I was able to do my best work."

"I don't need to know the details." I handed him the bottle. "How was Mr. Angelini involved?"

"Mid-level guys can't move stuff of that value themselves. Mr. Angelini is the most well-known fence on the East Coast. Word travels fast when a piece like that is on the move. Jack already knew it was in Chicago and had come here to . . ." He trailed off with a grimace, so I put him out of his misery.

"Reclaim it?"

"Yeah. That's it." Gage took a long sip. "Mr. X keeps tabs on Jack. He knew something was up. Sent out some feelers. Found out the necklace had been stolen and figured either Jack had it or he was after it, so it would be an easy win."

"That's why he sent the guys to my place." My lips curled into a smile. "They didn't think there were any good fences in Chicago."

"They're idiots," Gage said. "Angelini is big-time."

"After the beating they got at the butcher shop, I don't think they'll be bothering us again."

"No, but they'll still be after Jack. Him and Mr. X . . . that's personal, and Mr. X will be pissed he didn't get the necklace."

"I have a feeling Mr. Angelini was going to move the necklace to Berlin and Mario was in on it," I said. "It was an odd location for a honeymoon. I guess he wasn't prepared for his daughter to steal it right out from under his nose." I leaned against the house and stared up at the stars. "If I ever go on a honeymoon, it will be somewhere tropical."

"Beach girl?" Gage asked.

"I like heat."

"Figured as much when I saw you spending time with that cop." He drained the bottle, then tossed it in the garbage can.

"We're just friends."

"Not sure if he understands that," Gage said. "But he'll be busy now that the necklace has been stolen again."

"Someone stole it again?" I stared at him aghast. "How?"

"The private collector who had loaned it to the museum came to pick it up personally. Understandably, he changed his mind about leaving it with the museum for the exhibit. He had it authenticated by the insurance company when he arrived, and hired an armed car service to transport it. But when he got home, the necklace in the secure case turned out to be fake."

I went to get the bleach from Rose's kitchen. Her house was still and quiet. Was it only nine weeks ago that my life had been a disaster, and I'd almost killed Stan? Now I was debt-free. I had my own place, an event planning business, and a new group of friends. I'd found my passion and I'd found love, although not the traditional kind.

I flicked on the light, heard a scream. A groan. A thump.

Rose was on the counter. Her new male friend was on the floor.

It was save-the-naked-octogenarian time all over again. This time I didn't need Chloe. I could handle it on my own.

◆ ◆ ◆

"Do you have to leave?"

I rolled to my side in my new bed, watching Jack dress. He'd shown up at my door last night to say good-bye. I've never been a believer in karma or spiritual energy like my aunties, but I had known he was coming. I could feel a pull inside me. When I heard the rumble of a motorcycle outside, I opened the door because I knew it was him.

No one had ever looked at me the way he did that night. No one had ever seen me. I don't think an army of Mr. X's could have stopped him from coming through the door. When he wrapped me in his arms, something clicked into place—the other half of my soul.

"They'll be coming for me," he said. "If I stay, you'll be in danger. I should have left last night."

"Maybe you should have thought of that before you repossessed the Wild Heart." I pushed myself up to sit. "Don't look so surprised. When Garcia came to my office to tell me it had been stolen again, I knew it had to be you."

"Garcia was at your office?" He crossed his arms over his chest, his forehead creased in a frown. His jealousy was utterly endearing.

"We're friends. He brought me an office-warming gift to celebrate my new venture."

Jack muttered something under his breath that I couldn't hear. "What gift?"

"A Boston fern."

"A Boston fern?" Jack barked a laugh. "Are you working in a rain forest? They are incredibly hard to keep alive indoors. They're also outdated. It's not the nineties anymore. I was worried for a second, but a Boston fern . . . ?" He chuckled to himself, mumbling something about loser plants.

"What do you mean by 'I was worried'?" I knew exactly what he meant but I wanted to hear it.

"He doesn't just want to be friends," Jack said, pulling on his jeans.

"Is that a problem? You're going away and you can't tell me when you'll be back? Am I supposed to sit around waiting for you? I have needs."

"I thought I just took care of your needs," he said. "I didn't even get any sleep, you were so needy."

"What about tomorrow? Or next week?" I was teasing him. We hadn't talked about the future, but I didn't want to be with anyone else. Not even Garcia, who had made it clear with his gift he was interested in pursuing something now that I wasn't a thief.

"Simi . . ." A pained expression crossed his face. "I can't make you any promises, but there's no one else for me. I'm going to try and get out of the business, but it's going to take time."

I wrapped the sheet around my body and crossed the room. "There's no one else for me, either."

"No police boyfriend?" He wrapped an arm around my waist and drew me close.

"No one but you."

He buried his face in my neck and sighed. "I'll pick up a burner phone as soon as I land in Delhi. You'll always be able to contact me."

"India?" I pressed a soft kiss to his cheek. "Isn't that where the Wild Heart is originally from?"

"I believe so."

"I can imagine the Indian government would love to have a piece of such cultural significance returned to their country," I said.

"Countries are always very grateful to have their antiquities repatriated." He backed up another step. "Or so I've heard."

"Should we have code names if we have to communicate by burner phones? I'd like something daring and adventurous, something wild."

"Simi," he said. "That name ticks all the boxes."

"What about you?"

"I have a code name. Oliver Twist."

I wound my arms around his neck. "It's a good name because Oliver Twist had a hard life, but in the end, everybody lived happily ever after."

"Except Fagin, who was arrested and hanged, and Monks, who died in prison." His bitter tone told me everything I wanted to know. He hadn't shared any more about Mr. X, but I had a strong suspicion he was the Fagin in Jack's life.

"Where are you going after India?" I dropped my sheet and pushed him back against the door, hoping to chase away the shadows that had fallen across his face.

Jack responded with a growl of approval. "Egypt, and Greece after that. I get a new burner every time I hit a new country. I'll make sure you get my numbers. Keep an eye out for flower deliveries with secret messages."

"I remember seeing statues from Egypt and Greece in Mr. Angelini's office," I mused out loud. "When I went to see him to collect our money, he said they'd been stolen during the wedding." I rubbed up against him, eliciting a groan.

"That's quite a coincidence."

"Do you know what else is a coincidence?" I'd been waiting all night to share this with him. "Garcia told me that he received a tip that Simone's missing necklace from the charity ball was in Mr. Angelini's office safe, along with papers that showed he was guilty of loan sharking and forcing people out of their homes on the very block where your grandmother lived. He had planned to develop the entire area as a shopping mall."

"Garcia talks too much," Jack said, pulling away. "Maybe he should put some of that energy into learning about plants."

"He thinks Mr. Angelini will be going to prison. Thank God I already got my five-star review."

"He deserves far worse than prison." Jack pressed a soft kiss to my lips. "You are making it almost impossible to leave, but I can't miss this flight."

"I'll miss you."

"I'll miss you, too, sweetheart." He grabbed his bag from the floor. I'd tucked an envelope in it with the number of an account Chloe had set up that contained a share of the reward money and the wedding planning fee. Everyone had agreed Jack deserved it, even though he'd never asked for a cent.

"I've left a few plants at your new office so you don't forget me," he said. "Real plants. Not nineties throwbacks that are unsuited to an office climate. The moth orchid is finicky and the tillandsias can be particularly tricky. They don't grow in soil and instead need rocks or shrubs to cling to. They'll need several hours of indirect sunlight so don't put them on your bookshelf." He gave me one last, long kiss and opened the door.

"Jack?"

"Yes?" He looked over his shoulder.

"Why were you still in the bushes outside the museum if you knew the necklace was already gone?"

He turned fully to face me. "I was thinning the hellebore when I saw a woman in an oversize suit jacket and a fedora trying to throw a rope into a window two stories high to rescue her friend in the dark and rain. I've traveled all over the world and I've seen many things, but I've never seen anything like that. And then the alarm went off and she didn't run. She didn't give up. She refused to leave her friend and tried to scale a sheer brick wall with her bare hands. I didn't know love and loyalty like that existed. I only knew what it meant to be alone. I had to meet her."

"We didn't meet," I said. "You grabbed me and dragged me into the bushes."

"That's what you do when you find the love of your life," he said.

"You love me?"

His voice was soft as he turned away. "I think I loved you from the moment you threw that rope."

EPILOGUE

$\diamond\ \diamond\ \diamond$

JACK

SIX MONTHS LATER

Imagine you are just an ordinary guy. You have a good job. You came into some unexpected money and now you have a brand-new Ford F150 truck waiting for you behind your cousin's greenhouse in Chicago. Your *Acanthocereus tetragonus* cactus is thriving. You have your health. And you have found a woman to love and who loves you back. You call her every day just to assure yourself she isn't a dream, and also because she loves burner phone sexy times almost as much as you.

On a cool summer evening in New York, you repossess an incredible sixteenth-century bronze by Willem Danielsz van Tetrode. Don't worry. The collector is a bad guy. On your way to the airport, you are run off the road by four goons in a Mitsubishi Mirage. They have guns and tire irons and they look like they mean business. But this time you have not been cavalier about your safety. You promised your girlfriend you would come home to her alive, and she has threatened to withhold all sexy times if you get seriously injured. You are carrying the Sig Sauer 45 and two small Beretta M9-22s that your cousin gave you when you were last in Chicago. Your rental car is fully insured, and you are wearing the bulletproof vest your girlfriend bought you for Christmas.

You are also not alone.

After you get shot—but live thanks to your vest—Gage blows up their rental car and helps you beat them and break a few bones. You toss them in the ditch and tell them to pass along a message to Mr. X: *Watch out for Oliver Twist.*

You search their phones and pockets and discover the details of Mr. X's next target—a $50 million collection of Cambodian antiquities hidden in a secret gallery beneath a controversial billionaire's Chelsea home.

You tell Gage to use his special skills to question Virgil. He has always been Mr. X's weakest link. Also, you haven't forgotten that day in the butcher shop when he kicked you in the head. You call your boss, who green-lights the job. As always, it's off the books. No one can know what you do.

You have a good feeling about this one. After you repatriate the bronze to Italy, you make two calls. First, you call your cousin and tell him you're coming for your truck. Then you call your girl.

Unfortunately, your girl isn't interested in hearing about your exciting new job. You regret leading with the ambush, the blown-up car, the shooting, and the fight. You have to send her a "proof of life" picture and then fly all the way to Chicago to show her you haven't been seriously hurt. Gage comes along for the ride. There's someone he wants to see.

You drive up to a fancy condo building in Evanston and pick the lock on the back door. Old habits die hard. Ten stories of stair climbing later, you knock on her door. And there she is. Now your heart aches. Now your pulse beats strong and fast. You wrap your arms around her and kick the door closed. You are home. You lift her to your hips and carry her to bed. You don't talk because you need her lips on your lips. You don't breathe because you need her breath in your lungs. You rip off her clothes because you need her skin on your skin. She has awakened something inside you—something wild and forever.

When it is over—and it is many hours before you both collapse from exhaustion, because you are a stallion in bed—you lie under the sheets and hold her in your arms. You tell her you've got a job that could be your way out. A treasure trove in a secret gallery owned by a billionaire whose daughter just got engaged. But you can't do it alone. You need a team, people you trust, a leader to plan.

You need the Wedding Crew.

ACKNOWLEDGMENTS

◇ ◇ ◇

Every author needs a crew. In this case, instead of a heist, they helped to bring my story to life. Thank you to my editor, Kristine Swartz, for her keen eye, amazing insight, and belief in my crazy story from the start. Thank you also to my agent, Laura Bradford, for her support and patience and mad diplomatic skills. Thank you to the incredible design team at Penguin, and in particular Lila Selle, who made a cover that made me scream in delight, and a huge thank-you to Mary Baker, Stephanie Felty, and Daniela Riedlová and the rest of the Penguin team for helping to send my story into the world with a bang.

I'd like to give special thanks to all my plushies and stuffies for their sacrifice and bravery. It wasn't easy being dropped from a balcony with only a skipping rope to hold you, but now we're all prepared if we have to steal a diamond from a room filled with laser beams or if Tom Cruise needs a stand-in for his next *Mission Impossible*. You guys rock!

To Jamie, Sapphira, and Alysa for being my reason for everything. To John for being there, holding my hand, and carrying the load. And to Mom and Dad, who always have time to listen.

And finally, thank you, dear readers, for coming on this adventure with me and being the best crew an author could ever imagine.

TO HAVE

•◦• AND •◦•

TO HEIST

SARA DESAI

READERS GUIDE

QUESTIONS FOR DISCUSSION

◆ ◆ ◆

1. Simi's parents are so desperate to see her married, they ambush her with eligible young bachelors. How do familial expectations influence Simi's perspective on relationships? Why does she continue to meet the potential suitors despite having no interest in getting married?

2. When we first meet Simi, she comes across as risk averse. She is still living in the same city where she grew up. She has the same best friend. She remains closely tied to her family. And she has been through a number of dead-end jobs, each one very similar to the last. What motivates her to take the risk of getting involved in a heist with a man she barely knows? How does her life change once she starts taking risks?

3. Simi and Jack have their first fight after he abandons her during a break-in. He explains later that there was a very small chance the intruders would have hurt her because they were after him. He was also confident she could look after herself. Do you agree with his decision? Could he have handled the situation a different way? Was he sufficiently apologetic, or would you have expected more groveling?

4. Every heist needs a crew. Simi relies on people with whom she has a connection—however tenuous. Did all the crew members fulfill the roles expected of them? Did the members grow over the course of the story? Did you have a favorite?

5. If you had to assemble a heist crew from the people in your life, who would you pick and why?

6. Jack thinks of himself as a good guy akin to Robin Hood. He retrieves stolen jewelry and artifacts and returns them to their rightful owners. Nothing annoys him more than being called a thief. By law, two wrongs don't make a right. But is it morally wrong to steal back something stolen from you or, alternatively, to steal something to return it? Where does Jack fall on the spectrum of right and wrong?

7. Despite seemingly opposite personalities, Simi and Jack fall for each other over the course of the book. What fuels their attraction? Is it purely physical, or is there something more? Simi also had a flirtation with Detective Garcia. Do you think Garcia or Jack is the better fit for Simi?

8. Simi and her friends are saddled with debt; unable to accumulate wealth; and stuck in low-benefit, dead-end jobs. They see the reward money as a means of achieving the financial security that their parents, grandparents, and even older siblings enjoyed. For each member of the crew, how do you see the money changing their life? Do you think it will pave the way to a better future, or will they blow it all at once?

9. Near the end of the story, Bella steals the necklace and then callously shoots her lover. Do you think the theft was impulsive or planned? Did she truly love Ben, or was he simply an escape or diversion from familial obligation? Would you give up $25 million for love?

Keep reading for a preview of

THE MARRIAGE GAME

*by Sara Desai, available now
from Berkley Romance!*

When Layla walked into The Spice Mill Restaurant after yet another disastrous relationship, she expected hugs and kisses, maybe a murmur of sympathy, or even a cheerful *Welcome home*.

Instead, she got a plate of samosas and a pitcher of water for table twelve.

"There are fresh poppadums in the kitchen," her mother said. "Don't forget to offer them to all the guests." Not even a glimmer of emotion showed on her mother's gently lined face. Layla could have been any one of the half-dozen servers who worked at her parents' restaurant instead of the prodigal daughter who had returned to San Francisco, albeit with a broken heart.

She should have known better than to show up during opening hours expecting to pour out her heart. The middle child in a strict, academic, reserved family, her mother wasn't given to outward displays of affection. But after the emotional devastation of walking in on her social media star boyfriend, Jonas Jameson, as he snorted the last of her savings off of two naked models, Layla had hoped for something more than being put to work.

It was her childhood all over again.

"Yes, Mom." She dutifully carried the plate and pitcher to the table and chatted briefly with the guests about the restaurant's unique decor. Decorated in exotic tones of saffron, gold, ruby, and cinnamon with accent walls representing the natural movement of wind and fire, and a cascading waterfall layered with beautiful landscaped artificial rocks and tiny plastic animals, the restaurant was the embodiment of her late brother's dream to re-create "India" in the heart of San Francisco.

The familiar scents—cinnamon, pungent turmeric, and smoky cumin—brought back memories of evenings spent stirring dal, chopping onions, and rolling roti in the bustling kitchen of her parents' first restaurant in Sunnyvale under the watchful army of chefs who followed the recipes developed by her parents. What had seemed fun as a child, and an imposition as a teenager, now filled her with a warm sense of nostalgia, although she would have liked just one moment of her mother's time.

On her way to the kitchen for the poppadums, she spotted her nieces coloring in a booth and went over to greet them. Her parents looked after them in the evenings when their mom, Rhea, was busy at work.

"Layla Auntie!" Five-year-old Anika and six-year-old Zaina, their long dark hair in pigtails, ran to give her a hug.

"Did you bring us anything from New York?" Zaina asked.

Layla dropped to her knees and put her arms around her nieces. "I might have brought a few presents with me, but I left them at the house. I didn't think I'd see you here."

"Can we go with you and get them?" They planted sticky kisses on her cheeks, making her laugh.

"I'll bring them tomorrow. What have you been eating?"

"*Jalebis.*" Anika held up a bright orange, pretzel-shaped sweet similar to a funnel cake.

"Yesterday we helped Dadi make chocolate *peda*," Zaina informed her, using the Urdu term for "paternal grandmother."

"And the day before that we made *burfi*, and before that we made—"

"Peanut brittle." Anika grinned.

Layla bit back a laugh. Her mother had a sweet tooth, so it wasn't surprising that she'd made treats with her granddaughters in the kitchen.

Zaina's smile faded. "She said peanut brittle was Pappa's favorite."

Layla's heart squeezed in her chest. Her brother, Dev, had died in a car accident five years ago and the pain of losing him had never faded. He'd been seven years older, and the symbol of the family's social and economic strength; expectations had weighed heavy on Dev's shoulders and he didn't disappoint. With a degree in engineering, a successful arranged marriage, and a real estate portfolio that he managed with a group of friends, he was every Indian parent's dream.

Layla . . . not so much.

"It's my favorite, too," she said. "I hope you left some for me."

"You can have Anika's," Zaina offered. "I'll get it for you."

"No! You can't take mine!" Anika chased Zaina into the kitchen, shouting over the *Slumdog Millionaire* DJ mix playing in the background.

"They remind me of you and Dev." Her mother joined her beside the booth and lifted a lock of Layla's hair, studying the bright streaks. "What is this blue?"

Of course her mother was surprised. She had given up trying to turn her daughter into a femme fatale years ago. Layla had never been interested in trendy hairstyles, and the only time she painted her nails or wore makeup was when her friends dragged her out. Dressing up was reserved for work or evenings out. Jeans, ponytails, and sneakers were more her style.

"This is courtesy of Jonas's special hair dye. His stylist left it behind for touch-ups. Blue hair is his signature look. Apparently, it shows up well on screen. I didn't want it to go to waste after we broke up, so I used it all on my hair. I had the true Jonas look."

Unlike most of her friends, who dated behind their parents' backs, Layla had always been honest about her desire to find true love. She'd introduced her boyfriends to her parents and told them about her breakups and relationship woes. Of course, there were limits to what she could share. Her parents didn't know she'd been living with Jonas, and they most certainly would never find out that she'd lost her job, her apartment, and her pride after the "Blue Fury" YouTube video of her tossing Jonas's stuff over their balcony in a fit of rage had gone viral.

"You are so much like your father—passionate and impulsive." Her mother smiled. "When we got our first bad review, he tore up the magazine, cooked it in a pot of dal, and delivered it to the reviewer in person. I had to stop him from flying to New York when you called to tell us you and Jonas split up. After he heard the pain in your voice, he wanted to go there and teach that boy a lesson."

If the sanitized, parent-friendly version of her breakup had distressed her father, she couldn't imagine how he would react if she told him the full story. "I'm glad you stopped him. Jonas is a big social media star. People would start asking questions if he posted videos with his face covered in bruises."

"Social media star." Her mother waved a dismissive hand. "What job is that? Talking shows on the Internet? How could he support a family?"

Aside from her family's disdain for careers in the arts, it was a good question. Jonas hadn't even been able to support himself.

When the bill collectors came calling, he'd moved into the prewar walk-up Layla shared with three college students in the East Village and lived off their generosity as he pursued fame and fortune as a social media lifestyle influencer.

"That boy was no good," her mother said firmly. "He wasn't brought up right. You're better off without him."

It was the closest to sympathy Layla was going to get. Sometimes it was easier to discuss painful issues with her mother because Layla had to keep her emotions in check. "I always seem to pick the bad ones. I think I must have some kind of dud dude radar." Emotion welled up in her throat, and she turned away. Her mother gave the lectures. Her father handled the tears.

"That's why in our tradition marriage is not about love." Her mother never passed up an opportunity to extol the benefits of an arranged marriage, especially when Layla had suffered yet another heartbreak. "It's about devotion to another person; caring, duty, and sacrifice. An arranged marriage is based on permanence. It is a contract between two like-minded people who share the same values and desire for companionship and family. There is no heartache, no betrayal, no boys pretending they care, or using you and throwing you away, no promises unkept—"

"No love."

Her mother's face softened. "If you're lucky, like your dad and me, love shows up along the way."

"Where is Dad?" Layla wasn't interested in hearing about marriage, arranged or otherwise, when it was clear she didn't have what it took to sustain a relationship. No wonder guys always thought of her as a pal. She was everybody's wingwoman and nobody's prize.

She looked around for her father. He was her rock, her shoulder to cry on when everything went wrong. Usually he was at the front door greeting guests or winding his way through the linen-covered tables and plush saffron-colored chairs, chatting with customers about the artwork and statues displayed in the mirrored alcoves along the walls, talking up the menu, or sharing stories with foodies about his latest culinary finds. He was a born entertainer, and there was nothing she loved more than watching him work a room.

"Your father has been locked in his office every free minute since you called about that boy. He doesn't eat; he hardly sleeps . . . I don't know if it's work or something else. He never rests." Layla's mother fisted her red apron, her trademark sign of anxiety. Pari Auntie had given the apron to her to celebrate the opening of the Spice Mill Restaurant, and she still wore it every day although the embroidered elephants around the bottom were now all faded and frayed.

"That's not unusual." Layla's father never rested. From the moment his feet hit the floor in the morning, he embraced the day with an enthusiasm and joyful energy Layla simply couldn't muster before nine A.M. and two cups of coffee. Her father accomplished more in a day than most people did in a week. He lived large and loud and was unashamed to let his emotions spill over, whether it was happiness or grief or even sympathy for his only daughter's many heartbreaks.

"He'll be so happy that you are home to visit." Her mother gave her a hug, the warm gesture equally as unexpected as their brief talk. Usually she was full on when the restaurant was open, focused and intense. "We both are."

Layla swallowed past the lump in her throat. It was moments like these, the love in two sticky kisses from her nieces and a few powerful words from her mom, that assured her she was making the right decision to move home. She had hit rock bottom in New York. If there was any chance of getting her life back on track, it would be with the support of her family.

"Beta!" Her father's loud voice boomed through the restaurant, turning the heads of the customers.

"Dad!" She turned and flung herself into his arms, heedless of the spectacle. Except for his traditional views about women (he didn't have the same academic or professional expectations of her as he'd had for Dev), her father was the best man she knew—reliable, solid, dependable, kind, and funny. An engineer before he immigrated to America, he was practical enough to handle most electrical or mechanical issues at the restaurant, and smart enough to know how to run a business, talk politics, and spark a conversation with anyone. His love was limitless. His kindness boundless. When he hired a member of staff, he never let them go.

All the emotion Layla had been holding in since witnessing Jonas's betrayal came pouring out in her father's arms as he murmured all the things he wanted to do to Jonas if he ever met him.

"I just bought a set of Kamikoto Senshi knives. They go through meat like butter. The bastard hippie wouldn't even know he'd been stabbed until he was dead. Or even better, I'd invite him for a meal and seat him at table seventeen near the back entrance where no one could see him. I'd serve him a mushroom masala made with death cap mushrooms. He would suffer first. Nausea, stomach cramps, vomiting, and diarrhea. Then liver failure and death."

Laughter bubbled up in her chest. No one could cheer her up like her father. "Mom has made you watch too many crime shows. How about just shaking your fist or saying a few angry words?"

He pressed a kiss to her forehead. "If I have to defend your honor, I want to do it in a way that will be talked about for years, something worthy of the criminal version of a Michelin star. Do you think there is such a thing?"

"Don't be ridiculous, Nasir." Layla's mother sighed. "There will be no murdering of itinerant Internet celebrities when we have a restaurant to run. Things are hard enough with the downturn in the market. I can't do this on my own."

Frowning, Layla pulled away from her father. "Is that why the restaurant is almost empty? Is everything okay?"

Her father's gaze flicked to her mother and then back to Layla. "Everything is fine, beta."

Layla's heart squeezed at the term of endearment. She would always be his sweetheart, even when she was fifty years old.

"Not that fine." Her mother gestured to the brigade of aunties filing through the door, some wearing saris, a few in business attire, and others in *salwar kameez*, their brightly colored tunics and long pants elegantly embroidered. Uncles and cousins took up the rear. "It seems you bumped into Lakshmi Auntie's nephew at Newark Airport and told him you'd broken up with your boyfriend."

Within moments, Layla was enveloped in warm arms, soft bosoms, and the thick scent of jasmine perfume. News spread faster than wildfire in the auntie underground or, in this case, faster than a Boeing 767.

"Look who is home!"

While Layla was being smothered with hugs and kisses, her father ushered everyone to the bar and quickly relocated the nearest customers before roping off the area with a PRIVATE PARTY sign. The only thing her family loved better than a homecoming was a wedding.

"Who was that boy? No respect in his bones. No shame in his body. Who does he think he is?" Pari Auntie squeezed Layla so hard she couldn't breathe.

"Let her go, Pari. She's turning blue." Charu Auntie edged her big sister out of the way and gave Layla a hug. Her mother's socially awkward younger sister had a Ph.D. in neuroscience and always tried to contribute to conversations by dispensing unsolicited psychological advice.

"How did you come here? Where are you staying? Are you going back to school? Do you have a job?" Deepa Auntie, her mother's cousin and a failed interior designer, tossed the end of her *dupatta* over her shoulder, the long, sheer, hot pink scarf embellished with small crystal beads inadvertently slapping her father's youngest sister, Lakshmi, on the cheek.

"Something bad is going to happen," superstitious Lakshmi Auntie moaned. "I can feel it in my face."

Mehar Auntie snorted as she adjusted her sari, the long folds of bright green material draping over her generous hips. "You thought something bad was going to happen when the milk boiled over last week."

"Don't make fun, Mehar," Lakshmi Auntie said with a scowl. "I told you Layla's relationship wasn't going to work when I found out she left on a full-moon night."

"No one thought it would work out," Mehar Auntie scoffed. "The boy didn't even go to university. Layla needs a professional, someone easy on the eyes like Salman Khan. Remember the scene in *Dabangg*? I went wild in the theater when he ripped off his shirt."

Layla's aunties groaned. Mehar Auntie knew the moves to every Bollywood dance and the words to every song. She was Layla's favorite aunt, not just because she wasn't shy to bust out her moves at every wedding, but also because she shared Layla's love of movies from Hollywood to Bollywood to indie.

"Mehar Auntie!" Layla gasped mockingly. "What about Hrithik Roshan? He's the number one actor in Bollywood. No one can dance like him. He's so perfect he hardly seems human."

"Too skinny." Mehar Auntie waved a dismissive hand. "He

looks like he was shrink-wrapped. I like a man with meat on his bones."

"Mehar. Really." Nira Auntie shook a finger in disapproval, the glass bindi bracelets on her arm jingling softly. She owned a successful clothing store in Sunnyvale and her exquisitely embroidered mustard yellow and olive green salwar kameez had a fashion-forward open back. "My children are here."

"Your children are men in their twenties. They're hardly going to be shocked by my appreciation of a well-muscled man."

"If you spent less time dreaming and dancing, you could have had one for yourself."

Layla winced at the burn. Mehar Auntie was well past what was considered marriageable age, but seemed content with her single life and her work as a dance teacher in Cupertino.

"Layla needs stability in her life, not some singing, dancing actor with no brains in his head." Salena Auntie pinched Layla's cheeks. She'd been trying to get Layla married off since her third birthday. "What will you do now? What are your intentions?"

"I'm done with men, Auntie-ji," she said affectionately.

"Don't call me Auntie." She tucked her gray hair under her embroidered headscarf. "I am not so old."

"You are old." Taara Auntie pushed her aside and handed Layla a Tupperware container. "And you're too thin. Eat. I made it just for you."

"What's this?"

Taara Auntie smiled and patted Layla's hand. "I've been taking cooking classes at the YMCA. I'm learning to make Western food, but I've added an Indian twist. This is Indian American fusion lasagna. I used roti instead of pasta, added a little halloumi cheese, and flavored the tomato sauce with mango chutney and a bit of cayenne. Try it." She watched eagerly as Layla lifted the lid.

"It looks . . . delicious." Her stomach lurched as she stared at the congealed mass of soggy bread, melted cheese, and bright orange chutney.

"You're going to put me out of business." Layla's father snatched the container out of her hand and studied the contents. "What an interesting combination of flavors. We'll enjoy it together this evening when we have time to appreciate the nuance of your creation."

Layla shot him a look of gratitude, and he put an arm around her shoulders.

"Don't eat it," he whispered. "Your sister-in-law tried her chicken nugget vindaloo surprise last week and she was sick for two days. If you're planning to travel in the next week—"

"I'm not. I'm staying here. I'm moving back home. My stuff is arriving in the next few days."

"Jana, did you hear that?" His face lit up with delight. "She's not going back to New York."

"What about your job?" her mother asked, her dark eyes narrowing.

"I thought it was time for a change, and I wanted to be here so I could help you . . ." Her voice trailed off when her mother frowned.

"She wants to be with us, Jana," her father said. "Why are you looking at her like that?"

"We aren't old. We don't need help. She had a good job. Every week I time her on the Face and she doesn't say anything is bad at work."

"It's called FaceTime, Mom, and it's not as good as being with the people you love."

"She loves her family. Such a good girl." Layla's father wrapped her in a hug even as her mother waggled a warning finger in her direction. Emotional manipulation didn't work on her mother. Neither did lies.

"Tell me the truth," her mother warned. "When I die, you will feel the guilt and realize . . ."

"Mom . . ."

"No. I will die."

"Fine." Layla pulled away from the warmth of her father's arms. It was almost impossible to lie to her mother when she started talking about her own death. "I was fired."

Silence.

Layla braced herself for the storm. Even though her mother was emotionally reserved, there were times when she let loose, and from the set of her jaw, it was clear this was going to be one of those times.

"Because of the boy?"

"Indirectly, yes."

"Oh, beta." Her father held out his arms, his voice warm with sympathy, but when Layla moved toward him, her mother blocked her with a hand.

"No hugs for her." She glared at Layla. "I told you so. I told you not to leave. New York is a bad place. Too big. Too many people. No sense of family. No values. You had boyfriend after boyfriend and all of them were bad, all of them hurt you. And this one makes you lose your job . . ." She continued her rant, mercifully keeping her voice low so the aunties wouldn't hear.

All her life, Layla had wanted to make her parents as proud as they had been of Dev, but the traditional roads of success weren't open to her. With only average marks and no interest in the "acceptable" careers—doctor, engineer, accountant, and *lawyer is okay*—she'd forged her own path. Yes, they'd supported her through business school, although they hadn't really understood her decision to specialize in human resource management. Her father had even wept with pride at her graduation. But underneath it all she could feel their disappointment. And now she'd disgraced herself and the family. No wonder her mother was so upset.

"Go back to New York." Her mother waved her toward the door. "Say you're sorry. Tell them it was a mistake."

"I can't." Her mother couldn't grasp Facebook. There was no way she would be able to explain YouTube or the concept of something going viral. And the temper tantrum that had started it all—the utter disappointment at having another relationship fail again? Her mother would never forgive her for being so rash. "I've really messed up this time."

Wasn't that the understatement of the year. Although the police had let her go with just a warning, she had spent a few humiliating hours in the police station in handcuffs and her landlord had kicked her out of her apartment. But those were things her parents didn't need to know.

Her father shook his head. "Beta, what did you do that was so bad?"

Layla shrugged. "It doesn't matter. I wasn't happy at my job and they knew it. I didn't like how they treated the people looking for work like they were inventory. They didn't care about their needs or their wants. It was all about keeping the corporate clients happy. I even told my boss I thought we could be just as successful if we paid as much attention to the people we placed as the companies that hired us, but she didn't agree. Things started going downhill after that. I have a feeling I was on my way out anyway, and what happened just gave them an excuse."

"So you have no job, no marriage prospects, no place to live . . ." Her mother shook her head. "What did we do wrong?"

"Don't worry, beta. I will fix everything." Her father smiled. "Your old dad is on the case. As long as I am alive, you never have to worry."

"She's a grown woman, Nasir. She isn't a little girl who broke a toy. She needs to fix this herself." Layla's mother crossed her arms. "So? What is your plan?"

Layla grimaced. "Well, I thought I'd live at home and help out at the restaurant for a bit, and I can look after the girls when Rhea is busy . . ."

"You need a job," her mother stated. "Or will you go back to school and get a different degree? Maybe doctor or engineer or even dentist? Your father has a sore tooth."

"This one." Her father pointed to one of his molars. "It hurts when I chew."

Scrambling to come up with a plan to appease her mother, she mentally ran through the last twenty-four hours searching for inspiration, until she remembered toying with an idea on the way home. "I saw one of my favorite movies, *Jerry Maguire*, on the plane. The hero is a sports agent who gets fired for having a conscience. He starts his own company and he only has Dorothy to help him."

"Who is this Dorothy?" her mother asked.

"She's his romantic love interest, but that's not the point. I'm Jerry." She gestured to herself, her enthusiasm growing as the idea formed in her mind. "I could start my own recruitment agency, but it would be different from other agencies because the focus would be on the people looking for work and not the employers. You've always told me how in the history of our family, the Patels have always been their own boss. Well, I want to be my own boss, too. I have a business degree. I have four years of recruitment experience. How hard can it be?"

"Very hard." Her mother sighed. "Do you think you can just show up one day and have a successful business? Your father and I started from nothing. We cooked meals on a two-burner hot plate in a tiny apartment. We sold them to friends in plastic containers.

It took years to save the money to buy our first restaurant and more years and many hardships before it was a success."

"But we can help her, Jana," her father said. "What's the use of learning all the tricks of running your own business if you can't share them with your own daughter? We even have the empty office suite upstairs. She can work from there so I can be around—"

"Nasir, you sublet the office to a young man a few weeks ago. He's moving in next week."

Layla's heart sank, and she swallowed her disappointment. Of course. It had been too perfect. How had she even thought for a minute that it would be this easy to turn her life around?

"It's okay, Dad." She forced a smile. "Mom's right. You always fix my problems. I should do this myself."

"No." Her father's voice was uncharacteristically firm. "It's not okay. I'll call the tenant and tell him circumstances have changed. He hasn't even moved in so I am sure it won't be a problem." He smiled. "Everything is settled. You're home. You'll have a new business and work upstairs. Now, you just need a husband and I can die in peace."

"Don't you start talking about dying, too."

But he wasn't listening. Instead, he was clapping his hands to quiet the chatter. "I have an announcement. Our Layla is moving back home. She'll be running her own recruitment business from our office suite upstairs so if you know of employers looking for workers or people needing a job, send them to her."

Everyone cheered. Aunties pushed forward, shouting out the names of cousins, friends, and family they knew were looking for work. Layla's heart warmed. This is what she'd missed most in New York. Family. They were all the support she needed.

Her father thudded his fist against his chest. "Our family is together again. My heart is full—" He choked and doubled over, his arm sliding off Layla's shoulder.

"Dad? Are you okay?" She put out a hand to steady him, and he swayed.

"My heart . . ."

She grabbed his arm. "Dad? What's wrong?"

With a groan, he crumpled to the floor.

"I knew it," Lakshmi Auntie cried out as Layla dropped to her knees beside her father. "I felt it in my face."

SARA DESAI has been a lawyer, radio DJ, marathon runner, historian, bouncer, and librarian. She lives on Vancouver Island with her husband, kids, and an assortment of forest creatures who think they are pets. Sara writes sexy romantic comedy and contemporary romance with a multicultural twist. When not laughing at her own jokes, Sara can be found eating nachos.

CONNECT ONLINE

SaraDesai.com

Ready to find
your next great read?

Let us help.

Visit prh.com/nextread

Penguin
Random
House